Out Like a Lion

...

Tracy L. Thompson

Acknowledgments

IF YOU'RE READING THIS, I'VE ACTUALLY DONE IT! Completed my first novel. As a reader, I used to marvel at acknowledgments pages (yes, I read them), thinking, "How can they have so many people to thank? I don't even know that many people." Turns out, I do.

Always first in my heart and my life, and now in this long list of acknowledgments, my sons, Zane, Hayden, and Sam. I'm putting Zane first, because he's the middle child and never lets me forget it. These guys love me, and that's the most important thing I've ever needed. They have supported my efforts every step of the way.

Zane has been my editor and a co-author in some ways, helping me work through tricky plot points and character development during hours-long phone calls from wherever I was writing. And when he won the poker tournament at River's Casino, he showed up at my door in the wee hours of the morning to put cash in my pocket. Thank you, Z.

Hayden provided comic relief and financial support for a few of my writing retreats, sharing the proceeds from the sale of his beloved Jag. Always believing I'd do this.

Sam employed me and gave me shelter, making sure I wasn't a starving artist. He's my boss and my landlord. He's always encouraged me in the time and space I need to accomplish my art. Sam's wife Ang, and my grandbabies have kept me going, providing joy, distraction, and sometimes dinner. I wish for them a future of freedom.

I've had so many friends cheering on and providing emotional support for my efforts. Especially Bill P., Louise F., Karyn L., Helen K., Theresa M., Linda T., and Diane L.

I am so grateful to the many people and places where I've found inspiration. My book group, Wild Women, provided a playground for imagining writing, and an offshoot writing group helped me realize what was possible. Thank you to Brigid B. for inviting me to the group back in 2009, and to all of the members, Karyn L., Susan, S., Annette N., Nadine S., Meredith S., Andrea H., Susan R., Lois M., Amanda W., Amy A., Casey B., Janet R., Jody F., Sally R., Judy F. If I missed a wild one, let me know and I owe you a drink.

In my early exploits into long-form creative writing, I was certain I could only write when the muse visited. Then I took a fiction writing course in New Orleans given by Stephen Rea who taught me that I could actually write to a prompt and under a deadline. The needed thing is peer pressure.

In 2022, the idea for this book began to take place. In spring of that year, I gathered with a group of women friends/activists at a state park in Tennessee. It was a reunion of women who had all, at one time or another, served on the board of an abortion fund in Florida. It was the first of what has become an annual reunion. There, over coffee and wine and snacks, I shared with these dear and generous friends the idea of the book. I introduced them to Jules. I'm so grateful they urged me to do the work and didn't let me quit. I love them all! Lori G., Ronna M., Mary K., Elizabeth B., Betsy D., Jillian A., Jess M., and Ruth B.

My storytelling group has been a source of exploration. It is only through our stories that we truly know anyone, and we made the effort to dig deeper into knowing each other. Kathy C. and Lorraine H., thank you for being willing to share yours.

Another thank you goes to the writers who gather at Pyramid Lake. I began going to the poetry writing weekends there years ago, then shifted to the writing week in 2022, when I got serious about this book. Clif Travers has led a workshop every fall that has been instrumental in moving me forward. The group is usually 10-12 writers who, along with Clif, have provided incredible feedback and support, making me a better writer.

At Pyramid, I connected with so many talented writers and a few of us decided to help one another with our craft. Suzanne S., Beckie O., and Susan H. were instrumental in getting me to the finish line with our monthly writers' group. Thank you all for thoughtful and always loving feedback.

In 2022, I was accepted to the Colgate Writer's Conference. At that conference, I was struggling with my identity as a writer. Was this going to be a hobby or something more? Some new writer friends helped me see myself as a writer, especially Ann M. and Monica R.

My writing support group at Moch Lisa's, hosted by Rhonda R., kept continuity for me during some stretches on not writing regularly. Thank you, Rhonda, for your constant pursuit of all things and people writerly.

In my search for places to write among writers, I found a few wonderful spots. Good Contrivance Farm in Reisterstown, Maryland was a place apart for a solo retreat, and helped me really dig into Jules' family.

The Barn at Boyd's Mills, run by the Highlights Foundation (Highlights Magazine), has been a refuge. My joy at finding them on the table in my dentist's office as a kid has turned into joy at finding this haven. They nurture writers, body and soul. Three meals a day. Farm to table. And WRITERS!

In 2023, I was introduced to the Focus Retreat Center in Malone, NY, again by Rhonda. It's about as far north as you can go before Canada. Again, a place set apart for creatives to produce. Pete and Stella provided healthy food, great conversation, and even a sit-stand desk in my room (in every room) for the hours at work.

I have a special appreciation for my dear friend Dorothee Racette, whose coaching and approach to time management helped me "Take Back My Day" and finish the work!

This book is for my boys.

I'll like you forever.

Vote.

2016 - The Past
is Prologue . . .

UNITED STATES DISTRICT COURT, CENTRAL DISTRICT OF CALIFORNIA
CIVIL COVER SHEET

I. (a) PLAINTIFFS (Check box if you are representing yourself [X])

KATIE JOHNSON

DEFENDANTS (Check box if you are representing yourself [ ])

DONALD J. TRUMP and
JEFFREY E. EPSTEIN

(b) County of Residence of First Listed Plaintiff   SAN BERNADINO
(EXCEPT IN U.S. PLAINTIFF CASES)

County of Residence of First Listed Defendant   NEW YORK
(IN U.S. PLAINTIFF CASES ONLY)

(c) Attorneys *(Firm Name, Address and Telephone Number)* If you are representing yourself, provide the same information.
KATIE JOHNSON
6634 DESERT QUEEN AVE., TWENTY NINE PALMS, CA. 92277
(760) 401-0192
NO E-MAIL OR FAX

Attorneys *(Firm Name, Address and Telephone Number)* If you are representing yourself, provide the same information.

UNKNOWN

II. BASIS OF JURISDICTION (Place an X in one box only.)

[ ] 1. U.S. Government Plaintiff

[ ] 3. Federal Question (U.S. Government Not a Party)

[ ] 2. U.S. Government Defendant

[X] 4. Diversity (Indicate Citizenship of Parties in Item III)

III. CITIZENSHIP OF PRINCIPAL PARTIES-For Diversity Cases Only
(Place an X in one box for plaintiff and one for defendant)

	PTF	DEF		PTF	DEF
Citizen of This State	[X] 1	[ ] 1	Incorporated or Principal Place of Business in this State	[ ] 4	[ ] 4
Citizen of Another State	[ ] 2	[X] 2	Incorporated and Principal Place of Business in Another State	[ ] 5	[ ] 5
Citizen or Subject of a Foreign Country	[ ] 3	[ ] 3	Foreign Nation	[ ] 6	[ ] 6

IV. ORIGIN (Place an X in one box only.)

[X] 1. Original Proceeding
[ ] 2. Removed from State Court
[ ] 3. Remanded from Appellate Court
[ ] 4. Reinstated or Reopened
[ ] 5. Transferred from Another District (Specify)
[ ] 6. Multi-District Litigation

V. REQUESTED IN COMPLAINT: JURY DEMAND: [ ] Yes [X] No   (Check "Yes" only if demanded in complaint.)

CLASS ACTION under F.R.Cv.P. 23: [ ] Yes [X] No   [ ] **MONEY DEMANDED IN COMPLAINT:** $ 100,000,000.00

VI. CAUSE OF ACTION (Cite the U.S. Civil Statute under which you are filing and write a brief statement of cause. Do not cite jurisdictional statutes unless diversity.)
42 U.S.C. ; 1985 - CONSPIRACY TO DENY CIVIL RIGHTS

VII. NATURE OF SUIT (Place an X in one box only).

OTHER STATUTES	CONTRACT	REAL PROPERTY CONT.	IMMIGRATION	PRISONER PETITIONS	PROPERTY RIGHTS
[ ] 375 False Claims Act	[ ] 110 Insurance	[ ] 240 Torts to Land	[ ] 462 Naturalization Application	**Habeas Corpus:**	[ ] 820 Copyrights
[ ] 376 Qui Tam (31 USC 3729(a))	[ ] 120 Marine	[ ] 245 Tort Product Liability	[ ] 465 Other Immigration Actions	[ ] 463 Alien Detainee	[ ] 830 Patent
[ ] 400 State Reapportionment	[ ] 130 Miller Act	[ ] 290 All Other Real Property		[ ] 510 Motions to Vacate Sentence	[ ] 840 Trademark
[ ] 410 Antitrust	[ ] 140 Negotiable Instrument	**TORTS**	**TORTS**	[ ] 530 General	**SOCIAL SECURITY**
[ ] 430 Banks and Banking	[ ] 150 Recovery of Overpayment & Enforcement of Judgment	**PERSONAL INJURY**	**PERSONAL PROPERTY**	[ ] 535 Death Penalty	[ ] 861 HIA (1395ff)
[ ] 450 Commerce/ICC Rates/Etc.		[ ] 310 Airplane	[ ] 370 Other Fraud	**Other:**	[ ] 862 Black Lung (923)
[ ] 460 Deportation	[ ] 151 Medicare Act	[ ] 315 Airplane Product Liability	[ ] 371 Truth in Lending	[ ] 540 Mandamus/Other	[ ] 863 DIWC/DIWW (405 (g))
[ ] 470 Racketeer Influenced & Corrupt Org.	[ ] 152 Recovery of Defaulted Student Loan (Excl. Vet.)	[ ] 320 Assault, Libel & Slander	[ ] 380 Other Personal Property Damage	[ ] 550 Civil Rights	[ ] 864 SSID Title XVI
[ ] 480 Consumer Credit		[ ] 330 Fed. Employers' Liability	[ ] 385 Property Damage Product Liability	[ ] 555 Prison Condition	[ ] 865 RSI (405 (g))
[ ] 490 Cable/Sat TV	[ ] 153 Recovery of Overpayment of Vet. Benefits	[ ] 340 Marine	**BANKRUPTCY**	[ ] 560 Civil Detainee Conditions of Confinement	**FEDERAL TAX SUITS**
[ ] 850 Securities/Commodities/Exchange		[ ] 345 Marine Product Liability	[ ] 422 Appeal 28 USC 158	**FORFEITURE/PENALTY**	[ ] 870 Taxes (U.S. Plaintiff or Defendant)
[ ] 890 Other Statutory Actions	[ ] 160 Stockholders' Suits	[ ] 350 Motor Vehicle	[ ] 423 Withdrawal 28 USC 157	[ ] 625 Drug Related Seizure of Property 21 USC 881	[ ] 871 IRS-Third Party 26 USC 7609
[ ] 891 Agricultural Acts	[ ] 190 Other Contract	[ ] 355 Motor Vehicle Product Liability	**CIVIL RIGHTS**	[ ] 690 Other	
[ ] 893 Environmental Matters	[ ] 195 Contract Product Liability	[ ] 360 Other Personal Injury	[X] 440 Other Civil Rights	**LABOR**	
[ ] 895 Freedom of Info. Act	[ ] 196 Franchise	[ ] 362 Personal Injury-Med Malpratice	[ ] 441 Voting	[ ] 710 Fair Labor Standards Act	
[ ] 896 Arbitration	**REAL PROPERTY**	[ ] 365 Personal Injury-Product Liability	[ ] 442 Employment	[ ] 720 Labor/Mgmt. Relations	
[ ] 899 Admin. Procedures Act/Review of Appeal of Agency Decision	[ ] 210 Land Condemnation	[ ] 367 Health Care/ Pharmaceutical Personal Injury Product Liability	[ ] 443 Housing/ Accommodations	[ ] 740 Railway Labor Act	
[ ] 950 Constitutionality of State Statutes	[ ] 220 Foreclosure	[ ] 368 Asbestos Personal Injury Product Liability	[ ] 445 American with Disabilities-Employment	[ ] 751 Family and Medical Leave Act	
	[ ] 230 Rent Lease & Ejectment		[ ] 446 American with Disabilities-Other	[ ] 790 Other Labor Litigation	
			[ ] 448 Education	[ ] 791 Employee Ret/Inc. Security Act	

ED CV16-00797 DMG (KSx)

FOR OFFICE USE ONLY: Case Number:

CV-71 (02/16)   CIVIL COVER SHEET   APR 2 6 2016   Page 1 of 3

x

UNITED STATES DISTRICT COURT, CENTRAL DISTRICT OF CALIFORNIA
CIVIL COVER SHEET

VIII. VENUE: Your answers to the questions below will determine the division of the Court to which this case will be initially assigned. This initial assignment is subject to change, in accordance with the Court's General Orders, upon review by the Court of your Complaint or Notice of Removal.

QUESTION A: Was this case removed from state court?	STATE CASE WAS PENDING IN THE COUNTY OF:	INITIAL DIVISION IN CACD IS:
☐ Yes ☒ No If "no," skip to Question B. If "yes," check the box to the right that applies, enter the corresponding division in response to Question E, below, and continue from there.	☐ Los Angeles, Ventura, Santa Barbara, or San Luis Obispo	Western
	☐ Orange	Southern
	☐ Riverside or San Bernardino	Eastern

QUESTION B: Is the United States, or one of its agencies or employees, a PLAINTIFF in this action? ☐ Yes ☒ No If "no," skip to Question C. If "yes," answer Question B.1, at right.	**B.1.** Do 50% or more of the defendants who reside in the district reside in Orange Co.? *check one of the boxes to the right* →	☐ YES. Your case will initially be assigned to the Southern Division. Enter "Southern" in response to Question E, below, and continue from there.
		☐ NO. Continue to Question B.2.
	B.2. Do 50% or more of the defendants who reside in the district reside in Riverside and/or San Bernardino Counties? (Consider the two counties together.) *check one of the boxes to the right* →	☐ YES. Your case will initially be assigned to the Eastern Division. Enter "Eastern" in response to Question E, below, and continue from there.
		☐ NO. Your case will initially be assigned to the Western Division. Enter "Western" in response to Question E, below, and continue from there.

QUESTION C: Is the United States, or one of its agencies or employees, a DEFENDANT in this action? ☐ Yes ☒ No If "no," skip to Question D. If "yes," answer Question C.1, at right.	**C.1.** Do 50% or more of the plaintiffs who reside in the district reside in Orange Co.? *check one of the boxes to the right* →	☐ YES. Your case will initially be assigned to the Southern Division. Enter "Southern" in response to Question E, below, and continue from there.
		☐ NO. Continue to Question C.2.
	C.2. Do 50% or more of the plaintiffs who reside in the district reside in Riverside and/or San Bernardino Counties? (Consider the two counties together.) *check one of the boxes to the right* →	☐ YES. Your case will initially be assigned to the Eastern Division. Enter "Eastern" in response to Question E, below, and continue from there.
		☐ NO. Your case will initially be assigned to the Western Division. Enter "Western" in response to Question E, below, and continue from there.

QUESTION D: Location of plaintiffs and defendants?	A. Orange County	B. Riverside or San Bernardino County	C. Los Angeles, Ventura, Santa Barbara, or San Luis Obispo County
Indicate the location(s) in which 50% or more of *plaintiffs who reside in this district* reside. (Check up to two boxes, or leave blank if none of these choices apply.)	☐	☒	☐
Indicate the location(s) in which 50% or more of *defendants who reside in this district* reside. (Check up to two boxes, or leave blank if none of these choices apply.)	☐	☐	☐

D.1. Is there at least one answer in Column A?	D.2. Is there at least one answer in Column B?
☐ Yes ☒ No If "yes," your case will initially be assigned to the SOUTHERN DIVISION. Enter "Southern" in response to Question E, below, and continue from there. If "no," go to question D2 to the right. →	☒ Yes ☐ No If "yes," your case will initially be assigned to the EASTERN DIVISION. Enter "Eastern" in response to Question E, below. If "no," your case will be assigned to the WESTERN DIVISION. Enter "Western" in response to Question E, below. ↓

QUESTION E: Initial Division?	INITIAL DIVISION IN CACD
Enter the initial division determined by Question A, B, C, or D above: →	EASTERN

QUESTION F: Northern Counties?		
Do 50% or more of plaintiffs or defendants in this district reside in Ventura, Santa Barbara, or San Luis Obispo counties?	☐ Yes	☐ No

CIVIL COVER SHEET

IX(a). IDENTICAL CASES: Has this action been previously filed **in this court?**   ☒ NO   ☐ YES

If yes, list case number(s): ____

IX(b). RELATED CASES: Is this case related (as defined below) to any civil or criminal case(s) previously filed **in this court?**

☒ NO   ☐ YES

If yes, list case number(s): ____

Civil cases are related when they (check all that apply):

☐ A. Arise from the same or a closely related transaction, happening, or event;

☐ B. Call for determination of the same or substantially related or similar questions of law and fact; or

☐ C. For other reasons would entail substantial duplication of labor if heard by different judges.

Note: That cases may involve the same patent, trademark, or copyright **is not**, in itself, sufficient to deem cases related.

A civil forfeiture case and a criminal case are related when they (check all that apply):

☐ A. Arise from the same or a closely related transaction, happening, or event;

☐ B. Call for determination of the same or substantially related or similar questions of law and fact; or

☐ C. Involve one or more defendants from the criminal case in common and would entail substantial duplication of labor if heard by different judges.

**X. SIGNATURE OF ATTORNEY
(OR SELF-REPRESENTED LITIGANT):** _________________________   DATE: April 26, 2016

Notice to Counsel/Parties: The submission of this Civil Cover Sheet is required by Local Rule 3-1. This Form CV-71 and the information contained herein neither replaces nor supplements the filing and service of pleadings or other papers as required by law, except as provided by local rules of court. For more detailed instructions, see separate instruction sheet (CV-071A).

Key to Statistical codes relating to Social Security Cases:

Nature of Suit Code	Abbreviation	Substantive Statement of Cause of Action
861	HIA	All claims for health insurance benefits (Medicare) under Title 18, Part A, of the Social Security Act, as amended. Also, include claims by hospitals, skilled nursing facilities, etc., for certification as providers of services under the program. (42 U.S.C. 1935FF(b))
862	BL	All claims for "Black Lung" benefits under Title 4, Part B, of the Federal Coal Mine Health and Safety Act of 1969. (30 U.S.C. 923)
863	DIWC	All claims filed by insured workers for disability insurance benefits under Title 2 of the Social Security Act, as amended; plus all claims filed for child's insurance benefits based on disability. (42 U.S.C. 405 (g))
863	DIWW	All claims filed for widows or widowers insurance benefits based on disability under Title 2 of the Social Security Act, as amended. (42 U.S.C. 405 (g))
864	SSID	All claims for supplemental security income payments based upon disability filed under Title 16 of the Social Security Act, as amended.
865	RSI	All claims for retirement (old age) and survivors benefits under Title 2 of the Social Security Act, as amended. (42 U.S.C. 405 (g))

Case 5:16-cv-00797-DMG-KS   Document 1   Filed 04/26/16   Page 1 of 6   Page ID #:1

1 Name: KATIE JOHNSON

2 Address: 6634 DESERT QUEEN AVE.

3 TWENTYNINE PALMS, CA. 92277

4 Phone: (760) 401-0192

5 Fax: NO FAX OR E-MAIL

6 In Pro Per

7

8 **UNITED STATES DISTRICT COURT**

9 **CENTRAL DISTRICT OF CALIFORNIA**

10 CASE NUMBER:

11 KATIE JOHNSON

ED CV16-00797 DMG (KSx)

Plaintiff   To be supplied by the Clerk of

12 The United States District Court

13 v.

COMPLAINT FOR CLAIM RELIEF DUE TO:

14 DONALD J. TRUMP and

1. SEXUAL ABUSE UNDER THREAT OF HARM

15 JEFFREY E. EPSTEIN

2. CONSPIRACY TO DEPRIVE CIVIL RIGHTS

Defendant(s).

16

17

18 Plaintiff Katie Johnson, for causes of actions against Defendants Donald J. Trump and

19 Jeffrey E. Epstein, alleges as follows:

20 JURISDICTION

21 1. Jurisdiction is pursuant to the law of Diversity, 28 U.S.C. ; 1332, as plaintiff resides in the state

22 of California while defendants reside in the state of New York and the action is for damages above

23 $75,000.

24 VENUE

25 2. The venue is established as the Eastern Division of the United States Court Central District

26 of California because the plaintiff resides in San Bernadino County, State of California

27

28 1

PARTIES

3. The Plaintiff, Katie Johnson, resides in the State of California.

4. The Defendants, Donald J. Trump and Jeffrey E. Epstein, each reside in the State of New York.

FACTUAL ALLEGATIONS

5. The Plaintiff, Katie Johnson, alleges that the Defendants, Donald J. Trump and Jeffrey E. Epstein, did willfully and with extreme malice violate her Civil Rights under 18 U.S.C. ; 2241 by sexually and physically abusing Plaintiff Johnson by forcing her to engage in various perverted and depraved sex acts by threatening physical harm to Plaintiff Johnson and also her family.

6. The Plaintiff, Katie Johnson, alleges that the Defendants, Donald J. Trump and Jeffrey E. Epstein, also did willfully and with extreme malice violate her Civil Rights under 42 U.S.C. ; 1985 by conspiring to deny Plaintiff Johnson her Civil Rights by making her their sex slave.

7. The Plaintiff, Katie Johnson, alleges she was subject to extreme sexual and physical abuse by the Defendants, Donald J. Trump and Jeffrey E. Epstein, including forcible rape during a four month time span covering the months of June-September 1994 when Plaintiff Johnson was still only a minor of age 13.

8. The Plaintiff, Katie Johnson, alleges she was enticed by promises of money and a modeling career to attend a series of underage sex parties held at the New York City residence of Defendant Jeffrey E. Epstein and attended by Defendant Donald J. Trump.

9. On the first occasion involving the Defendant, Donald J. Trump, the Plaintiff, Katie Johnson, was forced to manually stimulate Defendant Trump with the use of her hand upon Defendant Trump's erect penis until he reached sexual orgasm.

10. On the second occasion involving the Defendant, Donald J. Trump, the Plaintiff, Katie Johnson, was forced to orally copulate Defendant Trump by placing her mouth upon Defendant Trump's erect penis until he reached sexual orgasm.

2

11. On the third occasion involving the Defendant, Donald J. Trump, the Plaintiff, Katie Johnson, was forced to engage in an unnatural lesbian sex act with her fellow minor and sex slave, Maria Doe, age 12, for the sexual enjoyment of Defendant Trump. After this sex act, both minors were forced to orally copulate Defendant Trump by placing their mouths simultaneously on his erect penis until he achieved sexual orgasm. After zipping up his pants, Defendant Trump physically pushed both minors away while angrily berating them for the "poor" quality of their sexual performance.

12. On the fourth and final sexual encounter with the Defendant, Donald J. Trump, the Plaintiff, Katie Johnson, was tied to a bed by Defendant Trump who then proceeded to forcibly rape Plaintiff Johnson. During the course of this savage sexual attack, Plaintiff Johnson loudly pleaded with Defendant Trump to "please wear a condom". Defendant Trump responded by violently striking Plaintiff Johnson in the face with his open hand and screaming that "he would do whatever he wanted" as he refused to wear protection. After achieving sexual orgasm, the Defendant, Donald J. Trump put his suit back on and when the Plaintiff, Katie Johnson, in tears asked Defendant Trump what would happen if he had impregnated her, Defendant Trump grabbed his wallet and threw some money at her and screamed that she should use the money "to get a fucking abortion".

13. On the first occasion involving the Defendant, Jeffrey E. Epstein, the Plaintiff, Katie Johnson, was forced to disrobe into her bra and panties and to give a full body massage to Defendant Epstein while he was completely naked. During the massage, Defendant Epstein physically forced Plaintiff Johnson to touch his erect penis with her bare hands and to clean up his ejaculated semen after he achieved sexual orgasm.

14. On the second occasion involving the Defendant, Jeffrey Epstein, the Plaintiff, Katie Johnson, was again forced to disrobe into her bra and panties while giving Defendant Epstein a full body massage while he was completely naked. The Defendant, Donald J. Trump, was also present as he was getting his own massage from another minor, Jane Doe, age 13. Defendant Epstein forced Plaintiff Johnson to touch his erect penis by physically placing her bare hands upon his sex organ and again forced Plaintiff Johnson to clean up his ejaculated semen after he achieved sexual orgasm.

3

1   15. Shortly after this sexual assault by the Defendant, Jeffrey E. Epstein, on the Plaintiff, Katie

2   Johnson, Plaintiff Johnson was still present while the two Defendants were arguing over who would

3   be the one to take Plaintiff Johnson's virginity. The Defendant, Donald J. Trump, was clearly heard

4   referring to Defendant, Jeffrey E. Epstein, as a "Jew Bastard" as he yelled at Defendant Epstein, that

5   clearly, he, Defendant Trump, should be the lucky one to "pop the cherry" of Plaintiff Johnson.

6   16. The third and final sexual assault by the Defendant, Jeffrey E. Epstein, on the Plaintiff, Katie

7   Johnson, took place after Plaintiff Johnson had been brutally and savagely raped by Defendant

8   Trump. While receiving another full body massage from Plaintiff Johnson, while in the nude,

9   Defendant Epstein became so enraged after finding out that Defendant Trump had been the one to

10   take Plaintiff Johnson's virginity, that Defendant Epstein also violently raped Plaintiff Johnson.

11   After forcing Plaintiff Johnson to disrobe into her bra and panties, while receiving a massage from

12   the Plaintiff, Defendant Epstein attempted to enter Plaintiff Johnson's anal cavity with his erect

13   penis while trying to restrain her. Plaintiff Johnson attempted to push Defendant Epstein away, at

14   which time Defendant Epstein attempted to enter Plaintiff Johnson's vagina with his erect penis.

15   This attempt to brutally sodomize and rape Plaintiff Johnson by Defendant Epstein was finally

16   repelled by Plaintiff Johnson but not before Defendant Epstein was able to achieve sexual orgasm.

17   After perversely sodomizing and raping the Plaintiff, Katie Johnson, the Defendant, Jeffrey E.

18   Epstein, attempted to strike her about the head with his closed fists while he angrily screamed at

19   Plaintiff Johnson that he, Defendant Epstein, should have been the one who "took her cherry, not

20   Mr. Trump", before she finally managed to break away from Defendant Epstein.

21   17. The Plaintiff, Katie Johnson, was fully warned on more than one occasion by both

22   Defendants, Donald J. Trump and Jeffrey E. Epstein, that were she ever to reveal any of the details

23   of the sexual and physical abuse that she had suffered as a sex slave for Defendant Trump and

24   Defendant Epstein, that Plaintiff Johnson and her family would be in mortal danger. Plaintiff

25   Johnson was warned that this would mean certain death for herself and Plaintiff Johnson's family

26   unless she remained silent forever on the exact details of the depraved and perverted sexual and

27   physical abuse she had been forced to endure from the Defendants.

28   4

MATERIAL WITNESSES

18. Tiffany Doe, a former trusted employee of the Defendant, Jeffrey E. Epstein, has agreed to provide sworn testimony in this civil case and any other future civil or criminal proceedings, fully verifying the authenticity of the claims of the Plaintiff, Katie Johnson. Witness Tiffany Doe was employed by the Defendant, Jeffrey E. Epstein, for more than 10 years as a party planner for his underage sex parties. Despite being subject to constant terroristic threats by Defendants Epstein and Trump to never reveal the details of these underage sex parties at which scores of teenagers, and pre-teen girls were used as sex slaves by Defendant Epstein and Defendant Trump, witness Tiffany Doe refuses to be silent any longer. She has agreed to fully reveal the extent of the sexual perversion and physical cruelty that she personally witnessed at these parties by Defendants Epstein and Trump.

19. Material witness Tiffany Doe fully confirms all of Plaintiff Katie Johnson's allegations of physical and sexual abuse by Defendants Donald J. Trump and Jeffrey E. Epstein. Tiffany Doe was physically present at each of the four occasions of sexual abuse by Defendant Trump upon the person of Plaintiff Johnson, as it was her job to witness all of the sexual escapades of Defendant Epstein's guests at these underage sex parties and later reveal all of the sordid details directly to Defendant Epstein. Defendant Epstein also demanded that Tiffany Doe tell him personally everything she had overheard at these parties explaining to her that "knowledge was king" in the financial world. As a result of these underage sex parties, Defendant Epstein was able to accumulate inside business knowledge that he otherwise would never have been privy to in order to amass his huge personal fortune.

20. Material witness Tiffany Doe will testify that she was also present or had direct knowledge of each of the three instances on which Defendant Jeffrey E. Epstein physically and sexually abused the Plaintiff, Katie Johnson. Tiffany Doe will testify to the fact that the Plaintiff, Katie Johnson, was extremely fortunate to have survived all of the physical and sexual horrors inflicted upon her by Defendants Epstein and Trump.

5

CLAIM FOR RELIEF

21.   The Plaintiff, Katie Johnson, asks the court for relief against the Defendants, Donald J. Trump and Jeffrey E. Epstein, in the amount of $100,000,000.00 (One Hundred Million Dollars) as a result of the Defendants aforementioned acts upon which they willfully and maliciously violated the Civil Rights of the Plaintiff as stated in 18 U.S.C. ; 2241 by sexually and physically abusing the then 13 year old Plaintiff Johnson under threat of harm to her and her family, and 42 U.S.C. ; 1985 by the Defendants conspiring to deny the Civil Rights of Plaintiff Johnson by making her their sex slave.

Dated: April 26, 2016   KATIE JOHNSON

By_______________________________

                                Plaintiff Katie Johnson

                                Appearing In Pro Per

6

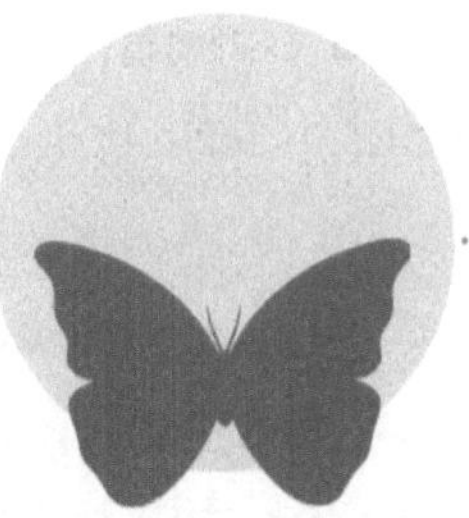

FEBRUARY 2022

IN THE WANING WEEKS OF WINTER IN 2022, Jules Campbell was longing for the spring more intensely than she had in recent memory. She was anxious. February's wicked weather had always made it feel the longest, rather than the shortest month in upstate New York. But this year, by the second week of February, Jules was already coveting the lamb days ahead, anticipating the wild yellow forsythia and timid purple and white crocus that always signaled spring to her.

Standing at her kitchen sink, steam from the dishes obscured the window, but not the view. At 5:45 pm it was already midnight-dark. She couldn't see anything out there anyway. As she settled a cup in the drainer, a familiar sound caught her attention, like a tennis ball gently bouncing atop a tight-strung racket. She wiped her sudsy hands on her jeans and opened the slider to let the cat back in.

Feinstein was an outdoor cat for as long as she could possibly stand to be. Then she would grudgingly come in to get warm and get food, sooner if she hadn't been successful in her hunt. She might even tolerate physical contact. Stroking her frigid coat as the cat crossed the threshold, Jules felt the contented hum beneath her fingers. She opened a can of Purina and watched the oily disc of mystery slurp into the cat's bowl. She rubbed her old friend between the ears as the cat ate, feeling grateful for the animal's forbearance, hoping to ease the chill from the fine bones beneath the damp fur. The woman and the cat were both gray now, where once it had been only the cat.

Jules had lured Feinstein from a feral life years ago, when the boys had both been in high school. They had all grown used to one another eventually. She wasn't a pet exactly, more like a beloved distant family member who occasionally crashed at their place. But age was forcing her inside more and more these days. Jules was secretly pleased. It was good to have another living soul under her roof.

She readied her coffee for the next day and set the timer for 7:30. The small luxury of waking to the aroma of her freshly brewed dark roast, ready for her to pour, was a simple pleasure she had come to appreciate. If she forgot, a tinge of disappointment would start her day instead. She finished tidying the kitchen, wiping down the counters and rinsing the sink.

With her meal over, Feinstein was curled up under the table to digest. She would stay inside now. It was still coming down outside. Big wet goose feathers. Suffocating. As soon as the weather broke, Jules planned to visit the grandchildren for a few weeks in Montreal. Standing at her kitchen window and cursing the snow, she could never have imagined that even before the lion could roar in, she would be planning murder.

• • •

Jules was jolted out of a dead sleep to the strains of Whitney Houston's "I Wanna Dance With Somebody," her ringtone for Ellie Chavez. She glanced at the clock, a relic from her childhood home, as she scrambled for her phone on the nightstand. The arms glowed green to indicate that it was somewhere before 6am. Jesus!

"Hey," she croaked into the phone, "did you forget? I'm retired!" An early call from anyone else would scare her. But Ellie lived life on a different schedule. She never seemed to sleep, and often forgot that other people did. Their pre-dawn chats had become routine.

"Damn! I'm so sorry, Boss!" Ellie was breathing hard, probably on the Peloton.

Even though Jules had been retired for years, Ellie still called her Boss. Ellie was second-in-command at Women Waging Peace and had been Jules' right hand, but she had never given Jules' successor Flora, her boss of the past five years, the same respect. Or even much of a chance. Her loyalty was with Jules, and she was loyal to a fault.

Jules had brought Ellie into the organization over a decade ago, proud to have wooed her away from a cushy job in academia before she became tenured. Ellie was smart as a whip. A peace and justice advocate who had come to the U.S. on her mother's hip from war-torn Guatemala in the late 80s. She was tenacious and rigorous. The two women made an excellent team and had grown close in their time together, despite the twenty-plus years that separated them. Jules considered Ellie her second-best friend, her girlhood friend Sally taking first place for decades.

Ellie should have taken the top spot at WWP when Jules retired, but she had declined the opportunity. She was still in parenting mode for her young kids then, and didn't feel she could give everything it required. She had come to regret that decision.

"That's ok, El. How's it going?"

"Did you hear about 'Truth Social?'"

"Tell me the latest."

"He's launching next week and Donny, Jr. 'leaked' his upcoming first post. "Get Ready! Your favorite President will see you soon!"" she mimicked in a lousy Trump impression, "I'm gonna lose my breakfast!"

"Well, what did you expect? Something creative? Brilliant? Insightful? Is everything spelled right?" Jules inquired.

"Um…well, looks like it, but he capitalized ready." They both laughed.

"How are the girls?" Jules asked as she emerged from the fog of sleep. Ellie had 12-year-old twins, Grace and Maria. They were fraternal and about as similar as Alaska and Hawaii, but they were each other's cheerleader and protector. They came as a pair.

"Ugh! They are so hormonal! I am just getting glimpses of what's to come. These teen-age years are NOT going to be pretty. Pray for me now and in the hour of my need!"

"It's not going to be that bad. They are good girls and they love you. You might be surprised."

"Says the woman who only raised boys." Ellie teased.

"And I got through it with no unwanted pregnancies, only a few rides in cop cars, and a few fender benders. Ben had that one bad wreck in his junior year but otherwise we made it. You will, too. It flies by! You know what they say; 'The days are long but the years are short!'"

She could tell Ellie was mulling that over.

"I never heard that before. That's going on my fridge."

Ellie's fridge was covered in layers of inspirational sayings scrawled on post-its, 3x5 cards, backs of envelopes. Whatever paper was at hand when she came across ideas she found noteworthy. Magnets held it all in place and allowed her to rearrange everything regularly, making room for something new or revisiting something that had given her strength in the past.

"How are the boys?" She asked Jules.

"All good. I miss them though. It was so nice having everyone home for the holidays. I got spoiled. I'm planning to visit Ben and his crew in Montreal sometime this spring, once the weather clears." Jules pulled herself into a sitting position, leaning against the headboard. "So, what else is going on? How's the Peace business?"

"Work's good. That's one reason I called. I was thinking about that piece you wrote a while back about the death penalty. It was about extending the holding of Roper to the age of 21, because of new brain science. Is this ringing a bell?"

"Of course. That was Bredhold. In Kentucky, believe it or not! I know it was appealed, but I don't know where that landed. I haven't really kept up with it in the last few years. What do you need?"

"I remember how much research you did on it and all the background material you had. I'm working on a death penalty program for a conference this summer and I'd really love to review all of that. It would save me a ton of time."

"Yeah, that was a white paper I wrote. Did you check the archive?"

"I did, but I can never find anything in there. I figured I'd save time by coming straight to the horse."

"Ok, if it's not on my laptop, I know I have a paper copy of everything from that project. I'll dig it out for you."

"Thank you! You're a pitch!" Ellie often mangled idioms or mixed metaphors.

"I think you mean 'peach.' Thanks, El."

"OK, peach. Call me when you find it and we can have lunch or something so I can grab it from you."

"If it's on my computer I'll just send it to you. But let's get together either way. I haven't seen you since before Christmas!"

"Sounds good! Love you!"

"Love you, too, El!"

It was just after 6am, but she doubted she'd be able to fall back to sleep. She flipped on her bedside lamp, opened the coffee app on her phone and started her brew. The thought of seeing Ellie soon gave her something to look forward to.

In her study, coffee in hand, Jules powered up her laptop. She doubted she would still have the e-files Ellie was looking for. Before leaving WWP, Jules had dumped everything on her personal PC into the organization's archives and wiped her hard drive. A quick search confirmed she was right; it wasn't there. She'd need to dig out her paper files.

Jules' generation were the straddlers; the only generation that knew the world before computers and the world after. She was mildly annoyed by the common characterization of this population as luddites. In her experience, most of her contemporaries were, like herself, quite adept with technology. Nonetheless, Jules had made it a working practice to keep paper copies of things she identified as particularly significant; work she couldn't bear to lose if e-files went missing. Her white papers, into which she put so much effort, were one of the things she kept.

Her filing cabinet was an old weathered oak one, probably from a lawyer's office or a bank. Jules had found it years ago on e-Bay when she needed a new one and couldn't stand to look at the ugly gunmetal ones from Staples for another second! They were so unimaginative, so utilitarian. Even though oak wasn't her first choice, it was a huge aesthetic improvement.

The drawers were organized in 5-year increments, going back to 2000. Older files were in the attic in four or five of the gray tin archives, probably moldering away. From the bottom drawer up she had: 2000-2004; 2005-2009; 2010-2014; 2015-. After leaving WWP, she hadn't kept any paper files, so this cabinet could probably join its ugly sisters in the attic. She made a mental note to task the boys with the job when they were next home.

Jules pulled open the topmost drawer and the whole cabinet jerked slightly forward. An avalanche of the magazines she'd stacked on top came sliding down. Jules attempted to catch what she could, but they were glossy and slick as fresh-caught fish. She laughed at how she must look, like a juggler dropping the spinning plates.

She gathered up all the issues and re-stacked them, moving them to the section of bookshelves where she kept her periodicals. Although she consumed most of her information digitally, there were three magazines that she still paid the upcharge for print: National Geographic, The New Yorker, and The Atlantic. Her other print indulgence was the Sunday Times. National Geographic was a lifelong love. Her grandparents had subscribed to it and she would pore over the pictures as a little girl, imagining places and people sometimes beyond belief. She would still get a little thrill seeing that yellow border in her mailbox. The other two came to her later in her life. She read all of them cover-to-cover and kept those she deemed worthy of taking up space in her home rather than being recycled. She reached for The New Yorker that had been on the bottom of the stack and was now on top. Although it was probably her favorite of the three magazines, she kept fewer of these issues since it was a weekly. She glanced at the cover to see why this one might have made the cut.

It was from November 2016. The first issue after the worst election in her life. On the cover is a man sitting in a subway car, briefcase between his feet. The newspaper he's reading is headlined "Oh, Sweet Jesus Please God, No." Further down the front page, "Anything but that." And near the bottom, "Come on." That's why she kept this one. As she set it back on top of the cabinet she noticed some paper that had been folded and tucked inside. She pulled it out and unfolded it.

It was a printout from The New Yorker website, dated Nov. 9, 2016. The day after the election. An editorial by David Remnick, titled *An American Tragedy*. Jules read:

> *The election of Donald Trump to the Presidency is nothing less than a tragedy for the American republic, a tragedy for the Constitution, and a triumph for the forces, at home and abroad, of nativism, authoritarianism, misogyny, and racism. Trump's shocking victory, his ascension to the Presidency, is a sickening event in the history of the United States and liberal democracy. On January 20, 2017, we will bid farewell to the first African-American President—a man of integrity, dignity, and generous spirit—and witness the inauguration of a con who did little to spurn endorsement by forces of xenophobia and white supremacy. It is impossible to react to this moment with anything less than revulsion and profound anxiety.*

Reading this, knowing with hindsight that the legacy of Trump's administration was actually much, much worse than anyone could have imagined then, it seemed almost naïve. Who would have thought that children would be separated from their families at the border? That kids would be kept in cages? Who would have thought that a President of the United States of America would mock the disabled? Who would have thought that America would pull out of the Paris Climate Accord? Or that Trump would publicly venerate Putin and Kim Jong Un? That he would foment an insurrection? She read on through the article, remembering viscerally that awful Wednesday. It was a turning point in U.S. history, Jules knew. It was the first day of the end of democracy.

Remnick wrapped up the piece with these words:

It is all a dismal picture. Late last night, as the results were coming in from the last states, a friend called me full of sadness, full of anxiety about conflict, about war. Why not leave the country? But despair is no answer. To combat authoritarianism, to call out lies, to struggle honorably and fiercely in the name of American ideals—that is what is left to do. That is all there is to do.

Jules had had the same conversations on that election night, and in the days and weeks that followed. She and her friends and colleagues, family members, all shell shocked. The unimaginable had happened. A know-nothing, do-nothing, blowhard was headed to the highest seat of power. Many people she knew seriously considered becoming expats. Two of her friends whose grandparents had been born in Ireland claimed their citizenship and moved abroad, each taking their families with them. Her own son, Ben, had left the country even before the inauguration, fleeing to Canada with his pregnant wife, Jess, and their two-year-old Tanner.

Jules re-read the final two sentences: *To combat authoritarianism, to call out lies, to struggle honorably and fiercely in the name of American ideals—that is what is left to do. That is all there is to do.*

She grabbed the scissors from her desk and carefully cut out these insightful words. She had finally found something fridgeworthy.

• • •

Jules had the death penalty research Ellie asked her for and they were meeting for lunch at a new Mexican food place on Wolf Road. She noticed Ellie's car in the parking lot as she headed inside. The smell of grilling meat engulfed her at the door, and she was suddenly famished. Ellie, waiting for her at a two-top near the bar, waved her over.

"Hey, Boss!" She always gave Jules a hard time about her hugs. She complained they lacked oomph. "It's like you're hugging your brother! C'mon, move in!"

Jules loved her friend's frankness. Ellie was always direct and rarely had a filter. She told it like she saw it. That was what had made her such an asset at WWP.

Jules handed over the file and they both took a seat. Ellie was short, maybe 5'4" in heels, and really had to boost herself up into the bar height seat. Her ink black hair was pulled back in a tight ponytail that fell halfway down her back. She didn't pay much attention to her looks, but she didn't need to. She was stunningly beautiful. Natural. She used no makeup. Anything she wore looked better for her having it on. Today it was simple black trousers and a cornflower blue, v-neck sweater that looked like cashmere but wasn't. She wore the same gold earrings every day of her life. They had been a gift from her Abuelita.

"So, other than the death penalty stuff, what else are you working on right now?" Jules asked. She tried to keep up on the work of the organization that she had steered for so many years.

"Well, we're still completely dedicated to the core mission and the major world peace initiatives that you know, but Flora is making a big push for us to take a more active and vocal role in domestic gun violence and gun control issues. I am really excited about putting more of our resources into that work."

"Wait, so you AGREE with Flora? AND, you're calling her by her first name?" Jules laughed. Ellie usually referred to Flora as Jefe. Not in a good way and not to her face.

"I have to admit it. She's good at her job."

"Well, it only took you about five years." Flora had been an excellent pick for the CEO slot, and she had continued to move the organization forward in meaningful ways. Jules understood the importance of the relation between the two, and she worked to never undermine that.

Their server came over and introduced herself. As Ellie ordered, Jules glanced around at the small early lunch crowd. It was a big space, seating for 200 or so, and well designed as an upscale Mexican spot. It wasn't a chain. The owners were local and had the bad luck of holding their grand opening in March, 2020. New York State went into lockdown on March 23rd that year. Somehow, they had survived and come out the other end. The place was packed from happy hour on, every day.

"So, tell me about the gun violence initiatives. I know the board was a little squeamish when we decided to take on the death penalty. Some members thought it was outside of our mission. Was this a hard sell?"

Ellie considered the question.

"Oh, yeah. I forgot that piece of history. Honestly, I think that made it an easier sell. World peace starts at home, right?"

"Amen!"

"I'll be honest, Jules, I really didn't know the extent of gun violence until we started down this path. I mean, I knew it was bad, but did you know that gun violence is the LEADING cause of death for children and young people in America? The leading cause! I was shocked to learn that. We're going to be working with March for our Lives. They're the ones who have brought the suit against that NRA guy. LaPew?"

"LaPierre."

"Right. They may be able to unseat him."

"Let's hope so. That 'non-profit' has been running the show with Republicans for way too long; lining their pockets to look the other way when we have yet another mass tragedy. I really don't know how those people sleep at night."

"The other partner we have in this is the Everytown Group. That's the one that was started after Sandy Hook. We're going to start with some grassroots stuff at the local level, bringing both groups into the community. Then we'll see where it leads."

"That sounds like fun! Good old street level work. If you hold any protests and need a sign carrier, call me. I'll bring my bull-horn." They laughed as the food arrived.

"Thanks, Boss. The work is going to be done by a subcommittee with lower-level staff support. I'm just glad we're dipping our nose in the water. Right now, my focus is on Ukraine."

"Toes."

"What?" Ellie glanced down at her feet.

"It's 'dipping our *toes* in the water.'"

"Oh, right." Ellie shook her head. "That makes more sense."

"So, what work are you doing in Ukraine? That's going to blow up any day. Things are really ramping up at the border."

"We're sending in aid along with some other NGOs. And we're trying to get women and children out ahead. It's hard, because so many Ukrainians are holding onto hope that it won't happen."

"I know. I get it, El. I'm still holding out hope! If Putin invades . . ." Jules trailed off, sighing under the weight of it all.

"It's hard to imagine where that will lead. And 45 is really looking like he's making a run." The two women shared a grimace as their food arrived.

They had sat together in the WWP offices late into the night of the election in 2016, watching the returns, both giddy with the thrill of electing the first woman president of the United States. A bottle of Dom Perignon sat in the office fridge, chilled for victory. Throughout the evening they each spoke to friends and family members on their phones, assuring them that these were just early returns. That it couldn't happen. Then they watched in horror as state after state was declared for Trump. It was after 2:30 am when Hillary conceded, and both women were in tears, shellshocked. Jules left the room and returned with the champagne bottle. She held it in two hands by the neck and hurled it with all of her strength at the wall-mounted TV screen, shattering both with a scream that came from her ancestors. Ellie gathered her up off of the floor and rocked her, waiting for her to return. To accept.

"No more shop talk!" Ellie declared. Jules gladly agreed.

They spent the next hour eating and catching up on personal stuff. Over the years the relationship had morphed from a professional one to a personal one. Jules was like a surrogate mother after Ellie's mom, Nikki, died. The twins were just toddlers then. Ellie, a single mom. Abuela was living with them to help out. She died in her sleep of a brain aneurysm. Ellie had been devastated by the loss. Her mom was a spitfire. A young 52-years with the energy of three women. Nikki kept the office fed, sending in amazing stews and breads. Everyone loved her.

Jules had been there for all of them in the weeks and months that followed. She had given Ellie as much support as possible, re-distributing her workload, flexing her hours, encouraging her to work from home before that was even a thing. Now that the girls were older, Ellie managed more easily. To Jules' surprise and delight, she had even started dating, though no one in particular. She shared a few horror stories over lunch that almost made Jules grateful that her own well was dry. The two women parted ways with promises to connect again soon.

• • •

Their conversation got Jules thinking about her own dating future. Driving up the Northway her mind started to wander. At 66, she was a woman who had learned to love herself. She had never really agonized over her looks, or her weight, or what people thought of her. She had a natural confidence that sometimes took her by surprise. She took care of herself for the most part. She dabbled in yoga, did a spin class 2 or 3 times a week. She walked for miles with her earbuds in, listening to e-books or podcasts. She didn't really diet but she didn't eat sweets except for a few times every year. She drank lots of water and very little alcohol. All of this kept her blood pressure in check and her heart healthy, but she still had a roundness. Menopause had not been kind to her metabolism, and she could probably stand to lose 20 or 30 pounds. "Rubenesque" was her go-to adjective in her pointless online dating profiles. Still, every time she saw herself in the mirror, excess pounds and wrinkles and dimples and all, she thought, "Not bad for everything we've been through together!"

She accepted that she might never have a romantic relationship again in her life, and she wasn't even sure she really wanted one. She had been a widow for decades, putting everything she had into her kids and her work, and maybe that door had closed. But she did believe in love, that it was attainable in many forms. She wasn't jaded. In fact, she believed love was the only thing that mattered. Who you love and who loves you. It had taken many years of self-discovery and seeking, but she had eventually settled on some truths that felt foundational to her; a worldview that had carried her through.

In her teens she tried embracing organized religion, the Catholicism she was born to, but in the end it felt ridiculous and she couldn't force it. When she studied philosophy as an undergrad in her 20s, there was the first glimmer of some palatable perspectives. What she landed on was something without a deity. It was a belief system that distinguished between the spiritual and physical planes and recognized the connectedness of all humanity. When she read Tolle's "The Power of Now," back when she was newly widowed and a young single parent, steeped in worry and fear, it had changed her life forever. She came to value peace, kindness, and love above all.

She had been so grateful for those first principles during the ongoing pandemic years. When the first stirrings of COVID appeared in early 2020, she was still struggling with life as an empty-nester. It had been a few years since Jax, her youngest, left, but she had never quite gotten her sea legs as a loner. She hadn't realized that the boys had been so central to who she was as a person. She was too busy raising them to see it.

In those days, she saw herself as a successful professional woman and single mom. Her kids were great, her work as the CEO at

WWP was fulfilling, and she thought she was killing it! She knew there would be some adjustment once they launched, but it had stretched into years and she had just never settled in to this new stage of her womanhood. She couldn't quite grasp her purpose now. She had been surprised by the intensity of her love for the kids when they came, and she was just as surprised at the void their absence left in her.

In 2017, with the boys launched, she had decided to step away from Women Waging Peace and try something new. She loved the work, but she had taken the organization a long way, and it was time for some new vision. With decades of experience and leadership to bring to the table to help other organizations, and after 30 years as a CEO, she wanted a more flexible schedule. So, after a hiatus of more than a year, Jules started her own consulting firm. It had been promising right out of the gate. Her large network and reputation as a visionary thinker and collaborative leader meant she had no shortage of clients. Of course, everything changed in 2020. Despite binding contracts and good intentions, COVID was running the show. All of her clients shelved their projects and sent their staff home. The world was closed for business.

One thing Jules knew was that work had always been central to her sense of self. While some people's nightmares featured monsters or murderers, hers featured unemployment. In her sleep she would find herself suddenly destitute and desperate to find a job. She came from a family where there were no extras, so she had worked from a very young age. When she was underage and wanting a mall job to buy makeup and clothes, her dad had proudly doctored her birth certificate and sent her off to the interview. The message was clear. Making a buck was more important than following the law. Jules got that first job at the Woolworth's cafeteria where she proved to be a lousy waitress. But with regular paychecks and tips, she bought those coveted platforms at Turtle Shoes, and the blacklight posters at Spencer's, and some make-up from her friend's older sister, who was an Avon Lady. Except for her maternity leave, and a few months after Mick died, Jules had worked ever since. Even through college and grad school she had a paycheck coming in.

COVID changed all of that. Suddenly, the stuff of her nightmares was coming true. From one day to the next, she had no visible source of income. Just like that. Luckily, she had a small safety net in her 401k. It was laughable to call it a retirement account; it would barely see her through six months if she was frugal. Which she had rarely been. She had put the boys through college with what remained of Micks' life insurance and what she had been able to accumulate through the years on her own and was just rebuilding her nest egg when this freshest hell hit the fan. But at least she had something to buy her some time. At least she could put off complete panic while she looked for that next opportunity.

Jules immediately refocused her energies on getting a job. It shouldn't be hard, even in a pandemic. She was a Navy vet, a first-generation college grad, and she held a graduate degree in poli sci. She was well-respected in her field and had a very marketable skill set. She freshened up her c.v., added recent accomplishments, publications, and presentations, and started the rounds. She put the word out in her spheres of influence, letting everyone know she was on the job market. She went back to all the old familiar places: Idealist, American Society of Association Executives, New York Council on Nonprofits, Execunet, Ladders. She went back to every executive recruiter who had ever reached out to her. She applied and applied and applied. She beefed up her LinkedIn profile and expanded that network. She put out all of her feelers. Eventually, she even started looking at Indeed and Craigslist. Nothing. Nothing was coming her way.

As weeks turned to months, the truth began to settle on Jules. Even with her resume, she wasn't in the right demographic for a new hire in the aftermath of the pandemic. She recalled her shock a few years earlier when a 59-year-old man had been hit by a car and the news had referred to him as 'elderly.' She was apparently beyond that threshold, no longer middle-aged. Unhireable.

She had felt that value shift in her social life, as well. At a certain point, women become invisible as sexual partners. They lose whatever power they may have had to attract the opposite sex. The men on the dating sites in her age group were all looking for young, thin women. "Vibrant." "Active." "High-energy." Code for young and thin. And Jules was neither. She had come to terms with it years ago, and she even understood it. After all, when she scrolled through the age-appropriate matches on Our Time or Meet Mindful or Plenty of Fish, she couldn't muster much interest in the 60- and 70-something men she knew were once active and attractive and who might find her interesting. It was one thing to grow old with someone and stay in love. It was quite something else to fall in love with an old person. Still, she held out some nugget of hope and continued to scroll.

But it had never dawned on her that she would become invisible in her professional life at this age. It had taken her so long to prove herself, acquiring her credentials and building her reputation over the course of the last thirty years. She saw herself as vibrant and engaged and still in the game, with so much more to offer. As often happened, she was surprised at her own naivete. In the beginning, it made Jules furious that she was being boxed out, especially in a country where 80-year-old white men are elected to run the country! But she couldn't stew. She needed to accept the current situation and find a solution. She was nothing if not a problem solver.

She was grateful that she no longer had to provide for her sons and needed only to generate enough income to meet her own needs. But that was not insignificant. She had her mortgage, insurance, car payments, utilities, gas, groceries, and on and on. And that was just necessities.

Thankfully, she didn't have any credit card debt. She and Mick had gotten that monkey off their backs early in their 20s. They could see the potential for financial disaster that those easy money schemes represented. As young marrieds, they wanted all the new and shiny things. And Mastercard and Visa, Discovery and American Express had gladly complied. The debt outlasted the stuff, and she hadn't fallen for it again. She paid cash or she went without. She kept one card with a $5,000.00 credit limit in case of emergencies.

And then there was her own student loan debt! She couldn't believe that at her age she was still paying off student loans. It was ridiculous. That debt alone was in the six figures. It was more than any house she had ever owned. She didn't think about it much because it was almost mythological. And she didn't share it with anyone. It was her dirty little secret. It had happened gradually, as she had requested one forbearance after another over the course of 20 years as she raised the kids alone. There were a lot of ways to put off the inevitable, and Jules had needed to put it off.

Over the years, as the nut grew from something under $100k for 7 years of education to something nearing the half-million-dollar mark, the loan servicers would call. She'd explain her situation and they'd find a loophole, adding to the magical number. It got to a point where the calls went like this.

"Hi, this is Jules."

"Ms. Campbell, this is so and so from the Bank of Make-Believe Money, calling about your student debt."

"Oh, sure! What would you like to discuss?"

"Well, your most recent forbearance ends next month and I'm calling to let you know that your first payment of $23,756. 92 will be due on the first of every month."

"Okay. Well, I make a little more than 3 times that amount in a year, so clearly I can't pay that. I already know two things from our years of conversations regarding this debt. One is that it can't be discharged in bankruptcy. The other is that it's forgiven when I die. I am (52, 55, 57, 59, 63, 66) years old now, and I've already educated my kids about the forgiveness at death. It's the only thing that lets me sleep at night."

Beat.

"Well, how much can you pay?"

"I can pay $300.00 a month."

"Ok, let me see if I can find a program that will let us work with this."

Hold. Hold. Hold.

"Ms. Campbell? Thank you for holding."

"No problem." She was always very accommodating to the debt collectors.

"I've found a program and if you can make the $300.00 monthly payments for the next 12 months, it will keep you out of default status. Does that sound okay with you?"

"Absolutely! Let's get me signed up immediately."

And this went on for decades. In around 2016 she'd finally gotten into a program where her entire debt will be forgiven if she makes a $500.00 payment every month for 10 years. Or so they say. By 2020, Jules had since become surprisingly comfortable with this sword of Damocles. But now, facing joblessness, that once meager monthly payment is suddenly daunting.

The money she'd need just to maintain her life, without having to move, was not insignificant. She'd cut back in lots of areas, like entertainment, travel, clothes, dining out. She did her own nails. All of this was easy as the pandemic wore on and those luxuries disappeared. She avoided online shopping. She didn't need cable, but she did need high speed internet access. Tightening the belt let her stretch that 401k money a little further. But as spring turned to summer, the pandemic settled in and paying work was not on her horizon. Her balance was shrinking, and it was getting harder to breathe.

In the fall of 2020, as the last of her miserable life savings dwindled, Jules applied for assistance in the form of unemployment benefits from the State of New York and Supplemental Nutrition Assistance Plan (SNAP), otherwise known as food stamps. She was humiliated but grateful for the state-issued debit card that gave her a few hundred dollars each month in grocery money, and the few hundred dollars each week direct-deposited into her bank account to cover some of her living expenses. She remembered the times when her dad, a teamster, had been on strike over one labor dispute or another. Her mom standing at the checkout, struggling with the booklet of food stamps, actual coupons that had to be removed and handed over to the cashier, obvious to everyone in line behind them. Technology allowed Jules to be more discreet in her pop-up poverty. And so she was able, like everyone else in these worst first years of COVID, to stave off hunger and homelessness through the largesse of the state. And of course, Ben and Jax made sure she was ok, constantly asking if she needed any money. She had been able to hobble through without resorting to that final humiliation, and their loving care and concern kept her from the depths of a despair to which she might otherwise have fallen prey. It was all so incredibly Orwellian.

The first year turned into the second year of disease, and by 2021 Jules had abandoned all of her preconceived notions of what her life was supposed to look like. She hadn't even been thinking of retirement, given her lack of any meaningful source of income. She knew she could start to draw her social security benefits since she was over 62, but she was hoping to hold off until 67 or even 70, to maximize her monthly income. As far as she could tell, it was all a crap shoot. If she lived into her 90s, she wanted to make sure she had the highest social security income possible from her years in the labor force. If she died in her 60s, before she started drawing, it was a lost opportunity to cash in as soon as she reached eligibility. Jules considered herself an intelligent and well-educated person, and she wondered how so many average people figured out this incredibly complicated system. After a little research, Jules decided to start collecting. Her situation was just too dire to wait any longer. If the pandemic passed in the next few months, she would return to her consulting work and try to pick up those pieces.

In the meantime, she needed to earn to fill in the gaps. She'd been able to hold the wolves at bay but now she was getting desperate. She was no stranger to hard work and manual labor, and she wasn't above whatever it took to make a legal buck. She decided to drive for Uber and Lyft. It was easy, flexible, and entirely independent. She joked with her passengers that she was the most highly educated driver they'd ever have. Sadly, she doubted that was true.

When Jules got home from lunch with Ellie, she filled her thermos with hot green tea. She slipped on her muk-luks, her driving coat and gloves, wrapped her neck with a scarf, and headed out for an afternoon of driving.

.   .   .

On Friday, Jules was meeting her lifelong best friend, Sally, for lunch at Barcelona. It was one of Sally's favorite spots, and Jules was treating her for her 66th birthday. She'd been squirreling away a little money from her driving gigs for the last few months to be able to afford this extravagance and had been looking forward to the treat.

Jules and Sally had grown up two houses apart. With paltry, unfenced backyards between them, and kids of roughly the same ages, the two families nearly merged, with any or all of them to be found in either house on any given day. Mrs. Adams, a widow with kids and grandkids who visited rarely, lived between them and gave up trying to keep them from crossing through her yard. The hedges she'd planted in a useless attempt to thwart this shortcutting never managed to fill in, avoiding that space where children passed through. In summers, a wide dirt path was worn between the O'Malleys' and the Campbells' back doors; in winters, a dirty, icy trench. To make up for the constant traffic of kids, bikes, and sometimes dogs or cats, their fathers took turns shoveling widow Adams' sidewalks and driveway every winter. In that way, a grudging truce was achieved through the years.

.   .   .

Jules arrived first and took a seat where she could watch for Sally, setting the beautifully wrapped gift she had for her on the table. It was covered in a glossy black, heavy paper and adorned with a handmade bow in Sally's signature color. It had taken three different Youtube videos before she was finally able to get that bow right.

Jules ordered two white sangrias and water, and the calamari appetizer. This was always the start of their meals here. Their tradition. Before lunch was over, Jules knew they'd be in tears laughing at something. No matter what had gone on in their lives, they'd always been able to laugh together. After they gave witness to the latest horribles in their lives -- deaths and illnesses and divorces and miscarriages and money troubles and infidelities and all of the things that make a life difficult -- they would swim to the surface, embrace the ridiculous. Before they parted ways, they would be doubled over, barely able to breathe, and more recently, peeing their pants. Tradition.

Jules waved when Sally walked in the door, stamping her feet and unbuttoning her coat. She was dressed head-to-toe in a bright but tasteful reddish orange blouse and pants. Tomato red. A color any fashion magazine would warn her against with that hair. Of course, that unsolicited fashion advice only made Sally want it more. It had become her signature color. The wide boat neck of the blouse exposed her still sharp clavicles, and a flowy abstract print scarf, the darling of every mature woman, covered her neck. Her long, pale-ginger hair was pulled back in a low pony. As she approached the table, she locked eyes with Jules and gave a little kick and a quick, shallow lunge. Not anything anyone else would even notice. If it wasn't Barcelona, she might have launched into her full scale, Sally O'Malley routine.

Ever since she had been made famous by Molly Shannon's Saturday Night Live character, Sally had milked it for all it was worth. Mostly just to goad her husband, Hemmy. They had gotten married in 1975. It was the era of the second wave of feminism. Betty Friedan's groundbreaking work, "The Feminine Mystique", was still in all of the front windows of the book stores. Young women were thinking differently about who they could become. Sally, at 20, decided not to become Sally Bledsoe. Hemmy didn't really have anything to say about it if he wanted her to meet him at the end of that aisle. Sally was born Sally O'Malley and she would die Sally O'Malley. They had never even discussed it as a couple. Then, in 1999, Molly's Sally, kicking and stretching and sporting a camel toe, appeared on their TV screen one Saturday night as they lay in bed watching. Hemmy, in a lapse of judgment he has regretted ever since, turned to his bride of nearly 25 years and laughing, roared, "See! You should have changed your name!"

Instead of responding to what Sally saw as her husband's biggest mistake, Sally simply embraced her great good fortune and became Molly's biggest fan. Jules never knew when SNL Sally might show up. It was mostly an inside joke. Family and friends kind of thing. Nobody looking at her now would get the reference, but Jules expected some big news. SNL Sally was usually a bellwether.

Jules stood and the friends hugged as they had thousands of times. It's not the hug of acquaintances. It's bone on bone. A full giving of self and acceptance of other. Religious. A hug that would make Ellie proud.

"You are a nut job, Sally O'Malley, and I love you!" Jules laughed. "Happy birthday, girl!"

As they sat, their appetizer and drinks arrived, and they clinked glasses.

"Chin-chin!" They chirped.

"To you, my dear friend! Happy birthday!" Jules took a sip.

Sally rolled her eyes. "It gets boring, doesn't it? Having to pretend you care about someone's birthday year in and year out? Just like assholes and opinions, everybody has one! Why can't we just do a blanket 'happy birthday everyone', from now until the end of eternity. One and done." Sally complained feebly.

"What would Hallmark do then, Sal? Plus, I love celebrating you. Would you deprive an old crone of that joy?"

"Ok I'll give you that. So how about this, other than immediate family, we only have to care about one other person's birthday. I'll pick you and you pick me. I mean, the Facebook birthday wishes? Really? How much effort does that take? With the push of one button you send a prefab message with a picture of balloons and cake."

Jules raises an eyebrow, "I sent you one of those!"

"You know what I mean, Jules."

"I do, but you're not usually this cynical. And I bet tomorrow you'll post how grateful you are for all of those wishes."

"You know I will. I'm just cranky today."

"Just your regular birthday blues or something more?" Jules asked.

Sally was quiet for a moment, looking at the woman who has been in her corner since the playpen.

"I don't know," she sighed "I just. . . How the hell am I sixty-six?" She looked at Jules as if she was pleading for something. Jules reached for her hand. I'm right here with you, she's saying.

"I know, Sal. I think about my age every. Single. Day. I don't remember when it started, and I don't know if it's normal or neurotic. It's like death. We just don't really talk about it in civilized society, even if it's all we think about. We're all supposed to be embracing the 'third act' or something. Christ. I guess that's better than the 'golden years,' but not by much."

They sipped their drinks and felt tired.

Jules continued, "It's just so weird feeling like the person you've always been on the inside, then looking in the mirror at what everyone else sees. Anyone describing either one of us would say "she's an elderly woman." Sally gave her a feigned look of shock. "Okay, maybe "older woman" if they were being kind. That's where we've landed. From here on out our deaths won't be 'tragic.' We won't be 'lives cut short.' There's just no other option. Well, except the eternal dirt nap."

They both laughed and leaned back, comedy masking their sorrow.

"I'm not as opposed to the dirt nap anymore," Sally shook her head.

"Mm. I can't pretend to be appalled and I know that's not a cry for help. Let's get martinis and right the world."

"Yes! As soon as we finish this!" Sally raised her glass to Jules. "But before we get too deep in our cups, I have news."

Jules looked up from the calamari she was dipping, "I knew it! What's wrong?"

"Nothing 'wrong' really. It's Claire." Sally had seven grandchildren, and Claire, the youngest, was the only girl among them.

At 16, Claire was Sally's youngest grandbaby. She was funny and bright, and about to graduate, having skipped a year in middle school. She would head to SUNY Purchase next year on a scholarship to study drama. Claire was very dramatic, in a good way, from a young age. At any family gathering, she would organize all of the older kids to perform. Not just her siblings, but any kid in attendance old enough to walk but not old enough for the grown-up table. Sometimes just a dance routine or a song. But at the big holidays, like Christmas or Thanksgiving, it was a full-blown extravaganza, with scripts and costumes. She ran a tight ship as producer, but even though *she* had everyone's lines memorized, she grudgingly let all of the 'actors' read from the scripts. Amateurs!

In elementary school she had the lead role in Peter Pan. In middle school she always auditioned for anything theatrical, and always won speaking roles. By high school she was a self-proclaimed theater geek. Any money she earned at her job at the bookstore went straight to tickets to some production at a small local theater, or The Palace or Proctors or the Cap Rep if there was something she couldn't miss. She never missed a free show at the Park Playhouse and had volunteered to work on a few of their productions over the last few years.

"Is she pregnant!?" Jules' first thought tumbled onto the table between them.

"No! . . . She's trans."

"Oh, thank god!"

"Jules!"

"Well, are you really that surprised? Our Carhart and flannels Claire-bear? With all those older brothers around, she probably saw the writing on the wall. She wanted the privileges of the forty-nine percent!"

"I hardly think that went into her calculations." Jules' teasing missed the mark.

"Sorry, Sal. I'm just kidding. But look, Claire couldn't be in a more supportive family to make such a big life decision. Right? How did you find out?"

"She just called me yesterday to tell me. After she told Erin and Sean, she asked them to let her tell me herself."

"How are Erin and Sean taking it? And the boys?"

Their waiter came over, filled their water glasses, and took their orders. Sally ordered the paella, and Jules the butternut squash ravioli. It was delicious here, and not too sweet like at most restaurants. They each ordered a Lemon Drop. Sally was usually a beer drinker, but birthdays called for extravagances.

"I called Erin after Claire and I talked. I mean of course they all love and support her no matter what. But there is a grief there for her. Or something like it. I actually think it's harder on Erin than Sean. And the boys, well, you know, this is their generation. They get it! People are people and love is love and so what? All this worry about who uses what bathroom is just not a concern they have."

"Oh my god. That tired chestnut. Do you know how many workplaces have unisex bathrooms? My last office building did. There are private stalls! With doors! If they're really worried about people being sexually aroused using the bathroom, by that logic, gay men should have to use the women's room and lesbians to the men's."

Their martinis arrived and they each raised their glass before a first sip. Sally's hand trembled slightly on its way to her lips, spilling a few drops on her scarf. She wiped at it with her napkin and Jules pretended not to notice.

"Okay, so the news is out and everyone is good for the moment." Jules chewed thoughtfully. "What does it mean for Claire? Is she going to change her name? Is she going to transition medically?"

"She, I mean HE, wants to use he/him pronouns. He is going to change his name to Eric. It's almost Claire backwards."

"I'm so glad she, *HE*, Eric, isn't opting for they/them. I just can't wrap my head around using they/them as a singular pronoun! It confuses the hell out of me and I always think I've misunderstood who is being spoken about. I wish we could just come up with some new, gender-neutral pronouns."

"I know. Something like knee/kner, maybe? Spelled G-N-E and G-N-E-R?"

"I like it. Or knee/knim?" suggested Jules.

"Surely some linguist somewhere is working on this."

"To the linguists!" Jules raised her glass.

"The linguists!" echoed Sally.

"So, what about the medical part? Has Cla . . . Eric made any decisions there? It's too late for puberty blockers."

"No, I think she wants to take it in steps and let it evolve. She's going to start as male-presenting at Purchase. She sent me a pic of the haircut she's going to get right before she leaves." Sally dug through her purse and grabbed her phone, holding it out to Jules after a few clicks. Jules leaned in to see.

"Oh, yeah. That will be cute on herrm? Damn. This is going to take some getting used to."

"Mm-hmm. She's really thought this through, Jules. I'm proud of her for that. She's going to bind for a while before deciding on top surgery. I swear, the serious issues our grandkids are dealing with is mind-boggling to me!"

"What do you mean? We had Vietnam and women's lib and abortion rights and Kennedy and Nixon! Jesus, Nixon." Jules vamped double peace signs with both arms stretched to the max. "We had our share of the shit show. And you mean HE'S thought it through and you're proud of HIM."

"Right! He, him, he, him." She sipped her Lemon Drop without a spill. "We did have our own fires though, didn't we. And we fought some good fights. We invented Earth Day, thank you very much! We must have at least slowed the climate crisis for our babies, right? Remember how much trash used to be along the roadways?"

"Yes! And what about smoking? We practically wiped it out."

"We've been busy girls!" Sally shook her head, laughing as their lunch arrived.

They pulled their chairs closer to the table and ate their first few bites in silence.

"This paella is delish! The rice is perfect. I love these crunchy bits." Sally pointed with her fork to the dark edges of the dish.

"Mmm. The ravioli, too. It never disappoints."

They ate appreciatively for a while, noticing their fellow diners. The room was a mix of ladies who lunch, suited deal-makers with goals and no time to spare, and a singlet here and there. If it were dinner rather than lunch, there would have been families and couples celebrating their special occasions. Barcelona was a special occasion kind of place.

"So, Sal, what are you worried about with Claire?"

"Honestly, the only thing I fear is her safety. I fear other people. I can't protect her from hate. Him. Eric."

"No, you can't. It's weird to think how much more progressive we were as a society ten, twenty years ago. Before that vapid asshole got elected. I know it's your birthday and I'm sorry to ruin it, but EVERYTHING is political now!"

"Yeah, the personal IS political. We invented that, and I've always known it. But it's magnified by the rise of these hate groups since Trump. People who traffic in hate have been freed from having to play nice. They don't need robes and hoods anymore. They have MAGA hats. And they want to overthrow democracy, for fucks sake!"

Sally's voice had risen and Jules glanced around to see if there were any kids nearby.

"Sorry," Sally calmed her voice. "But, seriously, these times we're in now? Did you see he's launching his own social media platform? 'Truth Social.' He wouldn't know truth if it bit him in the ass! We could never have imagined this! We all fought so hard for the ground we gained. It scares me, Jules."

"Me, too."

"Shit! You're not supposed to say that. You're the historian. You're supposed to tell me that this is just a stage in the life cycle of a healthy democracy, or something."

"I'm a political scientist, not a historian."

"Same thing. Just comfort me with your knowledge, for Christ's sake."

Sally hadn't gone to college, but she had a keen intellect and endless curiosity. It was never a bone of contention between the two friends, her lack of a higher education experience. From their shared upbringing, they both took as gospel that each person was presented with different opportunities and obstacles in their lives. Everyone had choices to make and a path to walk. Hemmy, with Sally's support and encouragement, had plodded his way through an undergraduate program on nights and weekends, and had worked most of his adult life in finance, earning a comfortable living for their family. She had seen her children and grandchildren earn their degrees. Sally joked that she was 'college-adjacent'.

"I wish I could help." Jules set her fork on her plate; she leaned towards Sally with no hint of a smile and dropped her voice. "But this moment looks different to me, Sal. And dangerous. Now they're reporting that he has all of these classified documents at his compound in Florida. Something like 15 boxes of stuff that could be top secret, just sitting there. And people in his administration are saying they saw him destroy documents in the White House before he left. It just makes me furious!"

A waiter came by to top off their water glasses. He was a young man, slight and dark skinned. He smiled at them both and wished Sally a happy birthday before hurrying off.

"We used to have first principles that were part of our national identity, y'know?" Jules continued, watching him go. "Things we accepted as true, at least publicly. Racism was bad. Full stop. Sexism was bad. Homophobia was bad. Xenophobia was bad. Now we have 'alternative facts.' It's okay to hate immigrants, or anyone for that matter, in the name of this "America First" agenda of the right."

"That's what I mean. Eric could end up a victim of that hate and I just can't help her! I have to let her live it."

"You do. Like we do with all of them, right? If we've done right by them they grow up to become their true selves. The best we can do is be their biggest champions. So that's what we'll do for him."

Jules reached over and laid her hand on top of Sally's. Both women looked at their joined hands, then up at each other.

"Isn't it strange seeing these old, wrinkled hands?" Sally lifted hers and turned the backs to Jules for inspection. "This is where I'm constantly reminded of my age, y'know? They're starting to remind me of my Tati's hands."

"But your Tati didn't have that killer French manicure!" Now Jules turned hers to Sally.

"Look at these! This raisiny skin. These inky veins and liver spots. But they've served me well and I love them for that. I heard "Grandma's Hands" on the radio the other day. I haven't heard that song in probably thirty years! Do you remember that one? Al Green, I think."

"God yes, I remember that! I loved it. It wasn't Al Green, though. He did "Let's Stay Together." Who the hell was it? The artist died recently." They both searched their own archives, neither reaching for a phone.

"Bill Withers!" Jules got it first.

"Yes! Bill Withers!"

"That song first came out when these hands were still juicy. But they were also boring. They hadn't really DONE anything or BEEN anywhere! When I heard those lyrics now, at this age, it really struck a chord."

The waiter arrived to take dessert orders. Birthday dessert was a must-have. It was the law. No pleading full or dieting or any other lame excuse. And no sharing. A full dessert, no fruit, and an Irish Coffee each. Tradition.

"So, we have these alien hands," Jules wiggled her fingers, "and we've EARNED them. Eric will need 'Grandma's Hands.' Just be there to 'pick him up when he falls down.'" She sang lightly.

They sipped their drinks and leaned back into their chintz covered armchairs, each with her own thoughts.

"Remember when we used to smoke, Jules? Sometimes, after a meal like this, I wish I still did. It was so therapeutic! Those deep breaths in and out."

"Yeah, with deadly toxins thrown in for good measure. No thanks. I'm so glad we both quit! Can you imagine if we were still smoking all these years later? What would these claws look like then! Or these teeth! We'd scare the grandkids to death!"

Laughing, Sally held a pretend cigarette in her right hand and brought it to her lips, inhaling the magical tonic and thoughtfully blowing the imaginary smoke away from their table.

"Aaahhhh," Sally sighed, "a girl can dream."

Jules picked up the gift that had been sitting on the table and passed it over to Sally.

"Here, open your gift before dessert."

"Thank you! It's beautiful," Sally remarked of the wrapping.

"What am I going to be reading this week?" Jules' go-to gift was always a book. She knew every independent, used, and antiquarian bookstore within a hundred-mile radius. And anywhere she traveled, she made sure to find the closest indy bookseller.

Sally peeled back the paper to reveal a mostly white cover featuring a worn pair of work boots, with a fluffy blue sky sailing above. Written in the sky, "Limbo," and just below that "Blue-Collar Roots, White-Collar Dreams," by Alfred Lubrano.

"It's non-fiction," explained Jules, "so you might not read it in a week. But I ran across this copy on one of my road trips. I have my own copy somewhere and when I saw this, I remembered how much it reminded me of us and our families, and so many people we grew up with. I think you'll really like it."

"I think I remember you mentioning this one before. The title sounds familiar." Sally began reading the cover copy. "Interesting premise. Relevant. I mean, look at us sitting here. You couldn't find two people with a more working-class pedigree. Our parents would have never come to a place like this! And in our lives, we just take this for granted. We expect it. What a huge difference in a single generation."

"I know. I don't think my kids feel any connection to a 'blue-collar' identity. In the same way I never felt connected to my parents' post-great depression identity. That's what we try to do, right? Bring the next generation along to something better."

Their treats arrived along with their whiskeyed coffees, topped with a generous froth of whipped cream.

"Mmmm." They both sat forward to avoid any drippage.

"Heaven!" They ate in sweet silence.

"Do you remember like twenty, twenty-five years ago when there was all of that research coming out about the four generations being in the workplace together? It was a few years after Tom Brokaw came out with his book about the greatest generation."

"Mmmhmmm." Sally's mouth was full.

"A lot of the work that emerged back then tied each generation to a single significant historical event that defined them. Like for our parents it was World War Two and the depression. For us it was Vietnam and Civil Rights. This was just after 9/11 when that research was gaining traction. I think a lot of it was out of Cornell. The expectation was that 9/11 would be the defining event for that generation. I sure thought it would be a dividing line in my life. Before 9/11 and after 9/11. But then the 2016 election happened. In my opinion, nothing in our history as a nation has posed a greater threat than 45." Jules went to great lengths to avoid calling him by name, while she had no trouble calling him names.

"Hm." Sally thought for a moment. "What about the Civil War?" she probed.

"I've thought about that a lot. As a country, we came out of that intact, and leaning into a more robust, egalitarian democracy. It took time, but good prevailed."

"Ok, but we survived Trump."

"Yeah, but the Washington Post reported he's planning another run for 2024. He hasn't officially announced yet, but he's pretty much committed."

"What?!? Jesus! I missed that." Sally's face fell and she looked away from Jules, off into some unimaginable tomorrow. She pushed her dessert plate away from her, unfinished. After a moment, she took a sip of her coffee and wiped her mouth with the linen napkin. She blinked to stave off the tears, then turned her whole body to face Jules.

"What do we do?"

• • •

On Thursday, February 24th, 2022, less than a week after Sally's desperate question, Jules suddenly understood her life's purpose. Something clicked inside her bones and a calm resolve warmed her through. She felt the return of a hope that had abandoned her completely on that morning in 2016, in the WWP offices, when she and Ellie first learned that Donald Trump would become the next President of the United States of America. In that moment, and in every moment since, she no longer recognized her country.

And now Vladimir Putin, Russian President and Trump's BFF, had lost his mind, invading a sovereign Ukraine after weeks of absurd cat and mouse. Until the very day before the invasion, the ridiculous dictator had insisted that the 150,000 plus Russian troops amassing at Ukraine's border were only carrying out 'planned military exercises,' drills, and were a purely defensive force. Nobody bought the lies but there was nothing to be done. Now the war had begun, and NATO allies were denouncing the aggression in the 'strongest terms possible.' As if that would deter this power-hungry maniac whose love for the former Soviet Union was nearly pornographic. For Jules, World War III seemed a very real possibility.

For years, Jules had been asking anyone who would listen the exact question Sally had posed at her birthday dinner, "But what do we DO?"

She asked it in the lead up to the 2016 elections. When an editorial in The Atlantic entitled "Against Donald Trump" had called him "a demagogue, a xenophobe, a sexist, a know-nothing, and a liar."

She asked it when he talked about grabbing women by the pussy.

She asked it when he mentioned killing people on 5th avenue.

She asked it when she discovered that DJT was a named plaintiff, along with Jeffrey Epstein, in a 2016 California lawsuit demanding $100,000,000.00 was brought by a woman named Katie Johnson, alleging that the defendants had raped her and used her as a 'sex slave' when she was just 13 years old. April of 2016! Mid-election cycle! Where were the headlines? The day Epstein 'hung himself'? Jules knew that caged bird was planning to sing.

She asked it the day after the election. When the results showed Hillary Clinton with nearly 3 million more individual votes than Trump, but him winning the election with 306 of the 538 electoral votes.

She asked it in the weeks leading up to the inauguration in January 2017, when she secretly hoped and expected that good people in places of power were doing something, anything, to right this ship. They were not.

She asked it throughout the months and years of Trump's smarmy presidency. When he separated families at the border; when he pulled the plug on climate policy; when he mocked the disabled; when he fomented racism, sexism, homophobia; when he cozied up to Putin and Kim Jong-Un and Tweeted Mussolini quotes. When he lied, and lied, and lied.

She asked the women in her book club. She asked her friends and neighbors. She asked her family. She asked the panel members of her favorite morning radio talk show, The Roundtable, on WAMC. She asked her circle of long-time activist friends. Men and women who, like her, were appalled at the state of affairs.

And every time she asked it, what she meant was, what do we, the good and peaceful citizens of a country under the control of a megalomaniac and under siege by hate and power run amok, and a blatant disregard for human rights and the rule of law, do? What the actual fuck do we DO??

Inevitably, the answer was vote. Go to the polls at every opportunity. Vote in school board and city council and library board elections, vote in the mid-terms. Get your kids and neighbors to vote. Vote as religiously as the Republicans vote! That was the answer for the liberal-minded, peace-focused crowds in which she traveled.

At some earlier time in her life that might have been enough for Jules. But now it seemed weak and entirely unpersuasive. The right was determined to undermine elections and question their legitimacy at every turn. And it was clear that foreign countries opposed to democracy were interfering in our elections.

Those who saw voting as the solution to saving the country were well-meaning but naïve. They were still operating under the old playbook. The pre-45 playbook. If his presidency had done anything useful, it had exposed our democracy for what it was. Until he took office, America was revered as a great nation, underpinned by an inviolable Constitution, three independent branches of government, and a dogged commitment to the rule of law. Now everyone could see that the only thing holding all of it together was an implicit agreement to play by the rules. He had refused. And now he was considering running in 2024.

Jules knew that she was not over-reacting. The situation was as dire as it seemed. The fact that all around her everyone continued on with their day-to-day life was, she realized, a universal coping mechanism. It's like Stockholm Syndrome writ large. It's whistling past the graveyard. She was done whistling and she was done asking. She knew what to do. She would kill the snake at the head. She would kill Donald John Trump.

MASS SHOOTINGS IN THE US
February 2022 - 36 total

A mass shooting is any shooting where four or more people, other than the shooter, are killed or injured.

1. February 1, 2022 – Milwaukee, Wisconsin – 5 injured
2. February 2, 2022 – Oroville, California – 1 dead, 4 injured
3. February 4, 2022 - Blacksburg, Virginia – 1 dead, 4 injured
4. February 5, 2022 – Corsicana, Texas – 2 dead, 2 injured
5. February 5, 2022 - Las Cruces, New Mexico – 1 dead, 4 injured
6. February 6, 2022 - Fort Lauderdale, Florida – 4 injured
7. February 6, 2022 – Romeoville, Illinois – 4 injured
8. February 6, 2022 – Fresno, California – 6 dead, 6 injured
9. February 6, 2022 – Wilmington, North Carolina – 2 dead, 2 injured
10. February 11, 2022 – Springfield, Missouri – 4 dead,1 injured
11. February 11, 2022 – Phoenix, Arizona – 4 injured
12. February 12, 2022 - Murfreesboro, Tennessee – 1 dead, 3 injured
13. February 12, 2022 - West Hollywood, California – 1 dead, 6 injured
14. February 12, 2022 - Little Rock, Arkansas – 5 dead, 19 injured
15. February 13, 2022 – Racine, Wisconsin – 4 dead
16. February 15, 2022 – Joliet, Illinois – 4 injured

17. February 16, 2022 – Miami, Florida – 1 dead, 5 injured
18. February 17, 2022 – Philadelphia, Pennsylvania – 3 dead, 2 injured
19. February 17, 2022 – Houston, Texas- 1 dead, 6 injured
20. February 18, 2022 - Temple Hills, Maryland – 4 injured
21. February 19, 2022 – Portland, Oregon – 4 injured
22. February 19, 2022 – Charleston, Missouri – 1 dead, 3 injured
23. February 19, 2022 – Turlock, California – 4 injured
24. February 19, 2022 – Durham, North Carolina - 4 injured
25. February 20, 2022 - Des Moines, Iowa – 4 injured
26. February 20, 2022 - Mccomb Mississippi – 4 injured
27. February 20, 2022 – Omaha, Nebraska – 1 dead, 3 injured
28. February 20, 2022 – Portland, Oregon – 5 injured
29. February 21, 2022 - Saint Paul, Minnesota - 5 injured
30. February 24, 2022 - San Antonio, Texas – 4 injured
31. February 25, 2022 - Baton Rouge, Louisiana - 4 injured
32. February 26, 2022 - North Charleston, South Carolina – 9 injured
33. February 26, 2022 - Las Vegas, Nevada – 4 dead, 1 injured
34. February 26, 2022 – Bogalusa, Louisiana – 4 dead
35. February 27, 2022 – Alexandria, Louisiana - 4 injured
36. February 28, 2022 – Sacramento, California – 4 injured

• • •

MARCH 2022

"I love you the most! Bye Jax!" Jules Campbell signed off the call with their running joke, hung up the phone and headed into the kitchen to fix herself some lunch.

She had spent the morning shoveling the driveway and sidewalks after another 'unprecedented' early March snowfall. Climate change was exhausting her. She had resisted a snowblower so far because she still loved working up a sweat in the cold air. It reminded her of when she used to run in the winter. When she had knees. When she was 40 pounds lighter. She'd dread leaving the house in single digit temps, but within the first few blocks that inner furnace would kick in, and for an hour or so she enjoyed being outdoors in her least favorite season.

And she hated the noise of the snowblower invading that perfect silence that's left after the snow stops. She preferred the rhythmic "shhkk . . . whoomph" of her and her neighbors out shoveling to free up their Subarus and Priuses and minivans before a winter workday commute. But she was seriously considering hanging up her shovel for good after this season. The snow was coming more often, and the accumulations were more intense. It had been a while since she'd seen a dusting. It was the end of winter now, so she could probably get a good deal on a used machine on Craigslist or Marketplace. She'd have two more winters to contend with and needed stay healthy to accomplish her mission.

After finishing the driveway and sidewalk, Jules showered and changed and was starting to feel a little hungry when her youngest son Jack had called to tell her about a promotion he'd just received at the museum.

"There were three of us who were finalists for the job. One was a woman from another museum in town and the other guy was from Ohio. Both older than me and really well-qualified." He'd said. Jules heard the pride.

She was so pleased for him and thrilled to see his life taking a shape that made him happy. At 27, he seemed suddenly grown up in a way she hadn't noticed before. He had a job he loved and a woman he loved in a city he was starting to love. She wasn't sure Austin would ever feel like home to him, an upstate New Yorker through and through, but she knew he would do his best to contribute to that Texas town's brand promise to 'Keep it Weird.'

As the new Outreach Coordinator, Jack would play an active role in expanding the Museum's reach. It was a good fit for him, an extrovert with decent academic credentials, a history of community relations and organization, and more than three years of experience at the Museum. They had created the position with him in mind, but it had been a competitive hiring process and he was more than a little relieved to have won the day. She knew he would work his butt off to make sure they never regretted their choice.

His relationship of more than a year now seemed healthy and stable. Kelly was a librarian at the University, and a woman after

Jules' own heart. She was sharp as a whip and paid attention to what was happening in the world. Jules had spent time with them together in Austin twice when she'd been down for visits as soon as COVID started to let up in 2021. She loved having them show her around and share their world with her. They introduced her to their friends, and she'd met some of Jack's colleagues when they visited the Museum.

Kelly and Jack had come to her place for both Thanksgiving and Christmas last year, and her oldest son Ben and his family had been in town for those holidays, too. Her happiest times were when everyone was together. Kelly fit right into the mix. Ben's wife, Jessica, was six years older than Kelly but the two hit it off, and even the grandkids seemed to love her energy. Piper seemed fascinated with the young woman who had Uncle Jack's heart. She spent their time together having Kelly read every book the kids had brought along, then she'd laugh and laugh at Kelly's Texas drawl! Kelly didn't take offense to the 6-year-old's poor manners and seemed truly delighted to put on the show. Tanner, at 8, was less obvious in his admiration, but Jules noticed he stayed in the room more when Kelly was around. The gaming consoles would wait.

Jules and Kelly had also become Facebook friends over the last six months, and she loved that Kelly trusted her enough to let her into that little window of her life. Her posts confirmed what Jules already knew from their conversations and interactions over the last year and a half. She was a kind and compassionate person, a humanitarian, and a liberal feminist, and Jules loved her for Jack. He needed a partner who wouldn't let him get complacent. She hoped that her kids would continue her legacy as a lefty.

• • •

Jules had been a liberal-thinking person long before she thought of herself as a political animal. In her high school talent show, she had lip-synched and vamped across the gymnasium stage to Helen Reddy's "I am Woman." An anthem for an era of 'women's libbers,' as they were called in those days. She'd worn an orange and green striped polyester jumpsuit from Fox Casuals and platforms from Turtle Shoes. Looking back, it still astonished her that she had found the confidence to make such a public statement at 16. She was never a theater, band, or chorus kid. Her family didn't encourage the kids to participate in extracurriculars, and she didn't like to draw attention to herself. She kept a low profile. But she could still remember the pride and power she had felt with the mic in hand, belting it out with Helen's voice in her mouth:

I am woman, hear me roar
In numbers too big to ignore
And I know too much to go back an' pretend
'Cause I've heard it all before
And I've been down there on the floor
No one's ever gonna keep me down again
Oh yes I am wise
But it's wisdom born of pain
Yes, I've paid the price
But look how much I gained
If I have to, I can do anything
I am strong (strong)
I am invincible (invincible)
I am woman . . .

It was a huge hit and she'd gained instant teenage notoriety that week, before fading back into total obscurity for the rest of her high school years. But those lyrics had awakened something in her that stayed in her bones for the rest of her days. She had lived as a woman who was strong and invincible. Who could do anything.

Jules and her friends, mostly women in their 50s and 60s, some even in their 70s and 80s now, had all been rabid activists in their own time. Protesting Vietnam, working on civil rights issues, fighting for choice, trying to pass the Equal Rights Amendment, denouncing violence against women, attempting to save the earth from climate crisis. They had done clinic defense, sponsored gun buybacks, held bake sales for LGBQT+ youth. They had burned their bras and gone to Woodstock. They had smoked illegal pot and had illicit sex.

They had all been to D.C. at some point or another, some of them many, many times. Attending Take Back The Night, or the Million Mom March, or some anniversary of Roe v. Wade; 10 years, 25 years, 40 years. They had closets full of witty signs made over kitchen tables with poster paper and sharpies they'd picked up at CVS or Walgreens; quick stops made between shuttling their kids to school or social activities to get the needed supplies for revolution. Every one of them had worked on someone's campaign somewhere, from their local school boards to state reps and governors, to presidential candidates. They remembered Shirley Chisolm and Geraldine Ferraro. Several of them had even been elected officials themselves.

They belonged to the ACLU, Planned Parenthood, the Southern Poverty Law Center, the Audubon Society, and then NOT the Audubon Society. They served on school boards and nonprofit boards and were radically pro-choice. They donated to abortion funds and feminist causes and the campaigns of like-minded candidates. But now they were tired, and many of them retired. They had gray hair and bad knees and bunions, and ran google searches like "hip flats" and "boho chic tunics." They had hoped to pass the rabble-rousing mantle to their children's and grandchildren's generations.

Yet they all agreed they weren't seeing that passion in the 20- and 30-somethings, even in light of the dangers the country was facing since Trump was elected in 2016. Everyone in her circles, including her kids and their friends, saw Trump and his ilk for the fascists they were. They recognized how close the young nation had come to ruin on January 6, 2021, when The Capitol was attacked. Despite that, the young people simply weren't out in the streets protesting, or traveling to D.C. to make their voices heard. They were working and raising families of their own, heads down, noses-to-the-grindstone. Dangerously oblivious.

. . .

So, Jules was thrilled that Kelly was helping to raise Jack's awareness and kindle his activism as a full-blown adult.

"We joined a counter-protest group at an anti-choice rally here a few weeks ago." He'd told her on the phone. "It was the Texas Rally for Life. Mom, these people are really out there. You should have seen the signs. They were disgusting."

"Yeah. I've seen the signs. They've been using them since the 70s. It's probably still the same people. Tell them I said hi next time." She joked.

"And mom, you wouldn't believe how many of them were strapped! I still can't get used to the gun culture here. It's crazy.

Kelly and I went for ice cream the other day and there was a guy in there with his kids open carrying this huge handgun around his waist. He's yelling at the kids and swatting them around. In New York I would have called DCFS. Here it's just another day in paradise."

Even though she had tried out for the rifle team in high school, and had been weapons qualified in the Navy, Jules had always hated firearms. When the boys were young there were no toy weapons in their home. Not even nerf guns. She had wanted to teach them peace and love. She didn't want them to equate firearms with fun. Violent video games were forbidden. She wouldn't have her boys playing games where murder or misogyny were rewarded. She couldn't keep them from that exposure beyond her four walls, but she could set the example and the expectation for them.

And she was genuinely afraid of guns. Despite the ludicrous attempts by the NRA and the right-wing 2nd Amendment crazies to gaslight the public, Jules knew that guns kill people. Accidents happen. All the time. One of her friends had made it her personal mission to post every single accidental killing of a child with a gun in the United States on her Facebook feed. It was easy not to know about the daily violences happening in every corner of the country, and Jules was grateful to be reminded and not fall into complacency. Kids in the shopping cart at Walmart who find mommy's handgun and kill themselves in the garden aisle. Kids who find daddy's service revolver unsecured and shoot their baby sister dead. Kids at sleepovers who discover that pistol tucked between the couch cushions and never come home again. She couldn't imagine the depths of despair.

The solution was so obvious. If you aren't exposed to a weapon, you can't accidentally be killed by a weapon. Period. But gun-loving America was beyond that logic. The Second Amendment itself had been weaponized. The NRA was so deep into the pockets of the powerful in D.C. that common sense gun control was entirely out of reach.

When the kids were little, Jules was that mom who called the family before her boys went to play. She wanted to know if there were guns in the home. She didn't care if it seemed judgey. She wanted her kids to walk back in the door after their playdates. Now Jack lived in a place where people wore guns like jewelry.

"Jax, you just need to be really careful. Keep a low profile and don't engage any of these people. You know there are a lot of them who can't wait to pull that trigger in 'self-defense.' Don't forget, they have Stand Your Ground laws in Texas." She knew her son wasn't the kind of guy to back down if someone pushed a button.

"I know mom. Don't worry. I'm almost a native now. I might get my permit."

"Yeah, right. And I might get botox."

"Love you, mom! Bye."

● ● ●

It was rare for Jules to talk to one of the boys without talking to the other very soon after. She needed to complete that circle every time. There was a through line from one to the other and her day wouldn't feel complete now unless she spoke to Ben. After her lunch, she rang him up.

"Hey, ma!" He answered on the second ring.

"Hi honey. How are you?"

"Great. Jack just called and told me his news." The brothers were close despite the age difference and they were champions of each other more now than they had been when they lived under one roof. Jules knew Ben would have been Jack's next call after they hung up earlier.

"You were right, Ben. Even after a national search the right guy for the job was already in-house!"

"Plus, they didn't have to pay relocation costs," Ben joked.

Jules glossed over the slight jab. There was always that shadow of adolescent competition.

"How are Jess and the kids?"

"Everybody's good. The kids are still bouncing between the classroom and homeschool on any given day. It's just crazy. As soon as there's an exposure in a classroom everybody is sent home. Tanner's home this week, but Piper's in school. We're taking turns working from home."

"Anything new on Piper?" They'd been having some evaluations done to see if she might be on the autism spectrum. She had hit all of her milestones so far, but they noticed some difficulties with social cues in the last few years, so they were paying attention.

"Nothing yet. We're still waiting for the results of the recent assessments. She's doing great, though. Happy as a clam."

"Good. Give her a squeeze from me. And let me know what you find out. If she's going to need any services or support, or an IEP, it's good to get those in place now. Little kids are much less stigmatized by that kind of stuff."

"Yeah, Jess's brother, Tim, has a son on the spectrum. Remember Connor? You've met them. He's been a great resource for us."

"Oh, right! I forgot about them. I'm so glad you have them to help navigate that terrain. They're in the same school system, right?"

"Same school, even. Connor's in 4th this year, but he's had an IEP since 2nd grade. He's been doing really well these last few years."

"I'm sure Piper will do fine, too. It will just be good to know if she has any needs that aren't being met for her at this stage. Any news on the baby front?"

They had been trying for number three, to complete the family, for a few months. Jules wondered if she'd ever see any other grandchildren now.

"No, Jess got her period last week. But we're not worried yet. It was something like six months we tried before Pipe."

"I remember," said Jules, "I'm sure it's just a matter of time. It will be so great to have a baby again! So, how are YOU Ben-jam-min'? What's exciting YOU this week?"

"Not much. I'm thinking about volunteering to help coach Tanner's hockey team."

"Really? Don't you have to be able to skate to coach hockey?"

"Very funny. I can skate."

"You can skate? Since when?"

"It's a requirement before you can move into the country. They have rinks at every border crossing and you have to exit the car, strap on the blades, and run a figure-eight forward and backward before they'll wave you through."

"I don't even know you, anymore." She deadpanned. "Seriously, that would be so good for you guys. I know he'd love it and if you can stay off your butt it'd be a good workout for you. Isn't it late in the season though?"

"It is, but one of the guys on the coaching team was just diagnosed with MS. He's had to resign and they need someone. If I step in now to finish out the season and I hate it, I can just not come back next year. And if I like it, I'll stay. That's one of the beauties of being a sub."

"Sounds like a good plan. I bet you'll love it, though. I was so glad hockey was never your or Jack's sport. I didn't have to spend endless hours in the freezing rink. You know how I love the cold. Speaking of which, do you guys have snow up there? I was out shoveling earlier today."

"Ma, it's March in Canada."

"Right. Never mind. I was thinking about getting a snowblower. I can't keep up with the clearing anymore. The snow seems heavier."

"Really? I never thought I'd hear you say that. You hate those things. The noise, the smell, the environmental impact."

"I guess aging is the mother of necessity!" Jules laughed.

"Well, if you can hold out for the rest of this winter I'll bring you my old one." Ben offered. "When I bought that Kubota a couple years ago, I kept the Troybilt."

After a beat, "I don't understand a word you just said."

Both Jules and Ben howled with laughter! It was one of their inside jokes as a family. A line from Napoleon Dynamite, a cult classic of her boys' time. When it had first been released, Jax was just nine and Ben was 14 and Jules had forbidden them to watch it. She wasn't sure why, it was a knee jerk reaction really. She assumed anything geared toward adolescent boys was most likely unredeeming. Then one night, when she was on a work trip, she watched it in her hotel room. She found it stupid but benign, maybe even charming and naïve, and she relented. When she got home, Jax watched it obsessively. He memorized every line. He had passed the time on a road trip once reciting the entire script! In the years since, Jules had grown to love the quirky characters and goofy non-sequiturs; "your mom goes to college." Every so often one of them would see an opening and drop a classic line, like this one.

"Keep jammin' Benny! I love you the most!"

"You, too, Ma."

They both hung up breathless, still giggling and savoring that sweet connection to their times together. Jules would miss these small moments. After. She could not bear to imagine it.

• • •

Once Jules had settled on her course of action, she knew beyond question that it was her destiny. With Trump out of the picture, she imagined his followers would be Scar's hyenas rather than the Wicked Witch's flying monkeys. They would slink back into their dark recesses and wait for the next opportunity to emerge, but in the interim they would comply with the norms of the truth and light. They would hide their ugly. Like they used to.

She didn't see the mission through some grandiose lens. Despite her military service, she didn't identify as particularly patriotic. The right-wingers had misappropriated patriotism and even the flag itself. Jules distanced herself from those symbols. And she wasn't delusional, seeing herself as a 'chosen one.' She was a very practical person, and simply recognized that she was in the right place at the right time, a time when the country was on the brink of madness.

For the past seven years she had expected someone to come along. Some John Wilkes Booth or Lee Harvey Oswald. But why did she expect grace to be delivered by someone else? She was the someone who had to act. She was through with casting about for a savior. She had always been most successful when she relied on her own wits and judgment to solve problems. It was her nature as a Leo, a leader, and she was a little surprised that it had taken her this long to realize it.

During the pandemic, Jules had her first taste of being vulnerable and dependent as an aging woman. She knew her privilege, an educated, cis, white woman in America. And from the outside her life looked fairly typical. The neighbors probably thought of her as an elderly, single woman who kept a decent home. She gardened in the good months, some veggies out back that she shared with them, and raised beds in the front with annuals and perennials in all shades of purple. She maintained her small but tidy brick home in good order. She was friendly and always waved when she drove by. She looked like someone who would have a retirement plan, some savings, investments that would mature at just the right time.

What they couldn't see, just below the surface, was her now very real fear of living longer than she could afford. Her grand-mothers had both lived into their 90s, God forbid. And med-ical advancements were extending life expectancies. Jules hadn't returned to steady work since COVID and she was flat broke now. Her 401k depleted. She'd given up looking for any professional opportunities in her field. She got the message. She was no longer viable. She had taken a gig in the first year of the pandemic doing contact tracing, but it felt futile and invasive, and she lasted only a few months. Her meager social security, what little she earned driving, and the income from an annuity she'd created with the insurance after Mick died were her sole sources of income. She was getting by. Skin of her teeth.

She knew her sons felt a responsibility for her that she hadn't felt for her own parents, and if she became sick or destitute, they would care for her. They would change their lives' trajectories to provide for her. She couldn't bear the thought. Like everyone she knew, she didn't want to become a burden to her kids in her dot-age. Jules was proud of the life she'd had and the life she'd made for the boys. She was satisfied with the choices she'd made. She was incredibly grateful for all of it.

• • •

There were several possible outcomes to her assassination plan. She'd be nearly 70 years old by the time of the Republican National Convention in 2024, where she would make the attempt. That gave her the longest lead time to prepare, and if things changed dramatically in the meantime, like he died or was imprisoned or his party woke up from their coma, it gave her the widest window to abort the mission. She'd love to abort the mission. If none of those things happened, and the day came, she would either succeed or fail in her attempt. She didn't intend to be stealthy, just find that one perfect opportunity for that one perfect shot. Or two. She might be taken out by Trump's security forces on the spot. Over, finished, done, as the boys used to say. Or, she might be apprehended. If she survived, she'd be thrown into a federal prison. She'd get three hots and a cot. She'd survived on industrial food before. She'd get access to health care. If she got dementia, her kids wouldn't have to change her diapers. Win/win.

Having made what would be the most important decision in her life, Jules started to map out her mission.

Over the last handful of years Jules had listened to the relentless parallels made by pundits, journalists, friends, and colleagues between current-day America and the lead up to Nazi Germany. She knew it to be true from her own studies in grad school. She was tired of knowing about it and doing nothing. The world had witnessed what seemingly 'good' people had done to enable Hitler to come to power. Nothing. Because every day is a day when it's not here yet. Until it is. And then it's too late.

Jules had felt for years that the country was moving toward civil war. She had started having those conversations in the days leading up to Trump's inauguration, but she found people unable to imagine such a reality in modern day America. The pols and the media pooh-poohed the idea back then. They were short-sighted historians who viewed cultural advancement as linear, and democracy as absolute, unmovable.

When in fact, as a functioning political system, democracy ebbed and flowed around the globe and across time. Jules still followed the work of the Center for Systemic Peace and the Political Instability Task Force. She knew the signs. She knew that the United States had been downgraded in 2020 from a +10 to a +6 on the Polity scale. That scale was developed by the CIA in the early 90s to help the government predict in advance where armed conflict might emerge. The scale is a 21-point indicator, from -10 (completely autocratic) to +10 (completely democratic). On the -10 side of the scale are North Korea, Bahrain, and the like. On the +10 side of the scale are Canada, Norway, New Zealand and the U.S. prior to 2020. This serious slip in the score moved the U.S. away from a democracy into the anocracy zone. That term defines a mixed form of government with both autocratic and democratic features. A government in transition, and at a "high risk of impending political instability." The rise of autocracies, internal conflicts, and now this power grab by Putin, hankering for the days of the Soviet Empire.

She saw Trump as an incredibly dangerous imbecile. Many people she knew, both on the right and the left, thought he was an evil genius, or at least a shrewd businessman with some grand plan. She knew better. Jules felt she knew him at a deeper level. She had seen him through the years in small, insecure men, always men, with a modicum of power. How they preened and bullied and stumbled into positions of more power. Hateful people who felt entitled and who operated from a base of fear. Fear that they would be exposed for the know-nothings and do-nothings they were. The Peter Principled impostors.

Trump was exactly this man. But with all of the money. That was all it took in a capitalist society with a hunger for mindless reality television. The working-class could get behind this hard-nosed, potty-mouthed millionaire with gold toilets while they sat in their midwestern split-levels, playing the lottery and imagining such a life. He said the things they were thinking, about women and immigrants and gays and America. He polarized the people in ways Jules hadn't seen in her entire life.

The Republican right-wing had been waiting for just this puppet. Someone to pit the commoners against one-another, to get them fighting in the streets, so that the powerful could advance their agenda of white, male superiority, while the 99 percent were duking it out. It was a shell game with historical consequences. Trump was no world leader. He was a barely literate buffoon who lacked any empathy and sought only to be stroked.

Jules knew that an 'elderly' woman, a grandma, was an unlikely assassin. That made her task easier. Her invisibility, that which had made her unhireable and undateable, had become her super power. And no one who knew her would ever imagine her taking this drastic step. She was a pacifist. She hated firearms of any kind. Deplored hunting. But she knew that a gun would be her weapon of choice. It was an elegant irony.

Jules would have to put aside all of her liberal ideals of peace and justice, her dogged commitment to the rule of law, in order to take on this responsibility. She had come to terms with that.

It wasn't just America that stood in the balance; she wouldn't die for her country. It was the Democracy that had been so hard won by the millions who had died or been wounded in defense of it in the wars since Independence. It was the democracies that had flourished across the globe in imitation of what was recognized as the best political system available to human beings of this time. It was moving away from nationalism, fascism, and isolation and toward a future of human rights and dignity for all people. A world in which borders fell away. Those were the things for which Jules was willing to die.

• • •

By late March, Jules had begun working on the mission in earnest, thinking things through with care and precision. She had a great deal of research to do. She needed to learn about weapons, event schedules, security details, and the layout of the streets surrounding the Fiserv Arena in Milwaukee, where the RNC would be hosted. Google Maps Street View would be a godsend. Planning, meticulous planning, would be her surest path to success.

Early Monday morning, Jules headed to the public library branch in Voorheesville. She had decided to use the village libraries around the area for her internet research. She had mapped out 10. In addition to Voorheesville she planned to use Watervliet, Ballston Spa, Altamont, Menands, Troy, Saratoga Springs, Guilderland, Bethlehem, and East Greenbush libraries. She would use each library only once. If her research extended beyond 10 library visits, she'd expand the list.

Her cunning was for several reasons. First, she didn't want to use her own computer just in case some of the searches she might do would attract attention. She could imagine her Facebook feed filling up with gun sales and doomsday preppers just as it did with sports bras and gluten free recipes. Jules was no conspiracy theorist, but she assumed for the sake of argument that all internet traffic was monitored. And she didn't want some meta-algorithm putting the pieces together and thwarting her mission, so she'd move around to minimize that risk.

Second, she wanted to limit her exchanges with people at the library as much as possible; not become familiar. She would be hard pressed to make small talk with a stranger while planning an assassination.

Finally, she planned to make every day of her research an outing as much as a chore. She wanted to see these places again and linger over lunches with a good book. She wanted to poke around in the places she had always intended to go one day. Her 'one days' were running short.

On this day, her focus was security for former POTUSes and their families. She had to understand what she was up against before she could plan how to thwart it. Who has secret service protection and for how long? What does that detail look like? Does Trump wear body armor? Was his schedule published somewhere or would she need to try to glean that through media and PR? She spent hours reading news articles, visiting the official government websites for DHS and the Secret Service, and watching video of former POTUSes in public settings after they were out of office. It was enlightening. She took copious notes.

Just after noon, Jules left the library and headed over to the Windowbox Café in Slingerlands. She'd been there only once before and she remembered their delicious-looking, over-sized pancakes. She hadn't ordered them that time because she tried to watch her diet when she could. Now she indulged. She had nothing to lose. The blueberry pancakes were golden and crisp around the edges. They hid the plate entirely and drooped slightly over the sides, forming a shallow bowl. She filled the hollow with butter and maple syrup, and when it all melted into the cakes, she filled it again.

She pulled out her yellowed paperback copy of Doris Grumbach's *Coming into the End Zone*. She had decided to read it again with her new worldview and see if it could provide some solace. Grumbach had penned the memoir when she was 70, and Jules remembered it as an honest book about life and living and dying and death. The author, writing in 1991, assumed her own death was near, and that many things she was doing were 'lasts.' Jules would be re-reading it more than thirty years later, knowing that Doris was still, stubbornly, alive somewhere in this world as she sat there eating her pancakes. Perhaps, Maine. Perhaps, Manhattan.

Driving home, Jules wished she could answer Sally's question, now that she herself had decided 'what to do'. Just pick up her phone right now and reassure her bestie that things would be okay again. But, as much as she loved her, and as close as they were, Jules would never let Sally know what she had finally decided to do. Sally would learn of her plan along with everyone else in the world. She tried not to imagine the day.

In the few weeks since she had devised the mission, Jules had been thinking about the idea of having collaborators. Selfishly, she wished she had at least one trusted confidante. Someone who saw the existential risk of this moment in time and would help her execute. But everyone she loved and trusted would do just the opposite. Try to talk her out of this and save her from herself. They might even think she had dementia or had simply lost her mind.

But she knew that history required disruptors. Ordinary people who found themselves at a moral crossroads. This was her journey. She had vowed to herself to tell no one.

She'd also ruminated about the possibility of somehow being found out. These were rabbit holes she had to explore, evaluate, and resolve. Then move past. She wasn't worried about after. Everything would be an open book after. But she needed to avoid detection in the months to come. Her research plan was part of that. She'd watched enough crime TV to know about the dangers of a digital trail. She also planned to be meticulous with her phone. No searches, maps, phone calls of any kind related to the project. Everything digital would be done on public devices.

When Jules got home, she dropped everything on her desk and went straight to her bookshelves. She knew what she was looking for. A book she'd read first during grad school, and then again either during the campaign or just after the 2016 election. It was a non-fiction account of a plot among a group of young Germans to assassinate Hitler. Obviously unsuccessful. But the story had stayed with her. They had risked and lost their lives. But only because they had been too late to the task. The masses had already drunk the kool-aid; fear, hatred, and cruelty had become the governing principles of the entire German nation. Jules hoped she would not be too late.

One of the young would-be assassins, Dietrich Bonhoeffer, was a Christian pastor from a privileged and educated family of eight children. As Hitler came to power, Bonhoeffer was stunned to watch his fellow men of God fold, in compliance to the Reich-skirche, Hitler's one national church whose allegiance was not to a higher power, but to him and his Nazi party. All religious symbols were ordered removed from places of worship, to be replaced with the Nazi swastika. Jules felt physically ill recalling newsreel images of swastika banners hanging in pulpits throughout Germany.

She found the thin volume easily thanks to its red spine, wedged onto a higher shelf among her other WWII works. It was *The Plot to Kill Hitler*, by Patricia McCormick. An unlikely hero, she called Bonhoeffer in her subtitle. Jules studied the young man's image on the cover. The colorized photograph showed a handsome face with a set mouth, a slight cleft in his chin. His sandy brown hair swept slightly across his forehead. His dance card would have been full, had he been a less serious person. A few lines have begun to form, worry lines between his eyes and just above the brows, in a face otherwise youthful. He looks far off to his right behind round, wire-framed specs. Jules wondered what hell those eyes had witnessed. He was executed in April of 1945, just two weeks before the camp where he was imprisoned was liberated, and three weeks before Hitler's suicide.

Jules was looking for a specific passage in the book. She remembered Bonhoeffer's struggle to justify his Christianity, his moral compass, with his intent to murder a human being. While she didn't share his Christian dogma, her moral compass pointed sharply away from killing people.

She found it in chapter 23, when the group of conspirators first realized that it would not be enough to overthrow Hitler. He would have to be killed. Dietrich's brother-in-law, Hans von Dohnanyi, asked what would become of their souls if they committed this mortal sin? Bonhoeffer answered that the special evil of the regime, of Hitler, had forced this upon them. He assured them, "God promises forgiveness and consolation to a man who becomes a sinner in bold venture."

"God promises forgiveness and consolation to a man who becomes a sinner in bold venture." Jules reached into the caddy on her desk, pulled out a pink highlighter and ran it across those words. "God promises forgiveness and consolation to a man who becomes a sinner in bold venture." She dog-eared the page. Definitely fridgeworthy.

Reading these words reminded Jules of John Lewis, the activist and freedom fighter from Georgia. A long-standing member of the U.S. House of Representatives who died just recently. He encouraged what he called 'good trouble,' disruption and disobedience for noble and right reasons. She scanned her shelves to find his words. *Walking With the Wind* and *His Truth is Marching On* were both there. She sat with them for a while and listened. And they took her to her poetry shelves, seeking Jane Jordan's *Things That I Do in the Dark*. There she read this poem:

I Must Become a Menace to My Enemies

JANE JORDAN
Dedicated to the Poet Agostinho Neto,
President of The People's Republic of Angola: 1976

1
I will no longer lightly walk behind
a one of you who fear me:
   Be afraid.
I plan to give you reasons for your jumpy fits
and facial tics
I will not walk politely on the pavements anymore
and this is dedicated in particular
to those who hear my footsteps
or the insubstantial rattling of my grocery
cart
then turn around

see me
and hurry on
away from this impressive terror I must be:
I plan to blossom bloody on an afternoon
surrounded by my comrades singing
terrible revenge in merciless
accelerating
rhythms
But
I have watched a blind man studying his face.
I have set the table in the evening and sat down
to eat the news.
Regularly
I have gone to sleep.
There is no one to forgive me.
The dead do not give a damn.
I live like a lover
who drops her dime into the phone
just as the subway shakes into the station
wasting her message
canceling the question of her call:
fulminating or forgetful but late
and always after the fact that could save or
condemn me
I must become the action of my fate.

2

How many of my brothers and my sisters
will they kill
before I teach myself

retaliation?
Shall we pick a number?
South Africa for instance:
do we agree that more than ten thousand
in less than a year but that less than
five thousand slaughtered in more than six
months will
WHAT IS THE MATTER WITH ME?
I must become a menace to my enemies.

3
And if I
if I ever let you slide
who should be extirpated from my universe
who should be cauterized from earth
completely
(lawandorder jerkoffs of the first the terrorist degree)
then let my body fail my soul
in its bedeviled lecheries

And if I
if I ever let love go
because the hatred and the whisperings
become a phantom dictate I o-
bey in lieu of impulse and realities
(the blossoming flamingos of my wild mimosa trees)
then let love freeze me
out.
I must become
I must become a menace to my enemies.

Reading Bonhoeffer and Lewis and Jordan gave Jules courage and a sense of righteousness. A certainty that she needed to stay the course. She would return to their words many times in the coming months, seeking comfort and assurance.

Jules placed the books on her reading table and sat down at her desk. The desire to do something to move the project forward was hard to resist. She grabbed the notebook she'd used at the library and read through her notes. She made some edits and added some observations.

She wanted to research. That was her comfort zone. She'd have to resist that natural pull. She couldn't double-check anything or explore the random questions that emerged as she planned. She had seriously underestimated how hogtied she'd be without her devices, and realized already that her ten-library agenda might not suffice. The library would become her second home.

She looked at the notebook that she had started that day and realized she would need to be careful with it. She didn't have a lot of visitors, but she couldn't afford to be careless. She might finally have a valid use for the small home safe Mick had purchased when they were young marrieds. When she bought her current home, she'd had the bookshelves built up around it. Cabinet doors covered its façade so you wouldn't even know it was in the room.

The combination was taped inside one of her desk drawers. She had taken all of her important information, like usernames and passwords, this combination, the garage code, the kids phone numbers and addresses, birthdates and written everything down last year when her laptop had suddenly died. It made her realize how dependent she had become on technology as a stand-in for memory. And she needed it even more as her own memory grew thin.

In the bottom drawer she came across her stash of old cell phones, chargers, and cables of unknown origin. Hers and the boys'. She always intended to take the phones to one of those machines at the mall, where you can get a few bucks for them after you've upgraded. Maybe enough for a Starbucks. But she'd never gotten around to it. There were probably 12, 15. Even a flip phone and her first Blackberry. Enough to fund a dinner out maybe? Looking at them, something clicked. Maybe one of these discarded devices could be her co-conspirator. Her confidante throughout the mission.

She shuffled through them looking for the newest old device. That turned out to be an iPhone 6 plus that was Jack's in high school. She could tell by the Van's stickers. Jules smiled for the first time all day remembering how he loved those shoes. She dug into the morass again to figure out if there was a charger that would work. After a few misses, she hit. She plugged the phone in to charge overnight while she dug out the safe combo and locked up her mission manual. Exhausted but pleased, she headed off to sleep well.

In the morning, Jules was happy to find the old cell phone had charged completely. She unplugged the phone and powered it on. It had no service, but she didn't need that. In fact, she didn't want it. All she wanted was the video functionality. She intended to create a video diary as she went along, which would become evidence after. This cell phone would be both her collaborator and her testimony. She couldn't be sure it would see the light of day when the mission was complete, but she'd make every effort to ensure that result.

Jules sat down at her desk and turned the video on. She did a quick sound check and recorded a short video to be sure everything was working. Satisfied, she began her documentation.

VIDEO DIARY ENTRY – March 29, 2022

"Hello. My name is Jules Campbell. I live in upstate New York. Today is Tuesday, March 29th, 2022. I'm making this video for two reasons. One is to have a sounding board for my work as I move through the next few years. Two is for the world to have a clear understanding of who I am and why I undertook this mission. This is the first time I am saying these words out loud, although I have been planning this in earnest since the invasion of Ukraine in February. I intend to kill Donald John Trump."

Saying it felt terrifying. Saying it felt empowering. She paused a moment, grounding herself.

"I am a mom and a grandma. I love my family fiercely. I am a political scientist and a humanitarian. I'm a widow and a veteran and a loyal friend. I'm not being treated for any mental or emotional conditions. I don't suffer from dementia. I am acting solely in defense of democracy against the forces of authoritarianism, totalitarianism, and fascism that threaten us in this moment. The protection of the future of my country is in the interest of global peace and unity. This is my fulfillment of the promise of generations; 'Never again.' That's all I want to say for right now."

She turned off the video and powered the phone off. It felt good to have this outlet. A place to organize her thoughts, defend her actions, share her insights and outrages.

* * *

Jules' life had unfolded in unlikely and accidental ways, and she was extremely proud but mostly enormously grateful for all of it. She knew she had beaten the odds and made it better for the next in her line. For her kids and grandkids, and those souls down the line whom she would never know.

She had been born on August 20th of 1955, a Leo on the cusp of Virgo, joining her three-year-old brother, Simon. The second of four children of John and Jayne Campbell; the first of three girls in a row. Her sisters Cassie and Thea completed the family by '59. They were a solidly working-class family in Albany, NY. The civil rights movement was in full swing, and the country was leaning into the social unrest of the 60s. It was a precipitous era, a time and a place that would come to define Jules in unforeseen ways.

The Campbells were a traditional family of the time. The kids were kids and the adults were parents. The adults set the rules and the kids complied, or else. There were few hugs and kisses. No family inside jokes. While they all knew they were loved, it was a joyless, plodding family life for the most part.

John had been a truck-driver and was gone for long stretches. He imposed arbitrary rules on the family at a whim. He was fastidious in his habits, and kept his hair short and his fingernails gleaming. He always carried a starched white handkerchief in the pocket of his company shirt. The creases in his slacks were as sharp as the straight razor he used to shave. He reached the million-mile mark before retiring and was awarded an unwieldy and inartistic oak and bronze plaque as commemoration of that achievement.

Her mom, Jayne, was wren-thin and lived on pretzels and diet-Pepsi. She was always home, always busy, flitting from one task to another. Cooking or cleaning or doing laundry. Ironing those trousers and handkerchiefs, and even her husband's boxers and blue jeans. She fed the family according to John's palate, meat and potatoes, and made chocolate cakes and pepper cookies and cherry pies that she never ate. There was always a lit smoke in the ashtray and she'd take a puff or two as she zipped by. She kept busy with crossword puzzles and solitaire on the nights John was gone. Sometimes she'd play Yahtzee with one of the kids. Jayne was a nervous woman for no obvious reason. She checked the clock often. Jules fantasized about her mom as a single mom. She'd probably be fun without the rules.

John's trucker paycheck covered all of their basic needs. The bills were paid on time, the pantry was full, the fridge was stocked with Utica Club, and they each got a carton of smokes every week; he smoked Kool Filter Kings and she smoked Virginia Slims menthols. But there were no frills. No movies or dinners out. No vacations.

They lived in a three-story pre-war house on a street of three-story pre-war houses, all pulled close to the sidewalk with a postage-stamp patch of grass in front and a bit more in back. They kept what yard there was respectable, raked the leaves that fell from the trees planted in the city's spit of land between the sidewalk and the street, and always cleared the snow before it melted. John and Jayne Campbell kept mostly to themselves. Other than the mandatory social niceties with neighborhood parents, Jules had never known either of them to have a true friend.

The Campbell kids didn't do outside activities, like dance or scouting. No extracurriculars at school, no chorus or chess club. Nothing that required money or time. They played in the neighborhood with all of the other kids. Especially the O'Malley clan, who lived just two houses away. Spring, summer, and early fall meant riding bikes, hopscotch, jump rope, freeze tag. Late fall and winter they built snowmen, had snowball fights, and went sled riding behind the church on their block. These were the relationships that fed them.

Their parents had never had any expectations for them beyond obeying the rules at home and submitting to authority figures outside of home. Grades only mattered in so far as they were standards imposed by an external body and by which the children were measured. A 'bad grade' would lead to punishment, usually grounding, chores, or the loss of phone privileges. There was only one phone in the house, attached to the wall in the kitchen, so monitoring everyone's telephone time was easy back then. A 'good grade' would earn a pat on the head, nothing more. The only reason for good academic performance was to avoid trouble.

Education was a rite of passage to adulthood, not a means to the end that would become your life. What was important to the Campbell's was getting a job. Life was earning money to pay your bills. The only message that was consistently driven home in her family was that you were expected to move out or start paying rent as soon as you graduated or turned 18, whichever came first. It was more of a threat really. But since this was all Jules knew, she never questioned it. Until Ben was born in 1989.

Jules was close to thirty-five when she became a mom for the first time. It didn't take long for her to understand that something huge had been missing in her own upbringing. The intensity of feeling she had for her children made her recognize its lack in her relationship with her own parents, especially her mom. As Ben grew, and then Jack came along, she could no longer justify her parents' apathy with the old standard on which she had relied for so many years, "they did the best they could with what they had." She knew this to be untrue, but she would never know why.

Both her parents were dead now. Her mom more than 30 years and her dad 8, so there were no answers to be had. Jules doubted she'd bring it up even if they were still alive. After all, she appreciated so much of what her early family life had taught her. She had of necessity been a rule follower and she had an unhealthy respect for authority back then. So much so that she joined the Navy right after high school. And although it was a culture shock in many ways, she knew that her rigid family life had prepared her well for the rigors of military service.

At 18, she was accustomed to being told where to go and what to do. She could have done those four years standing on her head. But by the time her enlistment was up, she was keen to move on. Once she reached 'short-timer' status, she eagerly counted down the last 60 days to her release. At the end of her four-year stint, Jules received an honorable discharge and, she had to admit, an incredible foundation for the rest of her life's journey.

Jules' last duty station was Charleston, S.C., where she started her civilian life and felt like an adult for the first time. At 23, she got a job in a small machine repair shop, making the most of the skills she'd acquired in the Navy. She found an affordable apartment and furnished it with second-hand finds from yard sales and flea markets. She felt a kinship with the young women she watched on T.V., Mary Richards and Phyllis Lindstrom and Rhoda Morgenstern, Ann Marie, Laverne and Shirley. Maybe mostly the last two, who worked with their hands on a brewery assembly line, but she hoped someday for the glamour of those other girls.

She loved living in Charleston. The City Market, Battery Park, the salty sea air, and the climate! Even though she missed New York, she never tired of the warm-all-year living. She still had Navy friends on base, and they loved getting out of the barracks even if it was just for T.V. at her tiny apartment or Pizza at Papillon. None of them had cars so she'd go and get them on weekends if they were off duty and they'd hang out at her place, envying her civilian life and fantasizing about their coming freedoms.

When she was younger, her dad had set up a target attached to a bale of hay in their backyard and the kids would shoot his bow and arrow. Jules became a pretty good shot. She had gone on to make the archery team in high school. It was one of the few things she thought her dad was proud of. She had good hand-eye coordination, and a knack for compensating for the distance to the target. She just naturally adjusted her angles, and the depth of her draw on the bow, and she found the bullseye more often than not.

Billiards was similar in a lot of ways. You had to adjust your angles, figure out the right amount of English and top spin, and use that cue like a bow. Usually, once Jules' first two quarters went into any table, she played for free, beating every comer until she gave up her spot to go to a party or head home. It gave her a confidence that little else did.

Jules kept playing and winning throughout her Navy days. She'd play for money and had a reputation as a bit of a shark at the clubs on base. So, she and her friends played off base. It was fun to pick a bar where they wanted to hang out for an evening. Jules would drop her quarters on the table they wanted, and after she ran the table, it was theirs for the night.

On one of those evenings, out with friends about a year after she got out of the Navy, she met Mick Jacobs. He wasn't the kind of guy she usually fell for. She tended to like the skinny guys, the ones who were more likely to have been on the track team than the football team. Mick had the football physique; thick arms and thighs that were bigger than his waist, stretching his Levi's to their limit. He wore a thin, long-sleeved Henley that hugged his biceps. He had shaggy, dark hair, definitely not Navy length. He was taller than Jules' 5'6", but not looming. Jules first saw him shooting with some of his friends on the table she wanted. She lined up her quarters above the coin slots and she and her friends sat down to watch the game in progress. Mick was seriously good.

It took Jules three games to get the table. After she won it, Mick hung around to watch her play. It was unusual for women to be as good as she was with a pool cue. He bought her a drink and asked for her number.

They were married within a year. Jules was 24 and Mick was 26. The two were well-matched in so many ways beyond just eight ball. Mick was from Rhode Island, so he had the same East Coast sensibilities that she had. He came from a working-class background and had a strong work ethic instilled from a young age. They shared a deep love and a strong bond, and they were the couple that everyone aspired to be.

Mick had been the only true love of her life. They shared a similar set of values, and while he may not have self-identified as a feminist, Jules recognized that he was always on what she saw as the right side of any important issue. He was pro-choice, pro-woman, anti-racist, pro-environment, and didn't care who loved who. He treated everyone with respect. He saw Jules as a wholly autonomous life partner. They had great fun in those early years, before kids, planning futures that wouldn't come true.

Jules and Mick moved back to Albany in the early 80s to settle down. They wanted to be closer to their families before they had kids. They agreed they wanted at least three, but Jules wanted to go to college, and she'd need the support of her and Mick's extended families to pull it off. She had come to recognize the significant lifestyle gap between the blue- and white-collar worlds, and she wanted to pursue a degree to help propel her family forward. She wanted her children to recognize education as an end in itself, not simply a means to a paycheck.

Mick didn't share Jules' interest in higher education, but he supported her goals. He found work for a start-up solar panel installation company as soon as they moved back to New York. The industry was still in its infancy and he loved the potential it presented. He talked a lot about being in on the ground floor, and she'd always joke that he was on the roof, not the ground floor. He earned enough for them to pay most of their bills, and she took out student loans for the rest.

Jules completed her master's degree in political science at SUNY Albany in 1990, with a minor in Women's Studies. She crossed the stage in her cap and gown with Ben in a baby sling across her chest and a fairly respectable cheering section, consisting of Mick and her parents and siblings and in-laws and nieces and nephews. She heard them hooting and shouting her name. Someone was ringing a cowbell. It was one of the proudest and most defining days of her life.

Her first professional position out of grad school turned out to be her only professional position. She was hired as the Executive Director of Women Waging Peace, a relatively new national non-profit think tank, policy advocacy, and activist group based in Albany, where she would thrive for nearly three decades. It was the perfect fit for Jules' skill set and credentials. She hit the ground running and never looked back.

Jules and Mick were social and outgoing as a couple, and quickly developed a vast network of friends and colleagues in the capital region. Her work kept her engaged with the area NGOs and politicos, and this exposed them to the movers and shakers in the business community. They lived busy lives as a young family, coming and going at breakneck speed.

Jules was pregnant with Jack the day she got the call to apply for a more prominent national position that would have them moving to D.C. The Board President had called. The current ED was retiring, and the Board had decided unanimously that Jules was their target candidate for the post. It was an incredible opportunity that she and Mick had to seriously consider. That night, after Ben was down, they sat down at the kitchen table to decide what to do.

Mick broke out the special high-balls, reserved for only such occasions, and poured them each a drink. Jules had purchased the beautiful Waterford glasses on their honeymoon trip to her ancestral home. She had never loved such things, cut crystal, China, fussy things. But in Ireland she'd watched the craftsmen in their apprenticeships turning lava into art, and she'd come to understand the magic. They had splurged on the two rocks glasses and they had set them back almost two-hundred dollars. They had become an intimate part of the couple's decision-making ritual over the years.

"Tell me what you're thinking." Mick started the discussion like he often did. He set her crystal glass of ginger ale on the table and took a sip of his scotch.

"I'm thinking it's exciting and insane! Professionally, it's an unparalleled opportunity. It's an organization whose mission I support and I know I can move their work forward, like I have at WWP."

"But? And?" He coached.

"But, I'm six months pregnant. But, you have work you like. But, we have a life and family and friends here. But, Ben is happy here. But, but, but."

Mick reached for the legal pad that they always kept near the phone.

"That's all true. All good reasons to stay. Let's make a list of pros and cons."

Mick was a list maker with a practical approach to making the big decisions in their lives. Jules was a more emotional decision-maker. She was grateful for his help.

"You already have work you love. You've done so much good at WWP, and you've built a culture that you value. How would you feel about going into a different culture? Would that be a pro or a con?"

"You know I love working on culture, so I'd be okay with that. I'd be bringing my own values system into that workplace. That's a pro. But it may be a slow ship to turn. It's bigger than WWP. There could be lots of resistance to change. That is a big con. I'm afraid I might choke the first of my new colleagues who says anything close to 'this is how we've always done it.'" Jules laughed but they both knew it was true. She hated that mindset.

"Mmm. You could start with a change management retreat. Pro?" He suggested. He'd learned a lot from her over the years.

"Pro," she agreed. "But, it's really more about whether I want to take on such a big job at this stage. It's hard not to just jump at the chance because it's on the table. I mean, wow, I am so honored that they've tapped me! Pro. But, I just don't think it's the right time. Con. Once this baby comes, I'm going to be relying so much on my sisters for help just to keep my work going at WWP. Can you imagine if we pile on a move - con, a new job for me - pro, you looking for work - con, AND we have no family or friends around for support - con? I just think it's too much. I mean, imagine how much child care for two kids costs in D.C.? – con." She was definitely stepping away from the edge.

"That's true. But you could take some time off between. I'm sure they'd agree to something like 6 or 8 months for you to start. You'd have to give at least a few months' notice at work. Right?" Mick could see possibilities.

"Definitely. I hadn't even considered that whole transition. You're right, they might even be willing to make it 10 or 12 months. They know I'm pregnant and we discussed that a little. That's a pro."

Mick added it to the tally.

"And with what you'll be making – pro - we'd be okay if I didn't find anything right away. If I stayed home for a year or two with the kids, you'd have the support you need at home – pro - and the kids wouldn't need to be in daycare - pro. It could take a lot of pressure off."

Jules hadn't thought of that idea. It had never been a possibility before. She liked the idea of Mick building that kind of bond with their kids. It was a rare opportunity.

That night they went to bed without having made a final decision. They would sleep on it, maybe for a few nights. They'd each consult trusted friends and colleagues. They would add to the growing pro and con list throughout the week. By the weekend, the pros outweighed the cons, and Jules had started to get excited about the move.

By that Friday, they set their sights on D.C and started making serious plans for their new life. Mick suggested that the exposure Jules would get in this new organization might someday even lead to a cabinet post. That seemed a stretch to her, but he had complete faith in her abilities and was her most vocal cheerleader. Being in the capitol would bring them closer to the seat of power. They would rub elbows and shoulders. Who knew what could happen. Anything was possible.

On the day of their 17th wedding anniversary, Jules was surrounded by cardboard boxes and waiting for the movers to arrive. Baby Jax, shiny and new, was sleeping in his bassinette under the front window, and Ben was at school. The next two days would be a frenzy of moving and goodbyes. Jules had found herself teary over the last few weeks, and she knew the days ahead would bring ugly cries. She hated crying in public!

She wiped her eyes as she packed up Ben's bedroom, where she had first been a mom. She remembered all the time she'd spent poring over wallpaper books to find the perfect border for her baby. She wanted gender-neutral primary colors. Jules had decided before she ever got pregnant that she never wanted to know her babies' genders. She wanted that surprise waiting at the end of the pain. She'd done the same for Jack, and when they were ready for number three, she had no intention to change the birth plan. So, Ben had ended up with balloons and the alphabet. It was starting to look too juvenile for a 5-year-old. In their new place they would let Ben help to create a room he liked. Maybe planets and stars. With Jack, they had already decided they were moving to D.C., so they hadn't done anything more than move the crib, changing table, and rocker into his nursery. In the new house she was thinking of either teddy bears or ducks for him.

When the doorbell rang Jules assumed it was either the movers or a flower delivery from Mick. He had sent her flowers on every anniversary of their married life. Mick knew that lilacs were her favorite, so he'd always send something purple since lilacs were impossible. At the door stood two uniformed cops, a man and woman.

"Are you Jules Jacobs?"

"Campbell, but yes."

"Is Mick Jacobs your husband?"

"Yes, why? What's happened?"

"I'm sorry ma'am. Mr. Jacobs was killed in an accident at his place of work this morning."

• • •

The evening of the funeral, after everyone had filled her refrigerator with foil-wrapped love letters, washed out their casserole dishes and headed home, and the boys were finally tucked in, red-faced and sweating in the way of exhausted babies, Jules headed to their bedroom for the first time without him. She had slept with the boys since the accident. It had comforted all of them and delayed this final concession.

She removed her widow's weeds, as she thought of them. A tasteful black sheath and forgettable black pumps. She stuffed them back into the Boscov's bag that still held the receipt from yesterday. They would be at the curb with tomorrow's trash. She slipped on Mick's extra-large ZZ-Top concert t-shirt from the 80s that had once been black. He hadn't worn it in years, but only because she had insisted it made him look unserious. Jules had turned it into a nightshirt along the way so it still smelled like him. Like them. It came to just above her knees and felt butter soft against her skin. She pulled on the threadbare UAlbany cotton boxers that she'd given him as a Christmas gift in her first year as an undergrad. Purple had always looked so good against his dark skin.

Their bed was a sacred place. It had been the safe place for their most important conversations. Whether to move back home, whether Jules should go to grad school, whether to buy the house, whether to have a baby, whether it was time to move Mick's parents into an assisted living facility, whether to have another baby. Jules lit a few candles and turned off the overhead lights. She settled back into the goose down pillows propped against the headboard of their shaker-style king bed. A stray feather poked the soft skin of her arm, and she drew it slowly from the pillow, watching it take shape as it emerged from the linen case.

In her imagination, she nestled into the familiar crook of her husband's arm, her head on his bare chest. They clinked glasses. Jules had Basil Hayden on the rocks and Mick had a Guinness.

But Jules sipped her bourbon alone.

"So, Mick" she whispered, "what the fuck do I do now?"

MASS SHOOTINGS IN THE US
March 2022 - 42 total

A mass shooting is any shooting where four or more people, other than the shooter, are killed or injured.

1. March 2, 2022 - Baltimore, Maryland – 2 dead, 3 injured
2. March 3, 2022 - Las Vegas, Nevada – 1 dead, 5 injured
3. March 5, 2022 – Glendale, Arizona – 4 injured
4. March 5, 2022 - Atlanta, Georgia – 1 dead, 6 injured
5. March 6, 2022- Minneapolis, Minnesota – 2 dead, 3 injured
6. March 6, 2022 - Hazleton, Pennsylvania – 1 dead, 13 injured
7. March 6, 2022 - Louisville, Kentucky – 1 dead, 3 injured
8. March 6, 2022 - Lubbock, Texas – 4 dead
9. March 6, 2022 - Chester, South Carolina – 6 injured
10. March 6, 2022 - Monroe, Louisiana – 2 dead, 2 injured
11. March 7, 2022- Knoxville, Tennessee – 4 injured
12. March 8, 2022 - Jacksonville, Florida – 6 injured
13. March 9, 2022 - Aurora, Colorado -1 dead, 8 injured
14. March 11, 2022 - Columbus, Ohio - 2 dead, 2 injured
15. March 12, 2022 - Baltimore, Maryland – 5 injured
16. March 12, 2022 - Autaugaville, Alabama – 7 dead

17. March 13, 2022 - Chicago, Illinois - 2 dead, 2 injured

18. March 13, 2022 - Rochester, New York – 2 dead, 4 injured

19. March 13, 2022 - Columbia, South Carolina- 1 dead, 3 injured

20. March 14, 2022 - Reading, Pennsylvania – 2 dead, 4 injured

21. March 15, 2022 - Ozark, Alabama – 5 injured

22. March 16, 2022 - Irvington, New Jersey – 3 dead, 2 injured

23. March 16, 2022 - Irvington, New Jersey – 4 injured

24. March 17, 2022 - Lansing, Michigan - 6 injured

25. March 17, 2022 - Chicago, Illinois – 6 injured

26. March 17, 2022 - Fort Lauderdale, Florida – 4 injured

27. March 18, 2022 - Fort Worth, Texas – 1 dead, 7 injured

28. March 18, 2022 - New Iberia, Louisiana – 1 dead, 3 injured

29. March 19, 2022 - Norfolk, Virginia – 1 dead, 3 injured

30. March 19, 2022 - Fayetteville, North Carolina – 4 dead

31. March 19, 2022 - Dumas, Arkansas – 11 injured

32. March 19, 2022 - Madison Heights, Virginia - 5 injured

33. March 19, 2022 - Dallas, Texas – 4 dead

34. March 20, 2022 - Milwaukee, Wisconsin – 1 dead, 3 injured

35. March 20, 2022 - Austin, Texas – 4 injured

36. March 20, 2022 - Houston, Texas – 4 injured

37. March 21, 2022 - Waterbury, Connecticut – 8 injured

38. March 21, 2022 - Chicago, Illinois – 1 dead, 7 injured

39. March 22, 2022 - Stockton, California – 6 injured

40. March 25, 2022 - Colorado Springs, Colorado – 2 dead, 7 injured

41. March 26, 2022 - Hollister, California – 4 injured

42. March 26, 2022 - Cleveland, Ohio – 3 dead, 1 injured

• • •

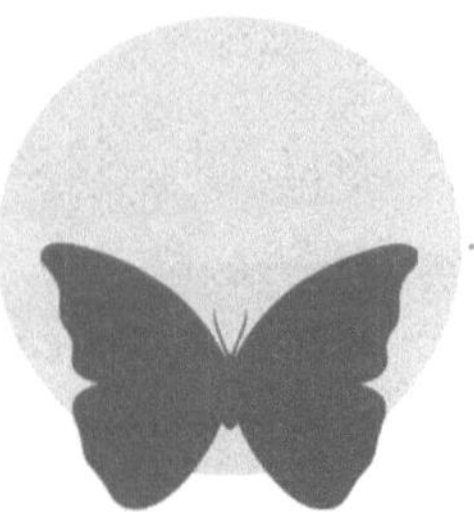

APRIL 2022

On the first Tuesday in April, Jules found a gun range in Troy that was just far enough away from her home that she wasn't likely to run into anyone who knew her. It was easy. Her search on the library computer was "gun range near me." It was called Troy's Inside Gun Range. Perfect. She wanted to train during all weather so she'd need to shoot indoors. There was no membership requirement, and you could rent guns and ammo or bring your own. She planned to rent until she decided what sort of equipment she would need for her mission. You didn't need an appointment. According to the website you could "just come on in and have some fun!"

Jules pored over the website. You could host birthday parties for kids 10 and over, have 'date nights' at the range. They even had 'ladies' nights.' As far as she could tell there was no alcohol involved in any of those events, but she couldn't be sure. No mention in the FAQs. None. Jesus.

The website said that only 'pistol caliber weapons' could be fired on the range. She wasn't sure what that meant, but she assumed it would be enough for her. She perused the 'equipment' that you could purchase on site. Glock, Sig Sauer, Colt, Bond Arms, Remington, Beretta, Savage, Ruger, Springfield, Smith and Wesson, Rock Island, Kimber. She'd heard of some of these but had no yardstick for comparing them. She found a book in the library's print collection entitled *Standard Catalog of Firearms*, which was published annually. The most current volume they had was from 2020, and Jules checked it out so she could study at home. She would have her work cut out for her trying to figure out what she'd need. Mostly, she needed to develop her accuracy.

She wasn't sure how much of a backstory to devise. Probably none. She planned to play it by ear. She wanted to avoid lying as much as possible. It would make it easier for her; the truth had always been easy. Besides, with the level of violence in the news it was no stretch to believe that someone like her might want a gun for protection. Her own father had been a firearms enthusiast and couldn't understand why she didn't have one in her house when the kids were little. It made perfect sense for a woman to want a gun in modern day America. It made her sad.

She turned left off the main road where she saw the sign and drove up a stone drive, past some power lines. The range was surrounded by a chain link fence, set back from the main road, behind a few other businesses. Jules assumed the motorized gate she drove through would be well closed and locked during non-business hours. Once inside the property, sheet-metal ads attached to this side of the fence read, GLOCK, and REMINGTON, and COLT, and BERETTA. She was surprised at the lack of artfulness. No tag lines, no flair, no design. Just letters spelling out words. Even the fonts were unimaginative.

A large American Flag hung from a pole attached to the building. There was plenty of parking and the lot was well maintained.

Cameras perched from every corner of the building, covering the entire perimeter. Jules was surprised at the size of the place. There were only six firing lines according to the website, so she was expecting something more like a storefront than the warehouse she was approaching. She parked her Jeep and crossed to the front door. Deep breath.

Inside, the sales floor was smaller than it had looked on the website, but there was plenty of fire power. An Irish Wolfhound the color of a dirty dishrag lifted his woolly bulk from the floor in front of a display case and slowly came over to check her out.

"Hi, baby!" Jules extended her hand for him to sniff, then rubbed behind his enormous ears. He could stick his nose in her armpit if he wanted.

"Who's this?" Jules asked the young man behind the counter.

"That's Bullet," he replied.

Of course it is, thought Jules. No subtlety should be expected. She finished greeting the store mascot and looked toward his owner.

"Welcome to TIGR, ma'am! How can I help you?" She'd seen that catchy acronym on the website.

He was in his late 20s, 30 at most, clean shaven and wearing what she thought of as sportsman clothes. Heavy khakis and a long-sleeved utility shirt with pockets and plackets that likely had some purpose. Boots that her father would have called 'shit-kickers.' She remembered something on the website about appropriate clothing for shooting. Hot brass and casings would be flying around, so the less skin exposed the better. Jules was in a black turtleneck and jeans under her hideous but cozy puffy coat, and black fur-lined Uggs. In early April there was still snow on the ground.

"Thanks! Um, I'd just like to start learning a little about guns and getting some hands-on training."

"Great. Tell me a little about your experience with guns. Have you ever handled a gun?"

"Yeah, but it's pretty limited. I tried out for my school's rifle team when those things still existed. Do they still exist?" She wondered out loud. Was he too young to know about rifle teams?

"I went to Troy and we didn't have one. I think schools that still have 'em have switched to air rifles." He seemed disdainful. She was pleased to learn about this change to the sport, even though air rifles, even BB guns, could still be lethal.

"Did you make your team?" He asked hopefully.

"No, so I guess your work's cut out for you." Jules laughed. "I was also in the service and we had to be weapons qualified in boot camp, but that's really the extent of my gun experience."

"Well, that's something. At least you have some basic knowledge." He smiled at her encouragingly.

"Basic. That might even be generous. My dad was a gun guy and had a bunch of weapons, but I really don't know a pistol from an ouzo!"

"Uzi. It's called an Uzi." He corrected her. "I think ouzo is some kind of Greek liquor?"

"Yeah well, I've definitely spent more time in bars than I have behind a trigger!" She joked.

They were connecting and she was starting to feel comfortable. It wasn't nearly as hard as she had expected.

"So, what do you suggest? I'm not planning to buy anything yet." She glanced around at the stomach-turning display of lethal hardware. There was even a women's section, clearly identifiable by the pink camo displays.

"I just want to get comfortable with the idea of using a gun. Once I feel like I could actually protect myself in a dangerous situation I'll think about buying one."

"That's no problem. We don't pressure sell in here. We're not on commission. You can rent equipment from us and buy your ammo here whenever you come in to shoot. We even have a 'try before you buy' program. That will give you the chance to try out all different options and see what's comfortable for you."

"Yes! That's exactly what I want to do. I want to make sure that if I'm going to buy a gun I'll be able to use it. There's nothing worse than buying a pair of shoes because they look so great and then never wearing them because they're impractical or hurt like hell!"

"I'll take your word for it." He laughed. "If only shoe stores had a try-before-you-buy program, right? It lets you get a feel for the actions of different manufacturers and calibers. You can try out long guns and handguns. It's a great option for someone like you. Um, what's your name?"

"Oh, sorry, I'm Jules. And you?"

"I'm TJ. This is my family's place. Fourth generation. My great-grandad started the business here in the 20s." He was proud of the heritage. "Just about everybody working here is related." He glanced down to the end of the counter at an older guy, "Right, Dad?" he yelled.

Dad looked up from the clipboard in his hand. "What's up, Teej?"

"I was just telling Jules here that we're all family."

"That's right. Otherwise, I wouldn't be hanging around with you bunch!" Dad barked. Jules could see that father and son were dopplegangers separated by a few decades and fifty pounds.

"You can't choose your family, right?" Dad walked toward her, smiling, hand extended. Jules could tell it was a gesture as natural as breathing to this guy.

"Tony Graybill. Nice to meet you, Jules." The two shook hands. She was surprised at both his firm grip and the softness of his working-man hands. She noticed his nails were clean, maybe even manicured.

"You, too. This is my first time in and I was just learning a little about the place from TJ."

"Oh, great!" He glanced at his son and she could see the warmth there. "He's a pro. Let me know if I can help, Teej. Nice meeting you."

TJ went on to explain all of the package options, and before the hour was up Jules had forked over almost five-hundred bucks for an annual membership. It gave her unlimited range time, a discount on ammo, and try-before-you-buy on the guns she might consider. She had charged the whole thing to her sole credit card; the one she kept for emergencies. Jules considered the possible collapse of civil society a worthy emergency.

She was shown to a small cubicle where she watched a range safety video before she could go in. It made her feel physically ill to realize that she would soon be entering a space where everyone was carrying loaded weapons. She could feel her heart beating in her ears. The video narrator reminded viewers that "when you are on the range you are a range safety officer," and "anyone can call for a cease fire at any time if they see anything amiss. For example, if someone drops their weapon or steps into the firing line." She started sweating, but her hands were steady. She could do this. She would do this.

After the video, TJ provided her with a beginner's lesson on pistols. He explained double action and single action and showed her the differences. Some of the guns, the single actions, had a barrel that she had to pull back with her thumb before she could pull the trigger. These were out right away. She'd need something that had the least probability of going wrong. The fewer steps she had to take the more likely she'd be successful in her mission. So now she knew she only wanted to work with double action models.

Then TJ explained what made a gun semi-automatic. That term meant that after a bullet was discharged from the gun, another round would chamber automatically. The trigger had to be pulled again for that next shot, but the ammo was ready. He explained that fully automatic weapons, like machine guns, fired more than one bullet with a single trigger pull. These were typically military use weapons, TJ told her. And the weapons of choice for mass casualty assaults in America's schools, grocery stores, shopping malls, and movie theaters, she thought. A semi-automatic was going to be her choice.

TJ explained the basic differences between rifles, shotguns and handguns, and the appropriate use-case scenario for each. Jules said that her primary concern was protection in the home. She was looking for something to keep by the bed.

"A shotgun is best for home security," TJ explained. "It has two key benefits. First, it doesn't require any accuracy. If an intruder breaks into your house at night, all you have to do is shoot in his general direction. He's either goin' down or beatin' feet! Second, everybody knows that trademark sound of a shotgun being racked."

He lifted the closest to hand and racked it back to demonstrate.

"TSCHK-TSCHK!" went the death stick.

"Any perp hearing that would think twice about crossing the threshold. Right?" TJ asked.

It made good sense but it wasn't in her playbook. She wanted to get straight to the easily concealed weapons and quickly make a pick for the mission at hand.

"I think I just want to start with the handguns and get a sense of how it feels to fire a weapon. I'm a little intimidated by the long guns." Jules and TJ walked back over to the pistol case.

"Of course. I get it. You can work up to these after you're more comfortable. I advise everyone to have a handgun, a shotgun, and a rifle at least. But you'll get there!" He encouraged.

"For now, we'll start slow." TJ recommended that she start that with a .22 caliber handgun. He pulled one from the display case.

"This is a Ruger SR-22." He explained, checking the chamber to make sure it was empty.

"Are you right-handed?"

Jules nodded.

"Okay, take your right hand and place it like this." He showed her the grip and she imitated it.

"Never put your finger on the trigger unless you're ready to fire! You keep your trigger finger aligned down the side of the barrel, like this." He instructed. She followed suit.

"Now take your left hand and fit your thumb into this space, and wrap your fingers underneath the barrel, like so. Your two thumbs should be in a line here, see? Relax!" The tension he saw in her white knuckles radiated into her neck and shoulders and would throw off her aim.

Jules took a deep breath and tried to match his grip.

"That's it! Great." He said.

"Now, lift the gun and look down the sights. Right! That's it. The two sights closest to you should be blurry, and the sight at the tip of the barrel should be in sharp focus. Got it?"

Jules pointed the gun across the store with her arms extended and locked, and looked down the top of the barrel. She shifted the gun a bit to get the right focus. The far sight was painted green. Go.

"And when you want to fire, you're going to squeeze the gun first, then squeeze the trigger, okay? Your hand is going to act like a vise, holding the gun in place so that you can fire accurately. It also minimizes kickback, which won't be bad with a small piece like this. But it's a good habit to build. Squeeze the gun, THEN squeeze the trigger."

Jules steadied herself and pulled the trigger. CLICK.

"Yes, that's it. We'll work on your stance once we're on the range." She hadn't realized he'd be the one accompanying her in. She was slightly relieved not to have to tell her story to anyone else that day.

TJ laid the pistol into a carrying case that was used to transport weapons safely onto the range. He grabbed a box of 50 rounds of ammo.

"Put on your ears." He instructed, pointing.

Jules donned the sound dampening earmuffs that were mandatory beyond the door. She was able to use her own glasses as eye protection. As TJ reached for the door, Jules had a momentary sensation of kinship with one Alice who had gone through the looking glass into a topsy-turvy world.

The range itself was as she expected from the videos. Shooting lanes separated by plexiglass dividers. There were two men and a young woman already shooting. No one looked their way as they entered. The shooters' focus was down range, on their imagined threats. The floor was littered with spent shells, more leaping to join them as each shot echoed in the small room. TJ grabbed a push broom that was kept just inside the door for such purposes and swept some of them deeper into the shooting lanes and out of the foot traffic area. There were thousands of spent casings. Jules wondered how often they were cleared out. Could all of this be just from today?

Each lane had a shelf for the shooter to place their weapon and ammo. She had been given a target identical to the three that were already taking fire. A hulking, pink humanoid shape on a white background. In the center of the big, pink body, an X, marking the kill shot zone. Jules taped her target to the zip line and flipped the switch at her left shoulder to run the target down the overhead track. When it got about a quarter of the way down, TJ reached over and stopped it.

"You start at about this distance." He said. "Then as you improve you move the target further down range."

"Oh, okay. How far will this gun shoot?" Jules asked.

"A handgun can hit a target a mile away."

"Really? Wow! I had no idea." That should be sufficient, Jules calculated. She'd have no trouble getting to within a mile of her intended target.

TJ showed her how to load ten rounds into the cartridge. It worked kind of like a pez dispenser. Once all ten bullets were loaded, the whole thing slipped right into the base of the gun. He showed her how to rack the first round. Everything sounded very mechanical and operated with smooth action.

"Remember your grip. Don't touch that trigger until you're ready to fire. Line up your thumbs. Good! Now, line up that front sight like I showed you. It should be in clear focus."

"OK, I see it." Jules' hands were shaking. She squeezed the gun to help steady them.

"Relax. I can see you're nervous. Relax your shoulders or you'll be a mess when you finish your ammo. Good. Now, just aim the sight at the X and pull the trigger." He coached.

BOOM! It was high and slightly to the right.

"Good, now just adjust your stance a little. Place your feet shoulder length apart and slide your right foot back just a little."

Jules followed the instruction.

"Good! That's it. Now lean forward slightly. Don't drop your arms to aim, just line up the sights. Keep the gun up. That's it. Now, fire!"

She pulled. BOOM!

"Keep going," urged TJ.

BOOM! BOOM! BOOM! BOOM! BOOM! Click.

"OK," TJ stepped in, "Sometimes you get a misfire. Let me show you how to clear that."

He took the pistol out of her hands.

"Smack the bottom like this," he demonstrated, "Hear that? Then just rack it again and you're ready to shoot again." He handed it back.

Jules sighted the target and fired off the remaining two rounds. BOOM! BOOM!

TJ reached over and flipped the switch to bring her target in.

"You're doing good! After these first few shots were high," he pointed on the target, "you really started tightening up your aim." He indicated a galaxy of holes surrounding the X. At least she hadn't embarrassed herself.

TJ sent the target back down the lane to the same spot. Jules filled the clip four more times and cleared two more misfires before her box of ammo was empty and her time was up.

"That was really good for your first time!"

"Not bad, but next time I want to move the target further away," Jules told him. "I want to be accurate at least at the full distance of the shooting lane."

"So, we'll start next time at the halfway point. If you can keep every shot in the white for your first two clips, then we can move it all the way down. You really have to get a feel for how to make adjustments on your sighting at that distance. Even once you're accurate at full range, you should move the target to different distances to maintain your precision."

"That makes sense," Jules knew she'd need precision for the mission.

TJ retrieved the target and walked out onto the sales floor with her. He wrote the date and the weapon on the target for her to take with her. A souvenir. She hadn't thought about how useful that would be to track her progress and record her impressions of the various weapons she would handle in the coming months.

After leaving the range, Jules stopped in the ladies room. Taped on the wall near the hand dryer was a reminder about Ladies' Night. First Thursday of the month. She planned to attend. She wanted to see what weapons other women used and get some insight. She hoped to identify a few really talented shooters and take some informal lessons. She snapped a photo of the flyer with her phone as a reminder to add it to her calendar.

On her way out, she handed her ear protection to TJ.

"Thank you!" He smiled and handed her a paper. "Here's the regular schedule. It's on the website, too, but this one has more information for our members. It shows league nights, specials, stuff like that."

"Great! Thanks." League nights?

"And we'll send you emails and stuff now that you're signed up with us. That way if we have weather closures or anything you'll know before making the drive."

The door to the range opened behind them and TJ glanced over.

"Oh, hey Frank!"

"Hi TJ."

Frank had been one of the guys with his back to her when she'd entered the shooting range. Now she saw that he was probably late 50s. Slightly graying. An aging physique that had once been athletic. He wore a flannel tucked in over a navy t-shirt and dark, well-fitting jeans. Levi's if she had to guess. Old school. He wore those round-toed, tan leather ankle boots, like her father had worn. But she didn't peg him for a truck driver. No ball cap. Hair close cropped and clean shaven. Retired military, maybe?

"Frank, this is Jules. This is her first time in." TJ introduced them.

"Hi, Jules. Pleasure." They shook hands and he nodded toward her dated target on the counter. "Looks like you're a quick learner."

"There's room for improvement, for sure. I'm still just getting comfortable with a gun in my hand." She pointed out the shots that had gone wide. "I really want to tighten that up next time."

"So, you roped 'er in, TJ? Signed 'er up?" He laughed easily.

"Yeah, I'm a member now. I want to try different guns before I decide if I'm going to buy. If I'm going to own a weapon, I want to make sure I can use it for its intended purpose."

"Which is?" He asked.

"Just personal protection. Something to keep at hand."

"OK, I've been duly warned!" He put his hands up and stepped away from her.

Jules laughed. "Are you trouble?" She asked.

TJ chimed in, "Frank's no trouble. He's trouble's worst nightmare! Po-Po."

She was close. "Oh! I see. Albany, P.D.?" She asked.

"Retired from Schenectady." She was right on the retired part. "I come in to keep my skill level up, just in case I ever decide to go back. I hadn't really planned to retire. But the plague kind of blew up my life."

"Say no more! I get it."

Jules had known lots of area cops and firefighters. The Irish had a long history in both professions, and some of her extended family members had even answered that calling. She and Frank went through a lengthy who-do-you-know conversation and found they had many common acquaintances. A familiar exchange in a town known lovingly as Smallbany.

Jules grabbed her target and headed for the door, "It was nice to meet you, Frank. I'm sure I'll see you again before my membership expires."

Jules turned to TJ. "I'm planning to come to the next Ladies' Night. Do you work those?"

"Either me or Dad. One of us will be here!"

"My daughter Charlotte usually comes. I'll tell her to look out for you." Frank said.

"Sounds good. Thanks, Frank. Bye!" Jules waved and headed to her car. It was cold and the windshield would need defrosting. She cranked the blower on high and took a deep breath. She felt okay. She felt good! She had actually started implementing the plan. She needed to improve her skill, a lot, but she felt like it was doable.

She drove home adjusting her shooting stance in her mind.

●   ●   ●

VIDEO DIARY ENTRY – April 5, 2022

"Hello. It's Tuesday, April 5th. The investigation into Trump's involvement in the January 6th insurrection continues. They're reporting an eight-hour gap in his communications trail on that day. Reports from insiders indicate he was watching it all unfold on TV and yet he never stepped forward to tell his terrorists to stand down. Why? Because he wanted them to succeed! It's not difficult at all. Why are we playing dumb? He committed treason. His actions and the actions of

his followers are the textbook definition of treason. No, that's wrong. They are the CONSTITUTIONAL definition of treason.

"Let me read the specific language to you." Jules reached into a desk drawer and held her pocket copy of the Constitution up to the camera before finding her place. *"Article III, Section 3, Clause 1 reads as follows: 'Treason against the United States, shall consist only in levying War against them, or in adhering to their Enemies, giving them Aid and Comfort.'*

"The January 6ᵗʰ insurrectionists were enemies of this Nation, attempting to thwart our democracy and the peaceful transfer of power. Trump provided Aid and Comfort. Period.

"Let's do a thought experiment. Think back to January 6ᵗʰ and everything you may have watched unfold on that day. Now imagine that the person orchestrating it all was someone other than Trump. Someone like a Ted Kaczynski or a Timothy McVeigh. Someone claiming the election was rigged and that they were therefore justified in their actions. They would be charged with treason under these circumstances. Why is Trump, someone with a sacred duty to uphold the Constitution, and in a position of greater power and influence, held to a lesser standard?"

Jules laid the book on her desk and turned back to the camera.

"I made my first trip to the gun range today. I have a lot of work to do to be mission ready, but the skills are there. Archery, billiards, those other things that I've always been good at come into play here. There's just some kind of natural inclination, I think." She reached down to the floor to retrieve the target she'd brought home and held it up for the camera.

"You can see I have pretty good accuracy for a first session. I surprised myself. These few here are some of the first shots, wide and unpredictable. I tightened them up as I got more comfortable with the

weapon. That's what you see in this cluster here, where I start getting consistent," Jules demonstrated, pointing. *"Dad would be proud.*

"I plan to try out several different weapons in the coming months, based on some research I'm conducting to determine the best gun for success with the mission. I expect I will have a very limited opportunity to achieve my target. One shot, maybe two at most. I have to make it count."

Jules shut down the phone and placed it along with her target into the safe. She was on task and she felt great.

MASS SHOOTING IN THE US
April 2022 - 57 total

A mass shooting is any shooting where four or more people, other than the shooter, are killed or injured.

1. April 1, 2022 - Walterboro, South Carolina — 4 injured
2. April 2, 2022 - Shelby, North Carolina — 5 dead, 2 injured
3. April 2, 2022 - Monroe, Louisiana — 4 injured
4. April 2, 2022 -Colorado Springs, Colorado — 6 injured
5. April 2, 2022 - Shreveport, Louisiana — 1 dead, 3 injured
6. April 3, 2022 - Buffalo, New York — 5 dead
7. April 3, 2022 - Dallas, Texas — 1 dead, 3 injured
8. April 3, 2022 - San Francisco, California — 4 dead
9. April 3, 2022 - Sacramento, California - 1 dead, 3 injured
10. April 4, 2022 -Covington, Kentucky — 1 dead, 6 injured
11. April 4, 2022 - Hartford, Connecticut — 5 injured
12. April 6, 2022 - Philadelphia, Pennsylvania - 2 dead, 2 injured
13. April 9, 2022 - Miami, Florida — 4 injured
14. April 9, 2022 - Washington, District of Columbia - 1 dead, 3 injured
15. April 10, 2022 - Baton Rouge, Louisiana - 4 injured
16. April 10, 2022 - Cedar Rapids, Iowa — 4 dead

17. April 10, 2022 - Elgin, Illinois – 4 injured
18. April 10, 2022 - Willowbrook, California – 1 dead, 3 injured
19. April 10, 2022 - Indianapolis, Indiana - 4 dead, 2 injured
20. April 12, 2022 - Brooklyn, New York – 4 injured
21. April 12, 2022 - Bronx, New York - 4 injured
22. April 15, 2022 - Stockton, California – 4 injured
23. April 16, 2022 - Columbia, South Carolina – 2 dead, 2 injured
24. April 16, 2022 - Baltimore, Maryland - 1 dead, 3 injured
25. April 16, 2022 - North Las Vegas, Nevada - 5 injured
26. April 16, 2022 - Daingerfield, Texas – 5 dead
27. April 16, 2022 - Syracuse, New York – 1 dead, 5 injured
28. April 17, 2022 - Philadelphia, Pennsylvania -5 injured
29. April 17, 2022 - Portland, Oregon – 4 injured
30. April 17, 2022 -Furman, South Carolina - 4 injured
31. April 17, 2022 - Sacramento , California - 4 injured
32. April 17, 2022 - Miami, Florida - 4 injured
33. April 17, 2022 - Pittsburgh, Pennsylvania - 4 injured
34. April 17, 2022 - Baldwin, Louisiana – 4 injured
35. April 20, 2022 - Duluth, Minnesota - 1 dead, 4 injured
36. April 21, 2022 - Mountain View, Arkansas – 4 injured
37. April 22, 2022 - Petersburg, Virginia – 1 dead, 3 injured
38. April 22, 2022 - Washington, District of Columbia – 1 dead, 3 injured
39. April 22, 2022 - Cincinnati, Ohio - 1 dead, 3 injured
40. April 23, 2022 - Chicago, Illinois – 4 injured
41. April 23, 2022 - Rocky Mount, North Carolina – 4 injured
42. April 23, 2022 - Atlanta, Georgia – 4 injured
43. April 23, 2022 - San Bernardino, California – 2 dead, 3 injured
44. April 24, 2022 -Myrtle Beach, South Carolina -1 dead, 3 injured
45. April 24, 2022 - Lafayette, Indiana - 1 dead, 3 injured

46. April 25, 2022 - Birmingham, Alabama – 2 dead, 2 injured

47. April 27, 2022 -Chicago, Illinois – 5 injured

48. April 27, 2022 - Biloxi, Mississippi - 4 injured

49. April 27, 2022 - San Antonio, Texas – 5 injured

50. April 27, 2022 - Opelousas, Louisiana – 5 injured

51. April 27, 2022 - Phoenix, Arizona - 4 injured

52. April 28, 2022 - Bessemer, Alabama – 4 injured

53. April 29, 2022 - Jackson, Tennessee – 5 injured

54. April 29, 2022 - New Orleans, Louisiana – 4 injured

55. April 29, 2022 - Laurel, Mississippi - 2 dead, 7 injured

56. April 30, 2022 - Atlanta, Georgia – 4 injured

57. April 30, 2022 - Jackson, Mississippi - 4 injured

• • •

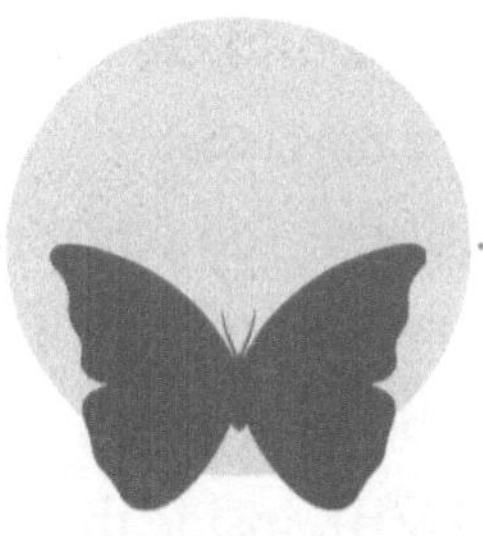

MAY 2022

Jules had been to the range several times on her own but had yet to make it to Ladies' Night. She had already tried a few different firearms, all semi-automatic 9mm pistols of different sizes and makes. In her research, she had learned the pros and cons of standard, compact, sub-compact, and micro sized handguns. She planned to avoid the standard size, because it wasn't as easily concealed, and could be unwieldy for her. The two smallest sizes reportedly lacked accuracy, but she tried them just to see. She really liked the smaller sizes and the ease with which she could handle them. But the pro's advice was to carry the largest gun you can that was still concealable, depending on your 'concealment method.'

There were a surprising number of concealment methods, and they fell into two different categories: off-body and on-body. Jules had already decided that she was going to carry a typical, nondescript black fanny pack around her waist. It would be part of her invisibility disguise. A gray-haired, MAGA-hatted, white granny in orthopedic shoes and a fanny pack over her sweats was entirely unremarkable in Trump world. It was the camouflage of syco-phants; the siren song to a narcissist.

Jules scanned the list of the 'top ten concealment methods,' and there it was, at number ten. Fanny pack. This was considered an 'unconventional' and 'off-body' method of concealment, following outside the waistband (OWB), inside the waistband (IWB), appen-dix inside the waistband (AIWB), and pocket carry method, which apparently didn't warrant an acronym. There were also ankle hol-sters, belly bands, and bra holsters. Backpacks, briefcases, and purses also made the list of off-body ways to hide your firearm.

On a website called pewpewtactical, seemingly named by 8-year-old boys with finger guns, she learned about deep conceal-ment. These are methods where concealment is the highest priority, over and above accessibility. The site's editor, a young woman, was pictured in a figure-hugging dress with a caption that challenged the reader to spot her 'deeply concealed' firearm. Jules wondered if it might require medical equipment. She was grateful quickly to back out of that site, since accessibility was paramount for her.

She had decided on either a 9mm or a .380., having ruled out smaller calibers, which were not recommended for self-defense. Even though the .22 was reported to have the least recoil, the 9mm seemed to be the preferred choice for their 'stopping power'. She could train to manage the recoil once she bought a gun, but she needed serious stopping power.

Jules pored over her firearms catalog to compare the two calibers that made her list. The .380 seemed to perform best at close range, meaning under 3 yards. She didn't want to take that risk. She wasn't sure how close she would be able to get on the day. A website she consulted at the library went so far as to call the .380 "underpow-ered and, thus, useless in most situations." Strike two. Whereas the

9mm "offers a perfect balance of power, concealability, reliability, and capacity." Also, she learned, the 9mm was the preferred caliber for both law enforcement and doomsday preppers. Sold.

Before her fourth visit to the range, Jules made a list of models she wanted to try out based on the research. Up to that point she had taken TJ or Tony's advice on what to try, and had even shot a few long guns. Just to keep up the façade. She decided to test a handful of 9mm pieces that day. She wasn't sure which, if any, TIGR would have, but TJ could probably figure out what they had in the store that measured up to these. She was interested in the Glock 19 (the 'gold standard'), Ruger Max-9 (sighting ease/accuracy), Smith & Wesson Shield EZ (oversized sights), and the Springfield Armory Hellcat 3" (micro-compact to try before ruling out the entire class of micros).

● ● ●

Pulling up to the gun range, Jules noted the parking lot was much busier than on her last visit. Lots of pick-ups and a few muscle cars. A mini-van. She noticed a bumper sticker on one truck that said, "I don't call 911" with a hand pointing a huge-barreled gun at the reader, finger on the trigger. There were a lot of "Let's Go Brandon"s. One that said something about prying a gun from cold, dead hands. That one was on the mini-van. She passed a no-nonsense "Fuck Biden" on one bumper and noticed a car seat in the back and a rosary hanging from the rearview. Family values.

Tony and TJ were both working, busy with customers on opposite sides of the store. Both men looked up as she entered, sounding the bell above the front door. Jules imagined they wanted to avoid anyone slipping in unnoticed. That could be a deadly mistake.

"Hey, Jules! Be with you in a minute," welcomed TJ.

Tony pointed to a far corner of the store, where there were seats for waiting customers, "There's coffee if you want some."

"Thanks!" Jules walked over and poured herself a paper cupful. A woman and a little boy, probably seven or eight, sat in one of the chairs. He was leaned against his mother's crossed legs, his eyes glued to a TV mounted on the wall. Jules felt like she was waiting for an oil change, except for the barely muffled sound of continuous gunfire.

The little boy had jeans tucked into worn cowboy boots, boots that looked like they did man work. His mom was lost in her pink camo covered cell phone; hadn't even looked up when Jules walked over. She was thin, dressed in dark wash jeans, a thermal vest over her flannel, with a little bit of lace from her yellow cotton tank top showing above the open buttons. Her brown hair was long and limp, and she kept pushing it behind her ears.

"Hi." Jules said to the pair as she took a seat. Mom joined the room.

"Hi." She replied.

They couldn't be waiting to shoot. He wasn't old enough.

"Do you know if there's a wait for the range?" Jules asked.

"I don't think so. My husband's in there and he got right in."

"Thanks." The little boy was looking at her.

"What's your name?" She asked.

"Kevin."

"Hi Kevin. My name's Jules. How old are you?"

"I'm seven. I used to be six, but now I'm KEVIN and I'm SEVEN! Get it?"

"That's a good one!" Jules laughed.

"Those boots look like you're a hard worker!" Jules pointed.

"I am!" he crowed. "We live. . ."

"That's enough, Kevin." Mom piped in sharply. Then to Jules, "This one will talk your head off."

"Oh yeah," Jules commiserated. "I know how that goes."

The door to the range opened and the third piece of the puzzle walked over. Tall and on the heavier side, bulky. Same puffy vest as her over a white long-sleeved thermal. He had his weapons in cases. Long guns and handguns from the looks of it.

"Let's go." He commanded. Mom put the phone away and grabbed Kevin by the hand.

"Bye, Kevin who's seven!" Jules sing-songed.

"Bye lady who's eighty!" He responded. Jules cracked up! But mom and dad didn't seem to find it funny. Mom shook his arm and gave him a hard look that said he'd pay for that later.

Tony came over to where Jules was waiting.

"Hey, Jules! What can I help you with?"

Jules pulled out her phone.

"Thanks, Tony. You guys are busy today! I've made a list of 4 guns I want to try out, if you have them." She read off her list.

"Okay!" replied Tony, "A woman who knows what she wants! I like it." He motioned for her to follow him to the display cases.

She glanced out the window to see Kevin and his family pulling away in the '911' truck. Kevin was standing in that space in a king cab behind the driver's seat, not even a seat belt, waving. Jules waved back and hoped he'd be okay. In a lot of ways.

"We have the Glock 19 and the Ruger, I know. You've shot the Glock here already."

"Oh, I thought so. It sounded familiar. I want to try it again today so I can compare it to the others."

Tony was opening the display behind him. "The Smith & Wesson isn't here, but we could get one in if you want to try it out. What is it about that one you're interested in?"

Jules consulted her notes while Tony pulled the two weapons from the display cases.

"Well, apparently it has oversized sights for people with limited vision? I wear glasses, but I thought the bigger sights might be helpful anyway."

"Okay. One option that might work is the Smith & Wesson CSX. Now that's a micro-compact, like that Springfield on your list. But it is known for its sighting ability. We have one here. Do you want to give it a try?" He pointed at the small gun.

"Yes, I'll try that. So maybe I don't need to try the Springfield then, because the reason it's on my list is that I wanted to feel the difference between a compact and a micro-compact."

"Gotcha. We don't carry that one anyway. But again, I could get it in if you wanted to try it out."

"No, let me try these three on the range today. Is there a free lane?" Jules inquired.

"There is. I'll put you in Lane 1, where Dave just finished." He nodded toward the parking lot, where Dave and his family were already gone. Tony consulted some paperwork and completed the records, checking Dave out and Jules in.

"You already signed a blanket release last time with TJ. That will cover you every time you come in until your membership expires. If you decide to renew, we'll have you sign a new release."

"Okay. That works. I'm still a newbie so I need one of you to come onto the range with me again." She gestured toward TJ, working with two other customers. "He looks like he's still tied up. I need to learn how to load each of these, and a little safety refresher would help, too. Do you have time?"

Tony handed her ear protection and a box of 9mm rounds.

"No problem. I'll take you in." He put on his own ears, picked up the weapons, which he'd placed in a case lined with Styrofoam egg crate, and walked her in to shooting Lane 1.

Within the hour, she had almost perfected her stance, im-proved her consistency at the half-way point, moved the target to the full length of the range, and tested out all three guns. Her clear winner was the reputed gold standard, the Glock 19. She did wish it was a little smaller, but she felt it was the right weapon for her mission. She would focus on that model from now on, aiming for accuracy at the mid- and furthest points in the lane.

Tony had left Jules on the range after he saw she was in a groove. She could load the weapon and clear a jam quickly and safely. She had given him a thumbs up when he signaled that he wanted to return to the sales floor.

"You're looking really comfortable in there!" He said to her now as she removed her ears. "That didn't take long."

"I surprised myself!" she admitted. "I think I'm going to go ahead and bite the bullet."

Tony's eyebrow shot up, "No pun intended?"

"Oh, it was intended all right. I've been holding on to that one since the first day." She laughed. "It was between that and 'pull the trigger'."

"Ok. Don't quit your day job." He joked. "So, the Glock 19, then?"

"Yeah, that really felt the most manageable for me. What's it going to run me?"

"That model is $395.00. It comes with three magazines, the standard 17-round and two 17+2 round magazines. And the standard case," he reached under the counter, "is this gray one. They call it coyote. You can upgrade the case for a small charge." He pointed to the blingy cases displayed in the 'women's' section. Lots of pinks and purples and silver.

"No thanks. I like the gray one. I think coyotes are romantic. And I need some rounds, too. The smallest box you have." Tony pulled a box of 9mm rounds from the stack behind him. They were $20.00 for 50 rounds. Jules had no idea if that was a good price. She had her plastic out and handed it over. She only had $500.00 in credit on it, and had paid the balance off, anticipating this purchase. Still, she was relieved when the charge went through.

Tony loaded her new purchases into a TIGR plastic merch bag, stapled the receipt to close the top of the bag, and placed it in a bin behind the counter with other similar packages.

"Ok, now the real fun begins. Compliments of your New York State legislature." Jules hears the eye roll in his voice. "Things are supposed to really tighten up later this year with Hochul in office, so I guess you're lucky. If this was September, you'd have to complete a 16-hour safety course before you could even apply for your permit."

"Lucky me!" She hoped he didn't register her sarcasm. One of Jules' points of pride as a New Yorker was her state's response to gun violence. Immediately after the Sandy Hook shooting in 2012, Governor Andrew Cuomo had taken decisive action, putting in place first-in-the-nation legislation to crack down on gun violence.

Jules started on the paperwork that Tony presented.

"Are you going to want to get concealed carry, too?" He asked, reaching for more paper.

"No, I'm just going to keep the thing at home. Probably in my nightstand."

"Ok, then you won't need that." He put the form back in its slot. "Now, you have to complete all of this and submit it to your local police agency. They're the ones who do the investigation. Do you live in Troy?"

"No, I'm in Saratoga County."

"Right. Just do it as soon as possible. It can take months to get your permit, sometimes close to a year."

"Really?" Jules was surprised but pleased at that news. She was glad to have made the purchase then, rather than waiting. She had plenty of time before the 2024 RNC.

"Yeah, we'll hold your purchase here for you until it comes in. Then just bring your permit here for our records, and you can take your new best friend home with you!"

"Got it. Thanks, Tony. I'll see you soon." The bell jangled over the door as she made her way out to the parking lot. It had been a productive day.

* * *

VIDEO DIARY ENTRY – May 12, 2022

"Hello. It's Thursday, May 12th. Here's where things are. Last month, in an interview with The Guardian, Trump slipped up. He admitted, for the first time as far as I know, that he didn't win the 2020 election. Of course, he has back pedaled since then, but it does seem like a chink in the armor. Not one that anyone seems to be exploiting.

"I went to the gun range today and had a good session. I decided on the best weapon for my mission and purchased a Glock 19. Once I have my license from the state, I'll be 'legal'. As I understand it, that

might take a while. New York has gun laws that are considered to be strict by U.S. standards. Of course, that's a very low bar.

I never thought I'd be a gun owner. But then, there is so much in these recent years that I couldn't have imagined."

• • •

MASS SHOOTINGS IN THE US
May 2022 - 64 total

A mass shooting is any shooting where four or more people, other than the shooter, are killed or injured.

1. May 01, 2022 - Lafayette, Louisiana - 4 injured
2. May 01, 2022 - Springfield, Ohio - 5 injured
3. May 01, 2022 - Tarpon Springs, Florida - 4 injured
4. May 01, 2022 - North Charleston, South Carolina - 1 dead, 3 injured
5. May 03, 2022 - Cowley (county), Kansas - 4 injured
6. May 03, 2022 - Baton Rouge, Louisiana - 2 dead, 2 injured
7. May 03, 2022 - Beaumont, Texas - 4 injured
8. May 05, 2022 - Sunnyside, Washington - 4 dead,
9. May 06, 2022 - New Orleans, Louisiana - 1 dead, 3 injured
10. May 07, 2022 - Miami, Florida - 4 injured
11. May 07, 2022 - Lexington, Kentucky - 4 injured
12. May 07, 2022 - Garland, Texas - 3 dead, 3 injured
13. May 08, 2022 - Clarkston, Georgia - 2 dead, 2 injured
14. May 09, 2022 - Detroit, Michigan - 2 dead, 2 injured
15. May 09, 2022 - Tuscaloosa, Alabama - 1 dead, 1
16. May 10, 2022 - Baltimore, Maryland - 1 dead, 3 injured

17. May 10, 2022 - Chicago, Illinois - 2 dead, 4 injured

18. May 10, 2022 - Chicago, Illinois - 2 dead, 5 injured

19. May 10, 2022 - Philadelphia, Pennsylvania - 7 injured

20. May 10, 2022 - Baltimore, Maryland - 4 injured

21. May 10, 2022 - Brookshire, Texas - 3 dead, 2 injured

22. May 11, 2022 - Chicago, Illinois - 2 dead, 2 injured

23. May 11, 2022 - Indianapolis, Indiana - 5 injured

24. May 11, 2022 - Saint Louis, Missouri - 4 injured

25. May 11, 2022 - Paterson, New Jersey - 2 dead, 2 injured

26. May 12, 2022 - Hot Springs National Park, Arkansas - 1 dead, 3 injured

27. May 13, 2022 - Napoleonville, Louisiana - 2 dead, 2 injured

28. May 13, 2022 - Milwaukee, Wisconsin - 4 injured

29. May 14, 2022 - Buffalo, New York - 4 injured

30. May 15, 2022 - Laguna Woods, California - 4 injured

31. May 15, 2022 - Winston Salem, North Carolina - 4 injured

32. May 15, 2022 - Elizabeth City, North Carolina - 2 dead, 2 injured

33. May 15, 2022 - Houston, Texas - 6 injured

34. May 15, 2022 - Amarillo, Texas - 1 dead, 3 injured

35. May 17, 2022 - Palo Alto (East Palo Alto), California - 6 injured

36. May 18, 2022 - Philadelphia, Pennsylvania - 3 dead, 1 injured

37. May 19, 2022 - Chicago, Illinois - 2 dead, 5 injured

38. May 20, 2022 - Highland, California - 3 dead, 2 injured

39. May 20, 2022 - Kissimmee, Florida - 1 dead, 4 injured

40. May 20, 2022 - New Orleans, Louisiana - 1 dead, 3 injured

41. May 21, 2022 - Goshen, Indiana - 7 injured

42. May 21, 2022 - Tacoma, Washington - 2 dead, 2 injured

43. May 23, 2022 - North Charleston, South Carolina - 4 injured

44. May 23, 2022 - Cleveland, Ohio - 1 dead, 3 injured

45. May 24, 2022 - Uvalde, Texas - 4 injured

46. May 25, 2022 - Philadelphia, Pennsylvania - 2 dead, 3 injured
47. May 27, 2022 - Stanwood, Michigan - 2 dead, 2 injured
48. May 27, 2022 - Anniston, Alabama - 1 dead, 6 injured
49. May 28, 2022 - Chattanooga, Tennessee - 2 dead, 2 injured
50. May 28, 2022 - Fresno, California - 4 injured
51. May 28, 2022 - Malabar, Florida - 4 injured
52. May 28, 2022 - Colorado Springs, Colorado - 5 injured
53. May 28, 2022 - Merced, California - 1 dead, 4 injured
54. May 28, 2022 - Memphis, Tennessee - 4 injured
55. May 29, 2022 - Taft, Oklahoma - 3 dead, 2 injured
56. May 29, 2022 - Henderson, Nevada - 4 injured
57. May 29, 2022 - Chicago, Illinois - 4 injured
58. May 29, 2022 - Houston, Texas - 4 injured
59. May 29, 2022 - Phoenix, Arizona - 5 injured
60. May 29, 2022 - Chicago, Illinois - 6 injured
61. May 30, 2022 - Benton Harbor, Michigan - 1 dead, 4 injured
62. May 30, 2022 - Philadelphia, Pennsylvania - 1 dead, 4 injured
63. May 30, 2022 - Charleston, South Carolina - 1 dead, 3 injured
64. May 31, 2022 - Waco, Texas - 1 dead, 4 injured

• • •

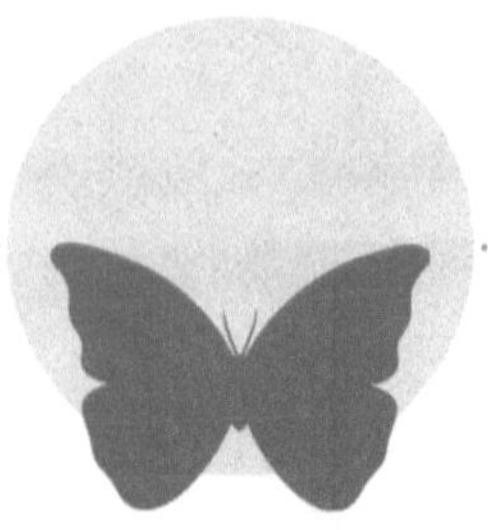

JUNE 2022

Jules was finally headed to Ladies' Night at TIGR. She hadn't been able to make it in either April or May, but she felt good having some solid range time behind her now. She could hold her own. The weather was finally lovely and that always lifted her spirits.

Her phone rang and she grabbed it from the console. It was Sally.

"Hey, Sal!" She answered as she closed the car windows and flipped on the A/C.

"Hey, Jules! What are you up to?"

An unexpected surge of panic welled up as Jules realized she didn't have a good lie prepared. She never had to have cover stories before, so she wasn't well-practiced. She quelled it quickly. She was being ridiculous.

"Oh, um, I'm just getting some gas and a few groceries. I'm in the car. What about you?"

"Hemmy and I are going over to Erin and Sean's for dinner. I was going to invite you to come with. Kids and grandkids are all coming."

"Thank you! I'd love to but I'm filthy from a full day of spring cleaning. By the time I get home with the groceries, shower, and make it to you, it would be late."

"Are you sure, Jules? Everyone wants to see you. We can wait for you."

"I'm missing everyone, too. Why don't we plan a barbecue at my house next weekend instead? I'll just do burgers and dogs and we can get the tribe together."

Sally was relaying all of this to Hem, and apparently he agreed.

"That sounds great. I'll tell everyone at dinner tonight."

"Perfect. I'll invite Simon, Thea, Cassie and all of their bunch, too. It's been too long since I've had a full house over here. Let's say Saturday at one. We can make it a leisurely day."

"Ok. I'll talk to you before then to see what we can bring."

By the time the call ended Jules was pulling into the driveway at TIGR. The parking lot was busier than she had ever seen it! A few 'ladies' were making their way to the door. Jules was in flip-flops so she had to change shoes for the range. She pulled on the socks and loafers she'd brought, and headed in.

"Hey, Jules!" TJ saw her come in and yelled over a few heads. "Glad you finally made it!"

"Thanks, TJ. I didn't realize the crowd you draw for this!" She made her way in his direction.

"This is always our biggest night of the month. Go over by the range door and you'll see some sign-up sheets. You can take up to two spots for the session."

"Ok. Thanks." She found a clipboard hanging from a rusty nail, with a pencil clipped to it. It looked like there would be eight shooting sessions, with six lanes for each. So, 48 spots in all. She guessed there were 15 or so women here already, and the sign-up sheet was looking pretty full. She took a spot in the 2nd session and one in the 4th. This way, she could either leave early or hang around to socialize if she felt comfortable. As she clipped the pencil back onto the board, she noticed the name Charlotte Bogardus. That must be Frank's daughter, she thought. She'd make sure to connect with her.

She glanced around the room. There were a few men in attendance, sitting over in the waiting area. She figured them for husbands or boyfriends. The shooters, the 'ladies', were a mixed bag. Mostly white, much younger than her, but a few gray-haired women who appeared to be here with a daughter or granddaughter. Even though every woman was visibly armed, Jules was relieved to see none of them holding beers or cocktails. She recognized Kevin-who's-seven's mom. The woman looked hollowed out. Jules caught the eye of a woman standing nearby. She turned toward her and extended her hand.

"Hi, I'm Jules."

"Hi Jules, nice to meet you! I'm Gloria. I've never seen you here before?" Her palm was warm and she shook with both hands. She was short, probably 5'3", with glossy black hair pulled back behind a rolled bandana tied behind her head. She had an olive complexion and a wide smile.

"Yeah, I'm a first-timer. I've been trying to come since April, but I always had last minute conflicts. I was adamant that I'd make it tonight. Big crowd."

Both women turned their attention to the rest of the room.

"This is about what a typical ladies' night looks like. I don't think we've ever had more than 20 of us here at a time. Everybody is real friendly."

"You know," Jules lowered her voice, "I actually thought there might be alcohol here. I'm glad to see I was wrong!" They both laughed.

"No, it's not that kind of ladies' night, but a group of us usually go out after. You should come! We go to Scotty's. It's just, like, the next block over, after the light at Walmart on the right."

"I've driven past the place but never gone in. Thanks for the invite. I'll probably join you."

"Good! Let me introduce you to a few of the ladies."

"Who's the woman in the red tank top over by the coffee? I've seen her here before."

Gloria glanced over, "Oh, that's Rebecca. C'mon."

She steered Jules over and introduced the two women. Jules extended her hand and Rebecca took it lightly between her thumb and two fingers, like you might hold a dirty diaper, shook it quickly and dropped it. She was clearly a woman unaccustomed to a handshake.

"Hi Rebecca. We met before when you and Kevin were here a few months ago." She gestured toward the waiting area. She noticed that Dave was one of the waiting group. "How is he?"

"Right. I thought I recognized you." Her tone wasn't hostile, but it wasn't friendly. She tucked a strand of loose hair behind her ear, then pulled a scrunchie off her thin wrist and arranged a ponytail. Her nails were bitten. She glanced toward her husband.

"Kevin's good. He's a good boy." She seemed guarded and uninterested in further conversation.

"Well, nice to actually meet you." Gloria had wandered off after making the introduction, so Jules was on her own. She met a few of the other shooters, and then finally Charlotte.

"So you're Charlotte! I met your dad the first time I was here back in the spring and he told me you'd be here. So nice to meet you!" The two shook hands. Charlotte was probably in her mid-40s. So Frank was older than Jules had guessed. His daughter was tall and solid-looking, with brown curls that stopped just below her shoulders.

"Right! I remember he mentioned it, but I've forgotten your name."

"I'm Jules."

"Nice to meet you, Jules. Is this your first Ladies' Night?"

"It is. I'm a little nervous. To be honest, I'm not very comfortable with firearms."

"Then what drew you here?" Charlotte asked.

"I just want to feel safe at home. Old lady living alone. I'd be an easy target. This will level the playing field."

"You'll be in good company here. A lot of the women who come to Ladies' Night live alone and have a gun for personal protection. I just read something that said women are buying guns in record numbers since the pandemic."

"Hm. What about you?"

"I live alone but I've always had guns. Cop dad, y'know? I've been shooting since I was a teenager."

"So, no fear then, huh?"

"Oh, I have a healthy fear. I never want to lose that. Has anyone invited you to the after party?"

"Yes, thanks. I met Gloria when I first got here, and she invited me."

TJ was near the range door holding up the clipboard and calling in the first group of shooters. Charlotte's name was called and she turned to Jules.

"I'm up! I'll see you at Scotty's if we don't get a chance to talk here. Good luck!"

Good luck? Suddenly Jules realized there might be some sort of competition involved in the evening; like a bowling league. It hadn't even occurred to her. She went back to the sign-up sheet and noticed a list of apparent skills with prizes attached to each.

1. Bullseye blowout (no black) - $200.00
2. Closest to bullseye at full distance - $150.00
3. Best 10-round heart - $100.00

TJ and Tony are the final decision-makers! No disputes!

She had a lot of questions.

• • •

Jules pulled into the parking lot of Scotty's. Her ears were ringing slightly, and she could still smell the unmistakable cloak of gunfire. It was in her hair and on her hands. That was the most she had ever shot in a single session. Thankfully, she hadn't embarrassed herself. She'd been able to shoot consistently at every distance. And she'd learned all the prize lingo. Her competitive streak was engaged. Maybe next time she'd leave with some cash in her pocket.

Charlotte pulled up next to her and they headed in together. Pointing to a black pick-up across the lot, Charlotte commented, "My Dad's here."

Jules was surprised but happy to hear that Frank was here. He had piqued her curiosity.

"He usually comes on Ladies' Night. It's one chance we have every month to catch up with each other."

They were just inside the door, letting their eyes adjust. It was bigger than Jules expected, and more modern. There were six or eight booths against the left wall, and the bar was against the right. It was long. Probably thirty or so stools. It looked like it came from somewhere else and probably had a story attached. The backbar was well-lit and well-stocked. Between the booths and the bar were a dozen four-tops, all at table height and well-spaced. Beyond the first room and separated by a pony wall was a brightly lit second space which boasted four regulation-sized pool tables. Two couples were playing against each other as teams. The restrooms were off the billiard room. The kitchen was on the other side of the backbar. She wondered what the menu was like. The music wasn't to her taste, but it was low enough that you could talk and be heard.

Frank was sitting at the far end of the bar, away from the door. They all waved and Charlotte headed in his direction. Jules waited at the door for some of the other women from the range to arrive. Charlotte turned back.

"Aren't you coming?" She asked.

"I don't want to interfere with your catch-up time. I'll wait for Gloria and the others to get here."

Charlotte grabbed her arm. "Come and say hi! You won't be interfering."

Frank stood up as they came over. The resemblance between the two was unmistakable. Jules saw that he was in fact older than she'd first thought. Maybe even 65. He wore army-green shorts that ended at his knees, leather sandals, and a loose, oatmeal-colored Henley, untucked, with the sleeves pushed up. He looked at ease with himself.

On the bar in front of him was a copy of Bob Woodward's *Peril*, which he'd put down to greet them. A bar napkin held his page somewhere deep into the heavy volume. It had just come out last fall and Jules hadn't opened her copy yet. It sat in her ever-growing to-be-read stack.

"Hey, Lottie." He kissed his daughter on the cheek and held a stool for her.

"Hi, Dad. You remember Jules?"

"Of course! Great to see you again!" He held out a hand to shake, then pulled out another stool for her. He smelled like sunscreen as he helped her onto the seat. Jules hated barstools. They were so ungainly. No grace. She hoisted herself up and let her feet dangle, not quite reaching that crossbar. At least these had backs. She hung her purse under the bar and tried not to feel like a six-year-old.

"I finally made it to ladies' night." She told Frank.

"Was it everything you hoped for?" He joked.

"Yeah, it was great meeting all the other women. And I feel pretty comfortable with a gun now. I'm no prize-winner yet but my consistency is improving with every visit to the range."

"The more you practice, the more confidence you build, the better your results will be. Keep it up."

"Thanks. Now I just need to be able to practice with my own gun. I bought a Glock from Tony in April but I'm still waiting for my permit."

"Where did you submit your application?"

"I'm in Saratoga County. Round Lake."

"I know some people there. I can check on it for you if that's okay." He offered.

"Yes, thanks! That would be really helpful. I think my gun rentals are funding TJ's vehicle upgrades. Did you notice his new tints and that detailing?" The three of them were laughing as the bartender approached.

Charlotte ordered a mojito, Jules a ginger ale with lime, and Frank still had a nearly full draft.

"How is it?" Jules asked, nodding to his book on the bar.

"Compelling. Comprehensive. His research is as good as it was with Watergate. Have you read it?" Frank asked.

"No, I hate to admit. I bought it but haven't gotten to it yet. Do you only read about political intrigue and failed politicians?"

"He reads cereal boxes if there's nothing else around!" Lottie offered.

"I can't even deny that. What about you, Jules? Are you a reader?"

"Guilty. I've always loved to read. It was free entertainment, and it was so . . . private? I don't know if that's what I mean. I just loved being inside of a story that's only on the page for you. If you watch a film or a show, you're having the same experience as everyone watching it. But with books, your experience isn't shared. It's sculpted by your history, your worldview, the path you've walked. Does that make sense? It's a romantic view, I guess."

"I don't read like my dad, not even close, but I do get what you're saying. If I read the same book as you, we can discuss it because we both know the context, the facts, the storyline. But my tall, thin man in a red hat will be different from your tall, thin man in a red hat. So, the experience of each reader is unique in that way. Am I close?"

"Exactly! Thank you, Charlotte! And I've always loved libraries and bookstores, too. It's my addiction." Jules was completely surprised and delighted by the conversation. It was far from what she had expected for the evening.

"What do you do, Jules?" Frank asked.

"I'm retired. I spent almost 30 years as the CEO of a local non-profit."

"Which one?" Father and daughter asked.

"Women Waging Peace, in Albany. It was rewarding work, but once the kids were gone, I wanted to switch gears. I had been running on empty for so many years and I just wanted to fill the tank. You know?"

"So, what would your Women Waging Peace think about you toting a Glock?" Frank asked.

"Probably the same thing some of your cop buddies would say about you reading Woodward." She lifted her glass in his direction and took a sip. He raised an eyebrow, along with his glass, and gave her her due.

"Touche!" Charlotte laughed and gave them both a look.

More of the ladies were arriving and the place was picking up. She saw Rebecca and Dave come in with Kevin in tow. Jules wondered where Kevin had been during Ladies' Night. Did they leave him in the car? Rebecca had been on the range with Jules for the fourth shooting round. She seemed to come alive behind the trigger. She knew what she was doing and had won the closest to dead center prize. That was the only prize that was always awarded each week. The other two skills were more difficult and often went unclaimed. Gloria said Rebecca won it a lot. She was a good shot. Most of the winners would buy a round at Scotty's if they came after. But Rebecca never did. And she was never without Dave. Gloria had told her all of this.

As Rebecca, Dave, and Kevin headed to a booth across the room, a small cheer went up among the ladies in recognition of her success of the evening. She flashed a quick and tenuous smile around the room, waved, and moved into the booth. Dave slid in next to her and Kevin sat across from them, alone. It was clear they were not going to socialize. Jules found that odd.

"I met Rebecca's son, Kevin, a couple months back while he was waiting for his dad at the range. He's so sweet." Jules directed her comment to no one in particular. She wanted to find out more about this family without asking. She saw Charlotte shoot a look at her father.

"That poor kid." Frank said quietly. "It's hard to watch."

"What is?"

"That family is a walking tragedy. Kevin shot and killed his baby sister, Angel, when he was three. She was only a few months old."

Jules gasped but resisted the urge to turn and look at them through this horrible new lens. She couldn't speak. She grabbed her drink in both hands, seeking its familiar shape and cool comfort. Here was one of the heartbreaking statistics in real life. The boogeyman she had dodged had visited that family instead.

"Jesus Christ!" was all she could manage in the face of it. She felt an unexpected panic rising in her gut and focused on maintaining control. The cold glass felt good pressed against her temple. She took a long drink and set the glass back on the bar. Hooking a piece of ice out with her fingers, she cooled her pulse points, her wrists, her neck, behind her ears. It was helping.

"It was Rebecca's gun." Charlotte continued. "They've just fallen apart ever since. I think Dave hates them both."

They sat in silence for a moment. All of them imagining. Jules spoke first.

"Kevin seems so . . . normal. So typically seven."

"He probably has no actual memory of it himself. But no one around him, around them, can forget it. He has a hard row to hoe. Once he's old enough to truly understand it, he'll have to deal with that for the rest of his life. Can you imagine?" Frank looked at Jules, anguished, and she just shook her head. Nobody could imagine. "It pains me to say, but my guess is we haven't seen the worst for that family yet."

"Refills, anyone?" The bartender stood in front of them. Saving them from their thoughts.

"Not for me. I'm going to head home." Jules said. She suddenly felt completely wrung out. Frank and Charlotte ordered another round.

"I have a bit of a drive. Thanks for showing me the ropes, Charlotte. I'll see you next month. I'm gunning for a money prize now. No pun intended. It was really nice to see you again, Frank." She stood and gathered her things.

"Let me get your number. I'll check in at Round Lake and see what's holding up your license, and I'll give you a call."

"Thank you. I really appreciate the help. Give me your number and I'll text you." Before she left, they had each other's contact information.

Driving home, Jules couldn't get Kevin and his family out of her mind. So much made sense now. Rebecca's remoteness. Dave's gruffness. The pall that hung over them all. But she couldn't make sense of why they would continue to embrace gun culture. Why would they expose Kevin to that after everything they'd been through? Maybe she'd continue that conversation next time she saw Charlotte. She felt a strange foreboding on Kevin's behalf, and she hoped he had some champions in his corner. He was going to need them.

. . .

The next day, Kevin's tragedy was still on her mind. Her dreams had been disturbing. She had accidentally shot and killed someone. It was the kind of vague someone that's a composite of many people in a dream; people she loved. The moment she felt the gun go off, her dream-self was overcome with grief and regret, overwhelmed by the knowing that there was no going back to one second ago.

She imagined a three-year-old Kevin would be incapable of that depth of feeling. He wouldn't have understood the devastation in the wake of his mistake. Jules felt a sense of relief for him in that way. But at some point, he would know. And there would be no going back.

She was surprised that the family's story didn't ring a bell when she'd heard it last night. She kept a close eye on gun violence incidents and thought she'd have noted one so close to home. She opened Facebook and went into her friend's archive of daily gun violence, curious if it had hit her radar. It would have been sometime in 2018, most likely.

The first thing she found was a post from early March of that year, when a two-year-old killed by his one-year-old brother marked the 123rd child hurt in gun related violence since Jan. 1 of that year. Not three months into the year and 123 kids had been shot. No wonder she hadn't registered Kevin's story. The extent of the bloodshed was mind-numbing.

Scrolling through the entries, she finally came upon it in June of that year. The post linked to the story in one of the local papers. It didn't name Kevin or his sister, but Rebecca and Dave were in the story. Rebecca Homer had left the kids in the car to run into Stewart's. Something many harried moms do on the way home from a long workday after picking up the kids at daycare. Jules had done it herself, when the boys were little and she was a young widow. Exhausted from holding up. She just couldn't bear to take them out of those car seats one more time, so she'd lock them in the car and run inside, keeping one eye out the store's window as she dashed around for the milk or bread.

Jules suddenly recalled Kevin standing up in the cab of the pickup, behind Dave's seat, at the gun range that day. He hadn't been in a car seat four years ago at Stewart's either. Rebecca's loaded semi-automatic pistol was in the glove box, in the direct sight line of a curious three-year-old. The shot had gone straight through the passenger seat and into the baby's car seat, killing her instantly.

Wiping tears from her cheeks, Jules did a little more research on the aftermath. Rebecca spent 18 months in prison for "criminally negligent homicide." Jules couldn't imagine a more tragic set of circumstances for a mother, a family. But why would they continue to embrace firearms after this? She would be sure to ask Charlotte next time they met. Or maybe Frank.

• • •

On Saturday, Sally and Hemmy and their whole gang would descend on Jules' place for a barbecue. Simon, Cassie, and Thea were all coming, and some unknown mix of their kids and grandkids. Jules had invited Ellie and the twins, as well. It was rare to find a day when so many of them were free. Everybody was so busy with work and kids and being busy. Jules was excited for the day.

The weather complied, and they'd be able to spend the day outside. She pulled out the mostly neglected tables and chairs from the garage and rinsed them down with the hose. They were left to dry in the sun. In the kitchen, she started a few dozen eggs to boil. Her deviled eggs, with capers and pine nuts, were always expected. She checked on the crème fraiche she had started the night before and saw it was coming together nicely. The strawberries, blueberries, blackberries, and fresh pineapple chunks created a beautiful trifle layered in with the crème. She topped it with some shredded coconut she'd roasted and placed it back into the fridge.

Despite the activity of the morning, she still felt unsettled. The façade was difficult for her. She was normally an open book, never thinking twice about what she was sharing or thinking. But everything was different now. She realized with a start that this would be the first stretch of time she'd spent with anyone who really knew her since she'd decided on her plan. She'd have to be careful not to let her two worlds collide from now on. The more her research and preparation was commandeering her time and attention, the harder that was going to become. If she'd met Kevin in any other way, she'd be sharing his tragic story, which she couldn't get out of her head. She would have told Sally and Thea and Cassie about Frank in any other circumstance. But all of this, and so much more, was now her secret. She needed to learn the fine art of deception. Or at least, omission.

Within the hour everyone was arriving, and her worries disappeared. She loved having the house full with this crew. Most of them had known each other since childhood, except for a few of the spouses and Ellie and her girls, but they all fit in seamlessly. She didn't have to play hostess with this bunch, and everyone was easy and fun to be around. They all called her Auntie Jules, even the grandkids. She so wished Jax and Ben were joining them. Maybe they'd all be together again for the holidays.

After hugs and kisses all around, getting everyone drinks and wiping down the few chairs that were still a little damp, Sally and Jules headed into the kitchen.

"Eric looks happy." Jules commented.

"Oh, he is! He's comfortable in his own skin in a way that Claire never was, you know?"

"I can see it." Jules was looking out the window. Eric's hair was cropped close and he wore cargo shorts and an oversized concert tee. Claire hadn't been flat-chested, but she wasn't more than a B-cup. It was easily camouflaged. He wore the ubiquitous Nike slides that Jules loathed, replacing Claire's beloved Birkenstocks.

"How has the social transition been? Has he had any issues?"

"Not really." Sally sounded mildly surprised. "Everyone has been great. The only thing that's creating a little concern is his dorm assignment in the fall. They haven't quite figured all of that out yet, but he may end up in the women's dorm for his first year."

"Hm. I hadn't really thought about that. What does he think about that?"

"Honestly, I think he hopes that will be the case. Since he's not medically transitioning, he told me he'd be more comfortable there. He thinks the girls will be less judgmental. I agree."

Sally's son, Patrick, came through the back door.

"Need any help in here?" He asked.

"Thank you, Paddy! Nice of you to offer. You could peel some potatoes for me. I'm going to do some fresh cut fries." Jules replied.

"There's some newspaper on my desk in my study. Can you grab it and spread it on the table for peels?"

"You got it." Patrick left the room, and Jules got out her good peeler and pulled a 10-lb. bag of potatoes from the pantry. As she set them on the table, she heard Patrick start laughing from her study.

She looked up as he came back into the room holding her mission phone.

"I can't believe you still have this thing! I remember Jax was so excited to get his first phone. And the Van's sticker. We loved those kicks." Patrick was focused on the device in his hand.

Jules felt a jolt of sheer panic. She couldn't believe she'd been so careless!

"Oh!" She flashed a smile. "Yeah, I'm rounding up a bunch of our old devices to donate. There are some nonprofits that will recycle them. Did you grab any newspaper?" She tried to sound casual as she reached for the phone in his hand and turned him back toward her office.

"If it's not on top of the desk, check my chair." She felt the color returning to her face as she slid the phone into the back pocket of her jeans. She wouldn't make that mistake twice.

The rest of the day was pleasant and largely uneventful. When they had such a large group together it was easy to relax and just enjoy the company. Thankfully, talk didn't turn to politics, even after a few drinks. Other than a few comments on the general state of world affairs, everyone was focused on relaxing. Cornhole isn't conducive to serious conversation.

That evening, after everyone had left and she had all the trash bagged and things fairly well in order, Jules grabbed her sleep t-shirt and leggings from behind the bathroom door to get ready for bed. Pulling her jeans off she heard a clunk and saw the forgotten cell phone on the floor where it had fallen from her back pocket. A return of her earlier fear washed over her, imagining what might have happened. But it didn't. She took the device to her study and locked it safely away.

*   *   *

The following Monday Jules hit the Ballston Spa public library to begin her reconnaissance on the 2024 Republican National Convention. Dates had yet to be announced but that was an almost negligible detail at this stage in her planning. She would start by studying past RNC schedules, security details, the Fiserv arena itself, and the surrounding area.

Based on tradition, the nominee speaks on the final night of the convention. Despite her complete inability to process the reality that this was going to be Trump, she knew that it would, even this far out. There was no other possible outcome. All of his bluster about rigged ballots and fraudulent elections was no more than the rantings of a narcissist, bent on convincing the masses to look the other way while he and his cronies actually rigged the ballots and engaged in fraudulent elections.

Jules had already decided to be at the convention from the start, dismissed as no more than another MAGA groupie, fawning over her hero. She would endear herself to the others she imagined hanging about outside of the venue, cheering their man on to victory. She might even bake cookies for them.

She had already planned a trip to the arena to see Brandi Carlile in August. She couldn't believe concert ticket prices these days. About two months' worth of groceries for her. But she didn't want Day Zero, as she thought of her target date, to be her first time at the venue. She needed an excuse to be there, and she loved Brandi's music, so it wasn't a complete loss. And she wanted to spend a little time walking the streets there and getting a feel for the place. Driving out would let her map the route, and then spend a few days in Milwaukee. She planned to sleep in the car and shower at a gym. She'd find a YMCA and maybe even hit a class or two. A hotel was out of her budget; even a Super 8 or Motel 6 were beyond her means. Her mind flashed to some of the particularly memorable 5-star accommodations she had enjoyed throughout her career. Fairmonts and Ritz-Carltons and Four Seasons and Waldorf Astorias. All of that was another time, another life.

The arena's website provided some good basic data and images. The building itself, completed in a mind-boggling two years. She couldn't imagine such efficiency. She was used to projects in the northeast, which lagged for years, typically running over budget and beyond all estimated timelines. The Big Dig, a notorious Boston project, had taken 25 years and been nearly 200% over budget!

The Fiserv Forum was a stunning piece of architecture, designed by local firm Eppstein Uhen Architects. It had just opened in 2018. The fact that the space was so new was a distinct advantage, Jules soon realized. There was an enormous amount of information available online because of the cutting-edge technology that had been employed in the design, marketing, and public communication about the project. She was able to get a much better feel for the space from just this single research session than she had expected. Everyone involved wanted to share what they were going to accomplish with this enormous investment in the city's future.

The arena, which had cost $524 million to build, was centrally located, had a capacity of about 18,000, and a dedicated VIP entrance. Thank you very much, thought Jules as she made a note. She'd need to scout out that entrance. The Fiserv had 34 large public restrooms, 19 for women and 15 for men. The women's line would probably still be ridiculously backed up while there was no line for the men's.

Jules took lots of notes but was realizing how helpful it would be to have some of the images and maps to study outside of the library. She would bring the mission phone next time and snap some stills.

Her watch revealed it was closer to dinner time than lunch time. The hours disappeared as she gathered more intel that day and she was pleased with her progress. And hungry.

She decided to leave her car parked at the library and walk over to find a place for a meal. Augie's was across the street, which she loved, but their large portions were better suited to group dining.

She resisted the urge to indulge anyway. A little further on was the Whistling Kettle. They had a wide tea menu and a Monte Cristo on their menu that was a special indulgence. And the vibe was pleasant. No pretense, good service, and usually an available seat at most times of the day. She chose the only unoccupied outdoor table, a small two-top near the door. After placing her order, she pulled a paperback from her bag. She had decided to re-read Anne Frank's Diary of a Young Girl.

· · ·

VIDEO DIARY ENTRY – June 20, 2022

"Hi. Today is June 20th, 2022. Here's what's happening in the news. Earlier this month, in the continuing January 6th hearings, many of the people who were in Trump's galaxy in the days and hours before the insurrection testified to trying to save him from himself. Even family members like Kushner tried to persuade him that there was no voter fraud and he had in fact lost the election. The Justice Department was debunking one claim after another, informing Trump that the information he was getting about lost or destroyed ballots was false. Barr, his own Attorney General, said Trump was 'detached from reality' if he believed the voter fraud narrative. Barr resigned after calling the voter fraud claims that Trump was embracing 'bogus' and 'bullshit'. He testified to the Committee that Trump was as mad as he'd ever seen him on election night, as the truth was emerging.

"Guiliana, on the other hand, apparently alcohol-fueled, was fomenting the Big Lie on election eve. He urged Trump to hold fast and was pushing ridiculous 'legal' theories. Trump grabbed onto Rudy's brass ring and has never let go, from that day to this. All of the infor-

mation I'm sharing in these videos is publicly available from reliable new sources. Which means not Fox News.

"No big surprise, but it came to light earlier this month that Fox has had a much bigger influence on the Trump administration than had even been suspected. Mark Meadows, Trump's former Chief of Staff, had something like 2,000 text messages that were leaked, showing Fox's communications to someone so high up the food chain. Hannity was even offering theories under which the election results could be undermined. So much for journalistic integrity.

"So, an update on my progress. I spent yesterday at the library researching the 2024 RNC, the arena where it's going to be held, and other details. I know this is going to be a difficult mission, and it may not succeed. There is a lot I'm not going to know, and I'll have to adapt as I go. I can do that. It's so strange having this weird covert life. Sometimes it seems ridiculous and implausible. But when I start to feel that way, I go back and study history. I remind myself that this is not new. Evil and empty people have risen to power all over the world with bad intent.

"I was reminded of this quote the other day and I dug it up to find out it's by Lord Acton in 1887, in a letter to Bishop Creighton. Even if you have no idea who either of them are, you'll know this quote. I'm going to read it straight from the text so I get it right. He said, 'I cannot accept your canon that we are to judge Pope and King unlike other men, with a favourable presumption that they did no wrong. If there is any presumption it is the other way against holders of power, increasing as power increases.' I'm skipping a bit here and this is the part you'll probably know, 'Power tends to corrupt and absolute power corrupts absolutely. Great men are almost always bad men, even when they exercise influence and not authority; still more when you superadd the tendency or the certainty of corruption by authority.

There is no worse heresy than that the office sanctifies the holder of it.' I'm going to repeat that last line. 'There is no worse heresy than that the office sanctifies the holder of it.' I leave you with that."

• • •

MASS SHOOTING IN THE US
June 2022 - 64 total

A mass shooting is any shooting where four or more people, other than the shooter, are killed or injured.

1. June 01, 2022 - Tulsa, Oklahoma - 6 injured
2. June 02, 2022 - Centerville, Texas - 1 dead, 4 injured
3. June 03, 2022 - Chester, Virginia - 4 injured
4. June 03, 2022 - Omaha, Nebraska - 1 dead, 3 injured
5. June 04, 2022 - Ecorse, Michigan - 1 dead, 3 injured
6. June 04, 2022 - El Paso (Socorro), Texas - 1 dead, 3 injured
7. June 04, 2022 - Philadelphia, Pennsylvania - 4 injured
8. June 04, 2022 - Macon, Georgia - 8 injured
9. June 04, 2022 - Phoenix, Arizona - 1 dead, 3 injured
10. June 04, 2022 - Summerton, South Carolina - 2 dead, 4 injured
11. June 04, 2022 - Hempstead, New York - 1 dead, 4 injured
12. June 05, 2022 - Saginaw, Michigan - 1 dead, 4 injured
13. June 05, 2022 - Mesa, Arizona - 1 dead, 6 injured
14. June 05, 2022 - Chattanooga, Tennessee - 4 injured
15. June 05, 2022 - Grand Rapids, Michigan - 4 injured
16. June 05, 2022 - Andrews, South Carolina - 4 dead,

17. June 07, 2022 - Portsmouth, Virginia - 4 injured

18. June 07, 2022 - Chicago, Illinois - 1 dead, 3 injured

19. June 07, 2022 - Baltimore, Maryland - 4 dead,

20. June 07, 2022 - Chicago, Illinois - 1 dead, 4 injured

21. June 08, 2022 - Yuma, Arizona - 5 injured

22. June 09, 2022 - Smithsburg, Maryland - 5 injured

23. June 10, 2022 - Decatur, Georgia - 4 dead,

24. June 11, 2022 - Alamogordo, New Mexico - 1 dead, 3 injured

25. June 11, 2022 - Detroit, Michigan - 1 dead, 5 injured

26. June 11, 2022 - Chicago, Illinois - 2 dead, 2 injured

27. June 11, 2022 - Atlanta, Georgia - 4 injured

28. June 11, 2022 - Antioch, Tennessee - 7 injured

29. June 11, 2022 - Louisville, Kentucky - 2 dead, 6 injured

30. June 12, 2022 - Los Angeles, California - 4 injured

31. June 12, 2022 - Roseville, Michigan - 1 dead, 3 injured

32. June 12, 2022 - Gary, Indiana - 4 injured

33. June 12, 2022 - Indianapolis, Indiana - 1 dead, 3 injured

34. June 12, 2022 - New Orleans, Louisiana - 5 injured

35. June 12, 2022 - Denver, Colorado - 1 dead, 4 injured

36. June 16, 2022 - Oakland, California - 2 dead, 2 injured

37. June 17, 2022 - Baltimore, Maryland - 1 dead, 4 injured

38. June 17, 2022 - Chicago, Illinois - 1 dead, 3 injured

39. June 18, 2022 - Pensacola, Florida - 4 injured

40. June 18, 2022 - San Antonio, Texas - 2 dead, 2 injured

41. June 19, 2022 - Washington, District of Columbia - 1 dead, 3 injured

42. June 19, 2022 - Miami, Florida - 4 injured

43. June 19, 2022 - Detroit, Michigan - 2 dead, 6 injured

44. June 19, 2022 - Grand Rapids, Michigan - 8 injured

45. June 19, 2022 - Walterboro, South Carolina - 1 dead, 3 injured

46. June 20, 2022 - New York, New York - 1 dead, 3 injured

47. June 20, 2022 - Staten Island, New York - 5 injured

48. June 23, 2022 - Chicago, Illinois - 4 injured

49. June 24, 2022 - Hopewell, Virginia - 1 dead, 4 injured

50. June 24, 2022 - Philadelphia, Pennsylvania - 1 dead, 6 injured

51. June 25, 2022 - Brooklyn, New York - 4 injured

52. June 25, 2022 - Houston, Texas - 4 injured

53. June 25, 2022 - Minneapolis, Minnesota - 2 dead, 2 injured

54. June 26, 2022 - Blakely, Georgia - 9 injured

55. June 26, 2022 - Sutherlin, Virginia - 5 injured

56. June 26, 2022 - Paterson, New Jersey - 4 injured

57. June 26, 2022 - San Antonio, Texas - 1 dead, 4 injured

58. June 26, 2022 - Winona, Texas - 5 injured

59. June 26, 2022 - Tacoma, Washington - 4 injured

60. June 27, 2022 - Charlotte, North Carolina - 4 injured

61. June 29, 2022 - Jersey City, New Jersey - 3 dead, 2 injured

62. June 29, 2022 - Philadelphia, Pennsylvania - 1 dead, 3 injured

63. June 30, 2022 - Allen, Kentucky - 4 injured

64. June 30, 2022 - Newark, New Jersey - 5 injured

• • •

JULY 2022

DRIVING TO HER SECOND LADIES' NIGHT, Jules realized she hadn't heard from Frank since she'd seen him in June. She wasn't really worried about expediting her permit, but she had hoped to hear from him. She wanted to probe a little more into the Kevin situation now that she had more information. Wait. Is that all she wanted? Was she kidding herself? She definitely found him attractive, but she was hardly available to even consider exploring anything there. It wouldn't be fair. She was a dead woman walking. She put the thought aside.

Jules turned into the parking lot and noticed that the range wasn't as busy as it had been for June's Ladies' Night. By this point she had more than a dozen sessions under her belt, and her hot pink target collection was growing. She rarely shot wide anymore and her consistency improved with every visit. Jules was comfortable at the facility and confident in her abilities. She walked in and headed for the sign-in sheet.

"Hey Jules! Glad you made it." TJ smiled and waved. "Everybody gets three spots tonight."

"Great! Thanks, Teej."

Jules selected her spots, choosing her third round in the last line up, and headed for the coffee. So far there wasn't anyone Jules didn't recognize, either from June or from her solo shooting sessions. Gloria was there, talking to another woman, and she waved when she saw Jules. Rebecca wasn't there yet.

Charlotte came through the door and headed for the sign-in sheet.

"Hey, Charlotte! Do you want me to pour you a cup?" Jules held the pot up.

"Yes! Thanks. Be there in a sec."

Jules poured them each a coffee and took a seat. Charlotte finished signing in and joined her.

"How've you been?" She asked Jules.

"Good. Just loving this summer weather! It's my favorite season. How about you?"

"I'm beat today. Work was pushing all my buttons!"

"What do you do?" Jules asked her.

"I work at a senior independent living facility. I'm a nutritionist."

"Oh, wow. I can imagine that could be trying." She couldn't. "How long have you been doing that?"

"Mm, I guess like, fifteen or sixteen years now. It's really a great job, but a national corporation is trying to buy the current owners out. We're in the middle of all of these discussions and negotiations. If they succeed, I may be looking for a new opportunity."

"Oh, will they be downsizing?"

"No, I just can't work for them. From everything I've seen they are completely bottom-line driven. No humanity. Our current owners are a family who started this business two generations ago. They're relationship based. They know all of the staff, all of the residents. It's been a lovely place to work. I've been spoiled."

"OK, LADIES!" TJ shouted, "First ups!" He grabbed the sign-up sheet and called off the names. Rebecca still hadn't shown up. Charlotte was among the first group of shooters.

"Are you coming for a drink after?" She asked Jules.

"Definitely. I want to talk to you about something."

Charlotte raised an eyebrow. "Mm. Sounds intriguing! I'll see you there."

Rebecca never showed up, and Jules was able to take the $150.00 prize for closest to dead-center. The money left after she bought a round would go into her mission fund. The irony didn't escape her.

She drove over to the bar after her last line-up. Charlotte was already there, as were all of the ladies who shot before the final group. She walked in to a light round of applause.

"Thank you!" She acknowledged the group with a wave and a laugh. "Beginner's luck. Round on me!"

She was glad that most of them were beer drinkers and Scotty's prices were neighborhood bar prices, not bougie hot spot prices. She figured she'd leave with at least $100.00 of her prize money in her pocket.

Charlotte and Frank were sitting at the bar with drinks already in front of them. She headed over to sit with them. Frank stood up as she got near.

"Hi Jules!" He pulled out the stool next to Charlotte.

"Hey, Frank. Nice to see you again." She climbed up on the seat and hung her purse beneath the bar.

"So, you won?" Asked Charlotte.

"I did! I can't believe it. Probably only because Rebecca wasn't there."

"It will be fun to see you two go head to head. She's not really used to any competition."

They all laughed and the bartender came for her drink order.

"I think I'll have a gin and tonic and a water. And the Range Ladies' all get one on me tonight. Can you keep a tab?" He knew everyone in the group.

"Sure, no problem."

Jules turned to Frank and Charlotte, then looked past them to the tables in back. "Do you guys shoot pool?" She nodded toward the other room.

In her teen years, one of Jules' and her friends' main hangout spots had been a pool hall in Troy called Rack 'Em. It wasn't a bar, so teens could get in, but they sold rolling papers and water pipes along with pro-quality pool cues, smokes, and sodas. Pot was illegal, but paraphernalia wasn't, so the cops kept an eye on place knowing what the clientele there was about.

Rack 'Em was owned by Larry, a guy in his 60s who turned a blind eye to anything that was going on in his establishment except violence. He wouldn't put up with that bullshit. When the occasional fight broke out, the offenders were banished for a few weeks if he knew them, for life if he didn't. Larry just wanted everything and everybody to be cool. Weekends and summers, it was the center of Jules' social life. She and Sally went there to hang out, smoke, and flirt with guys. Along the way she became an excellent pool player.

"Yeah, Dad has a table at the house and we all grew up playing on it. Do you want to play?"

"Yes! Let's get some quarters. We can play cutthroat if you're playing, Frank."

"I'm in. I want to see you in action."

Color rose into her cheeks and she was glad for the dim lighting in the bar area. She caught his eye and smiled. *Jesus*, she thought.

Jules racked the balls and invited Charlotte to break.

"You're one through five," she nodded at Charlotte. "Frank, you can shoot after her, and have six through ten. I'll shoot last, eleven through fifteen. Does that work?"

Everyone agreed to the order. Charlotte didn't sink anything on the break, but broke the tight triangle well, leaving Frank in good position. He lined up on the eleven ball in the corner and sunk it. Then he dropped the two in the side. He tried for the three ball all the way up the table and just missed it, leaving it a sitting duck on the rail. Jules sunk the easy three, then stepped back to survey the table.

"You said you wanted to talk to me about something." Charlotte said.

"Right." Jules looked around but there was nobody within earshot. She walked around the table to sink the six and followed that with the one ball. That left Charlotte with only two on the table. Jules took out Frank's nine ball before finally missing a shot on the four.

Charlotte stepped to the table to consider her shot.

"It's about Kevin and his family." Jules said quietly, "After the last Ladies' Night I went home and did some research. Jesus! What a tragedy for them! And then after all of that she ends up in prison."

"Yeah, she did a year inside and then probation." Charlotte sized up a shot on the thirteen. She made it in, but it clipped the eight ball on its way to the corner.

"Your shot, Dad. We don't play slop." She informed Jules.

"Absolutely." Jules respected that.

"But you know what's worse for Rebecca?" Charlotte was keeping her voice down. "That was Dave's gun in her car. She didn't know it was in the glove compartment."

Jules looked from her to Frank. He was leaning over the table for a shot at the four, but he looked up at Jules and nodded.

"Why did she do time then?" Jules directed this to Frank.

Frank knocked the four ball in and came over to where the two women stood.

"She was driving the vehicle." Frank held up one finger. "She didn't have Kevin in a car seat." Two fingers. "She left the babies alone in the car." Three fingers. "And the gun was in her possession, regardless of who actually owned it." Four fingers. "When they finally got to court a couple years after it happened, the jury took less than an hour. Guilty. Endangering the welfare of a child."

"But what about the fact that she didn't know the gun was there? Did that make any difference at all?"

"It came up at trial, but the fact that they are both owners of multiple firearms who spend so much time at the range, went against her. They felt she 'should have known' in legal parlance, to check for the presence of a weapon, since they were such a gun toting family." He reported.

"Which brings me to my next question. After all they've been through, why in the world are they still so gun happy? Why would they continue to expose Kevin?"

"Well, Dave's ex-Army. He did two tours in Afghanistan. I think he suffers from some serious PTSD from everything he's been through." Charlotte explained, glancing at Frank as he finished taking her out of the game.

"And don't forget. Guns don't kill people, right?" Frank rolled his eyes and cleaned the table, winning the game with his seven, eight, and ten balls still standing.

"But, how can she own a gun if she did prison time? I thought that was illegal."

"Only for felons. Rebecca took a misdemeanor charge. It was an accidental death, and no history of abuse or neglect. Every parent on that jury could probably imagine a moment in time when an error in judgment could have brought this to their doorstep. They found her guilty of the lightest of the DA's charges, but gave her the longest sentence allowable under the charge.

They racked their cues in the stand and headed back into the bar area. Jules paid her tab and was grateful to see it was under forty bucks. She'd still go home with more than $100.00 on the night. The three of them headed for the door together.

"Did you find anything out about my permit? I still don't have it." Jules asked Frank.

His face dropped and she could see he was caught off guard.

"Oh my god, Jules! I am so sorry! I completely forgot about that."

"It's no big deal." She assured him. "I just thought I'd ask."

"Do me a favor, will you? Call me tomorrow. I mean it. Call me so I don't forget again."

"I will. I still have your number from last month. Drive safe! You too, Char. See you next month." Driving home she realized she'd have to miss Ladies' Night next month. She would be on her first recon trip to the Fiserv Forum.

●　●　●

The next day she called Frank, as he had asked. She got his voicemail. She was both relieved and disappointed. Even though nobody listened to their voice messages anymore, she decided to leave one on the off chance.

"Hi Frank. This is Jules. I'm just calling to remind you about my permit. Thanks for anything you can do to move it along. OK, um, call me back. Or text me. Bye now!" *Ugh! Why had she left a message! She sounded like an idiot!*

Jules hadn't really had a serious relationship since Mick died. Almost thirty years ago now, she realized with a jolt. There had been a few men over the years that she'd dated for extended periods of time, but they usually ran their course and petered out. She'd almost been engaged in her early-40s, but she said no and broke it off.

It was the hardest thing about being a widow rather than a divorcee. She had never fallen out of love with Mick. Her love didn't die with him; love didn't work like that. It just had nowhere to land, like an albatross soaring over the sea for years, waiting to find safe ground. All these years later, and she was still aloft.

Most of her friends who divorced had a completely different experience. The love died long before the relationship did. They built up resentments and catalogued shortcomings. They could barely stand the presence of their once-beloved. They saw almost anyone else as a better potential partner than the one they had married. By the time they left the courtroom, legally divided, they could start again, begin the healing process. Find solid ground.

Where were these feelings coming from now? Jules wondered. Maybe it was simply a response to knowing she had so little time left to pursue anything life might offer. If she was completely honest with herself, if she let her guard down a little, she had to admit that she enjoyed feeling that attraction to Frank. She gave herself permission to enjoy her last crush.

Jules fed Feinstein and was making herself an omelet when her phone rang, startling her in the quiet house. It was Frank.

"Hey, Frank."

"Hi Jules. Listen, I just want to apologize for letting this fall through the cracks."

"Seriously, Frank. It's not a big deal! I am just surprised that I *still* haven't got this thing!"

"Do you have any felonies? That could be holding things up."

"Very funny. I don't even have a parking ticket. I'm an upstanding citizen!"

A sudden crash behind her made her jump. She turned to see Feinstein had knocked the empty cat food can onto the floor.

"What was that?" Frank asked, having heard the commotion on his end.

"Just Feinstein being a bad kitty." Jules grabbed the can and tossed it into her recycling bin. She grabbed a rag, dampened it at the sink, and wiped up the slimy residue that had spattered in the can's wake.

"Feinstein?" Frank laughed. "There must be a story behind that name."

"Not really. She's a strong-willed, independent kitty who doesn't take shit from anyone. End of story." They both laughed.

"That works. Listen, let me call over to Round Lake P.D. and see what I can find out. I'll call you back if I have any news."

"That would be great. Thanks so much, Frank! I'll talk to you soon."

Jules went to her study and got her mission notebook out of her safe. She was beyond pleased with her progress. Her research wasn't as daunting as she had first anticipated, she was getting more and more consistent with every visit to the range, and her trip to Milwaukee next month would help ease her anxiety about the venue. She planned to take lots of pictures and notes. She hadn't decided whether one site visit would be enough. She'd make that decision based on what she learned in August.

As she pored over her research notes, her phone rang again. It was Ben. Her momentary disappointment that it wasn't Frank was replaced by the joy of catching up with her oldest. She hadn't made the spring trip to Montreal that she had anticipated last winter. Her plans to save democracy had taken center stage in her life. But they still talked every few weeks.

"Ben! How are you?"

"Hi Mom. We're good. What are you up to?"

Jules glanced around her office, feeling guilty for the lie she was about to tell.

"Just a little yoga and stretching. Nothing too exciting."

"Are you getting outside and walking? I know you love this weather!"

"I am. It's been just beautiful this summer. I had a big to-do last month here with Sally and Hemmy and their group, and Uncle Simon, Aunt Thea, and Aunt Cassie and all of theirs. Everybody asked about you and Jax."

"That sounds so great! I really miss everyone. Which is why I'm calling. Jess and I have been trying to make holiday plans for this year. We'll do either Christmas or Thanksgiving here with her family, and then we'll come see you for the other. We're talking to Jax and Kelly, too, because we all want to be home at the same time. Do you have any preference?"

"What does Jess's family want to do?"

"They want you to have first pick, since we see them all the time and you get so little time with the kids."

"They are so kind! You really got lucky, you know?"

"I know, Mom. She got lucky, too, don't forget."

"That's true. We are a good family to marry into." She laughed, but thought with a heavy heart *until I kill a former world leader.*

"Ok, then I think I'll take Thanksgiving. There is less chance of any travel weather ruining our plans. Do you think you guys could make it here on Wednesday and stay through Sunday? We can put the tree up on Friday and have a pre-Christmas celebration on Saturday."

"That would be perfect, ma. I'll call Jax and see if they can make that work. Love you the most!"

"Hug Jess and the kids. Love you the most!"

Jules put everything back in the safe. It felt dirty somehow, having her mind in these two completely opposite realms. Mother and grandmother and potential date material on one side, cold-hearted assassin on the other. She decided to focus on the former today and left for a walk in the sun.

Jax called later that day to confirm the plans for Thanksgiving. He and Kelly were both coming.

"I'm so glad you can both make it! We had such a good time last year. What will you do for Christmas?"

"We're staying here in Austin. Kelly's mom will come in from Dallas." June was widowed, like Jules, but much more recently. The two women had met a few times and they had a lot in common. They got on very well.

"We were thinking you might want to come for Christmas, too."

"That would be so much fun! Let me think about it and see if I can work it out." The boys didn't know about her financial situation, had no idea she was driving Uber for extra money, and she would die before she shared that with them.

"June's going to stay at their condo. She says you're more than welcome to join her."

"Perfect. I'll check Southwest and see if I can make a reservation. It would be great to have it all planned this early in the year. Thank Kelly and June for thinking of me."

"I was involved." He deadpanned.

"Oh! I know you were, honey! Thank you, too!"

"Love you the most, Mom."

"Love you the most, Jax."

• • •

Later in the week Jules saw Frank's name pop up on her ringing phone. She felt a surge of adrenaline wash over her before she answered.

"Hi Frank! Any news for me?" She sounded cheerful.

"Hey, Jules. In fact, I do. Finally. Your outstanding warrant for drug trafficking is standing in the way of you carrying a firearm."

She played along.

"You've got to be kidding me? I don't understand why one thing should have any bearing on the other!" She sounded indignant. They laughed together.

"Seriously, it had just somehow fallen through the cracks over there. I think everybody is short staffed in the aftermath of COVID."

"I've noticed that everywhere. The world sure looks different on this side of 2020." She remarked. "I appreciate you going to bat on my behalf, Frank. I'll buy you a drink in September."

"You mean August, right?"

"No, I have to miss August Ladies' Night. I'm going to be away for a while."

"Oh. Anywhere fun?"

"I'm going to a Brandi Carlile concert in Milwaukee." She had already decided to be truthful with anyone who asked where she was going. The more she could lean on the truth, the better off she would be. Lies tended to trip her up.

"That's quite a trip for a concert! Are you a live music fan?" He asked.

"Not really so much. I like small venues and local artists mostly. But I love Brandi's music and I have a friend from my college days who lives out there. Two birds with one stone."

"A friend? Hmm. That sounds like fun." There was no mistaking the question behind his comment.

"Yeah, she recently went through a divorce so I'm going to provide some moral support and diversion for her."

"That's a tough time for anyone. It's nice that you can be there."

"Have you been divorced?" She asked.

"I was married for 17 years. Seems like a long time ago now. Been divorced longer than I was married. What about you?"

"My husband, Mick, was killed in a work accident when my kids were just babies. It was a long time ago."

"Oh, I'm so sorry. I hope you had moral support." Frank sounded genuinely concerned for her.

"I did. I'm lucky to have a fairly large safety net. Siblings, friends, and colleagues at that time. They all pitched in to get me through. As much as one can get through."

They were quiet for a moment. Acknowledging the enormity of the loss.

"Well, if you're not at Ladies' Night until September, would you want to buy me that drink before your trip?" He was asking her on a date. She nearly forgot how to respond.

"I'd love to. What are you thinking?"

"Let's go somewhere we can sit outside. I hate to waste these warm summer days."

"How about Carson's up on the Lake?" Jules suggested. "Maybe next Thursday? The weekends just get too busy up there. They'll probably have live music."

"I haven't been there in years. Sounds like just what I need. Does 6:30 work?"

"I'll call and see if they're taking reservations. If not, we'll just have to wing it. Either way, I'll meet you there next Thursday at 6:30. Sound good?"

"Great. See you then."

• • •

Mid-July in this part of New York meant one thing. It was track season at Saratoga. Horse people, sports bettors, and celebrities came from everywhere for this summer spectacle. Short term rentals commanded exorbitant rates and some homeowners locked away their valuables and booked themselves into distant hotels for two months to cash in on their family home. A modest property with proximity to the track could earn enough to pay the mortgage for the entire year. Most locals knew to avoid the area during that time, but Jules would drive it as much as she could when the horses were running. Picking up a winning player could mean a jackpot for her. Last year, a drunken high roller had tipped her $500.00 after she'd had to pull over to let him vomit on the side of the road. This year, she needed to maximize her earnings to afford the August recon trip to Milwaukee, so she was on site from day one.

In some ways, she enjoyed the diversion. It got her out of the house, and she met interesting people. Or at least observed interesting people. Some riders treated her like a person and engaged her in conversation. Typically, these were the single riders, headed back to their Airbnb after a day at the races. Others acted as if she wasn't even there, and continued on with their own conversations, either with the people they were with or on their cell phones. She had heard lots of interesting conversations from behind the wheel. At least the job wasn't boring.

She didn't have a passenger, so she waited, reading, within a block or two of the track to be able to respond quickly to any ride request that popped up on the app. She accepted the next one. 'Joe' needed to be picked up at the entrance by the Trackside Grill. With no traffic she'd be there in under a minute, but it was nearing the end of the race day, so things were picking up.

She rolled down the passenger window as she approached the curb and started calling for Joe as she rolled slowly, keeping an eye on the other rideshare drivers doing the same in front and in back of her. Joe raised a hand and headed toward her car. He was alone, probably in his 60s or 70s. Well-groomed and well-dressed. Part of the up-scale racing clientele, not the drunken college students or the desperate gamblers. Maybe an owner or co-owner.

He got in and she handed him a bottled water that she kept chilled for her passengers.

"Hi Joe." She knew his destination from the app, about twenty minutes away on the other side of downtown, but she always confirmed it with the passenger. If there was a change, she'd report that to Uber as a safety precaution. Joe confirmed and they pulled off, easing in behind the line of traffic leaving the area.

"Good day at the track?" She asked.

"So-so. I won't go hungry." He laughed. She could tell he had enjoyed a few adult beverages. His speech was cottony and his movements sloppy as he tried a few times to buckle his seat belt.

She asked if the temperature of the car was okay for him. It was. The two chatted amicably about nothing as they drove toward Broadway, the heart of downtown and the busiest tourist destination. It was lined with upscale boutiques, bars and restaurants, horse-related galleries. Summer traffic, both vehicle and pedestrian, was always hectic, but today they were at a complete standstill.

"Sorry for the delay. There must be an accident." Jules guessed.

"That's okay, sweetie. I'm enjoying the company." Joe reached up and patted her right shoulder with his left hand.

Oh, god. Really? Jules glanced in her rearview and noticed him looking at her. She didn't reply and returned her attention to the road. They were inching forward now and she could see that it wasn't a wreck but a protest that was gumming up traffic. Black Lives Matter. Some Saratoga leaders were under fire for harassing citizens connected to the BLM movement. Some of the activists had been arrested, and the constitutionality of the city's actions was in question.

"Christ!" Joe spat from the back seat, "ALL lives matter, you know? I hate this crap. We are not a racist nation!"

Jules said nothing as they eased past the protest, the heat creeping into her neck.

"I'm 78 years old. I've seen the change in this country. These people should be grateful for how far we've come. I remember segregation and we're past all that. We're a Christian nation! We need to get back to those roots. All this liberal bullshit is destroying America."

Jules still said nothing. The contradictions were lost on him.

"If the election hadn't been rigged, Trump would still be in office and we wouldn't have any of this. All of this is on Biden's shoulders."

Here we go! Jules thought, biting her tongue.

"I can't wait for Trump to get back in the White House. He puts America first and he doesn't back down. We have to close our borders if we want to keep these illegals from taking American jobs. We have to keep producing coal and oil in the U.S. so we aren't dependent on these Muslim countries! Trump thinks like a businessman, not a politician. That's what we need if we're going to maintain our position as the strongest nation in the world." He had seemed for a moment to forget she was there.

"You know what I mean?" He asked her, touching her shoulder again.

"Well, Joe." She was at a red light and turned in her seat to look him in the eyes. "All I can say is that we have very different world views. And please don't touch me again." She turned around and kept her eyes off her rearview mirror. She really didn't care to see his response.

At his destination, she unlocked the doors and bid him a good evening with a wide smile on her face. He slammed the door and was gone from her life. She figured she'd blown the tip. It was worth it.

• • •

Carson's wasn't taking reservations, so they'd have to get on the waiting list. When Jules arrived, the place was already packed. Standing room only outside. She added her name to the list.

"Outside or first available?" The host asked her.

"Outside please, but not too close to the band?" She had to yell a little to be heard.

"Ok, no problem!" He yelled back, handing her a pager.

Since there were no available seats, Jules walked to the edge of the lawn, overlooking Saratoga Lake to the north from the highest possible vantage point. It was smaller than Lake George, but still a huge attraction for every imaginable kind of watercraft, all of which appeared to be enjoying it today. You couldn't hear the activity from the lake, no loud motorboats or screaming-kid sounds reached this far up, so it was a perfect spot. She stood for a while, watching the lake buzz and enjoying the music. The band was playing covers that everyone knew.

Jules got in line at the bar. Maybe she could grab their drinks before Frank got here. She'd only seen him drink beer, so that's what she would get him. It was a safe bet. She was next in line when she felt a hand on her back.

"Hey, Jules!"

"Hi!" She turned toward Frank and they had an awkward hug. "I was just going to grab you a beer, but I'm glad you got here. I really have no beer knowledge. What do you like?"

She pointed to the extensive chalkboard menu of today's brews.

"Hmm. I guess . . ." The band started on a new song. Hendrix's *Foxy Lady*. Frank laughed. "That must be a sign! I'll have the Purple Haze."

Jules ordered the beer and a ginger ale for herself. She handed Frank the bottle.

"OK, now we're even. Thanks again for your help." They held up their drinks and tapped them. "Cheers!"

Frank noticed a couple about to vacate a pair of Adirondack chairs near one of the fire pits and he motioned her to follow. He had the kind of presence that moved people out of his way. *Must be the cop vibe*, thought Jules. He pulled the two chairs closer together, so they'd be able to hear each other without shouting. She appreciated the gesture. They sat with their drinks propped on the wide arms of their seats and enjoyed the scene for a moment.

"I don't know why I don't come up here more often. I kind of forget it's here. We used to bring the kids up to the lake a lot when they were young. I had a little boat we'd haul up and spend the day. There's a public launch on the other side of the lake." He pointed with his bottle.

"So, I've met Charlotte. Who else do you have?"

"Charlotte's twin sister, Carrie. She's out on the West Coast now."

"Any grandkids yet?" Jules asked.

"No, neither of the girls are married, or even in a long-term relationship. They both seem perfectly happy with their lives as they are. What about you? Tell me about your kids."

"I have two boys, Ben and Jax. Ben's married with two kids. They're in Montreal. Jack is the younger of the two, and he's in Austin. He has what's now becoming a long-term partner. They don't have kids yet, but I'm thinking that's where they are headed."

"It's nice having adult kids, isn't it? Kind of a reward." Frank commented.

Jules agreed.

"Mine are all coming for Thanksgiving. We made early plans this year. I'm going to Austin to spend Christmas with Jax."

"Charlotte and I are going out to spend Christmas with Carrie in Portland. Carrie works in public health so we haven't seen her since before the pandemic."

"Wow! That's a long gap! That should be fun for all of you."

"I'm hoping so. Their mother, my ex, is going to be there, too. We can tolerate each other so that's not a problem. I just prefer to avoid being in that situation. I try to limit it to weddings and funerals, and since we haven't had either of those, I've been able to keep my distance. But it'll be worth it to spend the holiday with my girls."

"Was it an ugly divorce?" Jules asked.

"As these things go, I guess not. I've heard some horror stories. Felicia just decided the life we had wasn't the one she wanted. I never saw it coming. But it's possible I wasn't paying attention. I was so busy on the job."

"Did she remarry?"

"No. She didn't want to be responsible for anyone else. That was one of the revelations she had after the kids came. She managed for a while, but ultimately it was just too much. She moved to New Mexico to pursue a more 'aligned' life."

"What about your girls?"

"Oh, they stayed with me. I got full custody. That was never even an issue in our split. Felicia wanted none of it. Just a clean slate."

"Ouch. That must have hurt. The girls."

"It did. We've all moved past it and made peace. She's back in the girls' lives now that they're adults. But believe me, there was therapy. Lots of therapy. And I still wonder to this day if that's why the girls haven't married."

"Are you sure they're straight?" Jules asked. Frank laughed.

"Trust me! They are. The string of boys who came through my doors through the years can probably attest to that, but I'd rather not know," He joked.

And if they were gay, neither one of them would be afraid to tell me. My youngest brother, Matt, is gay. He's been with Charles for over twenty years now and they have two bi-racial teenagers. They used donor surrogates so each of them has a biological child. Matt used a black surrogate and Charles used a white surrogate. They didn't want to have one white kid and one black kid, so they solved that problem."

Jules was taking the measure of this man again. As an ex-cop, she had pegged him as a hard-line right-winger. Although he'd quickly dispelled that idea the very first time they met, she still assumed he was at least leaning in that direction. Now she saw she was completely off base.

"Science," she said lamely. "It's amazing what we can achieve."

They sat listening to the music and enjoying their drinks on a beautiful summer evening. Jules focused on gratitude for the moment. It was close to perfect.

They were eventually shown to a table a comfortable distance from the band, where it was easier to talk.

"How's the shooting going? Have you gotten back out to the range since the last Ladies' Night?"

"I did. I got some time in on Monday. Honestly, I'm pretty pleased with my progress. I didn't expect to advance this quickly. Now my focus is mostly on consistency."

"Have you ever shot skeet?" Frank asked.

"Jesus! No. Don't you need long guns for that?"

"You do, but it's really fun. You'd be surprised. I belong to a club. Do you want to go sometime? Give it a try? I'll bring my shotgun for you to use. It's a completely different vibe and a nice change from the indoor range and static targets."

Jules had never even thought about it and realized that it could be a useful skill building exercise. Even with a different type of firearm she could learn some of the basics of sighting moving targets.

"I guess so," she said. "It would be a new experience and I'm always up for new experiences."

He met her eye and held it, "Good to know." They shared a flirty laugh.

Over the course of the evening, they started that well-trodden process of getting to know one another. They talked about the things they had in common, especially the realities of being a single parent. Books were another central talking point. They each took down several recommendations from the other. They talked about his life as a cop, and he shared how difficult he often found the work. He loved being on the job, but hated the culture. The toxic masculinity and thin blue line mentality, twisted to mean unconditional loyalty to the badge, of so many of the cops, even the women.

The check appeared on the table without either of them even noticing. Jules reached for her purse. On any of her exceedingly rare dates, she always intended to pay her own way. Frank waved her away.

"I've got this." He set his Amex on top of the bill.

"Okay," she relented, "but I'll get it next time."

"Since there's going to be a next time," Frank raised an eyebrow at the news, "I'll take you up on that offer!"

They walked to her car, Frank's hand resting lightly on the small of her back. Jules felt silly suddenly, awkward and giddy. She hadn't been in this situation in a very long time. She unlocked her car with a loud squawk and pulled open the door.

"Thank you, Frank." She turned to face him and took his hands in both of hers. "Let me know when you want to go skeet shooting?" She found herself hoping it was soon.

"I will." They shared a lingering hug and a kiss on the cheek. He smelled good and she was reminded how nice it was to be this close to someone.

On her way home, Jules was letting her mind wander over the evening. There was clearly an attraction between them. She felt it the first day when they met at the range, that unnamable chemistry that just feels comfortable. She felt it with him tonight. Easy to just be herself and enjoy the moment. No need for pretense . . . reality reached up and smacked Jules in the face as she sat at a red light.

What the hell am I thinking? OF COURSE there's a need for pretense! I have to NOT tell him I'm planning an assassination. I'm a walking deception from here on out. It's not safe to let anyone get close to me. I have to keep my distance.

It was hard for her to accept that the rest of her life would be living a lie. How would she manage? This woman who held truth and honesty among her highest values. She would need to build a hard shell around this secret and bury it under her authentic self if she was going to pull this off. She was facing two years of living this façade.

Her phone lit up. A text from Frank. Already. She could still smell him.

[Had a great time tonight. You owe me dinner. Sunday?]

[Yes!] She replied as the light turned to green. Fuck.

• • •

VIDEO DIARY ENTRY - July 29, 2022

"Today is Friday, July 29th, 2022. Here is what's happening in Trump world. In January 6th investigation findings, we learned this week that he watched the melee unfold from his dining room table in the White House on that day. As we already knew, people on his team begged him to act; to denounce the violence and call off his dogs. Even Ivanka tried. But he would not be deterred from enjoying the insurrection he had intentionally ignited. When he finally made his first public statement, more than 3 hours after the attack began, he told the attackers, "Go home. We love you. You're very special." I think that speaks for itself.

"Also this week, the Republican National Committee has threatened to stop paying Trump's legal bills if he runs for the office again. In a very confusing statement, they claim that their duty to remain 'neutral' would preclude them from continuing to foot his legal bills if he were a candidate. You can't make this stuff up!

"My work is on track and my progress continues. I've decided to try skeet shooting in an effort to further improve my skills, and practice on moving targets. Even though a long gun seems like such a different beast, I do think it will help with accuracy.

"Next month I'm headed to Milwaukee to explore the convention site and surrounding area. I can get a lot from Google Earth, which is absolutely amazing. The technology we enjoy today is beyond belief. But I want to get inside the arena and walk the streets.

"All for now. Peace."

MASS SHOOTINGS IN THE US
July 2022 - 89 **total**

A mass shooting is any shooting where four or more people, other than the shooter, are killed or injured.

1. July 01, 2022 - Chicago, Illinois - 4 injured
2. July 01, 2022 - Greenwood, Mississippi - 2 dead, 2 injured
3. July 01, 2022 - Chicago, Illinois - 1 dead, 3 injured
4. July 02, 2022 - Haltom City, Texas - 2 dead, 2 injured
5. July 02, 2022 - Corona, New York - 4 injured
6. July 02, 2022 - Clinton, North Carolina - 4 dead,
7. July 03, 2022 - Manassas, Virginia - 5 injured
8. July 03, 2022 - Mullins, South Carolina - 4 injured
9. July 03, 2022 - Surprise, Arizona - 4 injured
10. July 03, 2022 - Tacoma, Washington - 4 injured
11. July 04, 2022 - Boston, Massachusetts - 4 injured
12. July 04, 2022 - Kenosha, Wisconsin - 1 dead, 3 injured
13. July 04, 2022 - Minneapolis, Minnesota - 4 injured
14. July 04, 2022 - Sacramento, California - 4 injured
15. July 04, 2022 - Highland Park, Illinois - 4 injured
16. July 04, 2022 - Kansas City, Missouri - 1 dead, 4 injured

17. July 04, 2022 - Denver, Colorado - 1 dead, 5 injured
18. July 04, 2022 - Corona, New York - 3 dead, 2 injured
19. July 04, 2022 - Chicago, Illinois - 5 injured
20. July 04, 2022 - Richmond, Virginia - 1 dead, 3 injured
21. July 05, 2022 - Steubenville, Ohio - 4 injured
22. July 05, 2022 - Gary, Indiana - 4 injured
23. July 05, 2022 - Rochester, New York - 4 injured
24. July 06, 2022 - Saint Cloud, Minnesota - 4 injured
25. July 06, 2022 - Tampa, Florida - 4 injured
26. July 06, 2022 - Chicago, Illinois - 4 injured
27. July 07, 2022 - Chicago, Illinois - 4 injured
28. July 08, 2022 - Greensboro, North Carolina - 4 injured
29. July 08, 2022 - Detroit, Michigan - 4 injured
30. July 09, 2022 - Jacksons Gap, Alabama - 3 dead, 7 injured
31. July 10, 2022 - Crest Hill, Illinois - 1 dead, 3 injured
32. July 10, 2022 - Kansas City, Missouri - 4 injured
33. July 10, 2022 - Downey, California - 1 dead, 4 injured
34. July 10, 2022 - Brooklyn, New York - 7 injured
35. July 10, 2022 - Alvin, Texas - 1 dead, 4 injured
36. July 10, 2022 - Chicago, Illinois - 7 dead, 3
37. July 11, 2022 - Jackson, Mississippi - 4 injured
38. July 12, 2022 - Boston, Massachusetts - 1 dead, 3 injured
39. July 13, 2022 - Philadelphia, Pennsylvania - 4 injured
40. July 13, 2022 - Indianapolis, Indiana - 5 injured
41. July 13, 2022 - Minneapolis, Minnesota - 6 injured
42. July 14, 2022 - Chicago, Illinois - 4 injured
43. July 14, 2022 - Philadelphia, Pennsylvania - 4 injured
44. July 16, 2022 - Washington, District of Columbia - 2 dead, 4 injured
45. July 16, 2022 - Columbus, Ohio - 4 injured

46. July 16, 2022 - North Charleston, South Carolina - 2 dead, 4 injured

47. July 16, 2022 - Houston, Texas - 1 dead, 3 injured

48. July 16, 2022 - Monroe, Louisiana - 6 injured

49. July 16, 2022 - Philadelphia, Pennsylvania - 4 injured

50. July 17, 2022 - Mount Vernon, Washington - 1 dead, 7 injured

51. July 17, 2022 - Brooklyn, New York - 2 dead, 3 injured

52. July 17, 2022 - Detroit, Michigan - 3 dead, 5 injured

53. July 17, 2022 - Greenwood, Indiana - 9 injured

54. July 17, 2022 - Beech Grove, Indiana - 4 injured

55. July 17, 2022 - Grand Rapids, Michigan - 4 injured

56. July 17, 2022 - Milledgeville, Georgia - 5 injured

57. July 17, 2022 - Newark, New Jersey - 1 dead, 6 injured

58. July 17, 2022 - Vancouver, Washington - 1 dead, 7 injured

59. July 18, 2022 - Atlanta, Georgia - 5 injured

60. July 19, 2022 - Lincoln, Nebraska - 1 dead, 3 injured

61. July 21, 2022 - Los Angeles, California - 5 injured

62. July 23, 2022 - Richmond, Virginia - 8 injured

63. July 23, 2022 - El Paso, Texas - 4 injured

64. July 23, 2022 - Pinebluff, North Carolina - 2 dead, 2 injured

65. July 23, 2022 - Renton, Washington - 4 injured

66. July 23, 2022 - Chicago, Illinois - 2 dead, 2 injured

67. July 23, 2022 - Chicago, Illinois - 2 dead, 2 injured

68. July 23, 2022 - Rockford, Illinois - 1 dead, 3 injured

69. July 23, 2022 - Kalamazoo, Michigan - 1 dead, 8 injured

70. July 24, 2022 - San Pedro, California - 5 injured

71. July 24, 2022 - Atlanta, Georgia - 1 dead, 3 injured

72. July 24, 2022 - Fort Worth, Texas - 5 injured

73. July 24, 2022 - Bennettsville, South Carolina - 1 dead, 3 injured

74. July 25, 2022 - New Orleans, Louisiana - 4 injured

75. July 27, 2022 - Macon, Georgia - 2 dead, 2 injured

76. July 27, 2022 - Hahnville, Louisiana - 5 injured

77. July 29, 2022 - Baltimore, Maryland - 2 dead, 5 injured

78. July 29, 2022 - Albuquerque, New Mexico - 4 injured

79. July 29, 2022 - Cleveland, Ohio - 5 injured

80. July 29, 2022 - Miami, Florida - 1 dead, 4 injured

81. July 30, 2022 - Monroe, Louisiana - 3 dead, 4 injured

82. July 30, 2022 - Wheeling, Illinois - 4 injured

83. July 30, 2022 - Girard, Georgia - 2 dead, 4 injured

84. July 31, 2022 - South Bend, Indiana - 4 injured

85. July 31, 2022 - Orlando, Florida - 4 injured

86. July 31, 2022 - Detroit, Michigan - 2 dead, 4 injured

87. July 31, 2022 - Indianapolis, Indiana - 4 injured

88. July 31, 2022 - Decatur, Illinois - 4 injured

89. July 31, 2022 - Hartford, Connecticut - 1 dead, 4 injured

• • •

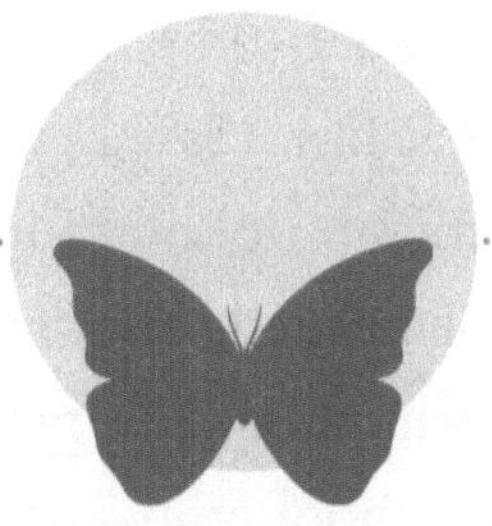

AUGUST 2022

Brandi Carlile was playing at the Fiserv arena on August 5th. Jules' first, and maybe only, reconnaissance trip would start three days before that. She had told everyone the same cover story. That she was going to see her college friend, Trish, who was going through a tough divorce, and that they were going to the concert together. Trish really was a dear friend from college who lived in Wisconsin, so it was a good cover, but Jules would not be seeing her on this trip. This was strictly a working journey.

She planned to stay off the toll roads to avoid having her license plate captured on camera. She would travel the old highways. The routes before the interstate system. It would add about eight hours to the trip. She hadn't booked any rooms, intending to just sleep in her car at rest areas or in parking lots. She could get a decent rest on the passenger side with the seat moved all the way back and fully reclined.

She also planned to only use cash for gas, food, and anything else along the way. She would buy her concert ticket at the box office. The cheapest tickets were $61.00, and she was hoping there would be some nosebleeds left on the day. Given the enormous capacity of the place, it felt like a safe bet.

She was taking the mission phone for pics and video, and to add to her video diary if needed. She'd also take her cell phone just in case of an emergency, but she planned to leave it off for the most part, using old school maps instead of GPS. She wasn't being paranoid with all of these safeguards, just overly cautious. She wanted to minimize any paper or digital trail of her trip just in case she was somehow thwarted before Day Zero. Better safe than sorry.

Although she hoped to be able to take her shot from outside the venue in 2024, she needed to get inside during an event to really understand the layout and try to see the VIP entrance from the inside. Jules had printed out every blueprint and floor plan she could find online at her most recent library session and had them in her bag for the trip.

She had packed lightly, not planning to have too many opportunities to shower and change. The small Coleman cooler was filled with food and drinks. She had some yogurt, a few sandwiches, some containers of fruit and veggies. Some cheese and hummus. In a grocery bag she had crackers, pretzels, Clif Bars, some nuts, and toilet paper. She was taking a light blanket and her pillow. She found an old soup thermos in the garage. It was red and black plaid with a beige screw-on lid that doubled as a soup bowl. She cleaned it up and filled it with coffee. Caffeine was her co-pilot, and she planned not to run out.

Feinstein would be stuck inside during her absence, maybe six or seven days, so Jules set up her automatic feeder, gravity water bowl, and two litter boxes. The cat knew the signs of her imminent detainment and kept her distance once she saw everything in place in the kitchen on Tuesday morning. Jules didn't dare let her out again after that.

With everything loaded into the Jeep, Jules settled into the driver's seat before 6:00 am. She was looking forward to the excitement of a long road trip alone. Especially the backroads and small towns. She always wanted to do that, but the convenience and efficiency of the mega-highways had always won out. Now she would be able to slow the pace.

Jules vowed not to eat at any chain establishment during the trip. She would be traveling almost a thousand miles on back roads, so there were bound to be more than enough mom-and-pop spots to grab a bite. She had a few novels with her and planned to get in some pleasure reading at her stops. Until she reached her destination, Jules wanted to feel like a tourist.

Over the next few days, she covered a lot of ground, watching the landscape unfold in ways that were impossible on the interstate. After traversing the entire width of New York on State Route 20, she drove along the edge of Lake Erie on Highway 5, remembering when it was considered a 'dead lake,' when the Cuyahoga River, feeding into the Great Lake, had caught fire and national attention. It was a shocking story to her as a little girl, imagining a lake on fire! They learned about it in school the next day, and it was the first time she ever thought about the by-products of human existence and advancement. She started noticing the trash, everywhere. She watched the grownups throwing trash out of their moving cars and saw it piling up on the sides of the roads. Remembering, Jules wondered how an entire population had ignored it for so long. Long enough for a lake to catch fire. Iron Eyes Cody, a fake Native American, appeared on their televisions, crying over the destruction of nature. The EPA was created.

Now the lake was crystalline as she drove its length from east to west. August sun blinding off its surface. Jules had the windows down and the warm air smelled like life. It wasn't perfect, still the most polluted of the Great Lakes, but it had come a long way.

Of course, Trump's one-term presidency had decimated environmental policy, and gutted the EPA. More than a thousand scientists and policy experts were eliminated. Nearly 100 earth-friendly policies reversed. He pulled America out of the Paris Accord, paving the way for corporate greed. What would happen if he cheated his way into the White House again?

She followed the Lake through Pennsylvania and Ohio, taking advantage of the long daylight of August to stay on the road. Driving at night had become difficult over the last 10 years or so. The glare from oncoming traffic made it tough. She planned to stop around 7 each evening, to catch the last of the light over dinner.

Leaving the lake shore behind near Conneaut, her mind began to wander to Frank. They had met for dinner on Sunday, and she'd had a great time with him. Again. They made plans to shoot when she got back. He was bright. Their conversations were substantive and compelling. She felt physically attracted to him, which she hadn't felt in years. He was kind and thoughtful, even noticing that she'd had her hair trimmed. He was paying attention to the world and had the right politics. He was woke. A title Jules embraced wholeheartedly, despite the right's efforts to demonize that term. He was exactly the type of person she would have hoped to meet, in another life. Before all of this. But here he was, and here she was, and Jules decided not to think too hard about it. It felt like a gift.

It was nearing 7:00 pm on her first day of driving. She was still east of Cleveland, and she planned to drive to the south of Cleveland, avoiding the city, and north of Akron the following day. She pulled off of 528 in search of food and a good sleeping spot and found both with ease. The fish and chips at a local diner was textbook, and she lingered over it, glad to be out of the car for a bit and stretching her legs beneath the table. She brushed her teeth in the bathroom and washed her face and hands. That was likely the best she'd get that day. Maybe she could find a shower tomorrow evening. Across the street from the diner was a small parking area for a trailhead. The perfect spot to spend her night.

• • •

The next morning, she woke to darkness. It was just after 5:30, but she'd slept long enough; out by ten the night before without even having cracked a book. She hoped every night would be as easy. After a long stretching session beside her car and a pee in the woods, Jules pulled back onto the road heading west. She planned for one more night on the road before reaching Milwaukee on the third day.

Being out of touch, off the grid, felt invigorating. Normally, she would listen to something on Audible to pass the time, but she was not using her phone, so that option was out. She had tried listening to the radio, but signals changed rapidly from town to town, and after spending too much time trying to dial in the local NPR station, she had just turned it off. She tried not to think about the purpose of her trip and just drive.

When she got west of Cleveland a few hours later, she decided to stop for a bite and fill her thermos. It was still early enough for breakfast and that was usually the cheapest and most satisfying meal of the day for her on a long trip like this. She found an old diner called Lou's Luncheonette a few miles off Rt 303 and pulled into the gravel lot. It looked busy, which she liked. She didn't attract as much attention, a single woman alone, in a busy place. She grabbed the thermos and one of her novels and headed in.

The breakfast smells were mouthwatering when she stepped inside. Bacon and coffee were the most prominent. She intended to have both. It was darker inside than out, and it took a moment for her eyes to adjust. As she was led to a small booth by the hostess, the interior started coming into focus. She realized too late that she was in enemy territory. 'Let's go Brandon!,' 'Trump 2024,' 'Make America Great Again!' Stickers and banners and propaganda plastered like wallpaper. All of the staff wore MAGA ball caps. Apparently, the owner had no concern about alienating diners who didn't share their politics. She wished it had been obvious from the outside; she hated spending money in Trump loving businesses. But she was here and she was hungry.

The menu was printed on her paper placemat, along with ads for local businesses. Many of these included American flags, the dog whistle of the right. She noticed a message in small print at the bottom of the menu: *Ask us about saving 20% on your order today! Her server, 'Barb' according to her name tag, came to take her order.

"Hey, Barb. How do I save 20% on my tab?" Jules asked, pointing to the menu.

"Oh. All you have to do is sign up for the Trump 2024 email list. Lou's Luncheonette is part of a national movement to grow the MAGA army. But it's on the honor system. If you're already on the list, we can't offer the discount."

"Thanks. I think I'll pass." Jules smiled at Barb and tried to keep the disgust out of her voice. Dishonorable people relying on the honor system. "I get so much email already!"

"Yeah, I know what you mean. So what'll it be?"

She ordered coffee and breakfast, and asked Barb to fill her thermos, before turning her attention to the book she'd brought in with her. She hoped to keep her mind distracted from her surroundings, but Fox news was blaring from two oversized flat screens mounted behind the counter. Earlier in the week there had been primaries in a handful of states and the talking heads were ecstatic.

Two big wins were being analyzed and Trump was front and center, taking credit for all of it. Tudor Dixon, a Trump-backed nominee, was going to face off against the incumbent Democratic Governor of Michigan, Gretchen Whitmer. In another Michigan race, Democratic Representative Pete Meier, an Iraq veteran, was being challenged by Republican John Gibbs, a former Trump cabinet appointee. Jules was both fascinated with and disgusted by women (Dixon) and people of color (Gibbs) who supported the right.

Jules kept thinking about that email list. As much as she hated the idea of being anywhere in their cybersphere, it was always good to know what the enemy was doing.

Barb came back with her order and Jules made a decision.

"Hey, Barb? I think I would like to get that discount. What do I need to do?"

"I'll bring you the check and there's a space right on the receipt for your email. Just fill that out and they'll take the 20% off at the register. Can I bring you anything else?"

Jules assured her she was fine and turned to her food. She finished her meal, wrote her junk mail email address on the receipt for the mailing list, and was out the door for under ten bucks.

The rest of the day was uneventful. Jules drove west, alternating speeds between 60 and 35 as she passed through small towns and villages. Some just farming towns with a single 4-way intersection and a flashing red-light. Almost always a church. Once she got past central Ohio, the vistas opened as the landscape flattened. The sun was undeterred. She was aiming to be south of Chicago before she stopped for dinner. Then day three would be just a little over a hundred miles to put her into Milwaukee.

Jules made her driving goal on Wednesday, crossing the width of Indiana and landing just south of Chicago in the village of Matteson, just off Rt. 30, by dinner time. She wasn't really that hungry, but she did want to stretch her body after two full days in the car.

Matteson was one of those sprawly suburbs that looked purpose built to serve as yet another Chicago bedroom community. Lots of flat, open space with new housing stock, big box stores, and chain hotels on its perimeter, surrounding a decaying downtown with local businesses holding their breath on some main street through the center of what was once downtown. Jules wouldn't get that far. A sign just off of the exit directed her to Governors Trail Park, less than a mile away. Jules parked the Jeep and headed for the Old Plank Trail. A placard at the trail entrance informed her that it was a 22-mile, paved rail trail that had once been the fur trade route for indigenous populations. It connected Joliet in the east to Chicago Heights in the west. Jules took a few good stretches, working out some stiffness in her back and shoulders, then headed off to the west.

It was later in the evening, and threatening rain, so the trail wasn't too busy. She generally avoided rail trails, mostly because of the bikers. She winced every time they came up on her from behind, shouting "on your left!" She'd had a few close calls and preferred dirt hiking paths, but here she was. She set off at a good pace, pumping her arms. It felt great to be moving and she hoped to cover 2 miles before she got back to the car. If the rain held off, she planned to eat her dinner at one of the many picnic tables in the park. She still had most of the food she'd started out with yesterday morning.

Because she didn't want to use her phone, she had to walk without any distraction. No music, no audible, just her and her thoughts. Despite her best efforts, her mind turned to the mission. To Day Zero. The enormity of what she was planning. She was able to keep those thoughts at bay most of the time, focusing only on each step of the plan rather than the outcome. But sometimes it overtook her. She realized that tomorrow would bring her to the place where her life would essentially end. One way or another.

In spite of the warm August air, Jules began to shiver. It started in the pit of her stomach and quickly spread, her arms and legs shaking under the weight of the thing she was doing. She didn't feel fear, though. That wasn't driving her body's reaction. It felt more like awe. A sort of spiritual awareness of her place in history. She didn't want it. In fact, she wished for any other outcome between now and then that would free her from the path. But she was prepared for the worst. Prepared to take that shot if the day arrived. And as prepared as could be to accept the consequences. Until Day Zero, everything about the mission, everything about her life, was personal and internal. Only hers. But once it was accomplished, she would belong to history.

Jules saw a bench along the trail ahead and made for it. She sat and tried to calm herself, taking deep breaths and focusing on her surroundings. For a moment, she thought she might be sick, but she was able to breathe through the nausea, and gradually her tremors subsided, leaving her wrung out and exhausted. She had no idea how long she had been walking, but she needed to turn back. She was suddenly ravenous.

That night, after wolfing down a PBJ and some cheese and crackers, Jules slept in the parking lot. She was out as soon as darkness fell, before 8:00 pm, her body demanding it. Her sleep was fitful. One nightmare featured her bleeding out on a sidewalk surrounded by women, all women, in black suits and dark sunglasses, guns drawn. Secret service. She could see the sun blazing in the sky as she looked up at them, faceless and looming above. Trump suddenly pushed into the circle.

"Nice job, ladies!" He bellowed with a smirk. Then he turned back toward the ring of agents and grabbed one of them by the crotch. In perfect lockstep, every other agent turned in his direction and emptied their weapons into his torso. He fell in a 350-pound heap on top of Jules, killing her instantly.

In another dream, she was being carried aloft through a city, maybe Chicago, in one of those colorful sedan chairs that used to transport royalty through the streets, and crowds were cheering and throwing flowers at her. She was waving and smiling in return. There were fireworks and circus animals lining the way. She looked to see who was carrying her and saw that it was Ruth Bader Ginsburg and Kathy Griffin. She was ecstatic. She had obviously been successful! She looked back down the street and saw they were nearing Trump Tower.

"No!" She shouted over the crowd. "Not there!"

She turned back to her sedan bearers to wave them off and saw they had morphed into Rudy Giuliani and Marjorie Taylor Greene. They were sweating and rushing her toward the Tower. The crowd was gone and there was no sound at all as they stopped before the entrance. Jules was in a panic. The door opened and Trump stepped outside. He pointed a gold-plated Desert Eagle .50 caliber handgun at her.

"See. I told you so."

The explosion was bone-jarring and Jules was flung from her beautiful silk-upholstered chair into the mean street. As she lay dying, Putin came from inside the hotel to stand with Trump and flung an arm over his shoulder. Kim Jong-Un emerged and stood to the other side of the failed President, completing the triumvirate of fascist dictators. The MAGA-bedecked masses oozed onto the scene from every nook and cranny, carrying signs and shouting 'four more years!' and 'let's go Brandon!'

She woke up crying from the sense of futility the dream had filled her with and felt a rush of relief when her eyes opened to the day. For some reason, this trip, more than all of her planning so far, was making it seem so real. She was glad for that. She needed to feel it and absorb the gravity of what she was doing. The task ahead was monumental.

Jules grabbed her mission phone and powered it up. She needed to talk to someone.

VIDEO DIARY ENTRY – August 4, 2022

"Good morning. It's the 4th of August. Happy birthday, President Obama! From a fellow Leo. Thank you for your years of service to this country. I only wish your legacy could have been continued, rather than destroyed.

"I'm somewhere in Illinois, on my way to scout the venue for the mission ahead. I'll reach the Fiserv in Milwaukee later today. I just woke up from a nightmare that really shook me so I wanted to record this. I want to remind you, whoever is watching this, about Trump's continuing admiration for the leaders of brutal regimes around the world. Not just Putin, but North Korea's dictator, and Duterte in the Philippines. He admired Xi in China when he was able to secure his

'presidency' for life. Trump said we might need to give that a try here in America. A lifetime term. Does that sound like democracy? And Erdogan. And even Hitler, for Christ sake! Adolf Hitler! Remember that Trump openly and publicly praised him for, in his words, 'doing good things.' I'm sharing this in defense of what I'm doing. It may seem crazy, but it feels like the sanest thing I've done since 2016. We are in such grave danger."

•   •   •

Jules shut off the phone and spent a few minutes in the parking lot stretching the sleep from her body. The echo of her nighttime sorrow still weighed her down, an invisible cloak. It was the kind of grief she sometimes felt when Mick came to her at night. So vivid. The love and loss enormous and unshakeable in her waking moments. Sometimes she cried through it.

In the park restroom, Jules freshened up for the day, brushing her teeth and doing what they used to call in the Navy a PTA bath. Pussy, tits, and armpits. It was the best she could do short of an actual shower. She was back on the road by 8:00 am, taking Rt. 30 west for a few miles before turning onto highway 50. She would reach Milwaukee in the early afternoon. As she drove, grief was replaced by purpose.

By 3:00 pm, Jules was pulling up to the Arena on Vel R. Phillips Ave. Vel Phillips was, she knew from her reconnaissance research, a civil rights activist, attorney, judge, and former Secretary of State of Wisconsin. She was the first black woman to graduate from the University of Wisconsin Law School and had died just recently at the age of 95. Would she be horrified at the thought of Trump bringing his hate-mongers to this sacred site? Jules imagined she would.

The arena itself was smaller than the blueprints made it appear. Jules circled it a few times, getting a sense of the layout, noticing the entries and loading dock areas. Bound by Vel Phillips, N. 6th St., W. Highland and W. Juneau Aves., the Fiserv was a gorgeous modern structure, all green glass and metal with a curvilinear roof of beige and brown panels that looked like wood. It sat comfortably in the heart of the city, in an area known as the Deer District, rather than in some remote urban-adjacent space. It was meant to be a jewel, not a blight, and it succeeded.

Jules parked on a side street several blocks from the arena, just to spend some time observing the area. She put some coins in the meter and took a few moments to stretch before getting back into the car. She was hungry. She'd had coffee and a muffin in the first hour of her drive, but nothing since. Her cooler food was edible, but not really appetizing. The cheese was hardening and the fruit was past ripe, soft. Her yogurt was room temp and watery but nothing she couldn't fix with a good shake. The apricot jelly had soaked through the bread on her last PB&J. She finished it all off from the driver's seat and promised herself a restaurant meal before the concert Friday.

• • •

The Milwaukee Museum of Art was less than two miles away and open late on Thursdays. They had a large Georgia O'Keefe collection, and Jules loved the exuberance of her work. They also had some Chihuly, another artist whose skill amazed her. She still had a few hours to tour the collection and grounds.

The building itself was architecturally stunning. In the photos it looked like a sleek jet about to take flight over Lake Michigan, which sat just beyond its doors. Saarinen built the original award-winning building in the 50s. The newest building, completed in 2001, was by a Spanish architect she didn't know, Calatrava. She had read that it had some sort of movable sunscreen, those 'wings' that made it look like a plane, which she couldn't completely envision and was excited to see for herself.

She parked downtown so that she could cross the suspension bridge to the museum campus. In the few blocks between her car and the bridge, posters freshly plastered everywhere invited Milwaukeeans to a Trump Rally in Waukesha the following evening. If only she were ready, she mused, he would be so close.

The view opened up in front of her when she reached the bridge. It was so purposeful and so well done. A panorama of the soaring gallery, the August-lush lawns and gardens, and the Lake beyond, alive with the kind of overly intent summer activity that only wintering bodies of water enjoyed. From this side it reminded her of a great ship with all of the rigging. As she crossed, she left behind the dark purpose of her trip and became a tourist for the evening.

The collection was comprehensive. Any art lover would be sated. Jules easily filled the few hours until closing, wandering the galleries. She was stopped in her tracks by a work from 1959 entitled *Congressional Gathering*, by Louis H. Draper. It was reported to be a gelatin silver print. Jules had no understanding of the process, but she understood the result. It was haunting. An image in blacks, whites, and grays of four figures filled the frame, fading into black top and bottom. They were cloaked in pointed white sheets, unidentifiable. Congress.

On another wall, a typewritten piece, *I want a president*, on onion skin paper, by Zoe Leonard. In 1992, she wrote:

"I want a dyke for president. I want a person
with AIDS for president and I want a fag for
vice president and I want someone with no
health insurance and I want someone who grew
up in a place where the earth is so saturated
with toxic waste that they didn't have a
choice about getting leukemia. I want a
president that had an abortion at sixteen and
I want a candidate who isn't the lesser of two
evils and I want a president who lost their
last lover to AIDS, who still sees that in
their eyes every time they lay down to rest,
who held their lover in their arms and knew
they were dying. I want a president with no
air-conditioning, a president who has stood on
line at the clinic, at the dmv, at the welfare
office, and has been unemployed and laid off and
sexually harassed and gaybashed and deported.
I want someone who has spent the night in the
tombs and had a cross burned on their lawn and
survived rape. I want someone who has been in
love and been hurt, who respects sex, who has
made mistakes and learned from them. I want a
Black woman for president. I want someone with
bad teeth ~~and an attitude~~, someone who has
eaten ~~that nasty~~ hospital food, someone who
crossdresses and has done drugs and been in
therapy. I want someone who has committed
civil disobedience. And I want to know why this
isn't possible. I want to know why we started

learning somewhere down the line that a president
is always a clown: always a john and never
a hooker. Always a boss and never a worker,
always a liar, always a thief, and never caught."

• • •

Jules slept in her car where she'd parked for the museum. It was free after 6:00 pm and it was well lit and busy. She felt safe. It was hot though, and she cracked the windows just enough for some airflow, not enough for a hand to reach in. She stretched out in the backseat this time, hoping to avoid anyone, police or otherwise, thinking she was passed out at the wheel. Sometime deep in the night, someone started trying to open her doors, hoping to find an unlocked vehicle and some treasure.

"Hey!" She bolted up and the thief stumbled back onto the sidewalk, as frightened as she was. A homeless guy or addict on his evening rounds. "Get out of here! I have a gun."

He took her at her word and was gone. She'd need a new plan the next night. No more city streets. She slept uneasily through the rest of the night.

On Friday morning she woke early to the hum of a busy workday in a big city. There was a YMCA on North Avenue that she hoped would give her reciprocity if she showed her Y Pass. SilverSneakers. She hated that demeaning characterization of every active person over a certain age. It was so fucking precious. Posters of women in bathing caps doing water aerobics. White haired couples wielding pickleball racquets. It was 2022 for god's sake! The bathing cap generation was gone, and everyone her age that played pickleball was a sweaty mess after a grueling match. But like so many other things about this stage of life, the AARP stage, she had to grin and bear it.

The front desk passed her right through when she flashed her ID. No questions. Jules wanted to do some yoga and get some miles in on a treadmill. The need to really move her body had accumulated after the days and nights in the car. A sauna and steam would really finish off her spa day before a long-anticipated shower. She had hours to spare, and this would be a good refuge.

In the early afternoon, feeling revived and ready to focus, she headed to the Fiserv. She found the parking garage that served the venue. The pre-concert crowd was already arriving and there were only a few spots left on the 4th level.

The garage was on the same side of the Arena where she had seen the box office entry. She took the elevator down, rather than using the skyway, and crossed the street. It was close to 2:00 pm and already crowded. The ground level of the arena and the surrounding area held lots of drinking and dining options. Shops to buy sports fan gear, Bucks and Brewers, were also plentiful.

Jules didn't stand out among this fan base. The pre-concert crowd was predominantly middle-aged and older women; women who grew up on Joni Mitchell and Joan Baez and Ani DiFranco and Stevie Nicks and Emmylou Harris and Linda Ronstadt. A crowd that reveled in activism and treasured a good lyric. The younger fans were there, too. Tuning in to this artist now that she had unwillingly crossed over into the 'pop' genre because of a Grammy nomination in the category.

The show goers donned pride t-shirts and hats, faded concert tees attesting to the wearer's excellent or exotic musical tastes, or Brandi Carlile swag from previous shows. There were even a few pink pussy hats. Jules had nearly forgotten that powerful symbol of female solidarity descending on D.C. and major cities around the world the day after Trump's inauguration in 2017. She had taken a bus into Manhattan with a group of local protesters that day and stood shoulder to shoulder in the streets with people from everywhere. It had all proven to be too little, too late.

As she had guessed, there were still cheap seats to be had. She picked up a $61.00 ticket at the window and headed back outside to walk the perimeter and see if she could locate that V.I.P. entrance from the exterior. It probably wouldn't be marked but she knew roughly where it should be from the floor plans she'd studied and would find it easily inside the arena during the concert.

New sidewalks circled the Fiserv, and she followed them around the building. It was so good to be out of the car and moving after the days on the road. The sunny day lifted her spirits despite the buzzing just beneath her flesh, an electric reminder that this would be her okay Corral.

There were quite a few entry doors, none of them marked except to say "No Entry." It was obvious where trash was removed. Oversized dumpsters stood empty, lined along a half-dozen concrete corridors that ran from the sidewalk down under the overhang of the building, awaiting the detritus of tonight's event. There were a few she guessed were employee only entries. Workers in a variety of uniforms were going in; scanning their badges to unlock the doors. There were loading docks, where everything needed for any given production would be delivered one day and retrieved the next. So much went into a single evening. Just past the first set of loading docks was a set of tall roll-up doors. Like garage doors but much taller. They were completely smooth and painted the same color as the wall into which they were set, and there were no handles or other external hardware. No signage. If you weren't looking you'd never notice them. The V.I.P. entrance. Jules noted their location on the street. This is where she imagined she'd get her opening.

There were, of course, security cameras everywhere. This was no surprise. Jules was grateful that she didn't intend to try to get away with anything. To disappear or go on the run, like Booth after Lincoln or Oswald after Kennedy. It really would be impossible. If she was able to get shots off here, and not get shot herself, she would drop her weapon and lay face down on the ground, spread eagle. She would be done. Mission accomplished.

• • •

The doors opened at 6:00 pm. Jules would have an hour to wander around inside before the concert started. She wanted to start by locating the VIP entrance and then work from there. Once inside the arena, she oriented herself to the surrounding streets and pulled up the exterior in her mind. It should be to her left at floor level. She headed down, hoping no ticket police stopped her short and sent her climbing back to where she belonged.

She reached the floor and found what she was looking for without any trouble. The discrete doors that she had seen from the outside led to this entrance. She turned to look out at the space, imagining where the dais would likely be erected to take best advantage of the 360° view. It was breathtaking to envision this enormous venue filled with Americans, powerful Americans, gathering to lift up a fascist. All while flying the flag of democracy. The lyrics of Dylan's *Sweetheart Like You* rose up from her memory; *Patriotism is the last refuge to which a scoundrel clings, steal a little and they throw you in jail, steal a lot and they make you king.*

Of course, she wouldn't be getting inside the Fiserv, and she could have no real certainty about how things would actually unfold on Day Zero. She knew that. But there were things she could know, and she needed as much intel as possible to play out different scenarios in the months ahead. She might not even get close to that exterior entrance. Some of the streets surrounding the venue could be closed to all traffic, including foot traffic, during the RNC. She had learned that had been the case at past conventions. If that happened in 2024, the V.I.P. entrance would be out of play. But she also knew Trump wouldn't be able to resist a photo op with his loving base during the biggest of his dog and pony shows. He needed to continue to pretend that he had the draw and could command bigger crowds than anyone. His pathetic need to be 'biggest' and 'best' was deep, and she hoped it would prove to be his undoing.

If she couldn't reach the arena on the day, she'd need to track down the Trumpsters. She knew they would be amassed somewhere nearby if they, too, couldn't reach the Fiserv. They fed off each other's vitriol and saw themselves as Trump's foot soldiers, waiting to do his dirty work, just as they had on January 6th. She knew she could find them. She knew she could infiltrate them. Hate was their siren song, and she'd be their shipwreck.

• • •

The concert crowd was pouring in and Jules headed up to find her seat. She planned to enjoy the music tonight and try to relax before hitting the road tomorrow afternoon.

• • •

The evening had been the balm she needed. Finding common ground with everyone present through language, through shared experience accompanied by sculpted noise. Magic. She decided to seek out more live music back home. Between now and then.

She spent the night in a little league field parking lot north of the city. It had a restroom she could use and she didn't think anyone would bother her parking there overnight. No signage warned against it. It was already near midnight when she pulled in, the beat and the energy of the crowd still with her. She read for a while under the dome light before sleep finally came.

The next morning was spent back downtown, exploring the blocks immediately adjacent to the arena, getting an actual feel for what she had already explored using Google Earth and Street View. Those were some amazing tools, and she felt like she had been here already. She sought out a shop called Insomnia Cookies that she had found in her virtual wanderings. They served warm cookies and she planned to indulge. Back in her working life, she'd loved the warm chocolate chips that every DoubleTree hotel desk provided to guests at check-in.

A friendly young guy behind the counter greeted her. He was thin, with a chic haircut. More Manhattan than Milwaukee. She felt his energy as soon as she walked through the door. Good energy.

"Welcome! Can I getchya a cookie?" His name tag introduced him as Jayme.

"Hi," she pointed to his name, "is it pronounced like Jane with an M?"

"No, it's Ja-mie. My dad is Jay and my mom is Melissa. Jay-Me."

"Sounds like you've explained that a lot." She laughed.

It was a small space and she was the only customer at the moment. Insomnia Cookies' claim to fame, their gimmick, was delivering warm cookies to your door in the wee hours, to satisfy the after party munchies or drunchies. The bars closed at 2:00 am. They delivered for an hour beyond that. Most of their business was either to-go or delivery, but they served coffee (and milk, of course) and had a few tables for walk-ins.

Jules placed her order.

"Were you at the concert last night?" He inquired as he readied her order. A large coffee and three cookies. One chocolate chunk to eat with her coffee, and an oatmeal raisin and lemon white chocolate to go.

"I was. It was great."

"Yeah, I was there." He said.

"Really? Are you a big fan?" She asked.

"Not really. I mean, I like her music and everything, but I wouldn't call myself a fan. She does soooo much for our community that I wanted to support her in my hometown." He pointed to a rainbow lapel pin as he handed her the coffee and cookies. "And I work at the Fiserv so I get cheap tickets."

"Oh, that's great. Good for you." She laughed as she took a seat, thinking this was fate, guiding her on her mission. Tread lightly, she counseled herself.

"So, you live in Milwaukee?"

"Yeah, born and raised. How about you?"

"No, I'm from Chicago." She had no idea why she lied. It just came out. But it felt like the right move. "We've been hearing so much about this arena since its inception, so I decided to come and see it when the Brandi tour was announced. I've been a fan of hers for a long time and I've seen her in concert in Chicago a few times. Those venues were much smaller, though. The Fiserv is huge!"

"Yeah, it's been a real boost to this area. This is called the Deer District." He indicated the surrounding area. "It used to be just like, a freeway with some old derelict businesses and warehouses. Now everything is new or re-purposed. It was really smart planning, in my opinion."

"Mmm," she agreed. "What do you do at the Fiserv?" Curiously. Innocently.

"I work in communications and marketing. I got an MBA with a concentration in marketing from UMW, and I worked here making cookies all during college. I've managed this location now for the past two years and I don't want to leave them hanging. They've hired my replacement, finally, and she starts next month. Then I'll be down to just one full-time job!" He laughed.

"Think of all the free time you'll have!" She dunked her warm cookie into her steaming coffee and took a bite.

The door opened and a family came in.

"Welcome! Can I getchya a cookie?"

While he filled their to-go order, Jules considered her next steps. She didn't believe in coincidence.

"I guess you've seen a lot of great events over there. Do you follow basketball?" She asked him as the door closed behind the cookie buyers.

"I'm not really a sports guy. I've seen a lot of Bucks games just because I happen to be in the office when they're playing. But we have huge screens on every wall, so I usually just watch from there."

"Who's been there in concert that you loved?"

"Oh my god, before COVID they had everyone! Cher came. Celine. Justin Timberlake. Um, the Eagles. Fleetwood Mac. Mumford and Sons. Panic at The Disco. Josh Groban. Oh, and Pink! This was all in the first year, 2018. Everybody wanted to play the new arena. Business here was great. We were slammed after every concert.

I was still a student then so I couldn't afford to spend much on entertainment, but stoned people are generous when you give them a warm cookie. So, I made it to Cher and Celine and Pink just on my tip money! I made more in tips that year than I did hourly."

"Wow. So, is it just music and basketball, or do they hold other events there?"

"No, there's comedy. Gaffigan was here that first year, too. We do Disney on Ice, motocross, rodeo. All of that kind of stuff. We're also the home arena for Marquette men's basketball. '18 and '19 were amazing. Then the pandemic hit and we basically went dark for almost two years. The Fiserv hired me in the summer of last year when everything started coming back. We still aren't up to the pre-COVID level of activity, but we're getting there."

"Sounds like a dream job. All that entertainment for free."

"Well, there are some drawbacks. Monster trucks," he laughed. "And WWE wrestling. I just hope we never do MMA. I can't stand that so-called sport."

"Amen! It's just brutal. I used to think boxing was the most violent sport until that came along." Jules agreed.

"Oh, and worst of all we're hosting the RNC in a few years. That's going to be a shit sh . . Whoops, sorry for the language. I get carried away." He was slightly red-faced at this snafu with a customer.

"No reason to apologize. I imagine it will be, um, quite a production. Will you be forced to attend or can you turn off the screens in your office?" She laughed.

He thought for a moment.

"Honestly? I've never seen them turned off. But I won't be there anyway. Most of us are getting paid time off for the entire convention. They bring a whole squad of people in to run things, including their own security detail. We'll have a small crew of our folks working with them. Most acts bring their own security, a few people who coordinate with our team to protect the talent, but we've never seen anything close to this. They have secret service and a massive private detail, too. They plan to close down a three-block perimeter for the entire four days."

"Oh, no! What will happen to business here?" The store was within that perimeter.

"I think we'll be okay, because we'll get the RNC crowd. I should say they'll be okay. I'll be gone by then."

The phone rang and he picked it up to take an order.

Jules finished her coffee, bussed the table, and waved to Jayme, mouthing 'thank you' as she headed out the door.

Back in the car, Jules powered up the mission phone.

VIDEO DIARY ENTRY – AUGUST 6, 2022

"Today is Saturday, August 6th, 2022. I went to the Brandi Carlile concert last night at the Fiserv. I feel more comfortable now that I've actually been on site. It all felt very familiar, and I know my way around. The only drawback so far is that I just learned they plan to close a wide perimeter around the arena during the entire run of the RNC. This is a slight obstacle. I'll need to alter my plan since I won't be able to get close to the venue. I'm working on it.

"Yesterday, Trump was in Waukesha for a rally. How ironic. Just 35 minutes away. There were signs everywhere in Milwaukee with the details. I might have gone if it hadn't been for the concert. I need to start infiltrating that community. Slowly. Showing up as one of them. Making a few blue-haired, black-hearted friends. It won't

take much. If I go to 4 or 5 events between now and the convention, some of his people will have seen me. Dismissed me.

"I'm heading back home today and really looking forward to my own bed and a home-cooked meal. I should get in late Monday. That's all for now. Peace."

· · ·

Jules spent the next few days retracing her trip west. She found new spots to eat cheap meals, and slept tucked away off the roads, undisturbed, for two more nights. Monday afternoon she pulled into her own driveway. She was glad to finally be home. The journey had been epic, and she had planned a hero's welcome for herself. She had champagne chilling in the fridge that she'd intended to open on her birthday in a few weeks, when she and Sally would celebrate, but she wanted to mark this moment. Her triumphant return from her scouting trip. She'd unpack the car later.

She opened her front door and Feinstein flew past her. She'd forgotten about the cat, or she would have been more careful. After that many days cooped up, she'd probably be in the wind for a while. Jules sent a silent wish out into the world for her safe return as she grabbed the mail and headed inside. She tossed the heap onto the kitchen counter and sifted through it. An official looking envelope from the State of New York caught her attention. Her gun license! Finally. Now she'd start training with her own weapon.

She dug her phone out of the bottom of her bag and realized how good it had felt to be unplugged for six whole days. There was a freedom in it that she had forgotten. She powered it up and grabbed the champagne, flashing back to the last time she'd held a bottle in her hands. Hearing it shatter against the TV in her office. Being saved from the brink by Ellie. Things were coming full circle.

It took a while for her to find a flute, deep in a top cupboard behind extra coffee mugs. She could have used any glass, it really didn't matter. But she wanted this to be celebratory. She rinsed and dried it, and poured a perfect measure, watching the bubbles subside just before spilling over the delicate lip.

"Peace." She said out loud, raising the glass in a mock toast to the world. She sat at the counter to sort through the mail and check her phone messages. There were eight from Frank, all since Friday. She felt a flush that might have been the bubbly or might have been Frank. She scrolled through his notes. "Hi. It's Frank. Call me when you can." "Hi, me again. Call me." All of them asked her to call him. Hm.

She noticed a few from Charlotte. Also starting Friday. Same message. Call me. She started to feel fear. Something wasn't right.

She rang Frank first.

"Jules!" He picked up on the first ring, "I've been trying to reach you. Are you home?"

"I just pulled in. Sorry about that. I forgot to bring my phone charger and it was dead the whole time I was away."

"Yeah, that's okay. Have you heard about Dave?"

"Dave? Dave who?" She couldn't think who he was talking about.

"Dave and Rebecca, Kevin's parents?"

"Oh no, what about him?" She couldn't imagine what he might have to tell her.

"He killed Rebecca and then shot himself in the head. Murder/suicide. It happened early Friday morning, after Ladies' Night."

Jules was stunned.

"Kevin!" She choked, not wanting to know.

"He's okay. Dave spared him. DCFS has him for now."

"DCFS? Oh my god. Where's his family? Grandparents? Aunts and Uncles?"

"Not yet. They haven't been able to connect with anyone for him. Nobody that will take him in, anyway. They've all been estranged for years. Dave did a good job of that."

Jules was crying now, imagining Kevin wherever he might be, grieving and alone.

"Are you ok?" Frank asked her. "Do you want me to come over?"

"Yes, come over." She gave him her address and hung up.

It would take him at least 30 minutes to get there. She needed to keep busy. Jules wanted to wait until Frank was here to look at the news coverage. It was too much to process on her own.

Her shirt was sweat-slick; she peeled it off and replaced it with a loose linen tank top. She'd turned the A/C down when she left for Milwaukee, and it was 82° in the house. She set it to 74° and waited for relief. Suddenly the heat was making her nauseous.

She dumped the champagne down the sink and rinsed the flute, all sense of celebration lost to grim reality. Her chest was tight. She sat on the floor and did some deep breathing, looking for her center. A few asanas helped her ground herself and quiet her thoughts, finally landing in lotus pose for a few moments of meditation. Her body felt heavy, as if a giant hand were pushing down on the top of her head, compressing her. She thought she might pass out if she stood too quickly, so she moved into child pose to push the blood into her head before standing.

She decided to unpack and get everything put away while she waited for Frank. Keep her mind occupied. It had started to drizzle but it was warm, and the mist felt good on her face. Six days of living in the Jeep, out of reach, had taken a toll.

Her car had turned into a rolling dorm room. Water bottles and coffee cups, food wrappers; the detritus of more than 2000 miles. It was a mess. After the trash was out, she grabbed her bags and her cooler, her pillow and blanket, and took those inside. To her surprise, Feinstein ran to her from somewhere across the street, zipping inside ahead of her, perhaps sensing Jules' need for connection. Jules stowed the linens away in the hall closet and rewarded the cat with a can of wet food, a delicacy after the days of kibble meted out from the feeding machine. She stroked its wet fur before attending to the litter box, then lit a few sticks of incense, hoping to abate the cat smell before Frank arrived. She secured all of her mission materials in her study and locked the phone in the safe. Putting things back in order helped to calm her.

Frank arrived as she was making a pot of coffee for them. She opened the door and neither of them said a word, acknowledging the horror of what they were about to discuss with their silence. They stood for a long moment like this before Frank stepped inside and drew her into a hug, then both were in tears.

Over coffee, Frank gave her the details. After Ladies' Night, everyone went to Scotty's as usual. Rebecca won all three prizes that night. First time it had ever been done. And, also for the first time ever, Rebecca ordered a round for the house. She was ecstatic over her win and she didn't hide it. Everyone was celebrating with her. Except Dave. He sat in the booth with Kevin all evening as Rebecca did victory laps among the women.

"How did he seem to take it?" Jules asked.

"He looked grim, but he always looks grim. He didn't make a scene or anything. He didn't try to stop her. He just watched her over the top of his beer. When he finished it, he went over to her, she was talking to some of the ladies over by the bar, and told her it was time to go. They left shortly after that, and then we all heard the news the next day."

"Anybody know what happened?"

"Dave didn't leave a note or anything. They don't know if it was premeditated or a heat of passion kind of thing."

"Passion?" Jules rolled her eyes.

"Everyone's speculating, but Kevin was the only one there. They don't know what he saw or heard, but he called 911 after. He sat there with them until a unit arrived."

She tried to imagine that little body trying to absorb the devastation as he waited. Seeing the only two people he could turn to lifeless and bleeding, leaving him behind.

"Where is he now?"

"He's with a local foster family in Albany. They're specially certified for trauma-informed care. It seems like a good solution for the short run and he seems better than I expected."

"You've seen him?"

"Yeah, Charlotte and I were able to go over on Saturday once they had him settled. I wanted him to see some familiar faces. We took him some books and toys. Legos. Crayons. Some clothes."

"How's Charlotte taking it? I saw she left messages but I haven't called her back yet."

"That's okay. I called her on my way here to let her know I had reached you. I think she's in shock. It's one of those things that ended exactly as you expected, but still you can't imagine it. You can't believe it. We all saw this coming. This or something like it. And there was just nothing we could do."

Jules wiped the tears that were still coming. Now anger mixed with her grief.

"Really? Was there really nothing? All of us in positions of power? We see with our own eyes the trajectory of this kid, and there's NOTHING we can do?!?"

Frank pulled her into his chest and waited, wrapping his arms around her as her rage played itself out.

"I know it's frustrating. There's just no system in place to catch these families as they fall. Now we're left with the aftermath, and Kevin's a statistic."

"What about the red flag laws? Aren't we one of the strongest red flag states?"

"Yeah, but it's still a high standard of proof. They have a right to due process. You have to prove that the person with access to the weapon is a threat to themselves or others."

"Couldn't we have tried that? Their baby was shot and killed for god's sake." She was disgusted with herself, with everyone, who watched this tragedy unfold.

Kevin, not Rebecca."

"It's just so fucking fucked up!" The tears started again, fueled by her sense of helplessness and failure.

Jules' phone rang and she went to the counter where it was charging. It was Sally calling.

[hey sal got back an hour ago great trip call you later x] Jules texted.

"Do you want coffee?" She asked Frank. He asked for it black, and they sat reviving themselves with caffeine.

Frank told her about the extent of the news coverage, and the funeral plans for Dave and Rebecca. They were having a joint service on Wednesday. If there had been any family on either side, Jules doubted that would fly. But a few of their friends, vets that had served with Dave, were coordinating the plans, and they decided to do it for Kevin's sake. One trauma instead of two.

"So, Kevin's going? Is that a good idea?" Jules asked.

"I think so. The worst is behind him, right? I think it will be a chance for him to grasp that his parents weren't just left where he last saw them. That they were cared for. Lottie and I are going to take him. It won't be a Mass. Just viewing hours at the funeral home, followed by the interment."

"That's still a lot for a seven-year old." Jules was worried.

"We're not going to take him to the cemetery. Just to the calling hours for a short stay. He'll have enough time to see any family friends who might be there. The cops who were on site at the house Friday are going to be there. They all want to see him. The scene was pretty rough; they want to let him know what a great job he did for his parents, and stand with him at the caskets to say goodbye. They're going to present him with Dave's flag, and then we'll leave. Thirty minutes, an hour tops."

Jules knew that the family of every military vet was presented with an American flag at their funeral, but found it hard to swallow in this case. Here Kevin, take this flag in honor of your father, who served his country and killed your mother.

"Do you know if Dave was being treated for PTSD?" She asked Frank.

"He wasn't. He'd never officially been diagnosed, but we all saw it in him after his last deployment. It got much worse after their daughter died. Apparently, he was self-medicating for a long time."

"Meaning?"

"He was drinking and taking oxys. That's what the toxicology report showed anyway. They found trace amounts of fentanyl. Who knows if he was doing anything else."

"Did they run Rebecca's blood?" she asked. "Anything there?"

"Yeah, they didn't find anything. Her BAC was under the legal limit and no drugs in her system."

Jules thought about that for a moment, wondering if it was good or bad for the poor woman.

"Do you know anything about the scene? Did she fight back?"

"I read the report. There weren't any signs of a struggle. She was sitting in a recliner in the living room and that's where they found her. They think she was probably dozing because she didn't pull away or try to deflect the gun. He shot her in the temple at close range, then shot himself where he stood and just dropped to the floor right there next to her. Kevin reported hearing two shots, one right after the other. He ran into the living room and found them like that."

They were quiet for a while, each in their own thoughts. Feinstein jumped into Jules' lap; something she'd never done before. Jules stroked the length of her and found it calming. The cat's warmth drove out the chill that had settled over her.

"Stay for dinner?" She invited. It was nearly 6:00 pm.

"No, that's okay. I know you just got home and you probably need some time."

"I unpacked while I was waiting for you. I'm fine. To be honest, I'd rather have your company than be alone with my thoughts right now."

"Okay, I'll stay, but let's just order in. I'm sure the last thing you want to do is cook."

She was grateful for the suggestion. She wasn't sure she could organize her thoughts enough to put together something that would pass as a meal.

By 8 o'clock, they'd finished dinner and cleaned up the Chinese takeout. Jules' fortune had read "Not everyday is good, but there is something good in every day." Frank's said "Take action. Make a change and never look back." As they shared their ancient wisdoms, Frank noticed the open bottle on the counter.

"Champagne?"

"Oh, I opened that when I got home earlier. I was going to celebrate my successful road trip."

Frank grabbed two juice glasses from the cupboard and poured them each a bit of the room temperature wine.

"A toast, to the good in every day!" He raised his glass.

"To taking action and never looking back!" She clinked her glass with his and they drank.

Jules poured them each another share.

"No, I'm good. I have to drive." Frank poured his into her glass.

"Do you?" Jules kissed him in a way she hadn't kissed anyone in a very long time. He had come here to sit with her grief, to cushion her fall. He could have texted her, or even left voicemail delivering this tragedy, but he knew that it would hit her hard and he'd wanted to be there while she processed it. She didn't want him to go, and he wanted to stay.

• • •

In her first moment of waking, Jules forgot that Frank was there. It had been years since anyone had slept in her bed, and hearing someone else breathing there next to her caught her off guard for a moment. Then she remembered the night before. At first, they'd been tentative, exploring the landscape of a new partner, checking in for confirmation. Permission. Then caution gave way to urgency. Jules was surprised by her body's response. Her desire had been dormant for so long, she'd wondered if it had fled with her youth. Now she knew it had simply been waiting for a worthy recipient.

"Morning." Frank threw his arm over her side and pulled her close.

"Mmm." She yawned and spooned into him. "Good morning. Did you sleep okay?"

"Great." He said as he kissed her shoulder.

Jules's phone rang, *I Wanna Dance with Somebody.*

"Hey, El."

"Hey, Boss. How was your trip?"

"It was good. I saw you left me a few messages. I forgot my charger and my phone was dead the entire time I was gone. Sorry."

"No, that's okay. I was calling to see if you heard the news about that murder/suicide in Troy?"

Jules had a momentary sense of two worlds colliding, one on the phone and one in her bed.

"Um, yeah. I did, just briefly. So sad." She leaned up on her left elbow, away from Frank.

"Tragic! The guy was a vet. There's a lot of history there. The family was really into weapons. We're going to stage a demonstration at the capital."

"Ellie, can I call you back? After I get a coffee?"

"Christ! I'm sorry, boss! I woke you up. You know me, the early worm."

"Bird." Jules corrected.

"What?"

"The early bird. Gets the worm."

"Hm. Okay. Talk to you later."

Jules rolled over.

"Ellie was my second at WWP." She explained. "They're taking up gun control as a new initiative."

"You didn't tell her you knew them." There was a question in his statement.

"I haven't told anyone that I've been learning to shoot. Or bought a gun. I don't want anyone to worry."

"Why are you? Learning to shoot, I mean? This is a pretty safe area."

"I just want to be able to protect myself. The older I get the more vulnerable I feel. I worry someone could see I'm alone and take advantage of that. Maybe follow me home. I want a fighting chance."

Frank nodded; he knew it happened. Strung out lowlifes with nothing to lose who needed to 'not be sick' as they referred to it. He'd seen elderly victims who fought back and lost. Her concern was legitimate.

"It's strange for me to feel this way. Once it started taking me a little longer to stand up, and I noticed I was driving slower, and taking more time to complete chores like shoveling the drive, I realized I could be an easy target. I lost my courage."

"Maybe that's a good thing." Frank rubbed her arm.

"Maybe. But I miss being fearless."

• • •

After Frank left, Jules thought about how she was going to walk this tightrope. She hadn't even considered that WWP might use this newsworthy tragedy to bring awareness to gun violence. It made perfect sense. There was bound to be a lot of media attention around the funeral tomorrow, but she wanted to go for Kevin's sake. He needed as many supporters around him in the coming days and weeks as he could get. How would she explain this to, well, to anyone really. She decided to just take her chances. She'd go to the visitation and let the chips fall where they may.

• • •

VIDEO DIARY ENTRY – August 9, 2022

"Hi. It's Tuesday the 9th. No Trump updates today. I want to talk about something else. A young man I met earlier this year, no, not a young man, a seven-year-old boy, became an orphan this week because of gun violence. His parents were both gun enthusiasts, and he was raised in that environment. Last Friday morning, his father, a vet who suffered from PTSD, shot and killed his mother, then killed himself. The boy was sleeping when he heard the shots and ran into the living room. He sat alone with his parents' bodies after calling 911. What do you think will become of him? Hmm?

"Do the research. Gun deaths are directly correlated to gun laws. You can look at it state by state, or country by country. The stricter the gun laws, the lower the gun deaths. The U.S. leads the world in gun deaths. This isn't a secret, and it's not a surprise.

"The Washington Post this year published the results of a study on gun violence in America. I pulled it up this morning to confirm the statistics. Every day 41 children lose a parent to gun violence! Every. Day. That's nearly 15,000 children every year. A small town. A college campus. Less than 3,000 people died on 9/11, and as a country we've been seeking to avenge those deaths ever since. At the same time, we make guns easier and easier to obtain. Why are we okay with this? Why?"

* * *

Jules pulled up to the funeral home and was struck by the turn out. Lots of cop cars. The ones that weren't cop cars looked like unmarked cars, except for the ones that looked like the cars and trucks of Republicans; American flag decals obscuring the rear views of pickups, anti-choice and homophobic bumper stickers (*It's Adam and Eve, not Adam and Steve*). Outside, a few smokers stood together near the entrance. Ladies' Night regulars.

Jules walked toward them and they each hugged her, everyone still shocked at what had transpired since they'd last seen each other less than a week ago.

"Is Kevin here?" She asked the women. She'd forgotten to look for Frank's car.

He had just gotten there, the ladies informed her, so she went inside to find him.

Inside, there were some people still wearing COVID masks. Widespread mask wearing had really diminished over the summer, but when groups gathered indoors people became more cautious. She'd stopped carrying them in her purse, but there was a box by the door. She slipped one on and walked down a thickly carpeted hallway.

She found the rooms where they were laid out. Rebecca was in the Serenity Salon and Dave was in the Harmony Room. There was an empty room between the two where more folding chairs were set up so that mourners could have neutral ground. Charlotte was in there with Kevin. Jules caught her eye and went in to join them.

"Kevin," Charlotte said as she approached, "Do you remember Jules?"

"Hi Kevin." Jules reached out and took the hand he offered. Someone had coached him, clearly. His eyes were red-rimmed, but he wasn't crying. He wore a navy suit with a light blue button-down shirt and a clip-on tie with a paisley design. Only his feet looked comfortable in his own sneakers. He'd had a haircut. He looked hollow as he met her eyes.

"Hi Kevin-who's-seven." She sing-songed, and pulled her mask away. "Now, do you remember me?"

"Oh yeah! Hi Lady-who's-eighty!" He sang back.

"Kevin, I just want you to know how sorry I am about your mom and dad." She held his eyes. He nodded and brought a crumpled Kleenex up to catch his tears. Jules grabbed a fresh one from a nearby box and handed it to him, tossing the used one in the trash.

Frank came across the room from Dave's side and joined them in the middle room. He gave her a peck on the cheek and she noticed Charlotte noticing.

"Are you doing okay, Champ?" Frank reached into his suit pocket and handed Kevin a small bottle of water. Kevin nodded as he screwed it open and took a sip. Some of the ladies from the range came in looking for Kevin and she stepped aside with Charlotte and Frank as they fawned over him.

"How's he doing?" She asked them.

"He seems okay right now. We picked him up from the fosters, and they were great. He's the only placement they have so he's getting all of their attention, which he needs right now." Charlotte reported.

"Are any of these people his family?" Jules glanced around the rooms.

"Nope. Nada. This is all friends and acquaintances. And cops."

There were lots of military uniforms in the mix. Jules saw a few kids, clearly friends from school or the neighborhood, come up to Kevin and give him some gum and a bag of Reese's Pieces. They seemed ready to entice him to run off to play, but the adults quashed that and moved them quickly through.

Someone from the funeral home came up and took Frank aside for a moment.

"They're here for the flag ceremony. I need to get the guys in here." He told Jules and Charlotte before going to round up the officers who had been first on the scene that night. He brought the four of them into the room and took them up front, posting Kevin between them. He leaned down and whispered something to the orphaned boy, hugged him close, then stepped away to join the rest of the mourners.

Three service members, in their razor-sharp dress blues and winter white gloves, Corfams gleaming, appeared at the entrance to the center room, and the bugler blew a call to order. Everyone fell silent and all of the men and women in uniform, police and military alike, snapped to attention and raised a salute in the direction of the three on death duty. Two of them held the flag that had been draped over Dave's coffin in the next room by its four corners. The third held the highly-polished, brass bugle in her right hand, and played a flawless rendition of Taps as the flag bearers performed the traditional folding ceremony, which ended with a field of blue stars in a perfect triangle, presented with the point toward the bereaved recipient. Kevin accepted the flag with two hands, one above and one beneath, exactly as it was handed to him. He was the only one in the room who wasn't weeping. The flag bearer saluted Kevin, then the three turned on their heels and marched out in formation.

The room sat in silence for a moment or two longer, everyone moved by the beauty and the sorrow of what they'd witnessed. No one feeling adequate to the task of helping this young boy find a way through. Frank stepped forward to stand with Kevin and thanked everyone for coming. He let them know that Kevin would be there for another few minutes if anyone wanted to speak with him. The crowd dispersed, some heading for Kevin, others finished with their mourning and heading into the summer sun, grateful to be on the fringes of this drama, and not in the leading roles.

Jules and Charlotte walked outside to wait for Frank and Kevin to wrap up. Jules had been there less than an hour and she felt wrung out.

"What's next for him?" Jules asked.

"I wish I knew. They've located some family members further upstate. Cousins of Rebecca with young kids. They don't want to take him. He has an uncle in Mass. Dave's brother. He's late-20s, unmarried. Seems like kind of a drifter. The best solution is going to be to find him a good foster placement and work toward adoption."

"Can he stay where he is now? That sounds like a good foster situation."

"It is, but they are meant to be an 'emergency' placement. A sort of stepping-stone to something permanent. That doesn't mean they can't agree to keep him, but they are usually a short-term solution."

"What do you think of them? Do they seem to like him?" Jules asked.

"They really do. They're a nice couple, nice house. Kevin has his own room and bathroom. He'll be able to start school there in a few weeks if he stays."

"Oh, right! I hadn't thought about that. It would be so good for him to start at a new school. Maybe he can leave some of his past behind."

"Hm. I can't decide if he'd be better off returning to something familiar. He's lost everything. Maybe it would be good for him to be in his own school with his old friends. It's hard to know."

Jules heard gravel crunching and turned to see Frank and Kevin heading their way. Kevin held the folded flag, now framed by a triangular glass and wooden case, under his arm.

"Okay, Lottie," Frank pointed his key fob and unlocked the truck. "Time to get the young man home." He stage whispered, "After ice cream!"

He opened the back door and Kevin climbed up into a child's booster seat. Jules recalled him standing, unrestrained, behind his father at the wheel, leaving the parking lot of the gun range. Kevin pulled the seat belt around himself and secured it with a click, his suit coat bunched up, the stiff shoulders swallowing him like a turtle shell. She started tearing up again and turned away to say goodbye to Frank and Charlotte.

"Do you want to come with us for ice cream?" Charlotte asked.

Jules followed them to an outside soft-serve stand and the four of them sat at a picnic table, competing to keep their cones from melting down their hands. Kevin had abandoned the suitcoat, shirt and tie, and looked like a regular kid in a tee shirt, but for the dress pants. The adults took their cues from him. He had some questions about the day. He was curious about the bugler and the song she played. He told them about the place he was living now. That he called his foster parents Megan and Mark, which was easy since they both started an 'M.' They asked him about school, explaining that where he lived now was a different school district, and that meant a new school and new teachers and new friends. He licked his cone as he considered this news.

"Well, I think that will be good." He pronounced, catching a chocolate river with his tongue. "Maybe nobody there will know I killed my sister."

• • •

In the days after the funeral, Jules watched the media coverage and was relieved not to have been captured by anyone on camera.

One station showed her car in the parking lot of the funeral home, but that was it. At least she could control the narrative.

She hadn't really had any time to debrief from her scouting trip. It had all been a whirlwind since she stepped through the front door on Monday. She'd spoken to Sally on Tuesday after Frank left, and they had made birthday plans for the 20th. Jules was turning 67. Of course, she hadn't shared anything about Frank or Kevin, and that was so hard. She was an open book with Sally and these were both momentous topics for discussion. She needed to talk to her best friend about them, and she was working on a story.

She thought it easiest to stick to the story she was telling everyone from her 'shooting life,' as she had come to think of it. Just let everyone know that she had been growing concerned about her safety as an older woman living alone and had decided to get a gun. She hadn't told them because she didn't want them to worry. It made perfect sense. Except it didn't. She was the most militant anti-gun person, and people closest to her wouldn't buy it. But where did that lead? What would they do? Try to talk her out of it? Think she was losing it? Okay, she could handle that. The best defense was a strong offense. Besides, coming clean about it now would let her drop a lot of the subterfuge.

In the week leading up to her birthday, she spoke with Jax and Ben, with Sally, with Ellie. She had avoided Ellie since she got home from Milwaukee. Hadn't called her back as she'd promised. She explained to all of them that she was becoming frightened. She never planned to use a gun, but if anyone ever broke in, she hoped to scare them off.

"Why don't you just install an alarm system, Mom?" Both boys asked the obvious. She told them she planned on it and had been researching them. It would be installed before the end of the year. Belt and suspenders, she said.

"First a snow blower, now a deadly weapon?" Ben was incredulous. "What the fuck, Mom?"

She could hear the concern in everyone's voices. They had to wonder if she was slipping. She kept her voice calm and rational as she talked about crime statistics she'd seen recently.

"In Saratoga County?" Jax prodded.

She reminded them that she'd used a gun before, and that she was pretty good with a bow in her youth. She shared her vulnerability. In the end, she was a grown woman making a choice for herself. She could withstand raised eyebrows to free herself from one set of deceits.

Sally understood immediately. In fact, she was relieved. The friends had shared their fears about losing the bravado of their younger selves. Sally knew that unwelcome helplessness. She had long worried about her bestie, alone at home and doing ride-share driving.

"Are you going to get a concealed carry permit? Then you can keep it in the car with you when you're working."

Jules' mind flashed to Kevin as a toddler, pulling a handgun from the glovebox.

"No. They have safeguards in place for drivers. I've never felt worried about that. It's just that sometimes I'll hear a noise at night, you know? Something that wakes me up. And suddenly my heart's pounding in my ears. And I'll lay there listening. Trying to convince myself it's just the cat, or just the house settling, or just the wind. I'll just feel less helpless if I can reach into my nightstand and pull out a bodyguard."

Ellie was the hardest. She answered on the first ring.

"Hey, Boss! How was your trip? How's Trish?" The two had met once when Trish had taken a train up from the city the year she came for the tree lighting at Rockefeller Center.

It felt like another lifetime since Jules had been in Milwaukee, but she'd only been home since Monday.

"Oh, yeah. Um. It was good. Trish seems like she's doing well, all things considered. And the concert was amazing. Very laid back vibe. Sorry I haven't called you back sooner."

"No worries, Boss. The reason I was calling was to see if you wanted to join a gun violence action in Albany on Sunday. We're pushing for stronger red flag laws in response to that guy who killed his wife. We'll meet at the capital and march down to the Governor's Mansion and back."

"OK, thanks for letting me know. Text me the details. I've been busy the last few days with some new developments in my life."

"I knew it!" Ellie sounded pleased with herself. "You sounded a little off when I called. Was someone there?"

"His name is Frank."

"OMIGOD! Who is he and where did you two meet? I need to get on that app."

"We met in real life, believe it or not. He's a retired cop from Schenectady. I met him in Troy." She was going to roll this out slowly.

"Hm. Doesn't seem like your type. A cop. How did you meet?"

"Well, this is another development in my life. I met him at Troy's Inside Gun Range."

"Troy's Inside Gun Range? That's where that couple went to shoot. The ones I was calling you about on Tuesday."

"Dave and Rebecca."

"Wait! You know them?! How?"

"I started going to the range in March to learn to shoot."

"A gun? YOU are shooting a GUN? Do you have a tooth loose??" Ellie's voice increased in volume and pitch.

"Screw." Jules said.

"Screw? What does that mean?" Another octave.

"It's a screw loose, not a tooth."

This had the desired effect of stopping Ellie from going off the register.

"Oh." She said. "Hm."

As Ellie considered this new information, Jules told her everything about her life at the gun range and why she had taken this up. She told her about ladies' night and Scotty's, and meeting Charlotte and Frank and all the shooting crowd. She told her about first meeting Kevin, and she gave Ellie the background on his baby sister. The media, in reporting on the murder/suicide over the past week, had spared Kevin, referring to him only as the couples' surviving son. They reported that Rebecca had been jailed for the accidental shooting death of her infant four years earlier. The truth without compounding the little boy's trauma. She told her about going to the service on Wednesday, and that she was meeting the ladies' night ladies that very evening, one week since the murder, to remember Rebecca.

"Are you still there?" El had been silent the entire time.

"Holy fuck, Boss! I don't know what to say. It's gonna take me some time. The only silver cloud I see is Frank." Jules didn't bother, smiling at the thought of Frank as a silver cloud.

"I know. Everyone is a little shocked. I'm sorry I didn't share it earlier."

"Hey, you're grown. You get to make those choices for yourself."

"Thanks, El."

"So, are you coming on Sunday? Or have you switched sides in this fight?"

"Ouch! Not at all. I'm even more convinced that our red flag laws need to be beefed up. Maybe Kevin could have been spared. Frank and I were just talking about this."

"Feel free to bring him along. I'll text you everything."

"Thank you, Ellie. I really appreciate your support in this."

"I don't know if I'd go that far. But I love you, Boss."

"Love you, El. Bye."

• • •

Gloria arranged the private get-together at Scotty's on Friday night. She asked everyone to bring a wrapped gift for Kevin, a book, and an item of clothing from a list with sizes and preferences. Jules learned that he wore boxers, not briefs, preferred black ankle socks over white, and needed a bathrobe and slippers. He was small for his age and was wearing size 5-6 now. They should buy him size 7 for the upcoming school year. She wished not to know these private little-boy details.

He liked Legos and Pokémon. Jules bought him some art supplies and a book about being the new kid in school. She went to Penney's and picked out some size 7 jeans and a Pokémon t-shirt.

At Scotty's, there were about 30 women, most of whom Jules had seen at TIGR at least a time or two in her six months of shooting. An 8x10 framed wedding photo of Rebecca was prominent on the buffet table. It was just head and shoulders, and she was smiling into her future, holding a bouquet of pale greenery and baby's breath with two white roses. She didn't wear a veil, and her wedding dress, the blush color that had become so popular with brides, was modest at the neckline. Jules had never seen her smiling in real life.

Next to the picture, standard bar fare was laid out for the group. Wings, nachos, chicken tenders. There were a few pitchers of beer on the table and some red solo cups. The mood among the group was mixed. Several of them were crying and hugging each other at one end of the bar, where a collage of pictures had been set up on a cork board. Jules realized that some of these women went way back with Rebecca, before she was married. Some even went to visit her in prison. They were all speaking openly now, about all of it. There was a lot of guilt.

Gloria was doing her best to lighten things up. She was telling a story about a camping trip that some of them had been on together where Rebecca's waders had filled up when she stepped in a hole in the river bottom. They had to go in and pull her drunk ass out and she lost one of her best fishing boots in the calamity. She took the other one home, filled it with potting soil and stuck it in the yard for her annuals. Ever since, she'd only wear bib waders in the river.

Charlotte and Frank arrived together and came over to join them. Frank greeted Jules with a kiss on the cheek again. He smelled like well-worn leather and something minty. His scent was still lingering in her bed and she'd caught herself breathing it in as she dozed off the night before. She saw a few of the ladies exchange looks, wondering.

Father and daughter had just come from seeing Kevin and gave the group an update. Things seemed as good as could be expected. The foster parents were doing great with him and he was settling into a routine there. Jules thought about the ability of a typical seven-year-old to manage such an enormous loss. The age of reason. That's what the literature said about that age. She imagined both that Kevin had figured a lot of things out a bit sooner than most, and that he would never be old enough to understand this.

The group talked about the change they'd seen in Rebecca when Dave came back from his deployment. He'd isolated her and kept her close. Their friendships had fallen off. Not just the way they do when you start a family of your own, naturally. The shift had been sudden and complete. Then when Angel died and Rebecca went to prison, she may as well have stayed there. Dave had her on lockdown for the rest of her short life. The telling got some of the women crying again, remembering another Rebecca.

Jules would never have imagined this depth to their relationships, given the distance, the coolness, that she'd witnessed between the small, insular family and this wider world. Rebecca was more animated to her in that moment than she had ever been in life.

The evening passed with more memories. The women seemed to be intentional in lifting her up, rather than engaging in petty gossip or speculation. Jules studied the pictures of Rebecca that had been pinned to the cork board. They were mostly from an earlier time, when she had been part of the social circle. Her face reflected a youth Jules hadn't known in her. In the few photos that included Dave, she appeared haggard and weary.

Frank came over as she was looking and touched her elbow as he stood next to her.

"How are you doing?" It wasn't a throw away question.

"It's been a long week," she turned toward him. "Remember the first time we met here and you asked me how my peacenik people would feel about me toting a gun?"

"I doubt I used the word peacenik, but yes. I remember."

"Well, I never told anyone I was doing this," she indicated the room at large.

"Oh. That's understandable, I think."

"Yes, but I've had to do a lot of explaining this week to a lot of people who love me. I swear, it's been like coming out." She glanced around the room and noticed people were starting to leave.

"I'm going to head home, Frank. Call me tomorrow if you can. I want to invite you to a gun violence action on Sunday."

"My 'coming out,' huh?" They shared a laugh and a hug. Jules said her goodbyes and called it a night.

• • •

The next few weeks were too busy to do much in service to her mission. When she had returned from Wisconsin, she'd found a flood of email from the 'Trump Café,' as she'd come to think of it. She had forgotten signing up for that list and now she had to manage that influx. She set up a file in her gmail and filtered all of that incoming mail from the listserv into it, unless the subject line contained a keyword from a short list she'd devised, any of which would sort those into her inbox so she'd see them immediately. These included 'Milwaukee,' 'Fiserv,' 'security,' 'New York City,' and 'Albany.' She added the last two in the hope that the RNC or the campaign would host an event nearby. If they did something in the city, it would be a chance for her to scout the security detail in a large metropolitan area. She could take the train in and make a day of it. Maybe grab a cheap last-minute ticket to something on or off Broadway. And of course, if they did anything in Albany, it would give her a chance to infiltrate the MAGA group close to home.

Her birthday was on the 20th, and she and Sally had lunch reservations at Barcelona. The six months between their birthdays was perfect. It meant they got to splurge twice a year at their favorite spot. Jules was looking forward to catching up and telling Sally about Frank. She had spent a lot of time with him since she got home.

He had stayed over again after the Red Flag Law protest march, which he'd joined with her the previous Sunday. It had been a perfect day for it. Some of his former cop buddies were on the security detail, and he'd stopped and introduced her a few times. They all knew about the Kevin situation and his involvement with it, and asked Frank how the boy was doing. Each time, they treated the conversation with the dignity it deserved.

She got to the restaurant ahead of Sally and started their birthday order with the server. When Sally arrived, Jules suddenly realized how long it had been between visits. The last time they'd seen each other was at the barbecue at Jules' house in the spring. Age was coming now like dog years, and gravity was winning its unending battle in even a few months. Jules imagined Sally saw the same in her.

"Oh my god, Jules! You look great!" Sally gushed, wrapping her up in a hug. "Maybe I'll take up shooting," she teased.

As they took their seats, Jules gave her a look.

"It's not the target practice, Sal," she gave her a cheshire cat smile.

"Oh my god! You're having sex!" Sally's enthusiasm was louder than it should have been.

"Shhhh!! Jesus." Jules noticed some of the other diners giving them the eye and she felt herself color. Blushing at 67 over a boy. And still planning an assassination. She couldn't decide if her life was completely fucked or completely perfect.

Their drinks came and over a long lunch she filled Sally in. When they had spoken on the phone about Jules' decision to learn to shoot, she hadn't gone any further than explaining her connection to Kevin and his family. That had been enough for that moment. She enjoyed sharing this unexpected development of Frank in her life. Sally approved on all fronts and was truly happy for her friend.

Before they parted ways, Jules opened the gift Sally brought. Inside a small, square box was a beautiful silver pendant, shaped like a small, smooth dogtag with a quarter-sized ring at one end and hanging from a silver chain. Jules put it on and it hung perfectly, just above her cleavage. It was simple and tasteful.

"Thank you, Sal! I love it."

"I found it on Etsy. If you pull hard on that ring," Jules moved her hand toward the ring, "NO!" Sally yelled, yanking her hand away.

"It's 140 decibels! They'd *definitely* throw us out of here!" She was whispering now, and both women were laughing at the disaster averted.

"If you won't get your concealed carry permit, at least wear this when you're driving, okay?"

"I will."

"Promise me! If you don't, I'm telling Ben and Jax that you're driving." She had Jules' hand in hers, and they swore a compact with their pinkies entwined.

• • •

Frank was picking her up for a birthday dinner that evening. They planned to go and see Kevin together first. Jules had a few things she'd picked up for him for the coming school year. Nothing that would excite him but things she knew he would need. A Pokémon backpack filled with school supplies, a 64-pack of Crayolas, some colored pencils, scissors, a few notebooks, and some construction paper. She was looking forward to seeing him and talking with his foster parents about his adjustment. It had been barely two weeks since his parents died. To Jules, it seemed such a long time. So much had happened in her life since. She wondered how it felt for Kevin.

VIDEO DIARY ENTRY – August 20, 2022

"Hi. It's August 20th, 2022. My birthday! I'm 67 today and having a lovely day. This morning, I read my horoscope and the characteristics of the Lioness. Here's what I found:

"As the fifth sign of the zodiac, fiery Leo is known for their ferocious and passionate attitude. Always one to embrace life to its fullest, the regal lion has a gregarious and jovial personality that others are often drawn to.

Their self-assured, easy confidence comes down to their ruling planet. Leos are ruled by the sun — making people want to bask in the warm, generous, giving light. Leos have a way of making others feel beautiful and special, which is why they tend to be social butterflies. Their charisma feels authentic.

Since Leo is a fixed sign, they tend to hew closely to their foundation — whether those are family bonds or values. It can take them a hot minute to change their minds. Always honest, this sign won't want to back down from a stance once it's been taken.

When angered, the lion's bark is just as big as their bite (you've seen "The Lion King," right?). Therefore, it's important to give Leos space to calm down before hooking them with matters that will irk or annoy them.

However, you will find that Leos are generally kind and tenderhearted, due to their sensitive natures. Yes, they can be a

*little dramatic and they do have a flair for over-the-top senti-
ments, but accept the whole package — and by doing so, enjoy
the attention that only a Leo can provide. Just remember to
give some attention back."*

*"If you are watching this, you will have witnessed my flair for the
dramatic. Over-the-top? Hardly.*

*"Anyway, it's been a few weeks since my last entry, on my way to
Milwaukee. That reconnaissance was a success. I learned a lot by being on the ground that I wouldn't get through Street View or Google
Earth. I don't think I'll need to make another trip between now and
the RNC in 2024.*

*"So much has happened in Trumpland this month. The FBI ex-
ecuted a search warrant for Mar-a-Lago a few weeks ago. Like most
things Trump-related, this is a first in our nation's history.*

*"They're looking for classified documents that belong in the Na-
tional Archives but may have made their way to his private residence.
It really is shocking. The level of indifference this former president has
displayed throughout his quote/unquote political career, is mind-boggling. His staff reports the White House was 'utter chaos' in the days
leading up to his eviction, and documents were stacked everywhere in
the Oval Office and outer Oval Office. The FBI indicated that there
may be documents related to our nuclear programs at his open-to-the-
public resort. Let that sink in.*

*"And then this week Liz Cheney lost her primary in Wyoming, so
she's out. That party has lost the only voice of reason crying into the
abyss. While I don't share her politics, I admire her bravery at this
moment in history. I just don't know what to make of the fact she
can't line up even a small cohort of 'patriots' to stand with her. Are
there really no more Republicans with the intellect and integrity to
stand against tyranny? It just doesn't add up. It can't be as simple as*

the desire to hold on to power. At what cost? I think there has to be more. Something we, the public, aren't privy to that is tying the hands of once honorable men and women. I just can't imagine what that could be. Maybe, by the time you hear my voice, some great truth will have been discovered.

"That's all for now. I want to go enjoy my birthday!"

And she did.

•   •   •

MASS SHOOTINGS IN THE US
August 2022 - 61 total

A mass shooting is any shooting where four or more people, other than the shooter, are killed or injured.

1. August 01, 2022 - Paramount, California - 7 injured
2. August 01, 2022 - Washington, District of Columbia - 2 dead, 2 injured
3. August 01, 2022 - Columbus, Ohio - 6 injured
4. August 02, 2022 - Albany, New York - 1 dead, 3 injured
5. August 02, 2022 - Orlando, Florida - 3 dead, 2 injured
6. August 03, 2022 - Panorama City, California - 4 injured
7. August 03, 2022 - Miami, Florida - 4 dead,
8. August 04, 2022 - Nashville, Tennessee - 4 injured
9. August 04, 2022 - Laurel, Nebraska - 2 dead, 2 injured
10. August 05, 2022 - Norfolk, Virginia - 4 injured
11. August 05, 2022 - Dayton, Ohio - 3 dead, 1 injured
12. August 05, 2022 - Milwaukee, Wisconsin - 2 dead, 2 injured
13. August 06, 2022 - Detroit, Michigan - 2 dead, 11 injured
14. August 06, 2022 - Detroit, Michigan - 1 dead, 3 injured
15. August 06, 2022 - Duquesne, Pennsylvania - 5 injured
16. August 07, 2022 - Cincinnati, Ohio - 4 injured

17. August 07, 2022 - Pittsburgh, Pennsylvania - 5 injured

18. August 07, 2022 - Atlanta, Georgia - 2 dead, 1

19. August 07, 2022 - Birmingham, Alabama - 2 dead, 2 injured

20. August 08, 2022 - Richmond, Virginia - 1 dead, 8 injured

21. August 10, 2022 - Winona, Mississippi - 1 dead, 7 injured

22. August 12, 2022 - Philadelphia, Pennsylvania - 1 dead, 3 injured

23. August 12, 2022 - Saint Louis, Missouri - 1 dead, 5 injured

24. August 13, 2022 - Cleveland, Ohio - 1 dead, 3 injured

25. August 13, 2022 - Raleigh, North Carolina - 5 dead,

26. August 13, 2022 - Atlanta, Georgia - 4 dead,

27. August 13, 2022 - Renton, Washington - 4 injured

28. August 14, 2022 - Phoenix, Arizona - 1 dead, 6 injured

29. August 14, 2022 - Chicago, Illinois - 2 dead, 2 injured

30. August 14, 2022 - Baltimore, Maryland - 9 injured

31. August 16, 2022 - Paw Paw, Michigan - 1 dead, 7 injured

32. August 16, 2022 - Philadelphia, Pennsylvania - 7 injured

33. August 16, 2022 - Memphis, Tennessee - 1 dead, 3 injured

34. August 17, 2022 - Chicago, Illinois - 4 injured

35. August 17, 2022 - Philadelphia, Pennsylvania - 1 dead, 5 injured

36. August 18, 2022 - Norfolk, Virginia - 5 injured

37. August 19, 2022 - Chicago, Illinois - 6 injured

38. August 19, 2022 - Chicago, Illinois - 1 dead, 3 injured

39. August 20, 2022 - Wilmington, Delaware - 4 injured

40. August 20, 2022 - Asheville, North Carolina - 1 dead, 3 injured

41. August 20, 2022 - Chicago, Illinois - 1 dead, 3 injured

42. August 23, 2022 - Philadelphia, Pennsylvania - 4 injured

43. August 24, 2022 - Chicago, Illinois - 4 dead,

44. August 24, 2022 - Washington, District of Columbia - 6 injured

45. August 24, 2022 - Milwaukee, Wisconsin - 4 injured

46.   August 24, 2022 - Baltimore, Maryland - 21 dead, 17 injured

47.   August 25, 2022 - Henderson, Kentucky - 5 injured

48.   August 25, 2022 - Spokane, Washington - 5 injured

49.   August 25, 2022 - Birmingham, Alabama - 1 dead, 3 injured

50.   August 27, 2022 - Brooklyn, New York - 4 injured

51.   August 27, 2022 - Spokane, Washington - 1 dead, 8 injured

52.   August 27, 2022 - Lexington, Kentucky - 1 dead, 3 injured

53.   August 28, 2022 - Clinton, Wisconsin - 1 dead, 3 injured

54.   August 28, 2022 - Bend, Oregon - 2 dead, 7 injured

55.   August 28, 2022 - Albany, New York - 5 injured

56.   August 28, 2022 - Denver, Colorado - 1 dead, 3 injured

57.   August 28, 2022 - Los Angeles, California - 1 dead, 5 injured

58.   August 28, 2022 - Detroit, Michigan - 7 injured

59.   August 28, 2022 - Phoenix, Arizona - 4 injured

60.   August 28, 2022 - Houston, Texas - 2 dead, 3 injured

61.   August 29, 2022 - Saint Louis (Jennings), Missouri - 1 dead, 4 injured

• • •

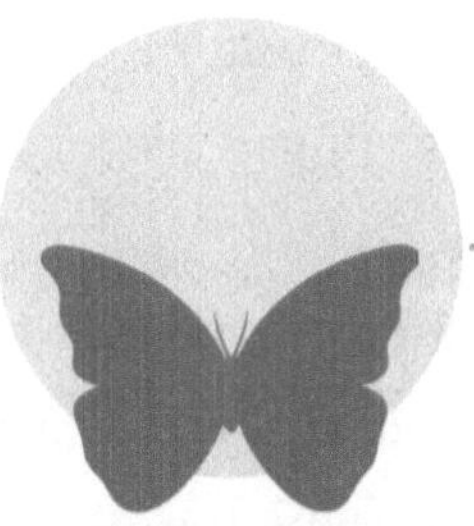

SEPTEMBER 2022

By the beginning of September, Jules and Frank were behaving more like a couple than simply friends with benefits. They were settling into a rhythm of knowing the details of one another's days, their likes and dislikes. They could order coffee for each other and get it right. Jules was conflicted about starting a relationship now, but she was trying to quiet that little voice in her head and give her heart free rein.

September was the first Ladies' Night since the murder/suicide, and Jules decided to get there early. It was strange how this tragedy pulled her closer to these women. She wanted to have time to check in with them and see how they were doing. Strangely, this group had been more intimately connected to the whole thing than anyone else, watching the family rise and fall.

There was already a good crowd when she arrived. Evidently they had the same idea. A need to validate what they had been through together and reconfigure the troupe with one woman down. She noticed a memorial sticker on someone's bumper, "Rebecca Homer – Angel born on August 5, 2022, R.I.P." It was pink and purple and showed a winged woman in white robes, looking skyward. Jesus, Jules thought.

Inside, the assembled group greeted her warmly. They'd spent a lot of time together in the past month. Between the funerals, memorials, and the march (which only a few attended) they started to know one another in a different way. The way that people who have brushed up against death together tend to do. Grief lays people bare.

Jules went to the sales counter and presented her long-awaited gun permit.

"It's official, everyone!" T.J. waved her credentials at the rest of the crowd. "Jules is a licensed gun owner!" A joking cheer went up.

"Yes, now please hand over my home security system." Jules teased, reaching her open hand across the counter.

T.J. turned to a wall full of purchases waiting for their buyers to become legal and pulled hers from its cubby.

"Here you go."

"Thanks, Teej. I'm excited to finally be able to work with my own gun. It might take a little getting used to."

She turned to the other shooters. "Ladies, I'm not sure I'll be buying tonight. I need to get the hang of my Glock." She showed it off like a new pair of shoes to the group.

After admiring Jules' purchase, they asked her about Kevin. Charlotte was there and she filled them in on what she knew, as well. She'd gone over a few times, with and without her dad. She raved about his foster parents, Mark and Megan. The first time she met the couple, she realized that she knew Mark from the senior residence facility where she worked. His grandmother, Gina Di-Marino, was a resident and Charlotte had chatted with him a few times when he had come to visit her. She remembers being taken by how involved he was, meeting with her to discuss Gina's dietary needs when his Gram was coming to spend a holiday weekend with him and Megan. Charlotte assured the group that Kevin had the perfect placement.

Jules went to the clipboard and chose her two range times for the evening. They were expecting a full house, according to TJ, so they were limited to two. Apparently, media coverage of the Homer family's tragedy was good for business. She noticed that there were already a handful of women whom she'd never seen before, and Charlotte didn't know them either.

The shooters were called onto the range. The first lane had been staged as a kind of memorial. Black crepe paper reminded Jules of crime scene tape. Two long guns formed an X in the space where Rebecca would have stood to participate. On the shelf, the letters R.I.P. stood in black cardboard. It looked like something from a Halloween display. Despite the macabre spectacle of it, Jules felt the void. Her stiffest competitor was gone.

Jules took the Bullseye prize for the evening. Despite having been away from the range for what felt like a very long time, she hadn't lost her touch completely. She planned to get back to her solo shooting sessions outside of Ladies' Night, a few times a month, to improve her consistency and accuracy.

Frank was waiting for her at the far end of the bar at Scotty's. She'd shot first and last, so a lot of the other women were already there when she walked in, waving her cash.

"I've got the next round!" They whooped and applauded her win as she crossed the room. Frank stood and kissed her, pulling out the barstool next to his. Charlotte wasn't coming. She had a date with someone she met on Tinder, and asked Jules to call in thirty minutes to give her the chance to bail if she needed an out. She'd set her alarm so she wouldn't forget and laid her phone on the bar.

"Remember when you mentioned going skeet shooting?" She asked.

"I do. Our first 'date.'"

"I think I want to give that a try. I just want to see what that's like and compare the two. I'm curious if my skills with a handgun will transfer."

"I'm sure they will. It's definitely a different experience, but if you're a prize-winning shot," he pointed to the cash she laid in front of her, "you'll probably get the gist of it pretty quick. When do you want to go?"

"Next week, maybe? After the holiday? Call and see what's available. Anything that works for you, I can make it work on my end."

"Okay. I'll call tomorrow. Now, spend some of that prize money." He motioned for the bartender and ordered a beer. Jules had a ginger ale with lime.

Sitting a little further along the bar were two women Jules had never seen before, who had both been at Ladies' Night. Jules raised her glass in their direction.

"Tradition is that the prize winner orders a round for the other ladies. Let Jimmy know that your next one is on me." She nodded at the bartender.

"Thank you!" They both responded.

"Was this your first time at the range?"

The woman closest to her replied.

"Yes, we were so shook about what happened!" Her friend nodded and Jules could see they were eager to talk. That primal urge to be part of the drama.

"Did you know them?"

"Yeah, they live in our neighborhood. We always thought something like this could happen. The way Dave abused that little boy was criminal!"

"Did you see it?" Jules asked.

"No, not directly, but you could feel it, know what I mean?" She looked at Jules, who nodded.

"Yeah," the other woman said, "if we saw them outside, Kevin kept his head down. No eye contact. And they weren't outside playin', throwin' the ball or anything like that. They were always workin'. Stackin' wood, workin' on cars, mowin' the lawn. That teeny little kid would spend entire afternoons pushin' wheelbarras full of grass clippings back to their compost pile. I never seen that kid with a smile on his face."

Jules imagined him with the big smile, the sense of humor, that she'd seen that first time she met him and Rebecca. And how uncomfortable Rebecca was with his playfulness. Jules didn't want to entertain the thought, but there it was, making a debut appearance on her frontal cortex. *Maybe Kevin would be better off without them. Maybe this was the best legacy his parents could leave for him.*

Her alarm went off to keep her from pursuing that line of thinking. It was time to call Charlotte to see if she needed saving. As it turned out, she didn't. She didn't answer the phone but texted back to say her date was going well, with a smiley face emoji.

• • •

The Memorial Day weekend followed Ladies' Night, and Kevin was scheduled to start the school year on Tuesday. Frank and

Jules were taking him out to dinner on Sunday. They took him to Friendly's, a favorite for most kids his age, which always included ice cream to finish the kid's meal. They were seated in a booth. She sat with Kevin on one side, and Frank sat across from them.

"You, you can sit on his side." Kevin stole a look at Frank.

"No, that's okay. I want to sit with you." Jules gave him a one-armed side hug, pulling him in.

"And when the ice cream comes, we're switching so I can sit with you." Frank declared, pointing a thumb into his chest.

"Well, we'll see about that!" All three of them laughed and color bloomed up the boy's neck and into his cheeks.

It was so good to see him opening up, and they talked about anything and everything within a 7-year-old's purview. He told them a lot about his new home. He really liked Mark and Megan, but Mark was the better cook. He had cooked asparagus one night, something Kevin had never eaten. It made his pee smell funny, he reported in a whisper, but it was really good! Megan had a vegetable garden and he had been a big help to her. They had lots of tomatoes and cucumbers, watermelon, and soon pumpkins would be ready. He told them that one of the bedrooms in the house had a crib and other baby stuff in it, because they wanted to have a baby. Well, they had a baby, but it died before they got to keep it. It was a girl so the crib room was all pink. He hoped the next one would be a girl, too, so they wouldn't have to change everything.

"Do babies go to the same place as grownups when they die?" He asked.

Jules was not prepared to answer that question for him, so she handed it over to Frank with her eyes. He smiled and took his time to reply.

"You know, Kevin, no one really knows. Nobody has ever come back from being dead to tell us what happens. But different people believe different things."

"Like heaven?"

"That's one. Some people think your soul, that very special part inside you that makes you exactly who you are? They think you get to bring your soul back to Earth and live in another body. And each time you come back, you learn more and more until you have nothing left to learn."

"Eww. What if I was a girl!" It was the worst thing that a 7-year-old boy could imagine, and it stopped him in his tracks. The ice cream came and proved to be much more interesting than dissecting death.

They dropped him at home and had a chance to chat with Megan and Mark. They were still considered the 'emergency placement' family, but they were all hoping to make it permanent. Not necessarily adoption, but at least permanent foster placement. His adjustment was going better than anyone had expected, and a move at this stage could be disastrous.

They wanted to let the couple know about the conversation they'd had with Kevin about death, just in case he raised it with them. He hadn't asked his foster parents anything about it. They'd been somewhat surprised by that and were relieved to hear he'd been able to begin to talk about it, even if only in theoretical terms. He did talk to them about his parents however, what they were like and that he missed them. He cried sometimes. They had a framed picture of Dave and Rebecca together, a wedding photo, in his bedroom, and Megan noticed that he turned it face down now and then. She asked them if they might be able to find individual photos of them that she could frame separately for him. They agreed.

They talked about the start of school coming up. Kevin's case worker, in consultation with them and working with his previous school's administration, decided it would be in his best interest to repeat first-grade. Learning new material at this stage could be too demanding, given the trauma he'd endured and the new school setting. And since he was small for his age, he wouldn't stand out in that age group. His first-grade experience at the previous school hadn't been exceptional. He'd missed a lot of school and was deemed to be socially immature among his peer group. Jules and Frank agreed it was a good decision for him to have a do-over. It could help him build self-esteem if he was a little ahead of the class, rather than trying to catch up. The last thing Kevin needed was a new disadvantage.

• • •

Frank had been able to book them some time at the Rod and Gun Club on Thursday afternoon. Jules was looking forward to trying a new skill. A moving target with a long gun was an entirely new challenge, and one that might prove valuable for her mission. But the thought of so many people wandering around with guns was unnerving. At TIGR everything was very restricted. Nobody came off that line with a loaded weapon.

"Do people ever wear bullet-proof vests at this kind of place?" She asked Frank on the way to the Club.

"Are you worried?"

"A little," she admitted. "I've gotten to the point where I feel fairly safe at the range. But this is different."

"I have seen people wearing vests, yes. I don't wear mine. And now New York has the most restrictive laws on body armor.

It just went into effect this summer. You couldn't buy a vest if you wanted to."

"Really? Why not?"

"They've limited ownership of it. Just cops, firefighters, military, that kind of thing. John Q. Public may not buy. Or Jane Q. Public for that matter." Frank laughed and reached over to rest his hand on her knee.

"Hm. That's so weird. I would have thought you could rent it at a place like a Gun Club, where there are so many firearms over such a big area." Jules made a mental note. She assumed you could buy the stuff at Walmart and was considering body armor for the mission. If she couldn't buy it in New York, she'd have to check the laws in neighboring states, or see if it was possible to buy online. It would give her a better chance of survival. If she decided she wanted that.

"Nope. But this place is what's called a 'cold club.' Weapons can only be loaded when you're on the line."

"Okay, well that's better than nothing, I guess." She still planned to keep her guard up.

When they arrived, Jules was surprised at the atmosphere of the place. It was a Rod & Gun Club, so it felt more sportsman-like and less like a concrete bunker. The parking lot was buzzing. Men and women in flannel, wearing utilitarian vests with pockets for ammo or lures or whatever was needed for their particular sport. People carried crossbows and compound bows. There was lots of green space and a few picnic pavilions that she could see spaced among some low-slung, shack-like structures. Colorful fishing and hunting advertising on the outside of the building made her think of Bass Pro Shops Outdoor World. This was going to be different.

Beyond the parking lot, Jules noticed that the shooters carried their weapons in a way that made her feel much more comfortable with the whole thing. They were sort of slung over their forearms, barrel down, with the action open and the butt of the gun under their arm. Less likelihood of an accident when you could see the gun like that.

"Is that what you mean about a cold club?" She asked Frank.

He looked to where she was pointing, across a field. "Yes, but also, all those guns have to be unloaded, not just open. Some people hate it because they have to load and unload all day, but it's safer."

Inside, they rented equipment for her and bought ammo. Frank had his own. They grabbed ear and eye protection and signed Jules up for the range safety instruction that all first-timers had to attend. There was an inside range where she would get to shoot a few rounds before going onto the field. As they waited for the instructor to arrive, Jules scanned the 'menu' of sporting options offered at the club. They also had Ladies' Nights there. Weekly during the season. She and Frank were going to do trap shooting. The other options included skeet, archery, and plinking.

"What's plinking?" She asked Frank.

"Oh, that's kind of fun. We should come back and do that one day. It's like, did you ever line up bottles in your backyard and try to knock them over with a rock or something?"

"My brother's had BB guns. They'd take my mom's empty bleach bottles and shoot at them because they were bigger targets." She laughed. "I haven't thought about that in years. And I had an archery set. My dad would set up a target on a hay bale in our backyard. I spent hours at it."

"On the plinking range, they have these big barrels, and you can set up bottles or whatever and try to shoot them off at different distances. It's fun. You can use a bow there, too."

"Okay," Jules said. "I guess we're coming back!"

After the safety lesson, they headed out to the trap field. She hadn't realized that it was structured like a competition. There were five shooting positions in an arc. Each shooter shot five targets, 'traps,' from each of the five positions. The best you could score was a 25. There was already a 'game' on the field, so she and Frank waited with some others who were there ahead of them. This gave her a lot of time to observe and try to figure out how not to embarrass herself.

The traps came from a single place, the 'shacks' she had noticed earlier, but they came from different angles every time. The shooters, all men, launched the targets by yelling 'pull!' when they were at the ready. Some in the group had a lot of experience, and it showed, but she was relieved to see some still learning. One in particular never hit a single trap.

She watched two who were more practiced. She noticed that they followed the trajectory of the flying clay with their guns, then shot slightly ahead of that, anticipating where their target would be when the bullet reached it. It really was an impressive skill.

The entire round took almost an hour. A few of the shooters had technical issues with their weapons, and something happened in the trap house that had slowed them down. When the group finally finished, the winner had scored 21, missing only four shots. The five moved off the range, congratulating the victor and paying off their friendly wagers.

Jules and Frank were up next. They shot with the two men and one woman who were ahead of them in line for the next round. As they'd observed the last game together, they had been chatting and commenting on stances and strategies. By the time she stepped up to take her first position, Jules' competitive streak had kicked in and she was ready to go. She told herself that the first round of five was her learning curve. She needed to get a feel for the gun, as well as the speed of the targets.

"Pull!" She yelled. Watching the clay in the air from behind the trigger was a completely different experience. She lost it in her sights momentarily and had to pull away to find it in the sky. She couldn't adjust quickly enough and her first shot fell well behind. She missed the second and third, but she was learning with each attempt. On the fourth try, she watched the clay fragment and fall.

"That's it!" She heard Frank encouraging her from behind.

She had to admit, it felt great.

"Pull!" Number five launched and she shot a little too early. But she was getting the swing of it.

They finished the game without any issues. Frank won with 24 points. He had downplayed his ability, and Jules appreciated that quality in a man. No bravado. As an ex-cop, she had expected him to be good, but not that good. Jules ended the day with 8 points, the lowest scorer in the group, but she was okay with that. She could only improve now that she had the hang of it. And she looked forward to honing the skill of sighting moving targets. It could serve her mission.

"What do you think? Would you come back?" They were sitting at a picnic table trying to cool off after the afternoon in the sun.

"Definitely. I enjoyed it. Plinking with a bow and arrow sounds like fun, too."

"I've never shot a bow. I'd be game, though." Frank admitted.

"Oh, I can show you a thing or two." She offered.

"You're on! This place is seasonal but they're usually open at least through Thanksgiving. Sometimes even into December. It just depends on the weather."

"I'm really looking forward to having everyone home for Thanksgiving this year. I know you're going away for Christmas with the girls. What about Thanksgiving? Do you have any plans?"

"Not yet. It will probably just be me and Charlotte at my place. We do pretty good together in the kitchen. She's a pie genius."

"Why don't you both come to my place? I'd love for everyone to meet." Jules invited. What was she thinking?

"Are you sure? I know you don't get to see them very often."

Jules had been struggling with this dilemma, and now she was going to have to decide. Was she going to work to keep Frank at arm's length? On the outside of her small circle? It felt wrong to intertwine everyone when she knew her time was limited. But maybe they would need one another, after Day Zero. Maybe they could help each other manage the unimaginable.

"Absolutely. I love having a full house these days. There are too many empty house days."

Frank reached across the table and held her hand.

"We'd love to, then. Thank you." His eyes met hers and held them briefly, acknowledging her admission.

After a moment, Jules broke the spell and asked, "Do you think we could have Kevin join us?"

"Hm, what a nice thought. I don't know. Would he be better off spending these first holidays with his foster family?" Frank wondered.

"Let's bring it up with them. My grandkids will be here and he might enjoy being with them. I've always wanted to need a 'kids table' at Thanksgiving."

"I'll call Mark and see what they think. It's a nice idea."

"If they agree, make sure it's what Kevin wants, too. He may not want to meet any more new people."

They grabbed a pizza on the way back to Jules' house and ate it, cold, in her bed.

• • •

Ellie called Jules to set up a time to get together for lunch. She'd met Frank at the Red Flag March, but she wanted to sit down with him and get to know him.

"I just had an idea." Jules offered. "Why don't we have lunch here next Sunday. I'll invite a few people. Sally hasn't met him at all, so I'll ask her and Hemmy. If the girls are interested, you can bring them as your plus-two. But I expect pre-teen girls have better plans on the weekend."

"Well, actually," she hesitated, "I'd rather bring my plus-one."

"Ohh, what? You're seeing someone? When did that happen?"

"His name is Reggie. We met on Tinder in July and started talking. We've only been dating for a few weeks. That's what I was calling you about when I caught you and Frank in a promising position." They both laughed.

"*Compromising* position. But it was pretty promising! Have the girls met him?"

"Yeah, he was over for dinner last week. They like him enough."

"Enough? What does that mean, El?"

"Enough to keep going, I guess. See where it leads. So, can I bring him Boss?"

"Of course! I can't wait to meet him. How about Sunday at noon. We can have brunch and I'll do mimosas and bloody marys."

"No offense but stick to the mimosas. I'll handle the big girl booze. Do you even know how to make those?"

"Tomato juice, gin, and a celery stick? How hard could it be?"

"Yeah, no. I volunteer. I'll bring everything but the blender. You have one, right?"

"A blender? Yes, I have a blender. For what?"

"Ay, Dios mio! Just make sure it's clean. See you Sunday!"

• • •

Jules was doing an easy brunch. A frittata, fruit salad, some homemade pecan rolls, a couscous with golden raisins, and some smoked salmon.

Ellie was the first to arrive. Reggie was tall, just over six feet. He towered over her, but they made a cute couple. Ellie introduced them and placed the grocery bag she brought in on the counter. It was overflowing with produce.

"Where's the blender, Boss. Oh, and I need a cutting board." Jules set up a workstation and Ellie got to work, while Reggie chatted with them both. He had a 17-year-old son who lived with his mother, Reggie's ex, in Raleigh. The pictures on his cell phone showed an athlete, tall like his father. In football gear taking a knee. In a tux on the way to prom, his date in a stunningly revealing gown that reminded Jules again how grateful she was to have had boys.

Sally, Hemmy, and Frank arrived together, and introduced themselves on the way in from their cars. They were chatting like old friends. The two men were sure they knew one another from somewhere and were playing the do-you-know game. Jules introduced everyone again and got started on some mimosas.

Ellie's cocktails were a huge hit. They looked like a meal in themselves; chilled shrimp on skewers emerging from the savory red-brown depths created from the host of ingredients that had been whirled up with ice in the vita-mix, and a wide array of add-ins from which to choose. Onions, olives, peppers (sweet and hot), baby corn, celery, cilantro, and several strengths of hot sauce.

It was nice that none of the men knew one another; it didn't put anyone at a disadvantage. Reggie was younger by two decades, but still fit seamlessly into the mix. Frank and Hemmy never decided how they knew one another.

The conversation turned to weapons when the inevitable topic of how they all met came up. She heard Hemmy and Sally's meeting story for the millionth time. Ellie and Reggie met on a dating app, now considered the 'old-fashioned' way. Jules shared that she and Frank had met through his daughter, Charlotte, who shot with Jules on Ladies' Night. She explained, for the benefit of Reggie mostly, that she hated guns, but had decided to get a weapon for self-defense.

That led Sally to ask about Kevin. Jules didn't feel comfortable sharing his story as cocktail party fodder, but she knew that wasn't Sally's intent. Everyone knew she and Frank were close to the situation. They gave a brief synopsis and let them know he was in a good foster home and doing well. No one prodded for more and they moved on to happier things.

The afternoon passed too quickly. Everyone had lots to talk about and there were no awkward silences among them. That would be impossible with Ellie and Sally in a group together. The two of them could host a stand-up routine, and Jules would pay good money to see it. She found herself gasping for breath a few times, her sides aching from laughter.

Frank stayed after everyone left to help Jules clean up.

"So," he teased, "do you think I passed?"

"Stop! It wasn't a test. I knew everyone would love you." She turned and wrapped her arms around him, leaning in and fitting perfectly into the space below his chin. He smelled so familiar now, that mix of spices that made up his cologne and summer still lingering on his skin.

He took her hand and led her to the bedroom. It was late afternoon; the sun was bright in the sky, but casting long September shadows. She closed the blinds before they undressed each other slowly, enjoying the luxury of time. Sex was something Jules hadn't expected again in her life. Even before she had devised her mission, she didn't see herself knowing that level of intimacy with anyone again. Frank was an unexpected gift. They were growing familiar with each other's bodies, their likes and dislikes, beyond the early uncertainties of new partners. The afternoon turned into evening, and they dozed, skin on skin, sated from the food and the booze and the sex. Especially the sex.

●　●　●

VIDEO DIARY ENTRY – September 21, 2022

"Hi everybody. September has been busy for me. I have been working on adding skills to my shooting repertoire. I'm learning how to shoot skeet. Moving-target practice with a rifle can only improve my consistency with a handgun. I'm trying to anticipate every scenario that I might face on Day Zero.

"This past Wednesday, the New York Attorney General, Letitia James, finally filed charges against Trump for his shady business

dealings, both overvaluing and undervaluing assets depending on the need. Ms. James has dubbed his actions "The Art of the Steal." I can only imagine she's had that one in her pocket since the investigation began 3 years ago. Can you blame her?

"Trump's response is of course an ad hominem attack, followed by cries of 'lies,' 'fake news,' and 'political stunt.' His M.O.

"I am watching all of these Trump cases coming through the justice system very closely. If he can be behind bars before the RNC in 2024, these video entries will never be seen. I am hoping and praying the system stops him, and planning the backup if it fails."

• • •

MASS SHOOTINGS IN THE US
September 2022 - 63 total

*A mass shooting is any shooting where four or more people,
other than the shooter, are killed or injured.*

1. September 02, 2022 - Fresno, California - 1 3 injured
2. September 02, 2022 - Minneapolis, Minnesota - 5 injured
3. September 02, 2022 - Brooklyn, New York - 11 injured
4. September 03, 2022 - Chico, California - 1 dead, 3 injured
5. September 03, 2022 - Yorkville, Illinois - 4 injured
6. September 03, 2022 - Birmingham, Alabama - 5 injured
7. September 03, 2022 - Capitol Heights, Maryland - 1 dead, 3 injured
8. September 04, 2022 - Norfolk, Virginia - 1 dead, 4 injured
9. September 04, 2022 - Charleston, South Carolina - 5 injured
10. September 04, 2022 - Fort Lauderdale, Florida - 1 dead, 4 injured
11. September 04, 2022 - Saint Paul, Minnesota - 6 injured
12. September 04, 2022 - Chicago, Illinois - 4 injured
13. September 05, 2022 - Hartwell, Georgia - 1 dead, 3 injured
14. September 05, 2022 - Kansas City, Missouri - 1 dead, 3 injured
15. September 05, 2022 - Cleveland, Ohio - 4 injured
16. September 05, 2022 - Saint Louis, Missouri - 5 injured

17. September 05, 2022 - Philadelphia, Pennsylvania - 3 dead, 3 injured

18. September 07, 2022 - Memphis, Tennessee - 4 injured

19. September 08, 2022 - Minneapolis, Minnesota - 2 dead, 3 injured

20. September 08, 2022 - Los Angeles, California - 2 dead, 2 injured

21. September 09, 2022 - Bronx, New York - 2 dead, 4 injured

22. September 09, 2022 - Elk Mills, Maryland - 5 injured

23. September 09, 2022 - Minneapolis, Minnesota - 4 injured

24. September 10, 2022 - Lexington, Kentucky - 5 injured

25. September 10, 2022 - Plainfield, Indiana - 5 injured

26. September 11, 2022 - Detroit, Michigan - 11 injured

27. September 11, 2022 - Santa Fe, New Mexico - 1 dead, 4 injured

28. September 11, 2022 - Grand Rapids, Michigan - 6 injured

29. September 11, 2022 - Durham, North Carolina - 1 dead, 3 injured

30. September 12, 2022 - Oklahoma City, Oklahoma - 4 injured

31. September 13, 2022 - Chicago, Illinois - 5 injured

32. September 13, 2022 - Oakland, California - 2 dead, 2 injured

33. September 14, 2022 - Milwaukee, Wisconsin - 6 injured

34. September 14, 2022 - Miami (North Miami), Florida - 4 injured

35. September 14, 2022 - Los Angeles, California - 1 dead, 3 injured

36. September 16, 2022 - Milwaukee, Wisconsin - 4 injured

37. September 17, 2022 - Blue Springs, Missouri - 4 dead,

38. September 17, 2022 - Minneapolis, Minnesota - 5 injured

39. September 18, 2022 - Corona (Queens), New York - 2 dead, 3 injured

40. September 18, 2022 - Kenosha, Wisconsin - 4 injured

41. September 18, 2022 - Las Vegas, Nevada - 1 dead, 3 injured

42. September 18, 2022 - Allendale, Michigan - 1 dead, 3 injured

43. September 19, 2022 - Swainsboro, Georgia - 2 dead, 3 injured

44. September 20, 2022 - Mount Vernon, New York - 2 dead, 2 injured

45. September 20, 2022 - Niles, Michigan - 4 injured

46. September 22, 2022 - Chicago, Illinois - 5 injured

47. September 23, 2022 - Castroville, California - 1 dead, 4 injured

48. September 24, 2022 - Columbus, Ohio - 1 dead, 5 injured

49. September 24, 2022 - Louisville, Georgia - 4 injured

50. September 25, 2022 - Harrisburg, Pennsylvania - 4 injured

51. September 25, 2022 - Hammond, Indiana - 4 dead,

52. September 27, 2022 - Corona (Queens), New York - 4 dead,

53. September 27, 2022 - New York, New York - 4 injured

54. September 27, 2022 - Goldsboro, North Carolina - 1 dead, 3 injured

55. September 27, 2022 - Jacksonville, Florida - 9 injured

56. September 27, 2022 - Philadelphia, Pennsylvania - 1 dead, 3 injured

57. September 28, 2022 - Oakland, California - 1 dead, 3 injured

58. September 28, 2022 - Columbus, Ohio - 2 dead, 9 injured

59. September 28, 2022 - Baltimore, Maryland - 5 injured

60. September 28, 2022 - Uniontown, Alabama - 9 injured

61. September 29, 2022 - Mc Gregor, Texas - 1 dead, 3 injured

62. September 30, 2022 - Tulsa, Oklahoma - 4 injured

63. September 30, 2022 - Marks, Mississippi - 1 dead, 6 injured

• • •

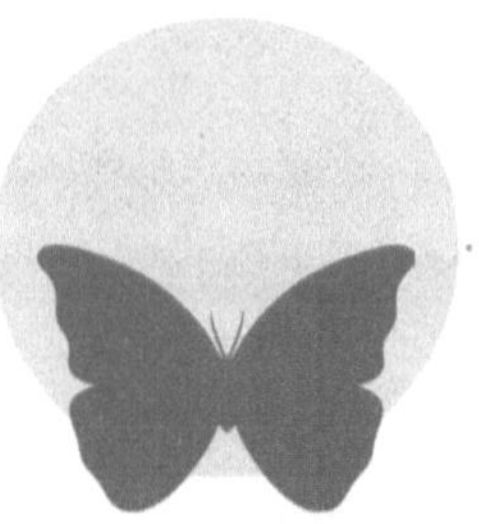

OCTOBER 2022

Ladies' Night was October 6th, and Jules looked forward to her first time on the range after the skeet. She had a whole new relationship with that part of her life. Since she was 'out' to her family and friends, she felt less anxious, no fear of being found out. And the vibe of the group had shifted as well. They were survivors of a shared catastrophe. They always would be.

She, Frank, and Charlotte had become the unofficial spokespeople for Kevin. They were the only ones who had spent any time with him since the funeral. In New York, foster placements were confidential. Frank's relationship to the family and to law enforcement, and the unique situation, meant that they had been given access where no one else would.

Jules greeted everyone she passed as she headed for the sign-up sheet. None of them were strangers to her anymore. She saw Charlotte chatting with a group across the room, and she joined them. The topic was, of course, Kevin. Charlotte looked relieved to see Jules, and she handed the conversation over like a baton in a relay race.

"Jules and my dad just saw him last week. How does he seem to you?"

Everyone shifted their attention.

"He's really doing so well. Beyond what I would have expected, under the circumstances. The foster family is amazing. And he has lots of additional supports in place. He has a case worker, and he gets grief counseling and psychiatric counseling services. He's making friends at the new school. The resiliency of kids always amazes me. I don't think you could ever put me back together if it had been me."

"I know. Poor little man. Does he need anything?" Gloria asked.

"No, he really doesn't right now. They are trying to minimize stimulation and keep him from getting overwhelmed. Trying to keep him on an even keel."

"I am praying the rosary for him every night. You let us know if he needs anything. You, too." She nodded toward Charlotte.

"We will."

"You know, we started a Gofundme page for him." Gloria told them, indicating the ladies in the room. "See those fliers?" Gloria pointed them out, at the cash registers, on the doors to the restrooms, in the waiting area. Pleas for donations for Kevin with a URL and a QR code.

"We set the goal at $5,000.00. We have almost $18,000.00 as of today. Whatever we raise is his."

Jules gasped. No words could squeeze past the goose egg that had formed in her throat. She felt the heat rise in her face and push out the tears that had been waiting there. She grabbed Gloria in a hug and Charlotte did the same.

T.J. called the first line-up and everyone dried their eyes. It was hard to sight a target through tears. Jules kept some tissues at hand just in case, but she shot well all evening. The skeet practice had been helpful, definitely, but it was the warmth and generosity of these women that was fueling her success. She took all of the prize money that night.

After buying the first round, where Jules offered up a toast in memory of Rebecca, she would donate the rest of her winnings to the fundraiser. The afterparty at Scotty's looked different since the tragedy, too. Everyone mingled rather than gathering in small groups of twos and threes around the space. They talked about the killings here and there. They sought out Frank for his confirmation of Charlotte's and Jules' reports, and maybe for a male's perspective on Kevin. They shared strategies for getting the word out about the Gofundme page. It had been shared on Facebook and Tik Tok and X many times. Some added the donation link to their social media as they stood at the bar. But they also talked about themselves, looking for common ground outside of the shooting range. Linked by a common grief, they sought out a deeper connection. People stayed later. There was more laughter.

• • •

By late-October, Eric had been on campus at SUNY Purchase for two months. He was enjoying the first freedom shared by so many freshmen. Every day was filled with promise. Anything was possible, and he loved the what-ifness of his existence.

He was studying a script for *The Book of Mormon*, hoping for the role of Elder McKinley, a part he was going out for in less than a week. If he could nail this, he could prove his chops right out of the gate in his first year. His phone vibrated and he reached for it on his pillow. He glanced at the display.

[Come hang! (Smileyfaceemoji)] – it was Cami.

[omw] – he texted back. He needed a break and Cami and her roommate, Jill, always had some good goss. He headed down the hall to their room and stuck his head in the open door.

"Hey!" It was just Cami.

"C'mon in."

He walked in a few steps and stretched out on Jill's ironic Hello Kitty bedding. "What's up? Are you going out?"

Cami was at the mirror working on her date-night hair and makeup, still in her robe from the shower.

"Jeff's coming by. We're going to Skip's to grab a bite. Come with us?" She invited. Jeff wasn't a student. He was a local guy that Cami, a sophomore, had started dating right at the end of last year. They'd picked up the romance again just a few weeks earlier.

"No thanks. I really need to work on my lines. But soon! I want to meet him. Maybe this weekend we can hang out. My audition will be over by then and I can chill."

"Cool. I think Jill will be free, too. Let's plan to meet at the Anchor around nine on Saturday. I'll tell Jill."

"I'll see if Kate wants to come, too. She might be going home for the weekend, but she'll probably come with if she's around."

Kate was Eric's roommate. They got along well so far, both from big Irish Catholic families. Hers was from Western NY, closer to Buffalo. Kate had no problem rooming with him. Of course, they'd had to address everything up front. The University wouldn't have matched them if Kate had objected. They were working hard to accommodate what was relatively new ground in modern campus life. Eric appreciated the effort. Kate joked that she was glad to have a roommate that didn't try to borrow her clothes!

"Sweet," Cami said. "I think we could all use a night out together. Dates encouraged. I don't want to be the only one there with a plus-one."

"Yeah, well, I'll be stag," he made a 'whatever' face at Cami in her mirror, "but I'll let Kate know."

Cami put down her eyeliner and picked a pair of earrings from a small, lacquered box that sat on her desk/vanity. "Have you asked anyone out yet, since we got here?"

"Nah, I'm just not there yet. I need to build my confidence." Eric confided, blushing.

"I get it. It must be hard. Like doing puberty all over again." They both groaned and giggled.

"Seriously, Eric, let me know if I can do anything to help. Like introduce you to someone, or, I don't know, help you make a tinder profile? Ooooh, that would be fun!"

"Dope." Laughing, he got up to leave just as a guy was coming through the door. "Hey, man! You must be Jeff? I'm Eric." He reached out a fist.

"Hey." Jeff tapped his fist reluctantly, looking confused.

"See ya, Cam! You guys have fun."

"Don't forget Saturday!" She called after him.

"See you then." Eric headed for his room.

"Who the hell is that?" Jeff demanded as he shut Cami's door behind him.

"He just told you! He's Eric. He lives down the hall."

"A guy? On this floor? I thought this was a chic floor?"

"Yeah, Eric's trans. He got assigned to the women's dorms for freshman year. You have to live on campus your first two years, and since he's early on in his transition, he wasn't ready to live on a guy floor. He's chill." She caught Jeff's face in the mirror as she adjusted her earrings. She didn't like what she saw.

"What?" She challenged.

"That's fucked up, is what. What's he doing in your room?"

"Just hanging out! Jesus, Jeff! What is your problem?"

"I just think it's all bullshit. Men are born to be men and women are born to be women."

Cami couldn't believe what she was hearing. It had never really come up before, and she was shocked at his homophobia.

"Are you kidding me with this? You know my brother is gay, right?" She realized he probably didn't know. And what did she know about him? She turned in her chair to face him and looked him in the eye. He suddenly seemed worth none of her effort.

"So you're going out with him on Saturday, huh?" Jeff didn't know when to stop.

"Yes. Yes, I am." She stood and walked to her door, opening it wide. "Who I'm not going out with is you. Ever. Bye, Jeff."

"C'mon, Cami! Is this guy really worth it?" Jeff's face was red with some misplaced emotion.

"Oh my god! This has nothing to do with any guy but you!" She stepped out into the hallway and raised her voice, "Just get out!" She crossed her arms over her chest and stared him down. A few residents stepped into the hallway, hearing the shouting, and looked Cami's way. Safety in numbers.

Jeff started toward the door, anger propelling him. He punched the door as he passed it and the sound was harsh, startling. Cami flinched and moved away from him.

"Cam, want me to call security?" Someone yelled down the hall.

"Fuck you!" He shouted at everyone and disappeared down a stairwell.

Cami leaned her back against the wall and slid down to the floor, taking deep breaths. She was shaken, but she had dodged a bullet. Maya Angelou's words came to her. When someone shows you who they are, believe them the first time. Amen!

• • •

When Eric got back to his room, he put the Saturday night plan on his calendar, then started working on the script again. This was a musical, so he'd have to sing and dance as well. He felt completely confident on that end of things, so he was focused on his lines and delivery at this stage.

He heard Kate coming down the hall, calling out 'hey!' and 'what's up?' as she passed other rooms. She came in carrying a small bag of snacks from the bookstore. Some trail mix, chips, a few yogurts, and her favorites, plain m&ms, the big bag.

"How's it hangin'?" She joked.

"It's not, yet." Eric's standard reply. "Hey, we're going to the Anchor Saturday at nine. Are you in? I told Cami you might be going home."

"Yeah, I'll go. I decided not to go home this weekend. I'm going to wait until Thanksgiving. Who's coming?"

"Cami and Jeff. Us and Jill. Plus dates if you want. I just met Jeff, by the way."

"Oh, you hadn't met him? I'm not a fan. What did you think?"

"Nothing really," Eric said, "He was coming in as I was leaving. He's hot."

"Yeah he is!" She agreed, "But I saw him off campus a few weeks ago? Guess what he was wearing?"

Eric closed his eyes, considering the options. "Wife beater?" He guessed.

"Worse. A fucking MAGA hat!"

"Jesus! Did you tell Cami?" Eric asked.

"I don't know her that well. You're closer to her. I figured she must know, right? I mean, they've been together long enough. You'd know something like that, right?"

Eric seriously doubted Cami would date some Cro-Magnon asshat, no matter how hot he was. Her brother was gay. Not that that meant anything, but he doubted Cami knew this guy was a Trumper.

"They were going out tonight. I'll talk to her tomorrow." He grabbed his phone and texted Cam –*[bfast tm?]* – ping – *[def]* was her reply.

"Will you run some lines with me?" He asked Kate.

• • •

Eric was tapped. He had the lines and delivery down, and now he was just over-thinking it. Kate had left an hour ago, telling him he had it.

"You're getting this part." She assured him. "No question."

He believed it was possible. He wanted it so bad. The idea of playing a repressed gay Mormon missionary tickled him. And he loved the costume. White shirt, skinny tie, neat trousers, nametag.

It was almost 8 and Eric was getting hungry. He decided to walk to a place just off campus for a burger and a beer, if he could get served. It was a large chain place that was known for its wings. The kids called it trip dubs. Walking over, he kept running through the script, memorizing cues.

It was busy for a weeknight, but no wait. There were a few parties ahead of him waiting to get seated, so he took his place in the line and glanced around. This was a fairly popular hangout for students and he expected to see some people he knew. He didn't expect to see Jeff at the bar. Cami said they were going to Skip's. She wasn't with him as far as Eric could tell. Hmm.

The hostess came and seated him at a table in the middle of the floor. He was going to text Cami and see what was going on, when he realized he didn't have his phone. It had taken some getting used to, not carrying a purse and putting everything in your pockets. He hadn't quite mastered that yet. He hated the weight of things in his pockets. Crap! This also meant he couldn't pay his bill without his apple pay.

"Sorry!" He said to the server approaching his table with her ipad, "I've got to run back and get my phone. I don't have any cash."

"No problem!" She replied brightly, full smile. "I'll see you when you get back!" She picked up the menus and walked away.

At the bar, Jeff, three beers and a Jamo into the evening, caught sight of Eric getting up from a table. He was alone.

Eric headed back outside into the dark. Luckily it wasn't freezing. Compliments of global warming, Fall had been mild so far. The walk would be pleasant, if inconvenient.

A block from the restaurant, he heard quick footsteps coming up behind him. He had just started to turn when he went down. Tackled, broadsided, from what felt like a freight train.

"You fucking faggot!"

The right side of Eric's head bounced off the pavement. The surprise attack gave him no time to brace for impact. Now that he was on the ground, he pulled up his knees and covered his face with his hands. He thought of the roly-polys they used to see in the yard when they were kids. Now he understood their instinct. He was being kicked repeatedly, everywhere. The back of his head, his kidneys, his stomach, his face. He tried his best to fend them off or protect his exposures. He looked up between his palms and realized this was Jeff. Motherfucking MAGA hat Jeff. A shoe found an opening and his nose exploded. Then, nothing.

. . .

Jules rounded the corner into the I.C.U. and almost ran into Sally's grandson, Patrick headed in the other direction. His eyes were red and his face was puffy and swollen with grief.

"Where is he?" Jules threw her arms around him and squeezed briefly, then headed towards the room where he'd pointed and stood just inside the door.

Everyone was there, but it was dead quiet aside from the machines. The drama unfolding here wasn't scripted even though Claire/Eric was at the center of it. He lay, unconscious, in the bed, a tube snaked from his mouth. His head was bandaged, and his face was plum-colored and ripe.

Sally turned around from the bedside when she heard someone come in. She looked wrecked. When she saw it was Jules, she dropped Hemmy's hand and reached the door in two strides. They hugged fiercely, quietly, and walked out into the hallway arm in arm.

"Can you step away for a minute, Sal? We can get a coffee?"

Sally nodded, "But, I need to pee first."

Jules scanned the hall and found the sign, "Over here." She led her friend down the hall.

While she waited, she found a coffee pot set up for visitors near the nurse's station and paid for two cups, dropping the money in a 'donations welcomed' basket on the table. She added cream and sugar for Sally and caught up to her just as she was coming out of the ladies.

"It's not very hot." Jules apologized as she handed over the paper cup.

"That's okay. I can drink it quicker that way."

They moved further away from the room and found a row of orange plastic bucket chairs down another hall. They sat in silence for a moment, sipping their coffee.

"So how is he doing? What are the doctors saying?" Jules turned to Sally.

"They're confident that he'll survive this, now that he's stabilized. But they're not sure about his brain function. They can't tell yet how much damage there is."

Jules absorbed that news. There was nothing more to ask. Nothing to say about Eric's condition.

"Have they charged anyone? Do they have any leads?"

"No. No witnesses have come forward, either. Yet. They're checking cameras, asking for information, canvassing the area near where they found him."

"Are they treating it like a hate crime? That's what it is."

"Those fuckers!" Sally broke down, tears fell into her coffee cup. Her hands began to shake, and Jules took the cup and placed it on the floor along with her own, then gathered Sally close.

"Okay. Okay." Jules rubbed her back, trying to convey a comfort she didn't feel.

They sat together for a few more minutes while Sally wept the tears she had and steeled herself to go back into Eric's room with her family.

There was contempt in her eyes as she leaned into Jules and whispered, "This is on motherfucking DeSantis. I lay this violence at the doorstep of his 'don't say gay' bullshit."

"I know. The lunatics are taking over the asylum. But just try to be with Eric right now. Surround him with positive energy. Have you talked to his roommate?"

"She called Erin to find out how it's going. They weren't together that night and she doesn't know who Eric was with. Or she's not saying, anyway."

"I'm so sorry, Sal. I know this is your worst nightmare."

"I wish it was a nightmare." Sally stood. "Walk back with me."

As they headed back toward Eric's room, Jules asked, "What can I do? What do you need? Anything."

"Yes, there is one thing." Sally glanced around and lowered her voice, "Eric didn't have his phone with him when they found him. The roommate told Erin it's still in her dorm. I know it's a drive, but could you go get it? And his laptop? We want to see them before they get confiscated."

"I can be back by dinner. Text me the roommate's information. And don't let her know I'm coming. Just in case." Jules headed toward the elevator.

• • •

Jules stopped for gas and a pee along 91, about an hour out of Albany. She checked her phone and saw the info Sally had sent. Eric's dorm info and roommate's name, Kate. Jules didn't have any reason to suspect her of anything, but she didn't have any reason not to, either. She was not giving anyone a free pass. Someone had attacked Eric. They were going to find out who.

Back on the highway, she called Frank to fill him in and get his help. They talked about the hate crime designation, assuming this was not a random act, but violence motivated by Eric's status as a trans man. She told him about Eric's precarious condition. They agreed to meet at the hospital in the evening. Frank wanted to be helpful to the family if he could.

Once Jules reached the campus, she found a parking spot curbside near the dorm. She wasn't sure if it was a legal spot, there weren't any meters, but she wouldn't be long. It was a weekday and there were kids everywhere. Still wearing summer clothes despite the calendar, keeping as much skin on display for as long as possible. She got to the dorm at the same time as two young women who held the door for her. It was easy getting into secure places when you looked like everyone's grandma.

She took the elevator up to the 4th floor and found Eric's room empty, door open. On his desk was the framed family photo from the party they'd had the weekend before he'd left for school. The last send off in a large family. Launched. Jules grabbed the laptop, covered in theater stickers, from that desk.

His side of the room was Broadway playbills and show posters, artfully arranged. It was vibrant and busy, but neat and tidy. Bed made, clothes hung in the small open closet on his side of the room. A plastic caddy held his deodorant and toothpaste, toothbrush, razor, and body spray. Another held over the counter meds and first-aid stuff, Tylenol, Band-Aids, Nyquil, Neosporin. Jules could picture Eric and his mom at Walmart making that list, anticipating every need of his first year away from home. But Walmart didn't have anything that could make this catastrophe better.

Kate came through the door and stopped hard, "Omigod!" She yelled, seeing a stranger in her room. She backed toward the door.

"I'm so sorry, Kate!" She reached out a hand to shake, "I'm Jules Campbell. A friend of Erics' family. The door was open." She explained.

"Jesus! You scared me." She sat on her bed, calming herself. "It's been crazy here since last night. Police talking to everyone. Not campus security, real police! It's so scary. I can't believe this happened! How is he? Is he okay? I heard they found him unconscious over near trip dubs." She was clearly shaken.

"I just came from the hospital. He's at Albany Med. They airlifted him last night. He's on a ventilator and hasn't regained consciousness yet."

"Oh my god!" Kate started to cry. "I called his mom but she's obviously a wreck. I couldn't get much from her. I just asked her to tell Eric we're all thinking of him. That we love him."

That did Jules in. She had come this far and kept it together, not even losing it when she saw Eric in that bed! But hearing the real love and concern in Kate's voice just flipped a switch. She dropped onto Eric's bed and began to sob, in sorrow and in hope, and in gratefulness for the young women who had embraced Eric on his journey. She had forgotten how quickly the young love. Kate came to sit beside her and handed her a Kleenex.

"Thank you, Kate. This is the first time I've cried, and I needed it. Eric is like a grandson to me." The two women hugged, then sat quietly for a minute or two.

"They feel confident that he'll survive. They just aren't sure about brain function yet. It's going to be a long recovery process." Jules stood up from Eric's bed and noticed that his cell phone had slid down from under the pillow when she sat down. She picked it up to take with her.

"Do you know anything about where he was last night?" She asked Kate.

"I left before he did. We were running some lines for a while, then I went to get dinner and hit the library. When I was walking home I heard the sirens. I had no idea they were for Eric! I just can't believe this."

"Is there anyone he's had trouble with? Giving him a hard time?" Jules asked.

"No, nothing like that. He's been having a great year as far as I could tell. He was so psyched about *The Book of Mormon*."

Jules gave her a stunned look, "The Book of Mormon? Was he exploring that?"

"Yeah, his audition is tomorrow. Was."

"OH! The musical. Christ. I can't even think straight. That makes sense. I thought you were talking about the religion." Jules felt churned. They didn't laugh; it wasn't funny.

"Is there anything I should take to him?" Jules glanced around the room. "Anything that is special to him that I could leave with him in the hospital?"

Kate was on her feet. Reaching to a shelf above Eric's desk she grabbed a Barbie-sized doll in braids, a blue-gingham pinafore, and ruby red slippers.

"Bring him Dorothy."

Jules held back her tears and hugged Kate one more time.

"OK, listen, Kate. If you hear anything, will you let me know? I mean anything."

"Of course. Text me now so I have your number." She held her phone out to Jules and Jules typed Kate's number into her phone, texting – [*Jules Campbell*].

"We're going to get whoever did this to him, Kate. They're going to face the music."

· · ·

Jules got back to the hospital in the early evening. Sally's whole family was still there. The doctors had removed the respirator and Eric was breathing on his own. He was still not conscious, but only because they were keeping him in a medically induced coma, hoping to minimize brain damage.

Sally followed Jules back to the plastic bucket chairs, where it felt like they'd sat years ago instead of just that morning. Sally looked worn out but better than this morning. Jules handed over the phone and the laptop. She pulled Dorothy from her purse.

"Kate said he'd want Dorothy. It can't hurt."

"Ohh!" Her eyes filled with tears. "Claire loved the Wizard of Oz! I didn't know she'd kept this. I took her to see it on stage one year at a local theater. I got this for her that Christmas." Sally put the doll down and turned to Jules.

"What did you find out? Did Kate know anything?"

"No. She said everyone loves Eric and he was having a great year. He had an audition lined up for tomorrow that he was really excited about. Sally, Kate is a real sweetheart. I think we can trust her."

"I trust you. Did you check out Eric's phone?" Sally held it up.

"No, I wanted to leave it to you. I don't even know if it's charged."

Sally touched the screen. It lit up with a choice between a 4-digit code or fingerprint access. Sally tried Eric's birth month and day. Nothing. Sally thought for a moment and tried 0220. Access granted.

"What's that number?" Jules asked.

"Eric's coming out day. He calls it his second birthday."

Sally opened his text messages. There were a bunch from worried friends all day long. Sally scrolled. Looking for messages from before the attack.

There were several between Eric and a few others about the auditions that day. Just making plans with them to meet before and run through a few things. Those were all between 6:30 and 8:00ish. Then Kate was texting him from 8:57 – *[dude]* -- 9:08 – *[dude wya]* – 9:53 – *[Im gunna crash door is unlocked gn! (Sleep emoji)]*. Then nothing until this morning. Okay, before 6:30pm yesterday, Sally saw a note from Cami. Eric said he was going to hang with her. And then not much later he texted her to join him for breakfast the next day.

"Here!" She pointed it out to Jules. "This Cami was probably the last person he saw before Kate. We need to talk to her. What should we do?"

"Why don't we just text her from Eric's phone?"

Sally looked relieved and terrified, "What should we say?"

After a moment, "Let's just text 'hey' and see what happens."

Sally typed in – *[hey]* and hit send. They waited, but not long.
[OMG E YOU OK!!!]

"What should we do now?" Sally was completely out of her element.

"Just tell her who you are. Try to find out if she knows anything."

[This is Eric's Grandma, Sally. I'm at the hospital with Eric and the family. I know you guys hung out last night and I'm trying to find out if you know anything about what happened?] – send

The wait was interminable.

[I'm so sorry! Please let Eric know we are all sending love. He came to hang out with me for a few yesterday in my room. He was fine! I asked him to come get a bite with us but he was studying some script. We made plans to go out on Sat. night instead] - send

The second she hit send, Jeff's fury over Eric loomed up in her mind. She hadn't even connected those dots. She'd been so distraught since yesterday, first over Jeff (mostly at herself for not seeing him sooner), then over Eric. There's no way they could be related. Right?

Jules said to Sally, "Who's 'us.' She says come and get a bite with us. Was someone else in her room?"

[Who else was going to get a bite?] – send

Cami went cold from head to toe. It felt like all of her blood had just evaporated, leaving her freezing. She obviously wouldn't protect Jeff, but if Eric was at death's door because of him? And she had put Eric in Jeff's crosshairs? She felt like she was going to puke.

[Jeff McEvers. He's not a student. He lives in town.] – send

Sally and Jules both read.

"Ask her if the police have interviewed her? My guess is no."

Sally typed, *[Have you spoken to the police?]* – send

[No] – send

"She should call the police and give a statement. Tell them she saw Eric in the time leading up to this and give them any information she has." Jules directed.

[Please call the police and give them this information. It could be useful. Thank you for your help. I'll give Eric your best.] – send

[heart emoji] – send

• • •

Cami walked down to Eric and Kate's room. The door was open and Kate was at her desk.

"Knock, knock." She said as she walked in. Kate startled.

"Jeeze. I'm so jumpy! C'mon in." She pointed at her bed, inviting Cami to sit.

"I was just texting with Eric's grandma. They asked me to call the police and give a statement."

"Why?" Kate asked.

"Because I was one of the last people to see Eric besides you. They think it might be helpful to the investigation."

"Makes sense. They interviewed me this morning. I don't think I was any help. And I think they talked to a few others on our hall who were around at the time. Have you called them?"

"Not yet. I wanted to talk to you about something first. It's kind of weird but it came to me when I was texting his grandma."

"Ok, what?" Kate closed her laptop, giving Cami her full attention.

"So, when Eric was in my room yesterday, Jeff came in. We were planning to get dinner. I asked Eric to come with us, but he wanted to work on his lines."

"Right. Eric told me they'd met. And that we were all going to The Anchor Saturday." Kate confirmed.

"When Eric left my room? Jeff went ballistic! All this typical macho bullshit. 'Who's that guy? Why is he in your room?' When I told him who Eric was, it went next level. 'Men are men' homophobic trash." Cami looked at Kate and saw that they were thinking the same thing.

"Christ, Cami! What did you say?"

"I told him to leave. He slammed his fist into my door on the way out. We're done. I can't believe it took me this long to see it!" Cami shook her head, embarrassed at her hot guy blindness.

Kate sat with her in silence for a moment, knowing that what she was going to share would be another blow.

"So, when Eric told me he had met Jeff, I shared something with him that I probably should have told you sooner. I don't know why I didn't. I just felt like it wasn't really my business? Like, maybe you already knew? I don't like to make assumptions about people's politics."

"What is it?" Cami pressed.

"I saw Jeff in a bar off campus a few weeks ago." Kate began. "He was wearing a MAGA hat."

Cami was quiet, trying to put the pieces together. Her breath started to come in little gasps, and she dropped her head to her knees, arms reaching toward the floor, seeking calm. Kate waited. After a time, Cami sat up and drew a few deep breaths.

"I think it was him," she decided. "I think Jeff did this to Eric. And I introduced them! Ohmigod!" Cami moaned and held her stomach, tears starting.

"It's not your fault, Cam. Don't even go there. Jesus, how could you have ever imagined anything like this? And we don't know for sure. We're just spit balling. Jeff could have nothing to do with this. He could be just a run of the mill pig."

"Come with me, Kate? I need to go talk to the police."

Kate opened a drawer in her nightstand and pulled out a small card.

"This is the Detective who talked to me this morning. She left her card and said to call if anything came up" She glanced at the card, "Detective Rodriguez. Maria Rodriguez. Let's call and let her know we want to meet."

"Good. Go ahead and call."

Kate punched in the officer's number on her cell.

"Detective Rodriguez." The officer answered in a flat, matter-of-fact tone on the second ring.

"Oh, hi. This is Kate Collins. Eric's roommate? You came to my dorm this morning?"

"Sure, hi Kate. How can I help you?" Her voice was softer now, a quick shift from civil servant to conciliator.

"I'm here with one of our dorm mates, Cami. She saw Eric last night and wants to talk to you. We're going to come over, but I wanted to make sure you were there first."

"Thank you for reaching out, Kate. I'm at the station. I can send a car to pick you up. They should be there in about ten minutes."

"Okay. Thank you." Kate clicked off.

• • •

Erin's cell buzzed in her pocket. She had turned the ringer off when she was in Eric's room to avoid startling anyone. They were all at the ends of their ropes. The display indicated it was Detective Rodriguez. The two had spoken earlier in the day regarding the investigation into her son's attack. Erin walked into the hallway to take the call.

"Hi, Detective." She answered on the fourth ring.

"Mrs. Evans?" She asked.

"Yes, it's me. Do you have news?"

"I do. How is Eric doing?" Rodriguez inquired.

"Better. Thank you so much for asking. He's breathing on his own and they are slowly bringing him out of the coma. We expect to have him completely off the propofol later today. The EEG is giving us hope. There seems to be strong brain activity."

"That's so good to hear! I hope that trajectory continues. He's going to be an important witness. On our end, we've made an arrest. A local man named Jeff McEvers. He met Eric the night of the attack in the room of one of Eric's dormmates."

"Oh my god! Has he confessed?"

"No, not yet. But we have videotape and some pretty damning statements from several of his friends and acquaintances. And if Eric can identify McEvers as the man who attacked him, it will be pretty airtight."

"Ok." Erin took a deep breath as she absorbed this news. "Are they treating this like a hate crime? You know it was. I don't want this kid getting a slap on the wrist as if it was just a random street fight."

"Given everything we have on him, I think the DA will charge it as a hate crime. First degree assault, which is what we've got him with, is a Class B felony. The hate crime designation won't affect that, still a Class B, but it will affect sentencing."

"Ok. That's something. What happens now?"

"He'll be arraigned tomorrow and then we'll know for sure. Someone will call you after the arraignment to let you know what's going on. If Eric regains consciousness, please call me as soon as possible. I'll text you my cell number. Call anytime. We'll need to get someone out there immediately to take his statement about the attack."

"Thank you, Detective! I'm sure there's still a long road ahead, but this has given me such a sense of relief and I can't wait to share this news with my family."

"Glad to help. Bye for now."

Erin went back into her son's hospital room and filled everyone in on the arrest. There was a collective sense of relief at the news that someone was in custody and a shared, fervent hope that Eric would be able to testify.

• • •

Frank met Jules in the hospital cafeteria. She wanted to fill him in outside of the family's orbit to spare them from the re-telling. She told him about the arrest, and he put the attacker's name into his phone to research later.

"Hate crimes are notoriously hard to prove. Unless this McEvers guy is affiliated with some kind of hate group, Proud Boys or something. Or if he has some sort of manifesto that he's touting. If not, Eric is going to be a crucial witness here."

"One of the girls in the dorm was dating the guy. He walked into her dorm room yesterday when Eric was there. After Eric left, the guy sort of flipped out on her."

"That could be good or bad. His defense could say it was just jealousy that triggered the attack. Nothing at all to do with transphobia."

"He told her that 'men should be men.' She has a brother who's gay, so she kicked him to the curb." Jules reported what she'd heard.

"That will help. Let me do some research on this guy. Is he a student there?" He asked.

"No. He's a townie."

"Good. So likely not from out of state. I'll let you know if I find anything on him. Are Sally and Hemmy upstairs?"

"They're all on the 4th floor. ICU."

"Okay, I just want to say hello. Are you coming back up?" Frank stood up from the table and held out a hand.

"Yeah, I'll say good-bye. I'm exhausted."

In the elevator he pushed 4 and wrapped his arms around her from behind. She leaned against him and the adrenalin of the day started to ebb. She could have fallen asleep standing there.

As they neared Eric's room they heard a buzz of activity. Sally and Hemmy and some of their grandsons, Eric's brothers, were hurrying from the room.

"Eric's awake!" She called as she saw them approaching. "He just woke up and the doctors are in there with him now."

Jules grabbed her in a hug.

"That's great! Oh my god, Sal! Is he talking?"

Everyone was in tears, crying with the joy of hope.

"I don't know! We called for help as soon as he opened his eyes. They only let Erin and Sean stay in the room. The neurologist is on her way, so we should know more soon."

They wandered a bit down the hall and took up all but one of the visitor chairs. Eric's brothers were convinced that all would be well. They couldn't entertain any other possibility.

They unpacked the events of the day, comparing notes. It had been barely 24 hours since the attack. They talked about the perpetrator, speculating about the kind of person who would do this. Frank let them know that he would see if he could find anything on this guy. They all turned to look as the double doors at the other end of the hall opened and a white-coated, name-tagged woman in loud heels came through and headed to Eric's room.

"That's the neurologist." Hemmy reported. They stared at the door long after she'd entered, unsure if a long stay or a short one was a better sign.

"I'm going to go and run this guy's background," Frank stood. He hugged Sally and shook hands with the men. "Nice to meet you, guys." He said to Eric's two brothers.

Jules couldn't bring herself to leave now. She needed the news, good or bad, so she walked Frank to the elevator and kissed him goodbye.

"Call me if you find anything."

She sat with them in the hallway again, and Sally's grandsons teased her about Frank. They thought of her as family and had never seen her with anyone before. She took their joking as a good sign and answered their questions.

"Cougar!" They laughed when they learned he was three years younger than her.

"What does he do?" Patrick asked.

"He's a retired cop." She told them.

"Oh! So he's packin' heat!" Jules felt the color creep into her face. Sally swatted a hand at him, reprimanding, but the joking lightened the mood.

Soon Erin and Sean came out of Eric's room with the neurologist. The three of them were talking intently but quietly, just out of earshot. Everybody stood up and headed toward them, anticipating some news. The doctor shook hands with the parents and headed down the corridor, the way she had come.

Jules hung back, letting Eric's family have the moment.

"Oh, thank god!" Sally threw her arms around Erin and everyone was crying again. Jules joined them, knowing she would be celebrating rather than grieving.

• • •

She called Frank with the good news as soon as she got clear of the parking lot. Eric was awake and talking a little. His throat hurt from the intubation. There didn't appear to be any signs of brain damage at this point, but they would need a few more days of testing and observation to be certain. They asked Eric if he'd be able to answer questions for the police tomorrow. He nodded. They asked if he remembered what happened. He nodded, then asked for more pain meds. He was sleeping when she left.

Frank was happy for the outcome, and he sensed the relief in her voice, too. Eric would need time to recover, both physically and emotionally, but anything on this side of dead was a win.

After leaving her at the hospital earlier, Frank had done some background on this McEvers kid. He filled her in, and Jules couldn't believe what he found.

"You're kidding me!?!"

"No, he was arrested with the January 6th crowd in D.C. He was charged with obstruction, assault, and attempted insurrection. He hasn't gone to trial on any of them yet."

"Wow. That's great intel! I mean, for the hate crime designation. Right?"

"I think so. I'm going to call Rodriguez and fill her in on what I found. Professional courtesy. My guess is she already knows, but I want them to know that the family knows. I don't want anything to be overlooked."

"Thank you, Frank. You don't know how much your help means to Sally and Hemmy. To everyone, really. This is going to make the case."

"Have they talked to the D.A. in Westchester, yet?"

"I don't think so, but I'm not positive. They've spent the last 24 hours in crisis mode. That will probably be a tomorrow task."

"Makes sense. Just make sure they share with her the January 6th connection."

"I'm going to call Sally as soon as I get home and fill her in. Thank you, thank you, thank you! I'll call you tomorrow. 'Night."

* * *

MASS SHOOTINGS IN THE US
October 2022 - 62 total

A mass shooting is any shooting where four or more people, other than the shooter, are killed or injured.

1. October 01, 2022 - Philadelphia, Pennsylvania - 1 dead, 4 injured
2. October 01, 2022 - Oakland, California - 2 dead, 2 injured
3. October 02, 2022 - Nashville, Tennessee - 1
4. October 02, 2022 - Seattle, Washington - 1 dead, 3 injured
5. October 05, 2022 - Baytown, Texas - 4 injured
6. October 06, 2022 - Louisville, Kentucky - 3 dead, 9 injured
7. October 06, 2022 - Washington, District of Columbia - 2 dead, 4 injured
8. October 07, 2022 - Portland, Oregon - 2 dead, 5 injured
9. October 07, 2022 - Fort Worth, Texas - 1 dead, 5 injured
10. October 08, 2022 - Hurtsboro, Alabama - 4 injured
11. October 08, 2022 - Saint Joseph, Missouri - 4 injured
12. October 08, 2022 - Berkeley, California - 4 injured
13. October 09, 2022 - Inman, South Carolina - 4 injured
14. October 09, 2022 - Miami, Florida - 1 dead, 3 injured
15. October 09, 2022 - Henryetta, Oklahoma - 4 injured
16. October 09, 2022 - Jacksonville, Arkansas - 1 dead, 16 injured

17. October 09, 2022 - Tampa, Florida - 2 dead, 2 injured

18. October 09, 2022 - Beaumont, Texas - 6 dead, 11 injured

19. October 10, 2022 - Delano, California - 1 dead, 3 injured

20. October 13, 2022 - Raleigh, North Carolina - 1 dead, 4 injured

21. October 13, 2022 - New Bern, North Carolina - 4 injured

22. October 13, 2022 - Lanett, Alabama - 1 dead, 3 injured

23. October 14, 2022 - Philadelphia, Pennsylvania - 4 injured

24. October 15, 2022 - Denver, Colorado - 2 dead, 3 injured

25. October 15, 2022 - Worcester, Massachusetts - 4 injured

26. October 15, 2022 - Itta Bena, Mississippi - 2 dead, 2 injured

27. October 15, 2022 - Freeport, New York - 1 dead, 3 injured

28. October 15, 2022 - Pittsburgh, Pennsylvania - 4 injured

29. October 16, 2022 - El Paso, Texas - 2 dead, 2 injured

30. October 16, 2022 - Atlanta, Georgia - 4 injured

31. October 16, 2022 - Lancaster, California - 4 injured

32. October 16, 2022 - Harrisonburg, Virginia - 1 dead, 3 injured

33. October 17, 2022 - Woodbridge, Virginia - 3 dead, 2 injured

34. October 20, 2022 - Cleveland, Ohio - 3 dead, 3 injured

35. October 21, 2022 - Cleveland, Mississippi - 1 dead, 26 injured

36. October 21, 2022 - New Orleans, Louisiana - 1 dead, 4 injured

37. October 21, 2022 - Hartland, Wisconsin - 1 dead, 9 injured

38. October 21, 2022 - Baton Rouge, Louisiana - 1 dead, 3 injured

39. October 22, 2022 - Milwaukee, Wisconsin - 5 injured

40. October 22, 2022 - Oxford, North Carolina - 4 injured

41. October 22, 2022 - Cordele, Georgia - 4 injured

42. October 22, 2022 - Phoenix, Arizona - 2 dead, 2 injured

43. October 23, 2022 - Brownsville, Texas - 1 dead, 3 injured

44. October 23, 2022 - Chicago, Illinois - 1 dead, 3 injured

45. October 23, 2022 - Milwaukee, Wisconsin - 5 injured

46. October 24, 2022 - Chicago, Illinois - 1 dead, 3 injured

47. October 24, 2022 - Saint Louis, Missouri - 7 injured

48. October 25, 2022 - Hamilton, Ohio - 2 dead, 2 injured

49. October 25, 2022 - Greensboro, North Carolina - 1 dead, 4 injured

50. October 27, 2022 - Broken Arrow, Oklahoma - 3 dead, 1 injured

51. October 28, 2022 - Toledo, Ohio - 1 dead, 3 injured

52. October 28, 2022 - Pittsburgh, Pennsylvania - 2 dead, 2 injured

53. October 29, 2022 - Orlando, Florida - 1 dead, 3 injured

54. October 29, 2022 - Tallahassee, Florida - 1 dead, 4 injured

55. October 30, 2022 - Memphis, Tennessee - 4 injured

56. October 30, 2022 - Aurora, Colorado - 1 dead, 3 injured

57. October 30, 2022 - Philadelphia, Pennsylvania - 1 dead, 4 injured

58. October 30, 2022 - Covina, California - 4 injured

59. October 30, 2022 - Charleston, South Carolina - 4 injured

60. October 31, 2022 - Kansas City, Kansas - 2 dead, 3 injured

61. October 31, 2022 - East Saint Louis, Illinois - 4 injured

62. October 31, 2022 - Chicago, Illinois - 1 dead, 3 injured

• • •

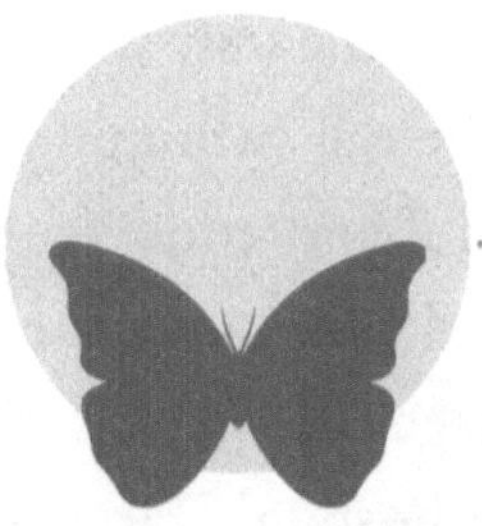

NOVEMBER 2022

By the first week of November, Eric was back home with Erin and Sean. He wasn't planning to return to campus until the following semester, or maybe even next fall. Or maybe never. They were taking things day by day. Physically, he was progressing. The bruises on his face and the black eyes had mellowed from angry reds and blues to healing yellows and purple-browns, like an overripe banana. They'd had to shave his head the night he was brought into the E.R.; a few lacerations from McEvers steel-toed boots needed stitches. The hair was growing back to camouflage the wounds. He still limped a little from the splenectomy pain, but no bones had been broken. By Christmas, his medical recovery would be complete.

The mental and emotional healing, the real work, would take years. He was in crisis counseling twice a week. His counselor was the woman he'd been working with before he left for college, so they already had a good therapeutic relationship. Eric would have happily gone to therapy daily, if the insurance had covered it. He wanted to be on the other side of this whole nightmare, psychologically speaking. But he knew that the only way to the opposite shore was to swim the channel, so he was swimming as fast as he could.

Eric was both grateful and annoyed by the level of love and support that surrounded him since the attack. After the new-found freedoms of college life, he was almost never alone since his discharge from the hospital. He suspected they were concerned about a suicide attempt, despite his assurances that he was not suicidal. In fact, he was more determined to live as his authentic self. But, to make sure he never had the opportunity, they passed him around like a newborn baby. Someone was always keeping him busy. He assumed there was a duty spreadsheet circulating among family and friends. Who has the Eric watch? Where is he? He expected a nanny cam to show up in his bedroom. That would be a hard no.

He accepted their diligence for what it was. Love. He would let them stand sentinel over him until he could stand on his own. It wouldn't be long, and he would look back with deep appreciation for the soft landing place.

• • •

VIDEO DIARY ENTRY – November 9, 2022

"Today is Wednesday, November 9th. It's only been three months since my trip to Milwaukee. Feels like a different lifetime. Violence has been an unwelcome guest in my life ever since I got back. Violence against innocent victims, caused by two angry people. Two people who have left devastation in the wake of their actions. The ripple effects of those acts are mind-boggling. If you've ever been impacted by violent crime, I'm sure you know what I mean.

"Speaking of violent crime, the journalist E. Jean Carroll continues her attempt to bring Trump to justice after he raped her in a department store fitting room. His defense? 'She's not my type.' What a sick and twisted response. How is it possible that any of you want this person to lead our country? Again?

"The good news today is that most of the Trump-backed candidates lost their mid-terms yesterday. The 'red-wave' that was expected, failed to materialize. We will likely hold the Senate. I don't want to get too excited about that, but it gives me hope.

"Still, Christian Nationalist and conspiracy theorist Marjorie Taylor Green was re-elected in Georgia. She's a QANON adherent. And Boebert, another MAGA mouthpiece, is in a tight race for her re-election in Colorado that hasn't been called yet, so she could also return. This one owned a restaurant in Rifle, Colorado, called Shooters. She encouraged her employees to open-carry at work.

"Trump has also now jumped on the QANON bandwagon with both feet. After years of dodging the issue, earlier this fall he showed up at an event wearing a Q pin. Have you heard "The Storm is Coming?" Go google it. This will help you understand the dangerous moment we are in as I record this.

"He was in Ohio yesterday during the mid-terms, desperate for attention as always, teasing a 'big announcement' coming on the 15th. I suspect it's just going to be his 'official' proclamation that he's running again. What a surprise.

"That's all from me. I hope you have a happy Thanksgiving. Peace."

●　●　●

Jules was looking forward to Thanksgiving, her favorite holiday every year. Jax and Kelly were coming from Austin, and Ben, Jess and the grandkids were coming from Montreal.

Frank and Jules had talked with Kevin's foster parents about him joining them for the holiday. Mark and Megan wanted Kevin with them for Christmas, when they planned to take him to meet his extended foster family, grandparents and cousins and aunts and uncles, who were all gathering in Ohio. But they agreed that a big turkey day feast with kids his age would be a fun diversion for him. They had arranged for him to spend the night. Kevin had been asking about Piper and Tanner ever since, and Jules was looking forward to them spending time together. It would be good for Kevin to see a functional family.

Jules called Jax to make plans for their visit. They were staying at her place, flying in on Tuesday and leaving Saturday evening.

"Does Kelly have any special requests for Thanksgiving? Any food traditions I can keep for her?" Jules asked Jackson on the phone.

"Well, there's one you're not gonna like." He laughed. "She likes the canned cranberry."

"Oh, my god! Have you met this woman's family?" She teased. "Listen, I'll serve it but I'm not going to leave it in that weird can shape. I'll put it in grandma's jelly dish so it looks like real food."

"Sounds good," he laughed. "If I can borrow your car while we're there, I want to go see everyone the day after." By everyone, he meant the aunts and uncles and cousins, and all of Sally and Hemmy's crew.

"Of course. It's all yours." She made a mental note to pull her rideshare signs out of the car.

"How's Claire doing?" Jax asked.

"Eric. He's had a rough time. Physically he's doing well, but there's a huge emotional toll with this kind of violence. When you're that young it can really skew your worldview. You'll have a chance to see him at Erin and Sean's. He's living there until he decides what to do."

"What's going on with the criminal case?"

"The guy is locked up. The judge set a high bail so he's probably going to stay there until the trial. They charged it as a hate crime, which increases the minimum prison time that he'll do. The trial starts in January and Eric will have to testify. I think that's going to be a setback for him, having to relive the attack in open court, with the guy sitting right there."

"I can't even imagine." Jax said.

They went through a few more logistics before hanging up.

Ben and Jess and the kids would drive down Wednesday evening. They were all staying with her, too, and she was looking forward to the full house. It had been too long since she had seen the grandbabies. Last Christmas. She had planned to visit Montreal over the summer, but her life hadn't cooperated.

"I'm bringing you the snowblower I promised you last winter." Ben told her when she called.

"Okay, I may need a quick lesson. I've never used one before, but I'll be grateful to have it. It's supposed to be a bad winter. We might even have snow before Thanksgiving."

"We had our first snow up here today," Ben reported.

"Well, as long as it doesn't keep you from making the trip. I can't wait to see you all!"

"I know, mom. Piper and Tanner are so excited. They want to play Scattergories again."

"Oh! I forgot how much fun we had with that. I'll dig it out. Frank and his daughter, Charlotte are coming, too."

"Good. We're looking forward to meeting him." Both boys had been in contact with Erin and Sean after the attack on Eric. They had received good reports on Frank.

"We're also having another guest. A little boy named Kevin. He's right between Piper and Tanner's ages."

"Is that Charlotte's kid?" Ben asked. While she had opened up about learning to shoot, she hadn't filled the boys in on Kevin's situation.

"No. Kevin's, um, he's a special kid. He's been through a lot. I met him and his parents at the gun range last spring." Jules proceeded to tell the sad story, from the accidental shooting of his sister to the murder/suicide of his parents.

"Jesus, mom! That's tragic."

"I know. He's in a good foster placement, though, and things are starting to settle down. We thought it would be fun for him to be with us for the holiday. He's an only child so he's excited about meeting the kids, and I'm excited about having a kids' table for the first time!"

When her parents were alive, they'd all gathered at their house for Thanksgiving. Jules and Simon and Cassie and Thea returning to their childhood home for the feast. The kids' table expanded year after year as they each grew their own families. And now they had become the matriarchs and patriarchs, welcoming in their scattered offspring. It was joy and sorrow.

She and Ben finished up their call and Jules headed out to drive for the evening.

●　●　●

Thanksgiving Day was sunny and warm. More August than November. Frank and Charlotte picked Kevin up and the three of them arrived together in the early afternoon. Jules made all the introductions and offered drinks. She had coffee brewed and homemade eggnog ready. There was beer in a cooler near the back door, and she had asked Frank to pick up some Beaujolais Nouveau. She loved getting a few bottles for this meal every year. There was something magical about a wine that was released precisely on Thanksgiving Day. The turkey had gone into the oven hours before, so the house smelled amazing. Charlotte brought three pies: pumpkin, pecan, and apple. They were still warm and added sweet notes to the meaty miasma.

Piper and Tanner's sleeping bags from the night before were still laid out on the living room floor, and a fort emerged from a clever arrangement which included pillows and couch cushions. Inside, the inhabitants took turns reading to one another from a stack of books Piper brought along. Tanner's flashlight created an eerie glow to the structure that Feinstein's curiosity couldn't resist, and she had materialized to join them in there. Although Piper was the youngest, she was clearly in charge, telling her brother and Kevin how things would go. Who would read what, and when. Neither of the boys challenged her. The three were already fast friends. Jules admired that about kids, how easy it was to open their hearts.

Jules had installed one leaf in the dining room table, which was set with mismatched place settings and the fabric napkins that only came out for holidays. It would be a tight squeeze for the seven of them, but they could make it work. The kids' places were set up on the living room side of the kitchen counter. She retrieved a third stool from her attic to join the two she usually kept there.

The unseasonable weather meant that Jules' guests could spill out into the backyard and leave the living room to the readers. Jax and Kelly had pulled out all her outdoor furniture, cleaned off the garage grunge, and set up the patio the day before. With the slider open, it was one large indoor/outdoor space and there was plenty of room for everyone.

Frank brought a Yankees cornhole set that his daughters had given him for Christmas a few years ago. Teams formed up and the play began. From the kitchen, Jules heard the *thunk-tsss* of the bean-filled pillows landing and sliding across the glossy targets, success or failure revealed by the response of the players.

Jules' kitchen was sufficient for the needs of one person, living alone, but not for Thanksgiving. She had to wash up a little between preparing each component. She needed the same pot and utensils for potatoes that she used for yams and stuffing and green beans and cranberries. At the sink, hands under the bubbles, she closed her eyes to just listen to the sounds of the day and took a deep breath to inhale the memory of every Thanksgiving of her life. She couldn't remember the last time she had felt so grounded, so rooted.

"Can I help with anything?" Jess had come in from outside. Jules didn't mind the interruption to her sensory meditation.

"Sure honey, can you grab that serving bowl over there next to the toaster. No, the blue one," pointing with her elbow. "Yeah, that one. The cranberries are cool enough to go in there now, and then you can stick it in the fridge."

Jess was efficient in the kitchen and Jules always enjoyed working with her.

"How are you guys doing? Do you still like living in Canada?"

"I've gotten used to it. The snow still surprises me sometimes. How much of it there is there. But I love how intrepid the people are. Schools don't close, businesses don't close. It's not like here, where every minor weather front is a full-blown crisis!" They both laughed at the truth of it.

"How are the kids doing in school this year? How's Pipe?" She glanced toward the living room. They were out of earshot and the kids were engrossed in their play, talking and laughing.

"She's made a lot of progress. Academically and socially. Ben and I have both relaxed a lot about her. We've decided just to give her time and see how she does in the next few years. We'll re-evaluate her in third grade."

"And the school agrees?" Jules asked.

"They do." Jess lowered her voice, "Listen to her reading out there."

Both women went silent and Piper's voice could be heard 'reading' to the boys. The book was *If You Give a Mouse a Cookie*, and she was clearly ad libbing sometimes, but she was sounding out words on the pages and asking Tanner for help. They heard Kevin chiming in, too.

"Ben told me Kevin's story," Jess whispered. The two women looked at each other, acknowledging the enormity with a quiet moment.

Jules turned back to the sink to finish her task. Jess picked up a kitchen towel to dry.

"How's the fertility stuff going?"

"Not good. We're trying to decide what to do. We didn't really want this much of a gap between Pipe and a newborn. Even if I got pregnant today, Piper would graduate high school before this one started middle school. They would hardly know each other."

"That's true."

"And me and Ben would be in our fifties when they finished school. It's just not what we imagined. We have these two amazing kids, things are stable. We might just count our blessings, ya' know?"

"Makes sense to me. Whatever you decide, you know you guys have my support."

"Thanks, Jules," Jess gave her a one-armed side-hug. "We really missed you this year. You have to come and stay this summer."

"I know. I missed you guys, too. Things were just a little crazy this year."

"So I see," the innuendo was unmistakable. "He's cute, Jules."

Charlotte walked into the kitchen.

"Can I help?" She asked.

"I was just saying to Jules how cute your dad is," Jess teased.

"They're a cute couple, right?"

The topic of them as a couple or a conversation about them being in a relationship had never come up between Jules and Charlotte. They just evolved into it being a fact that existed without comment. Jules was happy to hear Charlotte's take on the matter.

"Me and Dad just wiped the floor with your sons," Charlotte told Jules, laughing.

"Really?" Jules asked. "Expect a rematch. Those two are pretty competitive."

Despite the summerlike weather, it was still fall, and the shadows were already getting long as three o'clock approached.

"Mom, how long until dinner?" Jax had come to the open kitchen window to ask. Jules shot Charlotte an 'I-told-you-so' look.

"We'll sit down around four. Probably an hour or so."

"REMATCH!" Jax yelled back toward the yard.

"Jules, why don't you go play?" Charlotte asked. "Jess and I can manage."

"I'd love that. Thank you." Jules jumped at the chance. She

wasn't territorial in the kitchen. "The yams are ready to be mashed and then they can be baked in this." She reached for a casserole dish that held a bag of mini-marshmallows. "Do half with marshmallows and half without. Those potatoes can go on to boil anytime. Check the turkey in about fifteen minutes. The baster is right there," She pointed to where it stood in a measuring cup next to the oven. "Call me if you need anything."

She went into the living room and stuck her head in the fort.

"Hey guys. Come outside and root me on. I'm gonna play cornhole and I'm not very good. I need some cheerleaders."

Piper's hand shot up.

"I'll cheer for you, gramma! Come on guys!" They exploded through the roof of the fort, reducing it to rubble in a single motion, and followed Jules outside.

In the backyard, Jules announced that she'd take Charlotte's place and headed to her spot across from Frank. Ben and Jax were ready for retaliation.

"Kelly, why don't you take my spot and play on Jax's team? I'll go help in the kitchen." Ben handed her his bean bags. "This way if you lose again, I won't have to hear about it," He teased his little brother.

Jax shot back, "And if we win, I'll know where the weak spot is."

In the kitchen, Charlotte and Jess had returned to the topic of Kevin, and Ben joined them. Jess knew only what Jules had told Ben on the phone. His mom had spared him a lot of the story, just painting the big picture. Now they were getting more of it, the details, from Charlotte. Both of them were horrified at what this kid had already been through in his short life.

"Why isn't his family stepping in? Grandparents? Aunts and uncles?" Ben asked.

"You would think so, right?" Charlotte responded. "There's a grandmother on his mom's side, she's in memory care. There's some extended family in Jersey, and an unmarried uncle in Texas, but nobody is willing to step up. Dave really isolated them after he got back from Afghanistan and a lot of ties were cut. And I think there's a stigma, you know? Apple doesn't fall far from the tree kind of thing."

"It is sort of stunning that a single family could be subjected to so much trauma," Jess remarked.

"Well, not once you put an arsenal of firearms and a diagnosis of PTSD into the picture," Ben countered. All three of them walked over to the kitchen sink and looked out at Kevin. On the outside, he looked every inch the innocent seven-year-old he should have been, playing freeze tag with Tanner and Piper. Who knew what was going on on the inside.

●　●　●

It was dark by the time plates were filled and everyone was seated. Before starting the meal, they went around the table and each person was asked to share one thing they were thankful for that year.

"I'm so thankful we have Kevin here this year!" Jules began. Everyone echoed her sentiment, raising their glasses toward Kevin sitting at the counter with his new friends. "And I'm grateful that we made it through the pandemic!" Everyone cheered.

"I'm so grateful you invited Charlotte and me to join your table!" Frank smiled at her.

"Me, too! And I hope you're right about the pandemic." Charlotte passed the torch to Jax.

"I'm so grateful to Kelly for putting up with me!" Jackson raised his glass to his girl and kissed the air. "And for having a commander-in-chief who isn't a lunatic!"

"I'm grateful for this whole clan for welcoming me in!" Kelly looked a bit teary as she shared her gratitude.

"I'm grateful that we live in a democracy!" Jess shared.

"And that we're at peace!" Ben finished off for the adults.

"Ok," Jules turned to the kids' table. "Oldest to youngest. Tanner, what are you grateful for?"

Tanner lifted his water glass, "I'm grateful for Mario Kart!"

"That is a good one, bud," Ben confirmed.

"Kevin, what are you thankful for today?" Jules kept her voice light. All the adults felt the weight of the question on his skinny shoulders.

"I'm glad I get to spend the night tonight. This is my first sleepover!" Everyone relaxed.

"Really?" Piper was incredulous. "I'm only six and I've had lots of sleepovers already!"

"Ok, Pipe, what are you thankful for?" Jules asked.

"I'm thankful that Christmas is coming!"

Jules laughed, "Let's enjoy Thanksgiving first, though, okay kiddo? Cheers, everyone!"

While most families avoided discussing politics and religion at family gatherings, for Jules' family those were almost the only things worth discussing. Luckily, or perhaps predictably, everyone at her Thanksgiving table shared a value system. As they tucked in to their heaping plates, the talk between bites was lively conversation about the current political situation in America, Canada, and the world.

"There is just no way Trump can win again. Not after January 6th and all of the charges he's faced since he left office." Kelly claimed.

"Yeah maybe, but isn't that what we all thought the first time around? The *Access Hollywood* tapes?" Heads nodded at Jax's recollection. "Does anyone think he'll even be officially charged with anything?"

"I do," Charlotte said. "There are just too many slings and arrows headed his way. The thing with that journalist, the classified documents he hid at Mar-a-Lago, the insurrection, the fake electors. The list goes on and on. No matter how slippery the fish, eventually an eagle will dig its claws in."

"What do you think, mom?" Ben and the rest turned toward her. "Is it possible he'll be re-elected?"

"Sadly, I think it is." She glanced at the kids, who were deep in their own discussions about best friends and favorite colors and school. "I've never studied another point in our country's political history where the stakes are so high. Democracy hangs in the balance. No less than that."

"Isn't that overly dramatic?" Frank asked her.

"I hope so," she admitted, "but I don't think so. I just can't picture what happens if he gets in. His agenda is hate-based. Has anyone read the new book by Malcolm Nance? *They Want to Kill Americans?* It just came out this summer." Nobody had. "It's worth the time. He really takes a deep dive into the current threat. He's a journalist and a military intelligence guy, counterterrorism expert. I'll lend my copy to anyone who wants it."

"Is that the same guy who went to Ukraine to fight against the Russians? MSNBC guy?" Frank asked.

"Yes! Can you believe it? Sixty years old and the guy jumps into the fray. You have to respect that. He's a guest on the Roundtable sometimes and they announced it the day after he left. You could tell they were all just shocked. He's from Upstate. Hudson or something. He predicted the war would be over by now, Ukraine victorious. We can see how that played out."

"I thought it would be over by now, too, but I expected Russia to run right over Ukraine. Zelenskyy has put on his big boy pants. It seems like Putin miscalculated the country's resources." Ben said.

"It seems like democracies around the globe are at risk. My sister lives in Paris and she's seeing some of the same social shifts there. I'm not seeing that in Canada. Are you, Ben?" She asked her husband.

"No, I'm not. Not like here. We don't have anything close to the rates of hate crimes you have in the U.S. And we regulate guns at the federal level, which means gun violence is significantly less prevalent. It feels like we're still on the right trajectory. Both socially and politically." Jules tensed at Ben's mention of guns, but she saw the kids were clearly tuned out of the adult conversation.

"What's the abortion situation there?" Kelly directed this to Jess. "Can you believe they overturned Roe? I did not see that coming. Even with the Court's current make-up."

"It's legal and federally funded in Canada. Trudeau promised access to Americans as well after Roe fell. It's going to be a mess here in the states with everyone on their own. If Congress doesn't act to protect it, states could be swinging back and forth with administration changes. Can you imagine that?" Jess shook her head.

"It's banned in Texas. They started that even before the Supreme Court decision. Last year, a friend of mine at work found out she was pregnant at 11 weeks. That's too late under the state law. She had to go to New Mexico, which just added to the stress of the entire thing. Imagine a teenager trying to navigate that. Alone. It's really devastating that we're losing control over our reproductive health."

"Make America Great Again is just a dog whistle. Put straight, white men at the top of the world to control everyone else's destiny. The enemy list is short but encompassing." Jules held up fingers to count them off. "People of color, women, immigrants, and the LGBTQ-plus community. That's it. Control these four groups, which account for something like 70 percent of our population, and the remaining 30ish percent then hold 100 percent of the power."

The table got quiet for a moment, considering this. The kids' chatter filled the silence.

"Oh my gosh!" Jules suddenly stood up from the table. "I completely forgot." From the fridge she pulled a foil-wrapped cut crystal jelly dish and placed the canned cranberry on the table near Kelly, who caught Jackson's eye.

"If we're going to disagree about something, I'd rather it be food than politics!" Jules laughed.

● ● ●

MASS SHOOTINGS IN THE US
November 2022 - 43 total

A mass shooting is any shooting where four or more people, other than the shooter, are killed or injured.

1.   November 01, 2022 - Denver, Colorado - 4 injured
2.   November 01, 2022 - Baltimore, Maryland - 1 dead, 6 injured
3.   November 02, 2022 - Houston, Texas - 1 dead, 3 injured
4.   November 02, 2022 - Hattiesburg, Mississippi - 4 dead,
5.   November 03, 2022 - Chicago, Illinois - 4 injured
6.   November 04, 2022 - Orlando, Florida - 1 dead, 3 injured
7.   November 04, 2022 - La Plata, Maryland - 1 dead, 13 injured
8.   November 05, 2022 - Buffalo, New York - 9 injured
9.   November 05, 2022 - Philadelphia, Pennsylvania - 2 dead, 2 injured
10. November 06, 2022 - Chicago, Illinois - 4 injured
11. November 06, 2022 - Chicago, Illinois - 1 dead, 3 injured
12. November 06, 2022 - Tulare, California - 4 injured
13. November 06, 2022 - Gainesville, Florida - 1 dead, 3 injured
14. November 07, 2022 - McAllen, Texas - 4 injured
15. November 11, 2022 - Jersey City, New Jersey - 1 dead, 3 injured
16. November 12, 2022 - Sacramento, California - 1 dead, 5 injured

17. November 12, 2022 - Fort Worth, Texas - 2 dead, 14 injured

18. November 12, 2022 - Indio, California - 7 injured

19. November 12, 2022 - Paterson, New Jersey - 2 dead, 2 injured

20. November 12, 2022 - Memphis, Tennessee - 2 dead, 2 injured

21. November 13, 2022 - Philadelphia, Pennsylvania - 4 injured

22. November 13, 2022 - Enfield, North Carolina - 5 injured

23. November 13, 2022 - Charlottesville, Virginia - 1 dead, 3 injured

24. November 13, 2022 - Omaha, Nebraska - 1 dead, 3 injured

25. November 18, 2022 - Richmond, Virginia - 5 injured

26. November 19, 2022 - Washington Park, Illinois - 1 dead, 4 injured

27. November 19, 2022 - Philadelphia, Mississippi - 4 injured

28. November 19, 2022 - Colorado Springs, Colorado - 1 dead, 3 injured

29. November 20, 2022 - Hennessey, Oklahoma - 4 injured

30. November 20, 2022 - Dallas, Texas - 1 dead, 9 injured

31. November 22, 2022 - Chesapeake, Virginia - 4 injured

32. November 22, 2022 - West Palm Beach, Florida - 5 injured

33. November 23, 2022 - Temple Hills, Maryland - 2 dead, 2 injured

34. November 23, 2022 - Philadelphia, Pennsylvania - 4 injured

35. November 24, 2022 - Houston, Texas - 7 dead,

36. November 24, 2022 - Costa Mesa, California - 1 dead, 3 injured

37. November 25, 2022 - Atlanta, Georgia - 1 dead, 4 injured

38. November 26, 2022 - Atlanta, Georgia - 1 dead, 4 injured

39. November 26, 2022 - Chicago, Illinois - 5 injured

40. November 27, 2022 - Tallahassee, Florida - 1 dead, 3 injured

41. November 27, 2022 - New Orleans, Louisiana - 1 dead, 3 injured

42. November 30, 2022 - Lake Charles, Louisiana - 1 dead, 3 injured

43. November 30, 2022 - Mobile, Alabama - 3 dead, 1 injured

• • •

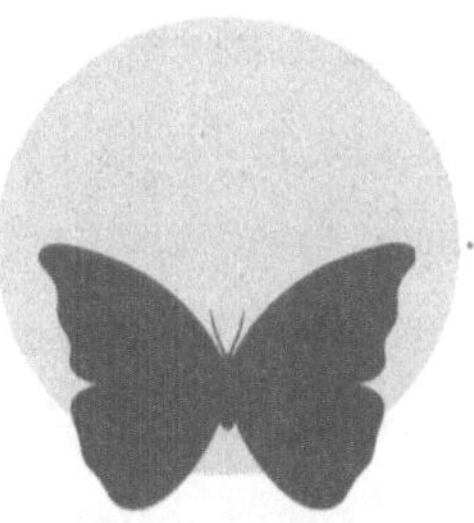

DECEMBER 2022

December 1st was a Thursday. Ladies' Night at TIGR. Jules had missed November because of everything happening with Eric and was looking forward to shooting again. She didn't want that muscle memory to fade. She planned to come to the range weekly after the New Year, then twice a week in the months leading up to Day Zero in 2024.

Charlotte wasn't coming. She'd taken a last-minute trip out west after Thanksgiving to see her sister. Jules didn't have any of the details, but she thought there might be some sort of family drama happening. Frank wasn't saying anything about it and Jules wasn't asking.

Christmas decorations were up in an attempt to make the place look festive. A small fake tree with white lights stood near the coffee station. The ladies had decided to do a Secret Santa and pulled names the month before. They would do the gift exchange at Scotty's afterward.

Even though she'd missed a month, Jules shooting was on point all evening. They had brought in special holiday targets that were Christmas wreaths instead of the standard bull's eye. She won the $150.00 prize for closest to bull's eye, which on the holiday targets consisted of a single cranberry set dead center within the wreath. They didn't award the top prize, bull's eye blowout, because a single shot would obliterate the small red fruit.

Frank was at Scotty's waiting for her, even with Charlotte away. They watched the ladies exchange their gifts. A ten-dollar limit had been imposed, so socks and scented candles, calendars and puzzles, scratch-offs and adult coloring books featured among the booty.

Jules looked around the room at these women and realized how much had changed in her life since she had begun her mission back in late February. As the year was coming to a close, war was still raging in Ukraine with no end in sight. The January 6th Committee completed its work back in October and a final report was expected before Christmas. Tensions were still growing between the U.S. and China. They were still hurtling toward destruction, and the preservation of American Democracy was crucial to stability worldwide. She knew she had to stay the course.

●　●　●

VIDEO DIARY ENTRY – December 5, 2022

"Hi. It's Monday, December 5th. Over the weekend, Trump made some bone-chilling statements that really don't seem to be getting much attention. On his Truth Social platform, he called for the suspension of everything that defines us as a Democracy. He said, and I'm quoting here:

"A Massive Fraud of this type and magnitude allows for the termination of all rules, regulations, and articles, even those found in

the Constitution. Our great 'Founders' did not want, and would not condone, False & Fraudulent Elections!"

She paused, looking straight into the phone.

"The termination of the Constitution." She let the silence expand around those words.

"This despot tells us time and again who he is and what he intends to do. Can't you see this? I can and I do. This is no less than the core of my mission. To protect our Constitution, our Democracy, and our way of life as Americans. Trump is a traitor, invoking the founders to support his planned overthrow of the very system of government that they created to protect us from the likes of him. Aren't you terrified? You should be."

●　●　●

On Saturday morning, Jules opened her email to find a message from the 'MAGA Millions.' The subject line was 'New York, New York!' She had almost forgotten about adding her name to their list last summer. She'd filtered everything into a separate mailbox except for those with certain keywords. 'New York' in the subject line landed this one in her inbox. It was an invitation to his followers to turn out at a rare Trump event on Tuesday, the 13th. Despite his deep ties to the city, he hardly bothered with New York as a political target. His time was spent in red and purple states.

Jules had been hoping for this opportunity. She would take the train into the city so that she could observe what went on around him at an event like this. It would be a learning experience. A chance for her to see what the security detail looked like and how close Trump let his true believers get. She couldn't imagine him mixing it up with the hoi polloi. He preferred the stratosphere of the rich and power hungry. But he was a narcissist, and she hoped his desire to be stroked would overcome his fear, and he'd let his guard down.

On Tuesday morning, Jules took the 6:55 train into the city. The event was scheduled for 1:00 pm, just after lunch. She'd arrive before 9:30, but she didn't want to take a later train and risk not making it. His people had chosen the 9/11 memorial, ground zero site, for this impromptu rally. Rudy Guiliani was going to introduce the failed president. These people really knew no bottom.

On the train, Jules had time to think about the mission. She'd been preoccupied over the weeks since Thanksgiving. Jax had taken her aside the day after to let her know he was planning to propose to Kelly at Christmas. He had booked them a post-engagement trip to Tahoe for a week of skiing. But for now, Jules needed to play along and act like she would be in San Antonio for Christmas with them, like they had planned. She drove them to the airport on Saturday, saying she'd see them soon. Jules was thrilled for them and excited for their future together. Even though she wouldn't be there to share it with them. She hoped they would set a wedding date before July, 2024, so that she could dance with her son at his wedding.

Kevin had ended up staying with her through the entire holiday weekend. He seemed more at ease than she'd ever seen him, just being a kid with other kids. By the time Ben and Jess headed north on Sunday afternoon Kevin was calling Jules Gramma right along with Piper and Tanner. He gave her a big hug and thanked her before Frank drove him home. When she shut the door behind him and turned to her quiet house, she sat down and cried unexpected tears.

At the end of the next week, Ben called her.

"Mom, we had a family meeting, and we want to discuss something with you."

"Okay, what's up?" They didn't know about the pending Christmas engagement, and she was hoping they weren't going to propose spending it in San Antonio together.

"You know we've been trying to get pregnant."

"Jess and I talked about it last week. She told me you might be rethinking it, since the gap between Piper and a baby might not be ideal now."

"Yes, and we made that decision. It's just too much to think about going back into diapers and bottles."

"It is nice to have kids that are past that intense dependency stage. Tanner and Piper are so easy. I told Jess I'm supportive of whatever you guys want to do."

"We talked about that. We think we're going to try to adopt."

"Oh, wow!" Jules was surprised at the news. "How do the kids feel about it?"

"They were the ones who got the wheels turning. They loved having a third person in the mix. They loved having Kevin in the mix."

Jules finally understood what he was telling her.

"Kevin? You guys want to adopt Kevin?"

"Do you think we could? Do you think it's weird?"

"NO! I think it's great. I think it's wonderful. Oh, my god. You would be the perfect family for him!"

Jules talked to Jess, then the kids. They all seemed excited and committed. Jules gave Ben Kevin's case worker's contact information.

"Call her on Monday. I'm going to text her now and let her know you'll be calling her at the office."

Ben and Jess had already started the ball rolling, and the process was underway. Even though Montreal was only 3 hours away, it was still considered an international adoption, so that added a little complexity, but they were exploring it. Until they determined if it was feasible, everyone was keeping the plan quiet. They didn't want Kevin to face more disappointment if it couldn't be worked out. Jules hadn't even shared it with Frank.

Frank. She couldn't ignore the fact that they were in a relationship now. They hadn't named it or claimed it, but it was there, nonetheless. On one hand, she felt enormous guilt for letting him get close. She knew that everyone close to her was going to suffer so much grief and trauma in the wake of the mission. It had been hard enough to come to terms with that inevitable reality for her family. Intellectually, she knew that her mission was larger than herself and her life. It was in service to the greater good. The protection of Democracy, the rule of law, human rights. But pulling new people into her orbit seemed cruel.

On the other hand, selfishly, she was enjoying this last fling. She would get two years with him. And he was reaching places in her that lain dormant for so long that she thought she had lost them. Not just physically. Sex was great. But the emotional and intellectual connection was a gift that she hadn't known she needed to sustain her on this journey. She wondered if Frank would regret their time together. She hoped he would understand.

But all of this was taking her focus off the mission. She needed to pull that back. She was pleased with the progress she'd made in the course of the year, but she'd need to sustain that momentum for the next year and a half. This was a long-term project.

She needed to double-check that the mission phone was charged. She could plug it in for the rest of the trip if necessary, and that would be good enough. She wanted to record any thoughts from her recon trip in real time. She wasn't going to take any notes and didn't want to forget anything. Her own cell rang just as she plugged the other one in. It was Sally.

Jules didn't want to explain why she was on the train, so she texted.

[I'll call you back in a bit] - send

She waited as Sal texted back.

[OK. It's important. Need to talk.]

Shit. Jules checked her watch. It would be a little over an hour before they got to the station that she still thought of as Penn Station. They had renamed it and she could never remember what it was called now.

[OK. I can call you around 11. Can it wait?] - send

[Yes. It's about Eric. Call me when you're free.] - send

Oh no! *[Is he ok????]* - send

[Yes. He's fine.] - send

[OK, I'll call as soon as I can.] - send

Jules dropped her phone back into her bag. Dammit. What could it be? The criminal case had moved forward since the arrest, but McEvers hadn't yet been indicted. They weren't expecting that until at least late spring. The judge had set a high bail given his participation in January 6th, so McEvers was behind bars and would be indefinitely. They hoped it would come to trial in 2023. Everyone wanted that closure.

Ben and Jax and the crew had spent some time with Eric over the holiday weekend. Sally's kids had all met them over at Erin and Sean's house for a Friendsgiving lunch. They said he seemed to be in good spirits, joking and laughing. He'd even organized a brief stage performance for the affair that thrilled the grandkids. They all had parts. From all appearances he was recovering. There was no visible evidence of the attack; his hair had grown over the scars on his skull, and the bruising had healed. It would take much longer for the invisible wounds to heal.

They were pulling into Penn Station before she knew it. Jules found a quiet spot to make the call. Sally answered on the first ring.

"You're not going to believe this! The prosecutor is considering a plea!"

Jules caught the fury in her voice. A tinge of panic. She wanted to have a calming influence on her friend in that moment, but she couldn't believe a plea was on the table. She thought of Ahmaud Arbery, a black man who had been chased and killed by vigilantes. The prosecutor had offered a plea there, and that had been a murder case.

"That doesn't mean McEvers will get off, Sal. I'm sure he'll still do prison time. Do you know the details of the plea?"

"No." Sally took a deep breath and sounded a little more grounded. "We just found out a few hours ago. I didn't realize it would be up to the prosecutor to make that decision. He didn't even have to consult with the family about it! He's negotiating with the defense attorney."

"Do you know why?"

"I have no idea. I feel so frustrated. I want Eric to have his day in court."

"Well, even if there is a plea deal, Eric will probably have input. Are Sean and Erin talking to the prosecutor?"

"Yes. The two of them spoke to him this morning. They have a conference call set up later this afternoon so Eric will have a chance to speak to him before any agreement is reached."

"Ok, that's good. You could have some influence on the process. Think about what the family would want for Eric if it does come down to a plea deal."

"What do you mean, Jules?"

"Like the chance for him to make a victim impact statement

in open court. And an admission of guilt from McEvers as a condition of the plea."

"Let me write this down. I can't think straight. Okay, victim – impact – and what was the other?"

"Admission of guilt."

"Right. Admission – of – guilt. Thanks, Jules. This is so helpful. I'm going to call Erin and give her this. If you think of anything else, call me or text me."

"I will, Sal. Listen, I'm going to call Frank too and get his take on this. He might have some insight."

"Yes! Great. I hadn't thought of that. Let me know."

"It's all going to be okay. Breathe deep."

"Thanks, Jules. Bye."

"Bye."

She called Frank and filled him in on the latest. He seemed surprised at the possibility of a plea deal and promised to see if he could find anything out.

Jules took the subway down to the Chambers Street stop near the rally site. Like Penn Station, ground zero had also been rebranded. It was now the 9/11 Memorial and Museum.

She had come into the city about three weeks after the 9/11 attacks. Early October of 2001. She needed to see it for herself. The absurdity of it, the impossibility as she watched it unfolding on her TV screen, drew her to the place. She had to feel it and smell it, so that she could believe it. Construction fences had been erected all around the areas that were still off limits to everyone but the workers. The chain link of the fences was papered over with colored fliers made by grieving families, "HAVE YOU SEEN ME?" shouting at passersby above photos of missing loved ones, contact information below. Block after block of misplaced hope. It was soul crushing.

This was her first time to the memorial site. A sanitized and somber place of veneration. With tickets and tour guides. She felt sick as she walked toward the sculpture that stood at the center of the plaza. It was an enormous oblong dark granite pool, entitled *Reflecting Absence*. The names of every victim engraved into its four sides. She looked over the edge. A thin sheet of water glided across the sleek bottom surface and disappeared over the lip of a carved-out rectangle at the center of the monument and into an abyss. She felt dizzy and closed her eyes to steady herself, leaning against the edge of the horrible shrine. In her mind's eye, she saw those posters floating off of their fences and slipping into that void.

When she was settled, she looked around to see where the rally would take place. She noticed a grandstand and some audio equipment across the plaza. It was still several hours before people would gather. The weather was mild for December, but still too cold to stand around outside for very long. She planned to get a bite to eat and change into her MAGA wear. She would play the part. She had a ball cap, a sweatshirt, and her fanny pack.

She walked a few blocks south to George's Diner for breakfast. She ordered an omelet and coffee. The place was buzzing. The din was a balm. Jules was able to pass the time people watching.

She was startled when her phone rang. It was Frank.

"Hi, Frank." She answered.

"Hey, Jules. You won't believe this. I found out why they are pushing for a plea bargain. McEvers' stepfather is a big wig with a law firm that represents the RNC."

"Wow. That figures. But why would the prosecutor agree to it?"

"Well, he might not want to risk getting a sympathetic judge. Better to get McEvers some jail time than none."

"Do you think that could happen? That he could get off scot free?"

"It shouldn't be possible, I know. But if the judge is in their pocket, who knows."

"Shit. Okay. I'm not going to share this with Sally right now. I'm just going to let them get through the day and see how this shakes out. I'll call you later. Love you." Jules clicked off.

Oh, no. It had been a reflex. Something she said every time she hung up with the kids. She felt herself getting hot, her face reddening with embarrassment, vulnerability. Maybe he hadn't heard it. She was moving the phone away from her to hang up. Maybe he'd already hung up. Oh, god. She had to put it out of her mind and get back to the work at hand.

Jules paid the bill for her breakfast and went into the bathroom to get into costume. She'd purchased everything online at one of many MAGA gear stores that all claimed to be the 'official' site for authentic gear. She'd considered a hoodie that had a picture of Reagan and a picture of Trump that read "I like my presidents like I like my guns, 40 & 45," with 2 handguns rendered below the former presidents. She had been so tempted by the elegant irony, but worried that it might draw the wrong kind of interest. She ended up with a pink zip up hoodie, TRUMP 2024 emblazoned across the back, and the obligatory American flag on the chest. Her ballcap was red, white, and blue, MAGA embroidered in gold across the crown, and she had a black nylon fanny pack with TRUMP embroidered in gold to match. She looked perfectly ridiculous and perfect. She would blend in seamlessly with the 'basket of deplorables.'

As she approached the rally site, she joined the sea of supporters, all of them in high spirits and emboldened by the like-minded mob. She expected that some of these men and women had been involved in the insurrection. While they looked like domestic terrorists, Jules knew that there were doctors and lawyers and other well-educated citizens in this group, ready to worship at the feet of a fascist.

Some portable stanchions had been erected for crowd control. Absurd theater. She moved all the way up to the stanchions, near where she surmised Trump would mount the stage. There were already several white men in red ties and a black woman sitting on folding chairs on the dais. The underlings. Rudy was nowhere to be seen so she had a little time. She spotted his security detail, the guys with the earbuds. They were clearly alert, on edge. They were the best of the best that the Secret Service had to offer, and Jules didn't underestimate them. She hoped they would underestimate her.

A couple who looked to be in their early 40s came to stand next to her with their three kids, everyone sporting political gear. They stretched out a TRUMP 2024 banner and instructed their sons to hold the ends. The boys were pre-teen aged and clearly excited about the event. Their older sister looked maybe 14, and appropriately bored, scrolling on her phone as she leaned against her father's back.

"How much longer do we have to wait? I thought it was supposed to start at one." She whined to her parents.

"Stop, Hayley. It's not like the movies. The President is a very busy person and has a lot of commitments. We wait as long as we have to. This is a privilege for you to actually see an American President. You'll remember this day for the rest of your life." Hayley's mom glanced at Jules; for sympathy or support she wasn't sure. Jules caught her eye and smiled.

"We want our kids to be active and aware of what's going on in the world."

"Of course. That's what we all want. They are the future, after all." Jules was grateful her own kids were active and aware.

"We took the train in from Springfield to be here. That's why she's so cranky." She nodded toward her daughter. "The kids are all tired. But we felt like we might not get the chance if we didn't come see Trump here. We just found out about it Sunday."

Jules nodded.

"They're missing school, but I think this is sooo much more educational than anything they'd get in school, you know? Have you been to a Trump rally before?"

"I . . ." She was interrupted as a cheer went up, the crowd suddenly electric. Rudy was striding toward the podium.

The opening remarks were limited but enough to hype the crowd up. When the former Mayor of New York City finally announced, "PRESIDENT DONALD J. TRUMP!!!" they were in a frenzy, chanting "4 more years! 4 more years!" Trump materialized from Jules' left, pumping his fists in his awkward way and flashing the veneered smile. He was giving high-fives and fist-bumps across the barriers as he strode to the stage. He stopped a few times for selfies and autographs. Jules realized how easy it would be right here and now. There had been no metal detectors to pass through; the venue was too wide open. She put out her fist as he passed and he tapped it with his own as he looked right through her. She felt ruined by his touch.

Whatever garbage he may have spouted was lost to her. She stood, observing, until he was finished. She was satisfied that it could be done, although it would be harder at the Fiserv, no question. She'd have to get some good intel from the MAGA community when she was in Milwaukee. She was sure her list-serv membership would prove invaluable for that.

The crowd dispersed quickly after he left; it had gotten colder as the afternoon wore on. Jules headed back to the subway bound for uptown and caught it just before the doors closed. It was too early for rush hour so there were seats available. Two different women, each sitting alone, had moved their bags into the open seats next to them and avoided eye contact as she looked for a place to land. She dropped into the first seat available and settled her bag next to her.

For the first time since she talked to Sally earlier, she thought of Eric. There had been a few 'Lesbians for Trump' and 'Gay Republican' shirts and hats at the rally, and Jules wondered what McEvers would think about that. Personally, she couldn't imagine anyone in the LGBTQIA+ community supporting the Republican agenda.

It was before 3 o'clock when she got back to Penn Station to catch her train to Albany. She had some time before it would board, and she needed a water. The line at Dunkin' was long, and as she waited, she noticed people giving her dirty looks. It suddenly struck her that she was still in her disguise. Jesus. The women on the train, one Black and the other wearing a Hijab, saw her like this and refused to share a seat with her. Good for them, Jules thought, as she hurried to the closest restroom with her head down.

* * *

Christmas was just a few weeks away, and Jules hadn't done much planning. The boys weren't coming, and she wasn't going anywhere since her plans to go to Austin were canceled. Frank and Charlotte would be on the West Coast for the week between Christmas and New Years, spending time with Carrie and Frank's ex-wife.

Jules had a real tree and a few decorations up. Christmas was on a Sunday, and she planned a small dinner party on the Thursday before. Nothing overblown. She was going to make a lasagna and garlic bread and had charged her guests with the rest.

Frank was bringing a green salad. She had asked Sally and Hemmy to take care of dessert. Ellie and Reggie, who were still going strong, would bring a fruit salad. Jules had also invited Kevin's foster parents, Megan and Mark. She wanted the opportunity both to thank them and to get their take on Ben and Jess's bid for Kevin to join their family in Montreal. Before Thanksgiving, the DiMarinos had been considering making their foster placement more permanent or exploring adoption. Jules wanted to know how they felt about this new option. Their support for the move, while not the deciding factor for DCFS, would have some influence. As first-time guests in her home, she hadn't asked them to bring anything.

She really didn't know the DiMarinos all that well and found herself a little apprehensive as the party approached. She wanted to make a good impression; convince them that Kevin was going to be in a 'good family.' The absurdity of the situation struck her. An assassin trying to make a good impression. She suddenly thought of Kevin after the mission. His young life rocked by yet more violence. Would he be better off with the DiMarinos? She hadn't considered it until that moment, and she had no answers.

Frank arrived early to help with party preparations. He put the leaf in her table and set up the extra chairs, called into action for the second time in a month. He had spent more time with Mark and Megan than she had, and she asked him about them.

"I was surprised you invited them." Frank said.

"Well, there has been a development since Thanksgiving that I haven't shared with you."

Frank's look was inquiring.

"Ben and Jessica have applied to adopt Kevin."

Frank put down the chair he was carrying.

"Really?" He considered it a moment. "Wow. That's a lot to take on, but I think he'd be great with them. They really hit it off at Thanksgiving."

Jules told Frank about their fertility struggles. And how excited Piper and Tanner were about the prospect.

"But it is considered an international adoption. I don't know how that plays out in New York. If they're politically opposed to it and want to keep kids in the state," Jules said.

"How do Megan and Mark feel about it?"

"I'm not sure. I didn't bring it up when I called to invite them and I don't plan to bring it up tonight unless they do. It's not public knowledge and not my place to share it. Did they have their heart's set on keeping him?"

Frank thought about it for a moment.

"They have always been an 'emergency placement' foster home and Kevin is still considered to be in emergency status. They do care for him and I think they'd keep him rather than let him go into the system. But a great adoptive family is the best outcome for Kevin. He'd be a lucky kid to have you for a grandma." Frank pulled her close and kissed her, letting his hands rest in the small of her back. "You're one hot granny."

Jules looked at the clock on the microwave, then caught Frank's eye.

"We still have a few hours before everyone arrives."

• • •

Thirty minutes later Jules was seriously regretting having people over that night. She loved being skin to skin with Frank, draped over his body with her head on his chest. He smelled like woodsmoke and she breathed him in, still feeling the buzz and flush of sex. They were both dozy and could easily have drifted off were it not for the party. At least he would be staying overnight. It would be their last night together before his week away. She would miss him.

Frank kissed the top of her head.

"I do, too," he said.

"You do too, what?"

"I love you." They hadn't talked about her inadvertent confession of love on the phone. She tried to convince herself he hadn't caught it.

"You did hear that, huh?" Jules pulled away to look at him. "Oh, god. It's just an automatic response whenever I hang up with one of the boys. It just slipped out."

"Ouch!" Frank winced.

"No, I mean, I didn't mean to say it right then, as an afterthought. I want it to be meaningful. Look, I haven't said that to anyone since Mick. I wanted to be looking at you when I told you. I wanted you to see it on my face. I love you."

She knew it wasn't fair. To let him love her when he didn't really know her. But she felt it, and she was grateful for it. And she realized that nobody really knew her now, anyway.

They got up and showered together, then dressed for dinner. Frank made the salad with the cornucopia of ingredients he'd brought from Trader Joe's, while Jules pre-heated the oven for the lasagna. It felt different between them, like some invisible barrier was gone. It felt good.

It was nearly dark and freezing outside; they hadn't had any significant snowfall in the early winter so the roads were in good shape. Everyone was there by five, introductions were made, and drinks offered. Jules had a chianti to go with the pasta. Frank brought some whiskey to add to store-bought eggnog or coffee. Ellie and Reggie had brought a six-pack of Ommegang.

"Did you know they make this stuff in Cooperstown?" Reggie asked the group, holding up a bottle of ale.

"Really? I didn't know that. I'm not a beer drinker though." Mike told him. "I will have a shot of that Irish eggnog though, Frank."

Frank prepared drinks and Jules readied some appetizers. Mike and Megan brought a charcuterie board, which is just what she'd have asked them to bring if she'd given them an assignment. Jules added some fruit and yogurt dip she had prepped and set everything out in the living room.

"Merry Christmas, everyone!" Jules raised a toast. Everyone touched glasses and drank to the holiday.

"Thanks for including us, Jules. This is so nice." Megan said.

"Frank and I are so grateful for everything you guys have done for Kevin. He seems to be healing." Frank nodded in agreement.

"I think he is. It's going to be a lifelong emotional burden for him, though. He can never be a person who hasn't suffered these horrors. He has to figure out how to live with that."

"He's in therapy?" Sally asked.

"Absolutely," Mark replied. "He goes a few times a week. It's helping."

"Is he excited about Christmas? This will be the first one without his mom and dad."

"I think he is. We're visiting extended family in Ohio over Christmas and he's been planning the road trip for weeks. What to bring for snacks, what games we can play in the car. He'll get to meet all of my nieces and nephews out there and it's going to be utter chaos. We have five generations."

"That must be fun, though." Sally said.

"It's busy, that's for sure. Is it fun, Mark?" She asked her husband.

They shared a look and he laughed.

"I'm just the driver. It's all her family, so I do a lot of smiling and fixing things."

"They don't like you?" Ellie was always direct.

"They just think it's weird that I'm an R.N. They have, you know, Midwest sensibilities."

"So what?" asked Ellie, "They think you are hanging in the closet?"

"In the closet." Jules replied.

"That's what I said."

"Just 'in the closet,' not 'hanging in the closet.'"

"Okay, so is that what they think?" she pressed.

"Do they?" Mark looked at Megan.

"No, it's not that. They just have more traditional, you know, ideas. About gender roles."

"Oh, that's sooo 1980s." Sally piped up in her best valley girl accent, and everyone cracked up.

The discussion of gender roles led Jules to ask Sally and Hemmy about Eric, after a brief synopsis of his situation for everyone.

"He's doing as well as can be expected," Hemmy reported. "He's in therapy, too. Like you said about Kevin, Megan, Eric will never be a person who didn't experience this violence. And because he can't change the past, he has to figure out how to manage his future."

"Has he decided about returning to school?" Frank asked.

"He's going to wait until after the trial. We don't know when that will be yet, but he wants the closure." Sally said. "He plans to go back to Purchase though."'

"I love that kid!" Jules said. "He's so brave. All of the young people these days are so comfortable with diversity. Being who they are and letting others be who they are."

"Unfortunately, not all of them." Hemmy reminded her.

"Of course. You're right. I'm just so grateful Eric has you guys." Everyone agreed.

"So, what do you do, Megan?" Ellie asked, lightening the mood.

"I just work part-time so I can be more present when we have a foster placement. It gives me more flexibility. Luckily, I married for money." She nodded toward Mark and they laughed.

A pile of wrapped gifts, some elegant and tasteful, others not so much, were on the coffee table in front of them. They had agreed to do a Yankee swap with a $25.00 maximum. That simplified the worry about whether or not to bring gifts and for whom. Something that was a constant source of anxiety for Jules during the holidays. And it would help to break the ice before they sat down to eat. Jules guessed at least a few of them were books, or maybe journals. And there was definitely a bottle of something.

Frank passed around a bowl with slips of paper numbered 1-8.

"Remember, you can't pick the gift you brought. When it's your turn, you choose from the pile, or you can take someone else's open gift. If you take someone else's gift, they get to choose a new one from the pile. After the last person goes, the first person can either keep what they got on the first pick, or swap for any other gift, and then the game ends. Got it?" Jules looked around the room to make sure the rules were understood.

The next hour was filled with laughter and fun. When the game ended, Megan wound up with a very nice bottle of merlot.

"Anybody want this?" Holding it by the neck, she offered it up with a laugh.

"Not a wine drinker?" Reggie asked.

"Mark's not a wine drinker, and I can't drink. I just found out we're expecting."

Everyone spoke at once, offering congratulations and well-wishes. Jules thought of Kevin, and how this new baby might play into their thinking about his placement.

"Wow, that is so exciting!" Ellie was sitting next to Megan, and she reached over to squeeze her hand. She and Megan were close in age. "How're you feeling? Is everything good so far?"

"Yeah, everything's good. But it's unexpected. We didn't think we could conceive. Surprise! I'm due in late May."

"The twins will be thirteen by then. Perfect babysitting age. I want to keep them busy so they stay away from the boys, you know? Take my number."

Ellie and Megan grabbed their phones. Ellie read her number to Megan and Megan rang her phone.

"Gotcha." A few more taps and Megan was a new contact.

"I don't have you either, Sally."

"I've got everyone. I'll put us all into a group chat later. That merlot," Jules grabbed the proffered bottle, "will go great with the lasagna. Let's eat." The guests helped carry their chairs back to the table, where the rest of the evening disappeared.

*   *   *

In the morning, Frank and Jules ate cold lasagna and leftover fruit with their coffee. It had snowed a little overnight, not enough to shovel. It was the heavy, wet snow that stuck and turned the landscape into a blank slate, virgin white, until the world woke up to ruin it. Frank went out to warm up his truck, and cleared her Jeep while he was out there. Jules had forgotten how nice it was to have someone care in those small ways. To have someone thinking about her as they went about their day, wondering how she was and looking forward to being with her. She was starting to like it.

• • •

In some ways, Jules was looking forward to the time alone during the holidays. She had always made the season special for the boys. They chose a live tree from the same farm each year, the weekend after Thanksgiving. The farm offered horse-drawn sleigh rides and hot chocolate, and the tradition kicked off the month. She loved the hush of Christmas Eve, their wrapped gifts piled beneath the white-lit tree, the anticipation of their joy. But the over-commercialization of it had worn her down. It felt more like an Olympic sport than a time to reflect on love and peace. She supposed this happened with age, growing weary of things.

Without any commitments for the week, she planned to do as much driving as possible to get a cash reserve built up. People over-indulged during the season and she was their designated driver for hire. If she drove every day from 7:00 pm to 3:00 am, catching the closing time crowd, she calculated that she could make what she needed to increase her range time in the coming year, as the mission plan required. Tips were usually very generous that time of year, especially on Christmas Eve and Christmas Day. Frank would be back for New Year's Eve, and they planned to spend it together. The anticipation was delicious.

MASS SHOOTINGS IN THE US
December 2022 - 30 total

A mass shooting is any shooting where four or more people, other than the shooter, are killed or injured.

1. December 01, 2022 - San Antonio, Texas - 1 dead, 3 injured
2. December 04, 2022 - Zion, Illinois - 4 injured
3. December 06, 2022 - Bronx, New York - 1 dead, 4 injured
4. December 06, 2022 - Macon, Georgia - 4 dead, 1 injured
5. December 08, 2022 - Detroit, Michigan - 6 dead,
6. December 08, 2022 - New Orleans, Louisiana - 3 dead, 1 injured
7. December 09, 2022 - Phoenix, Arizona - 4 injured
8. December 11, 2022 - Chicago, Illinois - 4 injured
9. December 12, 2022 - Bronx, New York - 1 dead, 4 injured
10. December 13, 2022 - Rochester, New York - 1 dead, 3 injured
11. December 16, 2022 - Valdosta, Georgia - 1 dead, 5 injured
12. December 16, 2022 - Chicago, Illinois - 4 injured
13. December 16, 2022 - Dallas, Texas - 6 injured
14. December 16, 2022 - Memphis, Tennessee - 1 dead, 3 injured
15. December 17, 2022 - Atlanta, Georgia - 4 injured
16. December 18, 2022 - Santa Ana, California - 4 injured

17. December 18, 2022 - Oklahoma City, Oklahoma - 1 dead, 4 injured

18. December 19, 2022 - Lake City, Florida - 1 dead, 6 injured

19. December 23, 2022 - Wichita, Kansas - 2 dead, 3 injured

20. December 24, 2022 - Columbus, Mississippi - 1 dead, 3 injured

21. December 26, 2022 - New Orleans, Louisiana - 1 dead, 3 injured

22. December 27, 2022 - Washington, District of Columbia - 2 dead, 2 injured

23. December 27, 2022 - Columbus, Ohio - 2 dead, 2 injured

24. December 27, 2022 - Eureka, California - 4 injured

25. December 28, 2022 - Bronx, New York - 2 dead, 2 injured

26. December 28, 2022 - Dallas, Texas - 1 dead, 4 injured

27. December 30, 2022 - Memphis, Tennessee - 1 dead, 3 injured

28. December 30, 2022 - Humble, Texas - 4 injured

29. December 31, 2022 - Mobile, Alabama - 5 injured

30. December 31, 2022 - Phoenix, Arizona - 2 dead, 2 injured

• • •

"Congratulations, honey!" It was the first time Jules had talked to Jax since he and Kelly got engaged. He had decided to wait until they were in Tahoe and propose on New Year's Eve. He thought there was a slight chance she might say no. They hadn't discussed it at length, and she was fiercely independent and not very traditional. He knew it might be something she didn't envision for herself. If that happened, he wanted them to be at the end of a great time together and headed home.

"I knew she'd say yes. Have you set a date?"

"We're thinking about this October, leaf-peeping season." Jules was thrilled that she'd be able to share it with them.

"Are you going to do it up here, then?" Jules asked.

"We think so. I already asked Ben to be my best man. Him and Jess and the kids can drive down. There's only like, six of her family members from Austin that she's inviting. And then we have some friends here that we'll invite. But if we had it here, it would be more like 60 people who have to travel from New York to Austin."

"How big are you thinking it will be?' Jules asked him.

"It's probably going to be somewhere around 100, 120 people, but very chill. No church, no big hall. We're thinking about an outdoor wedding and a barbecue. Maybe a pig roast. Remember that time we roasted a pig at Uncle Hemmy's place? Do you know where he got that from?"

"I'll ask him and let you know. It sounds like fun. Is Kelly with you?"

"Yeah, she's here."

"Put her on speaker." Jules heard the click.

"Hi Kelly. Congratulations, honey! I am so excited for you guys. Did you expect it?"

"Thanks, Jules. I absolutely did not! It was a complete surprise. Did he show you the ring?"

"No, text me a picture."

"I will. It's turquoise and platinum. Jackson knows I'm not a diamond girl and he commissioned this from a local jewelry maker. It's perfect."

"I can't wait to see it. I know it's early days, but have you thought about a dress yet?"

"Honestly, I don't know the first thing about wedding dresses. I've been in some friends' weddings, but I've never thought about a dress for me. I know I want to wear my cowboy boots, so it will have to work with that. And Jackson isn't planning to wear a tux. We just want to have a fun and comfortable day with all of our people."

"That sounds like the best kind of day. You two let me know if you need any help with planning. I can scout venues for you, meet caterers, whatever you need."

"We will mom. Thanks. And call Uncle Hem for the pig roast deets."

"I will. Love you the most." Jules rang off just as Frank walked into the kitchen.

"She said yes," Jules sing-songed, snagging his waist and pulling him into a hug.

"Did you have any doubt?" Frank asked her.

"Not really. But who knows, people are unpredictable."

"Not you. I predict you'd like a cup of coffee."

"Yes, I would."

Frank had been at her house since he got back from California four days ago. They had fallen into a comfortable fantasy. The honeymoon phase of every new relationship. She knew it was fleeting, but she was throwing herself into it. He handed her a steaming mug.

"I'm going to have to get dressed tomorrow," she joked. They had spent the first days of the new year inside her four walls. Ladies' Night would be her first foray into 2023.

"Yeah, I should probably go home and collect my mail, water my plants."

"You have plants? No way they've survived all this time without you."

"They've gotten used to my benign neglect. A little water and some kind words and they'll perk right up in a day or two. Any plant I adopt has to have a certain level of gumption. I can't abide a hothouse flower." He joked.

"Well, you see I have no plants. I kill everything. I have a black thumb." She offered her thumb for his inspection.

He pulled her hand close to examine her thumb.

"Yup, I can see it. You're a plant assassin." He kissed the back of her hand.

• • •

Jules walked away with some prize money after the first Ladies' Night of 2023. It was a smaller turnout than usual, frigid temps and snow in the forecast kept the numbers down, so she had been able to shoot in four rounds. On her fourth leg, she noticed a slight tremble as she gripped the gun. She loosened her grip for a moment, checking it. The tremble became slightly more pronounced. She laid down her weapon and shook her hands out, wiggling and flexing her fingers. Lately, she had noticed more pins and needles when she woke up, and a longer recovery time. Neuropathy. A word that hadn't been in her vocabulary a decade ago.

This wasn't something to be ignored. She thought about Sally, who had been diagnosed with a condition called essential tremor. Jules had noticed her friend's hands shaking more these days. It wasn't life-threatening, but it could be debilitating. Sally was still self-conscious, but also resigned. Aging was a demanding sport.

Charlotte was still on the West Coast and Frank wasn't coming to Scotty's, but Jules needed to buy a round for the Ladies with her winnings of the evening. The snow had started earlier and wasn't expected to let up. She'd make a quick appearance and head home. They were calling for 10-12 inches by the next day, and trucks were already out preparing the roads.

Inside, the decorations were still up. It felt like months since Christmas.

"Hey, Jules!" Gloria waved her over. "Happy New Year!"

"Happy New Year! How were your holidays?"

"Exhausting. We really do it up. Fifty or sixty of us on Christmas Day. We rent the reception room in our church. Everyone cooks and cooks and cooks. Then we keep going through the week, visiting this one and that one. By this time I'm ready for some R&R, you know? I'd like to be lyin' on a beach somewhere," She looked around. "No Frank tonight, huh?" She looked at Jules with a smile, a raised eyebrow.

Jules laughed, "Is there a question there, Gloria?"

"I'm just curious. He's a handsome man. Are you 'an item' as they say."

"I don't think they say that anymore. 'Hanging out' maybe? I suppose we are doing that." In her mind, she saw him standing naked in her bathroom, shaving over the sink.

"Aye, Chica. Lucky woman. It's nice though. That tragedy brought you together. Joy from sorrow."

Jules hadn't really considered that, but it was true. After Dave and Rebecca died, she and Frank had joined forces as champions for Kevin.

"How's Kevin doing?"

"Honestly? I think he's going to have a rough few years before he finds solid ground. He has all of the resources and support he needs, but everything in his life is temporary right now."

"Hmm. I guess that's true for all of us, right?"

The whole way home, Jules turned the words over in her head. Joy from sorrow. That was the legacy she was hoping to leave. She measured the sorrow her mission would yield for the people she loved. It would be unforgivable but finite. She thought of the joy of future generations who would know nothing of her, but would know only Democracy, and not have suffered under fascism.

She slept well.

· · ·

VIDEO DIARY ENTRY – January 6, 2023

"Hi. Happy New Year. Today is January 6ᵗʰ, 2023. I'm recording this to remind everyone that it's the second anniversary of the insurrection at the Capitol. We can't let this date go unrecognized ever again. It was a day that almost swallowed our Democracy whole. It was a day when we were attacked from the inside! To my mind, a much more dangerous threat than any act of war from a foreign nation. This enemy wears our uniform, lives in our neighborhood, teaches our children, polices our street, and preaches in our pulpit. This is what we once would have called treason, and now we call it tourism.

"President Biden recognized some of the heroes of the insurgency at a White House event today, letting them know that history will remember their names. People died that day. People died after that day from the fallout and the trauma. Remember how we all felt, watching the attack unfold on live television? Remember that Donald Trump was the incendiary, urging them all to 'fight like hell.'

"Donald, I want you to know that you ignited me, as well. You, your hate-filled rhetoric, and your unchecked lust for power. You have set me on this path. I only hope I'm not too late."

• • •

After Ladies' Night, Jules knew she needed to see her doctor and get the tremor checked out. She could not afford to ignore it. If it was something degenerative, it could have a serious impact on the mission. She still had 18 months to go until Day Zero. A lot could happen.

She had done some googling and got the basics of things that cause tremor. Stress (check). Sleep deprivation (nope). Heredity

(?). Essential tremor disorder (?). Normal aging (check). Parkinsons (?). Medication side effects (nope). MS (?). Stroke (nope). TBI (nope). While she mostly eschewed the common practice of prescribing drugs as a solution to anything, she was glad to learn that there were meds that could control the shaking or slow the progression if the news was bad. She booked the first available appointment, February 24th.

• • •

"Hi Ben." Jules was hoping for some news about Kevin.

"Hey, mom. How are you?"

"I'm good. Socked in with a big snow. Did you get hit?'

"Oh yeah, we're deep in it up here, too. How's Frank?"

Jules was pleased that both boys asked about him when they talked.

"He's good. He's coming over later with some groceries. He's got that big 4-wheel drive. Have you heard anything about Kevin?"

"It's a process, but we're definitely on track. We've had a few phone calls with Megan and Mark. You know they're pregnant?"

"Yes, I found out in December. It was still kind of under wraps. Do you think that works for or against you getting Kevin?"

"I think they want to bring their baby home and focus all of their attention on him or her. They just didn't anticipate that it would ever happen, so they hadn't really thought about it. And now they are feeling so much guilt about the impact on Kevin."

"I can see that. I guess an outsider might think they are getting rid of him now that they have their own, but we all know that's not true. Anybody who really matters knows it's not true."

"That's what I told them. They've given him a soft landing place after an unimaginable trauma. They don't want people to think that they're afraid to have Kevin around the baby."

"Jesus! That didn't even occur to me." Jules' ire was up at the thought. "That was an accident, period. He was three, for god's sake. His parents' negligence put him in that position."

"I know, mom, but I do understand how they feel. They're good people doing good things. But they know how the haters can come out of the woodwork. There was so much press around this whole thing last summer, bringing up Kevin's history."

"Well, let them know we'll be behind them if they need us. Frank has a lot of connections."

"I will. DCFS is trying to expedite this, given the tragic circumstances of Kevin's case. If it gets approved, he can come and live with us right away, but it could take up to a year to finalize the adoption."

"When do you think that could happen? Any idea?" Jules asked.

"It could be any day. We've talked with his caseworker and we're all in agreement that sooner is better. Even if he has to change schools mid-year. At this point, he's been through so much upheaval it's unlikely to have a significant impact, especially since he's already comfortable with us."

"That makes sense to me. Also, I think it will be good for him to have a clean slate. Here, people see him through the media lens. There, he'll just be a new kid in class."

"That's what we're all hoping for. Exciting news about Jax and Kelly, huh?"

"Yes! I'm so happy for them. Selfishly, I'm looking forward to the after-wedding. Remember how much fun we had at yours? Ever since that day I've been excited about doing it again with Jackson. It's a special thing to experience with your kids. Seeing them with their person, committing to share their lives." Jules' voice caught in her throat, and she wiped unexpected tears with the palm of her hand.

"I agree. I think they make a great couple. He asked me to be Best Man."

"Of course he did! Who else would he pick?"

"Did you know he asked Eric to do a reading?"

"No, I didn't. That's really special. I'm sure he was touched." Jules heard Frank's truck in the drive.

"Listen, honey, Frank's here and I want to go help him bring the groceries in."

"Okay, tell him hi." Jules was pleased that both boys seemed to genuinely like Frank.

"I will. Hugs to everyone. Love you the most."

•   •   •

MASS SHOOTINGS IN THE US
January 2023 - 57 total

A mass shooting is any shooting where four or more people, other than the shooter, are killed or injured.

1. January 01, 2023 - Chicago, Illinois - 1 dead, 3 injured
2. January 01, 2023 - Miami Gardens, Florida - 9 injured
3. January 01, 2023 - Durham, North Carolina - 5 injured
4. January 01, 2023 - Oklahoma City, Oklahoma - 1 dead, 4 injured
5. January 01, 2023 - Allentown, Pennsylvania - 4 injured
6. January 01, 2023 - Ocala, Florida - 2 dead, 4 injured
7. January 01, 2023 - Columbus, Ohio - 1 dead, 4 injured
8. January 03, 2023 - Washington, District of Columbia - 1 dead, 3 injured
9. January 03, 2023 - New Orleans, Louisiana - 5 injured
10. January 04, 2023 - Cedar City (Enoch), Utah - 7 dead,
11. January 04, 2023 - Baltimore, Maryland - 1 dead, 4 injured
12. January 04, 2023 - Dumfries, Virginia - 1 dead, 4 injured
13. January 05, 2023 - New Orleans, Louisiana - 2 dead, 3 injured
14. January 05, 2023 - Miami Gardens, Florida - 10 injured
15. January 06, 2023 - Dallas, Texas - 3 dead, 2 injured
16. January 06, 2023 - San Francisco, California - 1 dead, 3 injured

17. January 07, 2023 - High Point, North Carolina - 4 dead,

18. January 07, 2023 - Huntsville, Alabama - 2 dead, 9 injured

19. January 08, 2023 - Minneapolis, Minnesota - 4 injured

20. January 08, 2023 - Albany, Georgia - 4 injured

21. January 09, 2023 - Philadelphia, Pennsylvania - 3 dead, 1 injured

22. January 09, 2023 - Minneapolis, Minnesota - 4 injured

23. January 09, 2023 - Philadelphia, Pennsylvania - 3 dead, 1 injured

24. January 09, 2023 - Denver, Colorado - 4 injured

25. January 13, 2023 - Cleveland, Ohio - 4 dead, 1 injured

26. January 14, 2023 - Saint Louis, Missouri - 4 injured

27. January 15, 2023 - Rockford, Illinois - 3 dead, 1 injured

28. January 15, 2023 - Houston, Texas - 1 dead, 4 injured

29. January 15, 2023 - Homestead, Florida - 1 dead, 3 injured

30. January 15, 2023 - Phoenix, Arizona - 4 injured

31. January 16, 2023 - Goshen, California - 6 dead,

32. January 16, 2023 - Sanford, Florida - 1 dead, 5 injured

33. January 16, 2023 - Fort Pierce, Florida - 1 dead, 7 injured

34. January 17, 2023 - Houston, Texas - 4 injured

35. January 21, 2023 - Monterey Park, California - 11 dead, 9 injured

36. January 21, 2023 - Yuma, Arizona - 5 injured

37. January 21, 2023 - Bronx, New York - 1 dead, 3 injured

38. January 22, 2023 - Shreveport, Louisiana - 1 dead, 7 injured

39. January 22, 2023 - Baton Rouge, Louisiana - 12 injured

40. January 22, 2023 - Robinsonville (Tunica Resorts), Mississippi - 4 injured

41. January 23, 2023 - Chicago, Illinois - 2 dead, 3 injured

42. January 23, 2023 - Oakland, California - 1 dead, 4 injured

43. January 23, 2023 - Half Moon Bay, California - 7 dead, 1 injured

44. January 24, 2023 - Red Springs, North Carolina - 3 dead, 1 injured

45. January 26, 2023 - Newark, New Jersey - 1 dead, 4 injured

46. January 26, 2023 - Lancaster, Pennsylvania - 4 injured
47. January 27, 2023 - San Diego, California - 1 dead, 3 injured
48. January 28, 2023 - Andrews, South Carolina - 2 dead, 2 injured
49. January 28, 2023 - Austin, Texas - 2 dead, 3 injured
50. January 28, 2023 - Beverly Hills, California - 3 dead, 2 injured
51. January 28, 2023 - Philadelphia, Pennsylvania - 4 injured
52. January 29, 2023 - Luttrell, Tennessee - 4 dead,
53. January 29, 2023 - Columbus, Ohio - 1 dead, 3 injured
54. January 29, 2023 - Greensboro, North Carolina - 1 dead, 6 injured
55. January 30, 2023 - Lakeland, Florida - 11 injured
56. January 30, 2023 - Dallas, Texas - 1 dead, 3 injured
57. January 31, 2023 - Durham, North Carolina - 2 dead, 2 injured

• • •

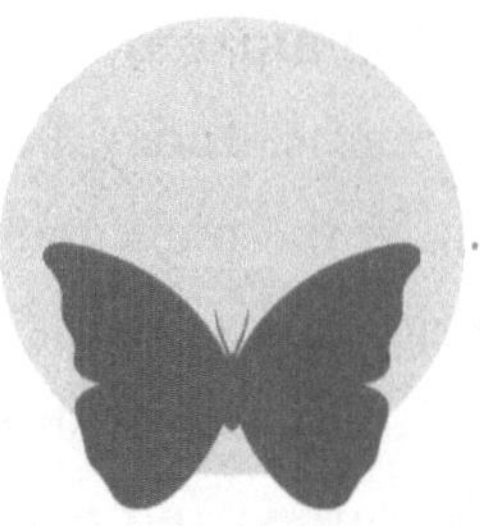

FEBRUARY 2023

ERIC'S DAY IN COURT WAS SCHEDULED for the first week of February. Jules and Frank were planning to be there, along with all of the family, to support him as he finally faced his attacker. Despite the family's opposition, a plea deal had been reached. The prosecutor felt that it was better than risking a hostile judge, one secretly friendly to the defendant. McEvers wasn't getting the maximum sentence he could have faced, but he would do prison time.

Eric had chosen to present his statement in open court, rather than with a video or a written statement. He wanted the last word. No notes.

"Thank you, your honor," Eric responded when the judge called him forward.

"My name is Eric Evans. I'm nineteen years old, and until *Hatred* derailed me," he looked pointedly at McEvers, renaming him, "I was a student at SUNY Purchase, a freshman studying drama. I first met *my attacker*," he nodded toward the defense table, "in my own home, my dorm, where he was visiting a friend of mine. Neither of us realized that we had opened our doors, exposed ourselves, to someone so vicious, so lacking in humanity. Jeff McEvers, this is the last time I will ever utter your name. Today, I am here to name you and shame you. To let you know the nightmare you were to me and to my family. My family," Eric's voice caught and he wiped away tears, "my amazing and loving family, my Irish Catholic family, who are all here with me today," he turned and pointed to the crowd behind him. "When I was on life support and in a coma, at death's door, when I struggled in the days and weeks after *your violence against me* to regain my ability to walk and talk, these people held me up. In the months since *your violence against me*, I've found inner peace again with my people at my side." McEvers was looking straight ahead. "Where are your people, McEvers? There is nobody here for you. Nobody who wants to witness your depravity. No one who wants to lay claim to your kinship. This is your legacy, Jeff McEvers. Your hate versus our love. Love wins. . . Love wins. . . Love always wins."

They stood as a group and followed Eric into the hallway, a sobbing entourage moved by an extraordinary act of courage.

• • •

Jules sat in the examining room, waiting for her doctor to show up and trying to empty her mind. In the weeks since she first noticed the tremor in her hands at the range, Frank had also noticed it, which had forced a discussion she preferred not to have. Frank's concern came from a place of love, and she knew that intellectually, but she wasn't used to having someone so close, seeing her need.

She had made the mistake of reading entirely too much about all of the possible causes, their symptoms, diagnosis, treatment, and prognosis. Even the most benign of these could seriously interrupt her mission.

Doctor Fritsch knocked twice, then opened the door.

"Come on in."

"Hey Jules! How are you? It's been a while."

Elaine Fritsch had been her primary care doctor since she finished her childbearing years. She had relied on her OB/GYN for everything back then, and Doctor Villanova had indulged her, over-indulged her, treating her with love after Mick died. She provided tele-health for Jules before it was even a thing. When Doctor V. finally pushed Jules out of the nest, she referred her to Elaine.

"Hi Elaine. Good to see you." They caught up with each other's families and personal lives in a few sentences.

"What brings you in?"

"Last month, I started to notice a slight tremor in my hands. I just thought I should have it checked out."

"I'm glad you did. Let's see what we can find out," Elaine glanced at her chart. "So you're, what, 67 now?"

"Yes, last August."

"Okay, hold your arms straight out, shoulder height, palms up," Elaine demonstrated. "We're going to hold this for 10 seconds. One, two, three, four, five, six, seven, eight, nine, ten. Okay, you can relax."

Jules dropped her arms and shook them out.

"Now same thing with palms down. One, two, three, four, five, six, seven, eight, nine, ten. And relax. Great." She made some notes in Jule's e-chart.

"Okay, now I want you to go palm to palm with me, elbow locked, and try to resist. Right hand first. Good. Now left. Good. Now you push and I'll resist. Push as hard as you can, right hand first. Okay, now left. Great."

"Now, let's talk about what you are seeing and when you are seeing it. Obviously, I'm not seeing a tremor during this exam and your strength and stamina seem age appropriate. I'm going to go through a series of questions that will help me decide on next steps, okay?"

Jules nodded.

"How often are you noticing the tremor? Is it daily? A few times a week? Less often?"

"I would say less often. Maybe a few times in the weeks since I noticed it?"

"Can you estimate how many times since that first instance?"

Jules thought back over the last five weeks since ladies' night in January; a few times in the shower, once over dinner with Frank, a couple times when she was reading, and when she was on her phone.

"Maybe a dozen?"

"That's more than a few. Starting today, when you leave my office, I want you to start keeping a log. Time of day, what you were doing, and how long it lasted."

Jules felt a prickle of fear and Elaine picked up on it.

"No reason to worry. This is just to help us with the work up. It's standard stuff." She laid a reassuring hand on Jules' forearm, and squeezed gently, looking directly into her eyes.

"Okay, now are you doing anything particular when you notice it? Are you holding a pen, or doing the dishes? Driving? Holding your cell phone?"

"The first time I noticed it I was gripping something very tightly, and I had to loosen my grip and shake out my hands. After a few minutes, the shaking dissipated."

Elaine was taking notes on the i-pad.

"So, is it only when you are gripping something? Or have you noticed it when you are at rest as well?" She looked at Jules expectantly.

"Um," Jules had to think about it. "I guess both. But, mostly when I'm holding something."

"Got it." More notes.

"Oh, and I've also noticed more pins and needles in my hands in the morning. I've had that on and off my whole life, but it seems to be more regular, and it lasts longer before I can finally shake it off and return to full feeling in my hands."

"Mhm. Are you a side sleeper?"

"Yes, but I switch sides."

"Okay, are you feeling that in your legs, hips, feet, arms, or just the hands?"

"My hands and wrists."

"Are you sexually active, Jules?"

"Yes, I am." Jules was surprised by the question.

"Good for you! Are you practicing safe sex?" Elaine asked.

"Elaine, I hardly think we need contraceptives." Jules laughed it off.

"No, but you still need protection from STDs. Older people tend to forget that. You know the old saying, you're sleeping with everyone your partner has ever slept with."

"Point taken. But Jesus, condoms? I think I was a teenager the last time I used one of those things. Sex with a new partner is awkward enough at this age. Adding that just seems, I don't know, cruel."

"I get it. They have made strides in that area and there are some day-after meds that can work for STD prevention. I'll give you some information." She made some notes in Jules' chart.

"Are you exclusive?" She asked. Jules nodded, assuming.

"Have you both gotten tested for HIV? That's a must. Do it together. That will give you a chance to open up about your sexual histories and health. Make it a date night."

"Sounds scintillating. Can we get back to this?" Jules shook her hands dramatically.

"Okay," Elaine laughed, letting her off the hook, "one last question. How much time do you spend on a computer or cell phone? I'm going to give you some options. Would you call yourself (1) a superuser – 6 or more hours per day, (2) a regular user – under 6 hours a day, (3) a casual user – a few times a week, (4) an occasional user – a few times a month, or (5) a rare user – less than monthly or never?"

"Definitely a casual user, now that I'm retired. When I was working, I would have said superuser."

"Got it." Elaine finished the notes, swiveled the screen away, and turned her focus to Jules. "Now, let's talk about what we might be seeing. I'm sure you've been on the google."

"Guilty. But it hasn't really been very helpful," Jules admitted.

"That's usually the case. It can be terrifying, right? But we're going to approach this with science instead of algorithms, okay?"

Jules laughed, relaxing in her friend's capable hands. Elaine explained that there are two primary types of tremor; rest tremors and action or intentional tremors. Rest tremors were a typical indicator of Parkinson's, among other possible diagnoses. If the tremor mostly occurred when she was holding something, contracting the muscles of her hand and wrist, that would be an intentional tremor. Intentional tremors could have physiological or environmental roots.

Elaine thought MS and Parkinson's unlikely, given her tremor type, but mentioned another possibility, FXTAS, Fragile-X Associated Tremor Disorder. It was a late onset disorder, more typical in men than women over the age of fifty, but still seen in women. If she had it, it would have come from her father. Fathers pass the gene to their daughters, but not their sons. Jules didn't remember her father having a tremor before his death. And neither of her sisters ever mentioned these kinds of symptoms, though she planned to call them to find out. It was entirely possible that they weren't keen to share this evidence of decay.

By the time she left, Elaine had reassured her. With no known family history of tremor-related conditions, the most likely diagnosis was the simplest. Jules was instructed to stop all caffeine intake, work on stress relief with meditation or yoga, and undergo a battery of tests. Elaine wanted to check her thyroid, sugar levels, and check for FXTAS. If her blood showed the genetic marker, an MRI would be indicated to confirm that diagnosis.

All Jules could do now was wait.

• • •

After leaving several vials of blood at the lab, Jules called Cassie. At 65, her sister was vibrant and fit. She still played tennis and was learning pickleball in preparation for the inevitable day when the tennis court finally beat her.

"Hey, Juicy!" Cassie answered, sounding upbeat as always.

"Hey, Mama." Jules had started calling her Mama Cass when the singer was a rising star in the sixties. That had been shortened to Mama when Cassie had her first baby.

"I've been meaning to call you. Drew and I want to come and visit." They had lived outside of Buffalo since the late 90s, when Drew got a job in manufacturing. He was still working so they didn't get away too often.

"I would *love* to see you guys. Just let me know what works with your schedule." Jules missed her siblings and was always happy to have them visit.

"But listen, I just came from my primary care doctor. I've started to notice a slight tremor in my hands occasionally and I'm having it checked out."

"Oh. I'm sure it's nothing. You know what they say, *getting old ain't for sissies.*"

Jules hated that cliché.

"Yeah, that's true. But one of the possibilities is a genetic thing. Something to do with Fragile-X. They're running tests and everything, but I wanted to check in with you to see if you've had any symptoms. This would have been passed to us from dad. Apparently, it only goes to the girls of the carriers, not the boys."

"Oh no. I hope you're okay. I've never heard of that. I haven't noticed anything at all. I'm still a machine on the court," Cassie laughed. "But you have a few years on me. You might be the first one to be affected. What is the prognosis? Is it treatable?"

Jules heard the sudden concern behind her sister's teasing.

"Yes, it's not a death sentence or anything. But it is progressive. Do you remember dad having tremors?" Their father had been gone for over twenty years.

"Hm. No, not that I recall. Have you talked to Thea yet? She spent the most time with him just before he died." Thea was a nurse and was the default family caregiver.

"I'm calling her next. I want to gather the family history while they are running the tests. But this could be as simple as cutting out caffeine and managing my stress."

"What about mom's side? Remember how bad Nana was when we were little? How her hands would shake so much?"

"I had completely forgotten that! You're right. I was always scared when she had a cup of coffee in her hand. Jesus, she must have been, what, late fifties? That seemed so old to us then, but now I'm realizing how young she was to be so debilitated. Mom never suffered like that though, so maybe it wasn't genetic."

"You should call Aunt Katie. She'd know for sure about Nana."

Their mother's sister, Kate, lived on the West Coast with their Uncle Ean.

"Good idea. After I call Thea. Listen, Mama, you let me know when you guys want to come out. I miss you!"

"You, too Juicy. Love you."

Jules' next call was to Thea.

"Hi, Juice." She answered.

"Hi, Three." Thea had become Three when toddler Cassie had mispronounced Thea as Three-a, and since she was the third sister, Three just stuck.

"Is everything okay?" Thea asked. Jules felt bad that a call from her was so rare that it would portend potential tragedy. She couldn't deny she'd been closer to Cass, which wasn't saying much.

"Oh yeah, everyone's good. Nothing to worry about. In fact, did you hear that Jax and Kelly got engaged?" She made a quick course correction and decided to start with some good news.

"No! That's so great. She's the one we met at Christmas a few years ago? The librarian?"

"Yes, that's her. They're thinking of an October wedding up here somewhere. As soon as I have a date, I'll let you know."

"We'll definitely be there. Spencer is kind of easing into retirement now and we're more flexible." Thea and Spencer lived a few hours southwest. They hadn't had kids of their own and had always made a fuss over all of their nieces and nephews.

"Bring your dancing shoes," Jules laughed. "I wanted to ask you about some health stuff."

"Okay, sure. What's up?"

"Well, I have started to notice my hands shaking occasionally. Just a slight tremor. My doctor is doing a workup and I'm trying to gather family history. You spent the most time with daddy at the end of his life. Did he have a tremor or anything like that? Anything you noticed?"

"Oh, no. He had good balance and coordination. We had to test that regularly as he declined to determine what supports he needed. His shortcomings were entirely cognitive."

"Well, that's good news. It's not definitive but it's a good piece of my puzzle. What about you, Three? Have you noticed anything like that? Shakiness in your hands?"

"Not so far. Are they doing bloodwork on you? What are they exploring?"

"She ordered lots of tests. Sugar levels, thyroid, and she's looking for some genetic markers. I'll let you know as soon as I have any results. It also could be environmental."

"You should cut out caffeine."

"Yes, that's my first step. Do you remember how bad Nana shook? I had completely forgotten that until I talked to Cass earlier. I don't know if she was sick or what. I was too young to even think about it. I just thought old people shook like that."

"Old people. We're both older than she was, Juicy."

"I know. Crazy, isn't it? Remember the housecoats she wore? The big pockets with bric-a-brac trim, stuffed with used tissues and butterscotch?" They both laughed at the memory, then fell quiet.

"I'm going to call Aunt Kate next week to see if she knows anything about Nana's health history. As soon as I have any more information to share I'll let you know. Hug Spencer for me. Love you."

"Stay Juicy."

VIDEO DIARY ENTRY – February 24, 2023

"Hi. Today is the one-year anniversary of Putin's invasion of Ukraine. February 24th, 2023. In the year since his ill-advised attack, Putin's Russia has lost more combat soldiers than in all combined wars since World War Two. He seriously underestimated Zelenskyy and the Ukrainians. A year ago, Volodymyr Zelenskyy pleaded with Putin to find a peaceful solution. "War is a huge calamity," he said, hoping to spare his people. But Putin would not be moved.

"So, today, a year on, over 100,000 Russians and 13,000 Ukrainian service members have lost their lives. More than 7,000 civilians, including about 400 children, have been killed in Ukraine. Collateral damage. What a disgusting concept. More than 8 million Ukrainians have fled their homes. And there is no end in sight. No peace talks. Just more death and destruction, more feeding the power-hungry machine that is Putin in his quest to remake the Soviet Union.

"Can't we evolve beyond the wars of men?"

•   •   •

"Hi, Aunt Katie. It's Jules calling. Sorry I missed you. I have some news to share. Jackson and Kelly are getting married! We're very excited. Watch for your invite. Second, I want to talk to you about some health stuff. Nothing alarming, but I'm looking at a possible neurological condition that might be genetic. Mom and dad didn't have any issues that we can recall, but we remember Nana having a bad tremor at a pretty young age. Do you know if she had a specific condition? My doctor is running some tests and I'm trying to gather family history to contribute to the big picture. Give me a call when you can. Say hi to Uncle Ean. Love you."

Jules read off her phone number, twice, slowly, before hanging up. Aunt Katie still had a landline and an answering machine. Jules would be a blinking red light on her kitchen counter in Del Norte, California.

.   .   .

MASS SHOOTINGS IN THE US
February 2023 - 41 total

A mass shooting is any shooting where four or more people, other than the shooter, are killed or injured.

1. February 01, 2023 - Los Angeles, California - 5 injured
2. February 01, 2023 - Texas City, Texas - 4 injured
3. February 04, 2023 - Huntsville, Texas - 2 dead, 2 injured
4. February 05, 2023 - Tucson, Arizona - 1 dead, 3 injured
5. February 05, 2023 - Newport, Arkansas - 1 dead, 4 injured
6. February 05, 2023 - Stockton, California - 1 dead, 3 injured
7. February 05, 2023 - Peyton, Colorado - 2 dead, 3 injured
8. February 06, 2023 - Corpus Christi, Texas - 1 dead, 3 injured
9. February 08, 2023 - Laurinburg, North Carolina - 4 injured
10. February 08, 2023 - New Orleans, Louisiana - 2 dead, 4 injured
11. February 08, 2023 - Elizabeth City, North Carolina - 4 injured
12. February 10, 2023 - Brooklyn, New York - 4 injured
13. February 10, 2023 - Bronx, New York - 2 dead, 2 injured
14. February 12, 2023 - Louisville, Mississippi - 1 dead, 5 injured
15. February 13, 2023 - Paterson, New Jersey - 4 injured
16. February 13, 2023 - East Lansing, Michigan - 3 dead, 5 injured

17. February 14, 2023 - Pittsburgh, Pennsylvania - 4 injured

18. February 14, 2023 - Buffalo, New York - 5 injured

19. February 15, 2023 - Baltimore, Maryland - 4 injured

20. February 15, 2023 - El Paso, Texas - 1 dead, 3 injured

21. February 17, 2023 - Coldwater, Mississippi - 6 dead,

22. February 17, 2023 - Columbus, Georgia - 9 injured

23. February 18, 2023 - Saint Louis, Missouri - 4 injured

24. February 18, 2023 - Columbus, Georgia - 3 dead, 1 injured

25. February 18, 2023 - Loris, South Carolina - 4 injured

26. February 19, 2023 - Chicago, Illinois - 3 dead, 3 injured

27. February 19, 2023 - Indianapolis, Indiana - 4 injured

28. February 19, 2023 - Memphis, Tennessee - 1 dead, 10 injured

29. February 19, 2023 - New Orleans, Louisiana - 1 dead, 4 injured

30. February 21, 2023 - Colorado Springs, Colorado - 5 injured

31. February 22, 2023 - Orlando, Florida - 3 dead, 2 injured

32. February 23, 2023 - Kissimmee (Poinciana), Florida - 2 injured

33. February 23, 2023 - Philadelphia, Pennsylvania - 7 injured

34. February 24, 2023 - Abbeville, Louisiana - 4 injured

35. February 25, 2023 - Saint Paul, Minnesota - 2 dead, 3 injured

36. February 25, 2023 - Machesney Park, Illinois - 4 injured

37. February 26, 2023 - Detroit, Michigan - 2 dead, 2 injured

38. February 26, 2023 - Pompano Beach, Florida - 2 dead, 2 injured

39. February 26, 2023 - Memphis, Tennessee - 1 dead, 4 injured

40. February 27, 2023 - Memphis, Tennessee - 2 dead, 2 injured

41. February 27, 2023 - New Richmond, Ohio - 3 dead, 1 injured

● ● ●

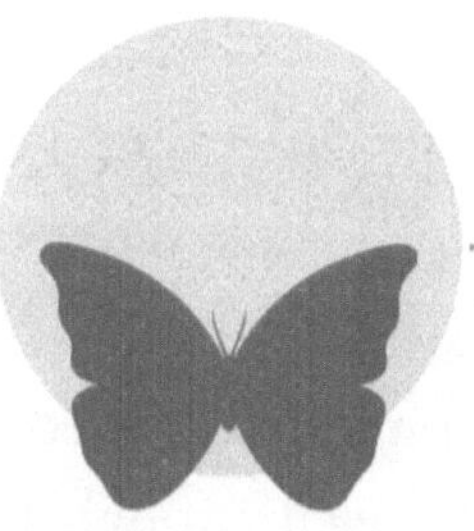

MARCH 2023

Even though Jules had increased her solo visits to the gun range, she still enjoyed the competition of Ladies' Night. And, she had to admit, the camaraderie. She walked in to a loud and rowdy welcome. In spite of herself, she had come to think of these women as her friends. She wondered what they would think of her after she accomplished her mission. Another tragedy from within their ranks.

For the first time since the new year, Jules was concerned about her ability to maintain her standing as the top shooter. A title she had held since Rebecca's murder. In these few months since she first noticed the weakness in her hands, the tremor had become a more regular visitor. She was tracking it in her logbook and noticed there didn't seem to be a pattern emerging. It happened randomly, sporadically, and lasted longer. It was affecting her consistency.

Jules was testing some over-the-counter remedies while waiting to hear back from her doctor. She hadn't seen any test results posted on her e-chart yet, so she decided to try a few things on her own. A little research suggested CBD in gummy or oil form might be helpful. So she was experimenting with that, as well as a supplement called Tremadone. These did seem to make a difference, at least in the moment.

"Jules! You're up this round!" T.J. called, reading off the clipboard.

She was still shooting well enough to take the cash, but the diameter of her target pattern was widening slightly. Not enough that anyone would notice. Anyone other than her.

● ● ●

March 4, 2023

Dear Ju-Ju-Bee,

I hope you and the boys and the grandkids are all doing great. It's been so hard not seeing everyone since before lockdown!!! I'm grateful that we had the holidays with you all in 2019. Wasn't that lucky? Who knew what lay ahead of us then!

Me and Uncle Ean hope to make a trip out soon to see everyone if the numbers stay down. Things seem pretty good right now. Of course, we're both keeping up on our shots, but given our age we worry about the risks of flying. All of that recycled air in such close quarters! And, neither of us is in great health. That's partly why I'm writing.

I got your message last week and decided to write rather than call. I have some health news to share, too. I saw the doctor last month and found out I have breast cancer. In a way, I've been expecting it for years. We've got those damn genes in our family, you know. I found it myself. Make sure you do your exams!

We haven't decided on treatment yet, but I'll be 82 this year. EIGHTY-TWO! She said I probably have 2-4 good years left with no treatment at all. If I start on chemo today, I might be able to double that, but I'd spend a lot of that time suffering from the treatment, not the disease. It hardly seems worth it, right? I'm not too keen on the idea of vomiting uncontrollably for days or weeks on end. I'd sooner slam my hand in a car door than throw up! And my hair is the only trace of the girl I once was. Aging leaves us so little. I know it's vanity, but I want to hold on to that. I hope you don't think that's foolish. I just want my dignity intact when all is said and done.

I'm glad your doctor is looking at family history to diagnose you. You're right that Nana had those shaky hands. Honestly, back then we didn't think anything of it. I doubt she even went to the doctor. And your mom and I didn't seem to inherit anything, but that isn't the whole picture.

I've been greatly blessed in this lifetime, beyond what I deserve. And beyond what most anyone knows. I've been agonizing over this letter, and what I am laying at your doorstep. But you need to know this now, before it's all too late. So, I will start with an apology. I apologize for the secrets that have been kept, the lies that have been told, and the damage that the truth will undoubtedly leave in its wake.

In 1955, I was a sophomore at St. Catherine the Divine. Your folks were already off and married, and Simon was two by that time. He was such a good baby! I was a built-in babysitter for Jayny and Johnny back then and I spent a lot of time with them. Uncle Ean and I were dating, but he was leaving for the Army, and we didn't know what that would bring. Of course, we planned to be together forever, but I still had 2 years of high school before we could legally marry without parental consent, and your Nana and Pappy weren't happy about the relationship. He was too old for me and they didn't see him at mass often enough. I think they hoped we would drift apart over time and miles.

But a few weeks before he was to ship out, we found out I was pregnant. A good Irish Catholic girl. In trouble, as they called it in those days. Of course, it was a sin, but it was also a black mark on the family. Daddy could hardly look at me and Mommy was stuck in the middle, trying to manage the crisis. Over the course of a terribly difficult week, we got everything figured out. Ean had no choice but to report for duty as planned. I was going to be sent to Most Holy Redeemer School for Girls outside of Philadelphia to have the baby, where it would be adopted by a loving Catholic family. If we agreed to the plan, and I returned to finish school, and Ean came back from overseas, they would give our marriage their blessing.

The key to all of this was secrecy. No one was to know. Not even family. They shipped me off quickly, before I started showing. I don't know what people were told. I don't know what they guessed. But somehow your mom found out. I have no idea how she did it, but she found out where I was and she just showed up one day! I was overjoyed and humiliated! I idolized Jayny. I wanted my big sister's approval, but I was afraid she'd never look at me the same way again. My weakness, my lack of moral fortitude, was a mark against all of us.

But as soon as she saw me, she burst into tears and pulled me close. There was no judgment in her. She was my sister.

You were born in August. John and Jayne, your mom and dad, were there with me. Not in the room, like they do today, but they were waiting for you. I never held you that day. You went straight from my body into their family. As we had all agreed.

Your mom and dad told anyone who was bold enough to ask that they had been trying to adopt through an agency and had been so lucky to get you as an infant. Even adoption was secret back then, closed, they called it. I'm sure people guessed at the truth, but any rumors soon faded as life went on. In time, most people become more concerned about keeping their own secrets.

Ean came home and we got married when you were almost three. I know you've seen the pictures. I wore white and Uncle Ean wore his dress blues. After a short honeymoon trip to the city, we left New York behind for good. It was an unspoken agreement that this would be the easiest thing for everyone. I know in my broken heart it was the right thing to do. I hope you can understand. Times were so different then.

Call me when you're ready. If you can. I love you.
Aunt Katie

• • •

Jules folded the letter and slid it back into the envelope. She had walked back into the house from the mailbox as she read and found herself standing in the living room, dazed. For a moment, nothing seemed familiar. Who bought that couch? Who chose this paint color? She half-expected someone to come from another room and welcome her to their home. Her breath was coming fast and she felt warm and dizzy as she dropped into a chair.

Focus, she thought. *Take slow, deep breaths. In through the nose, out through the mouth.* She put her head between her knees to keep from passing out. She thought of riding the Round-Up at

Coney Island when she was a girl; how the world kept spinning as she toddled off like a drunken sailor after the ride was over. But this lacked the euphoria of those summer adventures and Jules felt dangerously close to some point of no return. She closed her eyes and slept.

When she awoke, Feinstein was curled up next to her, warm and buzzy, attuned to her need. In that split second of first consciousness, she had forgotten. Her phone was ringing, and as she reached for it she saw the letter. The Letter. She needed time to decide what it meant to her. What did it change? What did it mean for her life? She'd had no inkling of it, ever. Never a hint that she was anything, anyone other than who she was.

Now she knew she had no blood siblings, and her siblings, Simon and Cassie and Thea, were her cousins. Her parents were her aunt and uncle, and her real parents, her biological parents, Katie and Ean, were still living. Her phone had stopped ringing; she hadn't even looked to see who was calling. She put the letter in her mission safe until she was ready to do anything more with it. The implications were overwhelming her, and she needed to sleep.

• • •

After a long night of vivid and unsettling dreams, Jules sat with a cup of decaf, assessed her situation, and made some practical decisions. She reminded herself that her mission was still, always, her priority. Selfishly, she wanted to abort it. She wanted to throw herself into a life with Frank, with her kids and grandkids. She wanted to help Kevin flourish. She wanted birthday lunches with Sal. She wanted to connect with Katie and Ean, *her parents*, to forgive them and get to know them. She wanted to see Eric thrive. But all of this, her life, her personal universe, paled against the threat of fascism. What was the value of these moments measured against the freedom of a nation?

With her commitment confirmed, Jules also realized she didn't want to share this news yet. Not with Frank, and definitely not with anyone in the family. It was too much for her, too much to manage. The only person she thought of calling was Ellie. Ellie had no stake in the truth of Jules' family tree, and she was always a trustworthy confidante. She could help Jules make sense of everything.

Jules' test results hadn't come back yet, but now she was more worried about the possibility of a genetic component to her condition. Cutting her caffeine hadn't seemed to eliminate the tremor. Maybe there was some history in Ean's family. She would find out when she was ready to call them. Her parents. She dialed Ellie.

"Hey, Boss!" Ellie sounded chipper, as usual.

"Hey, El." Jules sounded leaden.

"Everything good?"

"Well, I got some news and I need to talk it through. Do you have the time and brain space for some serious conversation?"

"Do you have to ask? You know I've got your back."

"Okay. Thank you, El. Here goes." She took a calming breath.

"You're scaring me, Boss. Are you okay?"

"I'm okay, but I'm not Jules Campbell."

Ellie was quiet for a moment.

"Hm. Is this some existential bullshit? Cause I know Jules Campbell, and you're Jules Campbell." Ellie tried for a laugh.

"I got a letter from my Aunt Katie this week. It turns out she and my Uncle Ean are my real parents."

"California Aunt Katie?"

"Yeah, you've met them before. They were here the Christmas before the pandemic."

"Wow. Wow. I remember them. That is a lot to unpack. Are you okay? I mean, of course you're not okay. What did the boys say?"

"You're the first person I'm telling. And the only person for the moment. I'm just not ready to share this. I need to talk it through and live with it for a while."

"Okay, let's talk it through. I'll keep it on my hat."

"Under."

"Under what?"

"Under your hat. You'll keep it under your hat."

"You know I will. I can't imagine how this must have rocked you! I mean, you are still *you* at the core, you've lived the life you've lived and had the experiences you've had, but the people you were raised with as your family of origin? They're your cousins, not your siblings. Hey, do you have any new siblings?"

"No. That makes me so sad, but maybe that's just what they wanted. I don't know any details. Maybe they couldn't have kids after that."

"Dios mio, that would be so tragic, no?"

"It all seems so tragic anyway. All of the secrets. The lies they all lived with." Jules' words caught in her throat before a sob could erupt.

"Do you want me to come over, Boss, or do you want to meet for lunch?" Ellie heard her sorrow.

"Aren't you at work?" Jules asked.

"I am, but I can get away."

Jules glanced out the window at the March snowfall ramping up as the temperature dropped, the lion roaring in.

"No, it looks like the weather's going to get bad."

"Okay, so let's talk."

They stayed on the phone into the early afternoon, reconstructing Jules' past, present, and future.

"Thank you, El. Thank you *so much* for walking me through all of this. I feel grounded. And I have a *plan*. You know how much I love a plan. I agree that it makes sense to wait until after I have all my test results back, just in case there's bad news to share. If everything's good, then I'll set up a zoom with the family to tell them about Katie and Ean."

They were quiet a moment.

"Love you, Boss. Call me any time you need to talk."

"Thank you. Love you, Ellie."

It wasn't hard to keep the news close to her vest, once she had a plan. She realized how good she had become at compartmentalizing. She had acquired so many new skills over the past year. But she was still struggling with the one thing Ellie couldn't help with; what did this mean for her mission?

• • •

By the middle of March, Frank was with her more often than not. That was a good distraction for her amidst all of the uncertainty. Her very real worry over her health provided good cover for the new anxiety over her family tree. Any difference Frank may have noticed, he contributed to her pending diagnosis. He was obviously concerned about her; anxious that her results hadn't come in yet. But he kept that to himself, knowing her disdain for dependence, and was just there, around and alert. Helpful. Jules knew what he was doing, mother-henning in a very unobtrusive way, and she was grateful. She needed him.

On Friday morning, Jules planned to check for her test results in her e-chart for the last time that week. Nothing got posted on weekends, so she'd have to wait until Monday if it wasn't there.

She saw it as soon as she opened her email; a message from the MAGA list. **Trump to Visit New York State Capital**, was the subject line. She felt a throbbing in her chest and heat rose into her face as she scanned the email. Trump was coming to the MVP Arena on Monday. She glanced toward the door of her study, listened to place Frank in the house. She heard the shower running. Good. She had some time.

She read the details. They were looking for a big turnout of the hateful. He would be taking the stage around 10:00 am. Come, kiss the ring.

The MVP was right here, right in her backyard. She still thought of it as the Knickerbocker, its original name, even though it had been the Times Union and the Pepsi Arena before the current, MVP iteration. It was a place she knew well. It was home territory.

Jules closed her eyes to try to cipher this message. She couldn't ignore the synthesis. She wasn't sure she'd be able to maintain her health, her acuity, through to the Republican National Convention in July of 2024. And here he was, coming to her. She could hardly breathe.

"Anything, yet?" Frank stuck his head in the door.

"No," she lied easily, having not even checked her e-chart. "I guess I'll have to wait until next week. Do you want coffee?"

Jules got up and went into the kitchen to brew a pot of decaf. Frank didn't seem to mind the change from full-strength, and he shared her morning brew most days. As she measured out the grounds, he stood next to her, wrapped in just a towel and with wet hair. She breathed him in and turned on the coffee. She had already made a decision.

"I'm going to have breakfast with Sally on Monday. I feel like I haven't seen her in way too long."

"Okay, give her and Hemmy my best. How's Eric doing?" Frank inquired.

"He's planning to return to campus in the fall, but not Purchase. He doesn't know where, yet. I think he's really doing well."

"Well, he's been a lucky kid to have the support he does. What do you want to do this weekend."

"I want to hit the range at some point. Maybe tomorrow. Then maybe a date night?" Jules suggested.

"Dinner and a movie? Are we already that predictable?" Frank teased.

"No!" Jules practically shouted. "Surprise me, sir. Give it your best shot."

"Challenge accepted, madam," Frank tipped an imaginary hat toward her and bowed low over it.

At the range on Saturday, Jules was consistent and unflinching. Her OTC meds were steadying her hands, and her hands were finding their target. She still had time to succeed. She could not let this opportunity pass.

When she arrived home, Frank had a plan. They were going to Lake Placid overnight. He had booked them a room at a very upscale resort and they were going to do some late winter skiing. Jules had skied before, but it wasn't really her forte. It was an expensive sport and she'd never really had the time for it. Now, she welcomed the chance to do something outside of her comfort zone. That was where she would be living for the next 48 hours, anyway. In the uncomfortable zone. "Bring it," she thought.

• • •

Jules had barely slept the night before the first day of spring, Day Zero. Monday, March 20th, 2023. She'd sent Frank home after their Placid adventure, encouraging him to water his plants, and had spent her last night home alone. Agonizing.

She had rehearsed her plan obsessively. She was as prepared as she could be, and she wouldn't turn back. She drew the sash of her oversized gray terry robe tight around her waist and stepped into her worn scuffs. The familiar felt exquisite.

This would be her last day of freedom, at best. As she put the non-decaf coffee on to brew, an indescribable sense of calm and resolve washed over her. Her mind went back to the moment, just a little more than a year ago now, when she had first understood her purpose. On that day and this, just these two, her soul felt aligned with the universe. Out the kitchen window, the blanket of late winter snow was comforting, muffling the Monday morning sounds of her neighborhood coming to life. Maybe it would be a snow day.

She filled her favorite mug, the one the boys had given her years ago on Mother's Day. It was white ceramic, emblazoned in black lettering, World's Best Mom. Part poking fun at itself and part an homage to The Office, one of their family favorite shows starring a clueless but well-meaning manager who unironically cherishes his World's Best Boss mug. She wrapped her hands around its warmth, and beamed her mother-love to Ben and Jax. She took a cleansing breath to fill her lungs and ground herself. The steaming dark roast was sharp in her nostrils.

Jules walked from the kitchen into her small study, her haven, and lingered on each artifact of the woman she had been. Books crammed the whitewashed bookshelves that encircled the room. She pulled the few volumes she needed and reached for the sealed envelope that lay on her desk. Her framed degrees hung on the wall over her chair. They would lend her some credibility on the 11 o'clock news. Her modest collection of beautiful things, collected and curated over the years, filled this room. A clay bowl Ben had made in second grade in which she kept spare buttons, safety pins, pennies. A bronze sculpture, no more than six inches tall, of a young boy in tattered knickers with his dog. She'd found it in a second-hand store in Dublin and it had delighted her. A milles flora paperweight exploding with color trapped inside a glass orb. On the top shelf of the bookcase nearest her sat her prized Waterford highball glasses. She'd only used them twice since the day Mick died, almost 30 years ago now.

Jules turned her whole attention to each framed piece on the walls. Photographs of the boys as babies, as kids, as teens, as young adults. Every graduation. Ben's wedding. Ben with his own family. Pictures of Mick from another lifetime.

Artworks of every stripe, from reproductions and prints of masters like Van Gogh, Picasso, and Matisse, to originals she'd purchased in galleries or art shows, filled the space. She bought the work of outsider artists she'd found online in the earliest days of e-Bay. She even had framed posters and greeting cards adorning the walls. Wherever her eye rested in this contemplative place, she had wanted to encounter beauty.

When she reached the safe, she unlocked it and removed her mission phone and her glock. The gun was cold and heavy. She loaded it with more rounds than she would need, and fitted it into her leather fanny pack. Reaching the door, she gave a silent prayer of thanks for each and every second captured here, and pulled it shut behind her.

Jules set her mug in the sink and placed her mission phone, the books, and the envelope on the kitchen table for her boys.

• • •

Dear Ben and Jax,

I've written this letter in my mind a hundred times. I've tried to figure out what your response will be to the news. You two, who know me better than anyone else. Will you be stunned that I resorted to violence? Will you understand why I sacrificed my soul when I pulled that trigger? What will you need in this unimaginable moment to bring you some comfort?

In the end, I decided that there are only two important things right now. Two things you need to know if we never speak again. Which is both possible and unspeakable.

First and foremost, know that I love you two more than I have ever loved any other human being on this earth. The word itself is painfully inadequate. How can I use the same word to describe a paint color, a pair of shoes, a pizza joint, and you? Until I became your mom, I didn't know my capacity for real love. Of course I loved your grandparents and aunts and uncles and cousins. And my many dear friends over the years. And I loved your father so much, the only man who ever really knew my heart. I still feel the void he left. But even those loves fall so far short of the intensity of my feelings for you boys. It has been effortless to love you. You have been my greatest joy and my proudest accomplishment. And I have always felt fully loved by you both in return. Thank you for that. Now be there for each other in the difficult days ahead.

Second, I want to answer your question, "Why?"

I'm sure some media outlets will make me out to be insane. Resist that easy account. You know who I am. I did not act impulsively. This was a hard-won decision. I brought out my 'fancy glasses' and talked to your dad in my study. I have given thousands of hours of thought, research, and planning to this mission. We've had so many conversations, stretching back even before the Trump election, in which I've shared my fears for this country and the world. For your future and your children's future. I see the terrifying parallels between Trump and Hitler. I see the rise of fascism around the globe. I see the hate that has been unleashed when permission is granted to the hateful.

We once agreed on right and wrong, on good and evil. We could discern truth from lies. We were leaning into a global community where human rights for all seemed attainable. But we have lost our true north. Our brave, new democracy is teetering on the brink. And, with Trump threatening to run again, I am afraid that if he doesn't prevail, he and his followers will take this country by force, another insurrection. A civil war seems not just possible, but probable. I have been waiting and hoping for a hero, someone to fix everything. I am tired of waiting. So, I felt called upon to act. To have the "courage of my convictions."

I am leaving three works here for you to read when you are ready. They have provided guidance and insight in the months leading up to this day. I have marked some key passages in each that I hope will help you.

I know my actions will bring you both hardship. That has been the most difficult part for me in all of this. Knowing that you are all going to suffer. For that I am truly sorry. But I expect you will be able to find your people. Our people. Who

know the arc of history and understand, as I hope you do, that
this is for the greater good. I beg them to circle the wagons.
  I love you the most!
  xxxxxooooo

* * *

Jules headed out to the garage. Her body felt anchored by the weight of history with each step. She left the house unlocked. She didn't want them to have to break in once they converged on her home.

She drove in silence for a while, visualizing the hours ahead. In less than three hours, her obscurity would be demolished. Everyone she loved would be absolutely shattered by the news. For a while. But over time, they would not just understand, but be grateful for her sacrifice. To distract herself, she switched on the radio. The Roundtable was a comfort.

Joe Donahue welcomed WAMC's Alan Chartock, former NYS Congressman John Faso, the rare republican on the show, Sarah Rogerson from Albany Law School, and Libby Post, a local activist and political commentator. Most of whom, excepting Faso, felt like old friends. The big news, of course, was the Grand Jury indictment of Trump purportedly coming out of the office of Alvin Bragg, the Manhattan D.A. sometime later that week.

Well, that was never going to happen. Jules was struck with an overwhelming jolt of adrenaline. She, alone in the world, knew something that was about to change the course of history. It was exhilarating and horrifying. Tomorrow, she knew, they would be talking about her. She began to sweat. An electrical current seemed to flow just beneath her skin, buzzing and thrumming.

Jules turned down the volume on the radio but left it on as background noise. She walked through the plan again, trying to anticipate any points of vulnerability. Any place where she might get tripped up and need to course correct. Her training would pay off today. Everything, everything was on the line.

Just before Jules hit the Twin Bridges, SCREEE, SCREEE, SCREEE, BEEEEEEEP. The Emergency Alert System screamed to life, nearly stopping Jules' heart with its intensity. For one wild moment, she thought that she'd been found out somehow. That something had gone wrong and a missing adult alert was about to be broadcast over the airwaves with her license plate number. Just as quickly she realized that was crazy. She gripped the wheel tightly and turned up the volume.

"This is a message from the Emergency Alert System. A private plane carrying Former President Donald John Trump and fifteen other passengers has crashed in Northern New Jersey's High Point State Park. Witnesses reported a loud mid-air explosion, followed by the aircraft's rapid plummet to earth. The cause of the explosion is as yet unknown. Anyone inside the park or within a 10-mile radius of High Point State Park is asked to shelter in place so that first responders and investigators can reach the scene to assist any survivors." SCREEE, SCREEE, SCREEE, BEEEEEEEP.

"This is a message from the Emergency Alert System. A private plane carrying Former President Donald John Trump and fifteen other passengers has crashed in Northern New Jersey's High Point State Park. Witnesses reported a loud mid-air explosion, followed by the aircraft's rapid plummet to earth. The cause of the explosion is as yet unknown. Anyone inside the park or within a 10-mile radius of High Point State Park is asked to shelter in place so that first responders and investigators can reach the scene to assist any survivors."

SCREEE, SCREEE, SCREEE, BEEEEEEP.

Before the final tones had sounded, Jules had pulled off the Northway, flung herself from the driver's seat, and vomited violently into the dirty snowbank. Her entire body convulsed in relief and protest. Her teeth were at war in her head. From somewhere deep in her ancient soul, a moan was emerging, a cataclysmic om. She wrapped her arms tightly around herself, holding her bones together as the moan became a howl became an atavistic roar. "The centre cannot hold" flashed through her mind. From Yeats' "The Second Coming." It was a poem she had returned to again and again since 2016, and almost daily in the last few months, and now that line came to calm her. Her 'centre' would hold.

Understanding started to rise up within her. Her mind began to process the new reality. A reality, a future that had been inaccessible for the past thirteen months. A freedom beyond anything she had ever known clenched her being. She started to laugh. She couldn't stop. It seized her like a boa constrictor. She doubled over, hands on her knees to keep her from toppling over. She couldn't get a full breath and long-denied tears were freezing on her cheeks. A few cars slowed to see if she was okay, but she waved them on and they happily complied, speeding up when they saw her in the grips of what must have looked like madness.

When hilarity finally relinquished its grip, Jules opened the passenger door and settled herself into the seat, seeking some warmth and respite before she could even think about what came next. In that moment, closing her eyes and leaning into the stiff headrest, she remembered how she felt right after each of the boys was born. Her body and mind stretched beyond their limits, the smallest comfort felt like great luxury.

She was vaguely aware that her phone had been ringing on and off since news of the crash was released. She needed to reclaim herself before she could move forward in this second life, this restored tomorrow. Gradually, her heart quieted and her breath returned.

NPR was now covering the story in minute detail. She reached down and turned it off. The sound of the traffic whizzing and shooshing along the slushy highway filled her ears. Horns had been honking on and off in both sorrow and joy, Jules imagined, since the news broke just a few minutes before. She stretched across the center console and laid on her horn in solidarity with the joy.

Her phone rang. It was the rest of her life.

MASS SHOOTINGS IN THE US
March 2023 - 43 total

A mass shooting is any shooting where four or more people, other than the shooter, are killed or injured.

1. March 01, 2023 - Cocoa, Florida - 4 dead,
2. March 04, 2023 - Selma, Alabama - 1 dead, 3 injured
3. March 04, 2023 - Los Angeles, California - 4 injured
4. March 04, 2023 - Douglasville, Georgia - 2 dead, 7 injured
5. March 04, 2023 - Cape Girardeau, Missouri - 5 injured
6. March 04, 2023 - San Pedro, California - 4 injured
7. March 05, 2023 - Bolingbrook, Illinois - 3 dead, 1 injured
8. March 05, 2023 - Capitol Heights, Maryland - 4 injured
9. March 05, 2023 - Lake City, Florida - 4 injured
10. March 05, 2023 - Shreveport, Louisiana - 4 injured
11. March 06, 2023 - Sacramento, California - 3 dead, 1 injured
12. March 06, 2023 - Memphis, Tennessee - 3 dead, 1 injured
13. March 07, 2023 - Memphis, Tennessee - 4 injured
14. March 07, 2023 - Pine Bluff, Arkansas - 2 dead, 2 injured
15. March 10, 2023 - Hialeah, Florida - 4 dead,
16. March 11, 2023 - Brooklyn, New York - 1 dead, 3 injured

17. March 11, 2023 - Vancouver, Washington - 1 dead, 3 injured
18. March 12, 2023 - Laredo, Texas - 14 injured
19. March 12, 2023 - Dallas, Texas - 4 dead,
20. March 13, 2023 - Lubbock, Texas - 1 dead, 3 injured
21. March 14, 2023 - Birmingham, Alabama - 4 dead,
22. March 15, 2023 - Portland, Oregon - 2 dead, 2 injured
23. March 15, 2023 - Modesto, California - 2 dead, 2 injured
24. March 18, 2023 - Columbus, Ohio - 2 dead, 4 injured
25. March 18, 2023 - Chicago, Illinois - 4 injured
26. March 18, 2023 - Dallas, Texas - 4 injured
27. March 19, 2023 - Philadelphia, Pennsylvania - 3 injured
28. March 20, 2023 - Milwaukee, Wisconsin - 1 dead, 5 injured
29. March 21, 2023 - Trenton, New Jersey - 4 injured
30. March 21, 2023 - Sumter, South Carolina - 4 dead,
31. March 23, 2023 - Baltimore, Maryland - 1 dead, 5 injured
32. March 24, 2023 - Shreveport, Louisiana - 8 injured
33. March 25, 2023 - Macomb, Illinois - 1 dead, 10 injured
34. March 25, 2023 - Hempstead, New York - 4 injured
35. March 25, 2023 - Shreveport, Louisiana - 1 dead, 5 injured
36. March 25, 2023 - Williamston, North Carolina - 5 injured
37. March 26, 2023 - Minneapolis, Minnesota - 6 injured
38. March 26, 2023 - Philadelphia, Pennsylvania - 2 dead, 2 injured
39. March 26, 2023 - Little Rock, Arkansas - 2 dead, 5 injured
40. March 26, 2023 - Minden, Louisiana - 4 injured
41. March 27, 2023 - Nashville, Tennessee - 6 dead,
42. March 27, 2023 - Milwaukee, Wisconsin - 5 injured
43. March 29, 2023 - Memphis, Tennessee - 2 dead, 4 injured

• • •

Epilogue

By Caroline K. Henning
From her blog, *Democracy in Demise*

Yesterday, a former President of the United States of America was killed in a plane crash while en route to Albany, NY. The cause of the incident is still under investigation, so I'm not calling it an assassination. Though I suspect it was. I was not surprised. In fact, my first thought was, how did he ever make it this far?

While such an event, the death of a former leader of the free world, would normally be shocking to our senses, yesterday, a burden was lifted. Sisyphus found the peak. Many of us who have feared for the survival of our Democracy since 2016 are grateful for this reprieve. I am hopeful that now we can stop bailing and right this ship that is America.

Under normal circumstances it is considered crass to speak ill of the dead. In poor taste and tacky. But to be frank, most people's lives matter very little in the grand sweep of history. Most people will have no impact on the course of humanity. That man, and many of those who perished on that plane, have already done great damage to our country and were poised and hungry to do so much more.

Our collective promise of 'Never Again!' shouted in solidarity against past horrors, had become no more than a bumper sticker. An easy shield to raise until we realized the enemy was at our backs. Then it became a silent plea, a whispered prayer, as we went about our daily lives, powerless against the powerful. Fascism knocking.

As Americans we have always held the Presidency in highest regard. We may feel an inclination to mourn as a nation. I urge you, dear reader, to resist that pull in this instance. This man had no regard for the office, for the people, for the Constitution, for truth. His lack of empathy combined with his lack of intellect left us with a playground-bully President. His only motivation in life was his own greatness. He does not deserve our grief. We deserve to be liberated.

I won't list all of the egregious things to which we were subjected by Trump and his administration, but please take some time to remember what we've been through. In a *Washington Post* article dated Jan. 24, 2021, they reported that Trump had made 30,573 false or misleading claims over the course of his Presidency. His lies ran the gamut from the pointless (it didn't rain during his inauguration) to the potentially catastrophic (the big lie—that he won the 2020 election—which nearly resulted in a coup on Jan. 6th and which he continued to peddle to his death).

On Jan. 19, 2021, the *New York Times* published the complete list of Twitter insults that Trump hurled at his perceived enemies from 2015 until he was banned from the platform on Jan. 8, 2021. They are arranged both alphabetically and chronologically and are stunning in their sweep.

Lies and insults speak to the character of the man. Trump's true character was also reflected in his public admiration of his many power-adjacent sycophants, until they showed the barest whiff of disagreement or independent thinking, in which case an infantile nickname was assigned and they were immediately subjected to his vitriol.

Trump's character was dangerous to Democracy. He showed us this in his overt praise for Putin and Kim Jung Un. Two dictators who couldn't believe their good luck when America elected a puppet. How quickly they all jumped into bed, stroking their egos, while Trump dangerously distanced us from our long-time allies. With Trump no longer in play, perhaps Putin will consider ending the war in Ukraine. No one else in contention is likely to serve up that sovereign nation.

Today is not a time for mourning. It is a time for action. Those of us with a better vision for our country and our world need to step into the fray NOW! We need to focus on two things: 1) getting a democrat elected in 2024; 2) addressing the lack of protections and checks and balances that left us in this position.

The left has laid out their fascist agenda in their plan entitled <u>Project 2025: Presidential Transition Project,</u> which was first made public in 2022. Very few people I speak to know about this frightening, publicly available statement (over 900 pages) that purports to be *Building now for a conservative victory through policy, personnel, and training.* This is a right-wing agenda for a Christian-based infiltration of our Democracy at EVERY LEVEL, with the President wielding outrageous power. Here is a just a taste:

> *Today, the American family is in crisis. Forty percent of all*
> *children are born to unmarried mothers, including more than*
> *70 percent of black children. There is no government program*

that can replace the hole in a child's soul cut out by the absence of a father. Fatherlessness is one of the principal sources of American poverty, crime, mental illness, teen suicide, substance abuse, rejection of the church, and high school dropouts. So many of the problems government programs are designed to solve—but can't—are ultimately problems created by the crisis of marriage and the family. The world has never seen a thriving, healthy, free, and prosperous society where most children grow up without their married parents. If current trends continue, we are heading toward social implosion.

Furthermore, the next conservative President must understand that using government alone to respond to symptoms of the family crisis is a dead end. Federal power must instead be wielded to reverse the crisis and rescue America's kids from familial breakdown. The Conservative Promise includes dozens of specific policies to accomplish this existential task. . .

In its opening words, Article II of the U.S. Constitution makes it abundantly clear that "[t]he executive power shall be vested in a President of the United States of America."1 That enormous power is not vested in departments or agencies, in staff or administrative bodies, in nongovernmental organizations or other equities and interests close to the government. The President must set and enforce a plan for the executive branch. Sadly, however, a President today assumes office to find a sprawling federal bureaucracy that all too often is carrying out its own policy plans and preferences—or, worse yet, the policy plans and preferences of a radical, supposedly "woke" faction of the country. . .

The great challenge confronting a conservative President is the existential need for aggressive use of the vast powers of the executive branch to return power—including power currently held by the executive branch—to the American people. Success in meeting that challenge will require a rare combination of boldness and self-denial: boldness to bend or break the bureaucracy to the presidential will and self-denial to use the bureaucratic machine to send power away from Washington and back to America's families, faith communities, local governments, and states.

Fortunately, a President who is willing to lead will find in the Executive Office of the President (EOP) the levers necessary to reverse this trend and impose a sound direction for the nation on the federal bureaucracy. The effectiveness of those EOP levers depends on the fundamental premise that it is the President's agenda that should matter to the departments and agencies that operate under his constitutional authority and that, as a general matter, it is the President's chosen advisers who have the best sense of the President's aims and intentions, both with respect to the policies he intends to enact and with respect to the interests that must be secured to govern successfully on behalf of the American people. This chapter focuses on key features of and recommendations for several of the EOP's important components.

This terrifying agenda directly addresses and attacks 'wokeness,' any sexuality other than hetero, gender non-conformity of any kind, women's reproductive and even social freedom, immigration, freedom of education. The list is long. I beg you, dear reader, to investigate this document for yourself. Share it far and wide to let your fellows know what is brewing. If the Republicans gain office in 2024, I doubt that our Democracy will live to see 2028.

Second, we must address, as a nation, the cracks in our system. We never imagined that a duly elected President would take office and simply refuse to play by the rules. Every President before Trump, regardless of party affiliation, respected the office and what it stood for; something so much bigger than themselves. But for Trump, there was nothing bigger than himself. He was king of the hill.

We learned the hard way that we, the American people, have no recourse when our leader is a clear and present danger. We must take steps to remedy that through legislative action.

I don't know what the coming days will reveal about Trump's death. And while I will be glued to the media like everyone else, I really don't care what happened. The decks are cleared and we have dodged a bullet. Take action.

TRACY L. THOMPSON is a mom to three amazing sons, a gaga to two remarkable grandbabies, and a dog mom to two listless lapdogs. She lives and writes in Schenectady, NY. Tracy grew up in a working-class family in rural Pennsylvania and has moved 28 times since leaving home to join the Navy. She holds a B.A. from the University of South Florida, where she majored in philosophy and women's studies, and a J.D. from Yale Law School. Her greatest wish is for people to live in peace.